T0267154

# Acclaim for
# ABERRATION

"In a time when defining the human condition has never been more difficult, McCrumb's follow-up to her debut novel cuts straight to the heart. *Aberration* is a rocket-fueled tale of hard truths, inalienable purpose, and enduring love that resonates far beyond the final pulse-pounding page."

— ANDREW WINCH, editor-in-chief of Havok Publishing

"In *Aberration*, Cathy McCrumb delivers a sympathetic look at humanity through the eyes of the Recorder, who has been systematically raised from birth to be dispassionate. The Recorder's persistent compassion and quiet heroism ignite glimmers of faith, hope, and love in a world that discourages all three."

— ROBERT MULLIN, author of The Wells of the Worlds series

"It's rare that one is able to emphathize with a character who once had no understanding of compassion, but *Aberration* succeeds beyond belief. Cathy McCrumb's lyrical prose dazzles, inviting the reader to join the Recorder on her journey to humanity and self-determination."

— ANNE WHEELER, award-winning author of *Treason's Crown*

"I've been on the hunt for great sci-fi, and I've found it in this series! Imaginative, immersive, and so, so good, *Aberration* is a worthy sequel. I highly recommend!"

— S.D. GRIMM, author of the Children of the Blood Moon series and *A Dragon By Any Other Name*

"Reading *Aberration* is like waiting for an impending storm to break loose. The storm clouds of events gather inescapable as the thunder of subtle tension raises hair on end. Anticipation and agony swirl together throughout, pushing and pulling you like a great wind. But you can't retreat, can't seek shelter elsewhere, because these characters are now your friends, your enemies, your frenemies, and you must know how they will fare, for good or for ill."

— CHAWNA SCHROEDER, author of *The Vault Between Spaces*

"Cathy McCrumb writes the way some people dream—in vivid detail and with an emotional punch. Her characters are unique and compelling. Her writing alternately rips your heart out and wraps you in the warmest hug. And her world building is phenomenally complex and real. One thing's for sure: after reading *Aberration*, I cannot wait for the next installment."

— LAUREN H. SALISBURY, author of *A Matter of Blood*

"Heart-stopping, captivating, and perfectly riveting . . . *Aberration* is a roller coaster of emotions from start to finish! McCrumb takes her rich cast of characters to even deeper levels and greater heights in this stunning sequel, weaving an exquisite tapestry exploring the true nature of love, freedom, and sacrifice. I am itching to get my hands on the final installment in the Children of the Consortium Trilogy!"

— J.J. FISCHER, author of The Nightingale Trilogy and
The Darcentaria Duology

# ABERRATION

# ABERRATION

CHILDREN OF THE CONSORTIUM | BOOK TWO

## CATHY MCCRUMB

For those whose stars sing silently
and those whose stars seem dim.

# 01

Solitude and its companion, apprehension, wrapped around me like a drone's tendrils. Air whispered through the vent over the holding-cell door, and quiet pressed through the walls to roar in my ears. Overhead, the red emergency light throbbed like the ship's visible heartbeat, and my imagination provided its sound—the faintest, gentlest click. I concentrated and uncurled my toes, pressing bare feet into the ribbed antistatic flooring, and the barely perceptible but steady rumble of the engines tickled my soles.

CTV *Agamemnon* was not dead, whatever might have happened to her crew.

For something had happened. I did not know why the ship's usual noises—conversation and the confident rhythm of people in a hurry—had been replaced by hushed footsteps and low murmurs. When trepidation had outpaced patience and I called out for food or news, no one answered, and eventually, even those sounds had disappeared.

Silence had been broken but once by a burst of weapons' fire and twice by faint screams, though no klaxon sounded. The emergency chemical system had not activated, so fire, collision, and piracy were improbable. Mutiny was unlikely with an Elder, Recorders, and their drones on board to maintain order. As members of the Consortium, we did not betray our own . . .

*Most* of us would not betray our own.

I had not intentionally done so. The loss of my drone on Pallas Station had been beyond my control, but my friendships—those were choices I would never rescind. Perhaps it was for the best that no one came. Starving alone in a holding cell would be preferable to spending the remainder of my life submerged in a medical stasis tank in the Hall of Reclamation.

Each time raw ache or hunger overtook dread, I drank some water then returned to my bunk. The recording device's lens no longer tracked my movements, but despite the Consortium's inattention, my uneasiness remained.

Loath as I was to consider another possible explanation for *Agamemnon*'s pervasive stillness, Julian Ross's words from six days ago rang through my mind: *"The Consortium, not the citizenry, is my target."* As a disgraced Recorder, an aberration, would I not be the perfect carrier for the bioweapon he had engineered on Pallas Station? But surely, Dr. Maxwell—Max—had known. I had warned the Elders. Surely, they had taken precautions.

Though I rarely risked a glance at the motionless camera, I paced the cell despite low blood sugar's dizziness and the sluggishness of fatigue. Three meters up, three meters down, over and over.

Then, the unexpected but longed for sound of footsteps brought my own to a halt, and muffled voices argued outside my cell. Someone knocked.

I pressed my left ear against the door's cool metal. "I am—"

A shot tore through the panel a mere half meter from my head, peppering slivers of metal into my neck, back, and left shoulder. I suppressed a cry and jumped away, pulse hammering painfully. The barren room had nowhere to hide, so I stepped to the middle, wiping away thin trickles of blood and tugging at my short top in a fruitless attempt to cover my abdomen.

Metal screeched against metal as a crowbar drove the door into its pocket.

Three young people—perhaps twenty years of age and wearing the olive-green uniforms of university students on a work-study tour—stood in the hall. The tall, slightly built young man in front tossed a metal crowbar away and fumbled for a sidearm. On the left, a stockier young man, whose hair escaped his braid in curly wisps, held a rifle. To the right, a young woman approximately my height aimed an unsteady weapon at me.

The first young man waved his sidearm without regard for safety protocol. His gaze darted around my cell from the bunk embedded in the back wall to the exposed personal hygiene facilities on my right before landing on my nearly three-centimeter-long hair. His eyes moved to my own.

"Recorder—or whatever you are—we need your help."

Though my breath came unevenly, I squared my shoulders. My previous assumptions must have been incorrect. Anxiety squeezed my chest like a steel band, but I stood tall. "I will not participate in mutiny."

"Mutiny?" The young woman's dark eyes widened. "Moons above, no."

The shorter man groaned, then cast a quick glance behind him into the hall. "I told you both, eh?" His voice held the odd lilt I associated with the mining platforms in the inner belt. "Space it, we're in so much trouble, and it's not even our fault."

"Easy, Eric," the other young man said, though he kept his eyes on me.

The one called Eric paid him no heed. "I've been on ships with mutineers, Recorder, and no one mutinied, I swear!"

"If this is not a mutiny . . ." I could not bring myself to voice my worst fear: that Julian Ross had succeeded in using me as a carrier for his bioweapon, and his engineered virus had spread through the ship. "There was no fire? No decompression? We were not attacked?"

In the flashing red light, it was difficult to ascertain if the taller one's eyes were dark blue, hazel, or brown. "Nothing like that."

The young woman glared. "Are you going to help us or not?"

Tension crept through me. "Without a drone, my standing as a Recorder is questionable, and since I have been kept in isolation, I cannot verify events. And so, I may or may not be of assistance, depending upon the situation."

She glanced down the hall and shuddered. "We need your help with the bodies."

Not-Eric cast a brief look at her. "We can handle the bodies." She began to protest, but he stopped her. "We need help with the drones."

The temperature seemed to drop several degrees when their words finally registered. "Bodies? And . . . drones?"

"Two of 'em," Eric said quickly. "One killed Jenkins."

"But their Recorders—"

"We haven't seen a Recorder in two days."

Not-Eric added, "We have to get to the bridge, but the drones won't let us."

"I tried to stop the one that killed Jenkins." Eric swallowed visibly. "I'm a good shot, but I couldn't."

"It wasn't your fault, Eric. You can't stop a drone without a Recorder." Not-Eric fixed his eyes on mine. "And that's why we need you. No one else answered. We even tried the Elder's quarters."

"We don't know if they're alive, dead, or hiding. We don't know anything." Eric's fingers tightened on his weapon. "We've only seen the drones. Been dodging them since Jenkins asked for our help, maybe six hours ago. They've been careening through the halls, waving those blasted tentacles like lightning—not that I've seen real lightning. When one grabbed Jenkins, I—"

"Don't say anything else, Eric," the young woman warned.

I hit my fist against my thigh. "If you consult with the captain—"

"You don't get it," Eric interrupted. "That's why we need to get to the bridge. No one's answering our comms. Ship's on emergency alert, probably drifting. Even the lifts are offline. Whoever's on the bridge is probably dead."

A chill swept down my spine.

"The point is, we don't know." Not-Eric moved toward me. "Recorder, can . . . *will* you help us?"

"What about a citizen request?" The young woman snuck another peek down the hall, then wiped away a thin glaze of sweat with her sleeve. "Can you do something if we specifically ask?"

My heart stilled a moment. Honoring a citizen's request had likely consigned my first friend—James, his name was James—to death in a medical tank. But, as I studied the three before me, their faces drawn and pale despite the jumping shadows cast by the emergency light, I decided.

"So be it. I am no longer a true Recorder, but I will not deny anyone assistance, whether they be citizen, Recorder, or Elder." Not-Eric's shoulders softened until I continued, "Please clarify the sequence of events and how the others died."

Eric began to speak, but the young woman shushed him,

confirming my fears, and that confirmation plunged through me like raw ore through water.

"When did they begin to fall ill?"

Eric narrowed his eyes. "How did you know?"

"Four days ago," the woman said, almost simultaneously. "The day after we left Lunar One."

"How many remain?" No one answered, so I tried again. "A transport vessel of this size would have a complement of at least twenty-eight, as well as the three Consortium members sent to retrieve me and possibly a ship's Recorder. Of those thirty-one or thirty-two"—I wrapped my arms around my bare waist—"how many remain?"

Eric's finger slid to the trigger. "Hands where we can see them!"

My mouth went dry. I raised my hands, keeping my palms open before me.

"Take a damper," the young woman said. "She can't—"

"She's one of them." Eric's voice was low and tight. "How else did she know about everyone getting sick before we told her?"

Very slowly, as if he handled a volatile liquid, Not-Eric holstered his sidearm. "It's all right, Eric."

He raised his hands, and the woman lowered her own weapon as well. Eric shifted uneasily, but he remained focused on me.

I lost my ability to see anything save the muzzle of his rifle, so I closed my eyes. "I would not, shall not harm you."

Harsh but indistinguishable words emerged from the argument that ensued and did nothing to allay my fears. Then, boots sounded, and someone touched me. I startled at the contact. My eyes flew open, focusing on the slim fingers on my bare forearm.

"I'm Portia Belisi," the young woman said. "You can call me Tia."

"Portia Belisi." My eyes lifted to hers. "Tia, I do not yet have a name to share."

Her forehead creased. "Yet?"

"That's enough, Eric," the taller young man said. "He isn't going to shoot you, Recorder."

"I still don't like it." Eric's weapon was no longer aimed at me, but when his gaze fell from my eyes to my undershirt, his ears reddened. "Do you . . . want to get dressed first?"

My face heated, and I folded my arms over my abdomen. "I have nothing else."

"But I saw you in Consortium greys when you came on board," Portia Belisi—Tia—said.

Eric's eyes widened. "You're a suicide risk."

I shook my head. "The Elder's assessment is and was incorrect."

Not-Eric shrugged his left shoulder. "It'll have to do, then. We'll find something for you eventually." He strode into the hall, pausing to check both ways before saying, "Recorder, watch the shards on your way out. You don't want to cut your feet. We haven't made it past the drones to the infirmary, so we don't know if it's open, and Dr. Smithson isn't responding."

As I followed them out of my cell, Eric exhaled loudly. "No one in the infirmary is. Not even Leslie. Probably dead."

Tia rounded on him. "Don't say that!"

We turned the corner, heading left to the forward lift. It was cooler in the hallway than my room had been, but my shivers were more a product of memory than of temperature. Despite the differences between *Agamemnon*'s clean hallways and the research station on Pallas, images of my failed assignment overlaid my vision, each one as vivid as if my neural implant were yet intact—

*Motes floating through targeting beams. Decimeters of insectile dust from decaying carapaces. The withered hands of the dead. A searing flash of light as my drone was destroyed—*

Then, in a sudden shift, the images were replaced by the memory of green eyes and perfect eyebrows. A separate pain replaced my fear, and I stumbled.

"Recorder?" A woman's voice, not Nate's. A hand grabbed my right shoulder, and I recoiled from the touch. Tia peered at me through the pulsing lights. "You still with us?"

"I am."

We reached the lift, and as Eric had indicated, its panel flashed a warning to use the ladder.

Not-Eric holstered his sidearm. "I'll go first this time." He grabbed the rungs and disappeared up into the flashing darkness. I forgot to count the seconds before his voice echoed down the metal shaft: "It's clear."

Tia motioned for me to ascend next. I took but three seconds to gather my resolve, then started up, the metal cold under my sweaty palms. Reaching the next level, I stepped from the ladder and froze. I had seen death before, both on the research station and in VVR reviewing records, but this was different. Bile rose in my throat.

The man—a thin, pale man in his early thirties, wearing engineering blue—lay in a contorted jumble of limbs, a drone's detached tendril entangled around his arms and torso. His vacant eyes stared past me. Despite the painful physical reprimands it would have unleashed for my emotional response, I found myself wishing for my drone's grounding, emotionless presence. Yet, a drone had done this, though drones were not programmed to take lives unless told to do so. I clenched my teeth, but nothing lessened the impact of the snarl on the man's face or the dark trickle leaking from his ears. The corridor seemed to heave about me, and I put my hand on the wall for balance.

"Jenkins." Not-Eric pointed his chin at the body. "This is why we need you, Recorder."

"I am no longer a Recorder," I said almost involuntarily.

Tia jumped from the ladder like a dancer, and Eric thumped into the hall after her.

I cleared my throat. "I understand your sense of urgency. There are two drones?"

"That we know of." Eric shot a look over his shoulder, but nothing was there. "They're roaming the halls around the bridge, though they must be using the ladders, too."

"Drones don't need ladders," Tia said.

"You know what I meant. They'd fit in the tubes."

Suppressing the urge to rock back and forth on the balls of my feet, I tapped my thigh. I had been trained to work with aberrant Recorders and their equipment, though without my drone and neural implant, my limitations surpassed my abilities.

I addressed the tall young man. "Her name is Portia Belisi. His name is Eric. I do not know yours. Not-Eric is insufficient."

A half-smile appeared for a half-second. "His name is Eric Thompson. I'm Cameron Rodriguez."

"Very well. Cameron Rodriguez, use your communication link to call the captain—"

"Space it, Recorder!" Eric blurted. "Weren't you listening? There's no answer!"

I held up a hand. "Yes, I recall. Ship-specific devices should still be functional, and internal communication on a Consortium transport vessel is automatically recorded. I wish to establish subsequent action as my responsibility, not yours."

The taller young man arched his eyebrows, but he tapped his communication link. "Cameron Rodriguez to Captain Stirling."

"Recorder Zeta—" But I was no longer a Recorder. "Identification designation Zeta4542910-9545E, speaking. Cameron Rodriguez, Portia Belisi, and Eric Thompson have released me. They have reported rogue drones, which have prevented them from accessing the bridge. As drones are Consortium property, I will attempt to shut them down. I accept responsibility for unsanctioned activity and request a full waiver of damages on their behalf. I shall endeavor to protect the interests of the Consortium, per AAVA sections 1.7.011, 5.32.19, and 8.11.04A."

When I fell silent, Cameron Rodriguez closed the link, but before he could speak, I cautioned, "Should the drone act aggressively, do not resist."

Unwilling to hop over Jenkins's limbs, I sidestepped his body and chose the longer route. The young people followed at my heels. We had only walked a few meters down the starboard corridor when the high-pitched whistle of a damaged drone set my teeth on edge. I held up a hand, and behind me their boots shuffled to a halt.

A Recorder's drone approached through the blinking red light, hovering one and a half meters in the air. The drone's primary gyroscopic stabilizer must have malfunctioned, for it listed backward, its underbelly showing as it lurched closer. Long, limp arms and a sparking tendril dangled below its belly, dragging on the black flooring. Eric swore quietly as the drone extended two tendrils, gathering speed as it approached.

I drew a deep breath, shook out my arms, and—hoping that my fatigue would not cause me to err—stepped forward to meet it.

In the time it took me to blink, the drone closed the distance. Two smooth tendrils twined around my wrists and tugged my arms further out. A thicker appendage wrapped around my torso like a safety harness, then encircled my waist.

Behind me, Eric swore. Cameron Rodriguez shouted him down. For seven rapid heartbeats, the roaring in my ears drowned their cries, even drowned the high-pitched whine of the damaged drone itself.

Eric's voice coalesced into words. "—just like Jenkins! It's gonna pull her apart."

"It's not the same," Tia protested. "Jenkins fought it, but she's— Eric, stop—"

A shot rang out. One of the drone's tendrils jerked back, and near my shoulder, beige paneling cracked around a small, dark hole. Bound as I was, I could not see the scuffle behind me, but something clattered to the floor.

"Let me go," Eric shouted. "It's gonna kill her if we don't do something!"

"Shooting the drone did nothing for Jenkins." Rodriguez's words echoed down the hall. "She told us to stay calm."

The tendrils squeezed my wrists, and my fingertips went numb. Pressure on my ribcage mirrored the fear constricting my lungs, but when a tentacle gently touched my cheek, an anthropomorphic and illogical thought flashed through me. The drone sought solace—it searched for its Recorder.

This was not discipline but comfort, like a weighted blanket. Relaxing my spine, I called up memories from university, when my shadow drone sensed anxiety and draped itself soothingly over my shoulders. The pressure eased, and the drone released me. I stumbled around to access the side control panel, but lightheaded from hunger, I was too slow. My fingers caught nothing but air, and I lost my balance. My knees smacked the floor as the drone resumed its lopsided course.

Bracing myself against the wall, I called, "Remain calm."

Eric did not listen. He dove to the floor and snatched up his rifle, then rolled to his stomach and fired, again hitting the drone's damaged tendril. It sparked, and the projectile ricocheted into the ceiling. He sprang to his feet, aimed, and fired again. The tendril flew off with a crack, hit the wall next to me, and writhed on the floor like a living thing, still trying to obey whatever final commands it had been given. I scooted away from it.

Rodriguez wrested the weapon from Eric's hands, but the drone must not have interpreted Eric's now unarmed state as cessation of aggression. All ten remaining appendages reached forward as it accelerated.

I hurled myself onto the drone, which dipped under my weight. Though my arms could not reach all the way around it, my fingers found purchase on the slight lip encircling its widest point. Muscles burning, I pulled myself up and wrapped my arms around its body, ignoring the way the metal rim bit into my bare midriff.

The drone's microantigravity unit whined. Halted in its forward momentum, it wobbled as its thicker tentacles coiled around my hips. The cool surface heated against my skin, but though a current tickled my hands, no true correction ripped through me. The drone's jointed arms locked around my calves and tugged. I tightened my grip.

Footsteps thundered, and Rodriguez leapt at the drone, which dipped again. He pulled himself over the top, his torso pinning my arms against its sides, though not even his longer arms reached all the way around it. It released my legs and grabbed him instead. A sharper electrical current pulsed over the smooth silver surface and stung us both, tearing a scream from his throat. He released the drone and slid to the floor. Twenty-four years of experience with reprimands, however, granted me a higher tolerance, so I merely gritted my teeth and held on.

The data-entry pad was only a centimeter out of reach. I stretched, and my fingertips brushed the access panel. With a gentle shush, it opened.

Tia hooked her elbows under Rodriguez's arms and dragged him down the hall, but Eric shouted incoherently and raised his rifle. The drone rotated.

My muscles burned while I struggled to keep from falling, and I gasped, "Do not shoot."

As he closed the distance between us, Eric flipped the weapon around. Holding the muzzle like a club, he swung the stock at the drone. It hit a decimeter below my wrists, and I lost my hold once more. I fell, landing awkwardly and twisting my ankle. Eric swung again. One jointed arm sparked, then a long tentacle yanked the weapon from Eric's hands and smashed it against his arm with a sickening crunch. He dropped with a cry. Tendrils reached for him.

The memory of Jenkins lying on the floor by the lift brought me to my feet.

I dove back at the drone, throwing my arms around its dangling appendages. Despite the bite of a true reprimand, I hauled myself up and strained again for the panel. My fingers found the keys and entered the emergency stop code.

Time seemed to slow, and the drone sputtered. Then, as the microantigravity shut down, its high-pitched noise softened to a quiet whir. Slowly, casually, like a sheet of paper falling, it drifted to the floor. I hopped out of its way, keeping my weight off my ankle. The drone settled beside me, spooling its tendrils and tentacles into interior pockets, folding and telescoping undamaged arms into tidy cubes.

I sank with it, closing my eyes to block the way the hall tilted. My attempt was unsuccessful, since the spinning worsened, so I opened them and focused on a scuff mark where the drone's tendril had dented the paneled wall. The ongoing pulses of red light did nothing to help. I leaned forward and rested my forehead on the drone's rapidly cooling surface and struggled to even out my respiration.

Loss rippled through me—loss of my previous life, loss of my new one, loss of this drone.

"Did you kill it?" Eric lay not too far from me, his face pale then ruddy in the flashing light, his breath coming in unsteady gulps. He sat up, cradling his left forearm close to his chest.

Still leaning against the drone's smooth shell, I swallowed down any hint of unreasonable emotion. "It was never alive."

Several meters down the hall, Rodriguez grunted, and Tia watched me closely, one hand on her weapon.

"Zeta? Are you all right?"

My gaze ranged over all three. "Zeta is not my name. It is merely a small part of my identification designation."

Rodriguez cleared his throat. "That's all names are. Designations."

"Not the point." Eric's voice sounded sharp. "You all right?"

The hallway tipped again when I tried to stand, but Tia caught my arm. No one spoke for what might have been a minute—I did not count that time.

"I have felt better."

"I'd take that bet. Can't believe you held on through that. Unless . . ." Rodriguez squinted at me through the emergency lights. "You're . . . used to it?"

I did not answer his question, only said, "We must see to Eric Thompson."

Tia released me to kneel at Eric's side. Rodriguez joined her, and together they helped him stand. Eric shook them off but went utterly pale at the motion. A grimace twisted his face.

"We need to go to the infirmary," I insisted. "His arm requires treatment."

Eric shook his head. Flashing red highlighted the trickle of sweat running down his cheek like a tear. "Bridge first."

"Eric," Tia protested, "your arm—"

"The bridge and the drones. Whole reason we got her out."

"That and the bodies." Rodriguez's mouth twitched. "All right. Tia, watch our six. Zeta, you keep an eye on—" His gaze darted to Eric Thompson. "Keep an eye out. Eric . . . watch over Zeta. We'll need her again if we come across the other drone." He turned to head down the hall.

"No, Cameron Rodriguez," I said. "Not yet."

He glowered at me over his shoulder. "What?"

I bent down and picked up the broken tendril. Eric cringed when I extended it in his direction. As gently as I could, I said, "This is not the best choice, but we should attempt to keep your arm from further damage. Since you elect to eschew the infirmary—"

"Gotta turn the ship. Besides"—his words hissed through clenched teeth—"my guess is the infirmary's full of shells."

Tia's lips pursed, but her eyes grew wide. Suddenly, she seemed very young. They all did. Next to these three, I felt old.

"What if they're contagious?" she asked.

Rodriguez frowned. "We're breathing the same air they did. Whatever it is, we've already caught it."

Ignoring their mild subsequent bickering, I folded the thicker end of the drone's tendril along Eric's forearm like a splint, then wound the thinner end around and around to stabilize it. Heat radiated through his sleeve, his respiration seemed shallow, and he kept his eyes on the ceiling. I finished, using the thinnest end to secure his arm at an angle across his chest, and patted his opposite shoulder, as Max would have done. Eric's eyes dropped to mine. For five seconds, he studied me, then walked to where Cameron Rodriguez waited.

Eric paused and turned. "Thank you."

"It is well."

Tia motioned me forward, and I limped after the young men.

"Zeta?"

I sighed. Evidently, my nameless state remained insufficient. She matched her strides to mine, a fairly easy task, since my throbbing ankle slowed me, and she was but two and a half centimeters shorter than I.

"Why did you tell Eric not to shoot?"

While I was uncertain about revealing the information, I also did not want to lie. "Drones are connected directly to their Recorder's neural implant. Their destruction can kill the Recorder, and I did not wish to take the risk, though there seems little chance this drone's Recorder yet lives."

"Stars," Tia exclaimed. "But what you did was all right?"

"Yes. Deactivating the drone merely leaves the Recorder without external input. Some even deactivate their drones at night for more restful sleep." I watched my bare toes and her black boots, almost in unison, even with my limp: left, right, left. "The drone was unaccompanied. It is probable the Recorder has succumbed to illness."

"What about damaging its arm-thing?" She glanced behind

us at the flashing hallway. "Will Eric be in trouble? Even though it killed Jenkins?"

"That is why I had Cameron Rodriguez attempt to contact the captain." What was done was done. "I shall assume responsibility for that."

"If the second one is unaccompanied, too, is its Recorder dead?"

"I cannot know."

Ahead, the two young men turned the corner to the bridge's double doors, and for a moment, she and I were alone. She touched my arm, and I stopped.

"What happened to you? Where's yours? Why aren't you dead?"

Again, the last, splintered moments of my shadow drone's destruction filled my mind. I shut my eyes and inhaled through my nose. "It was not my doing, as I told the Elder and before that, Captain North—" My whole body tensed at the thought of that man, and I rapped my fist against my thigh.

Her gentle alto broke through my memories. "It's all right. You don't have to say."

"There was an accident. Nate—" I caught myself before I revealed too much and tried to reframe my explanation. "A teammate—a team *member*—carried me out and put me in a medical tank. I was dying. The doctor took it upon himself to save me. I believe—I hope—they will not be prosecuted." I did not manage to keep the concern from my voice. "I hope he will not . . ."

Her dark eyes grew round. "You have friends."

Panic shot through me. My words might have betrayed them. If we were recorded . . . I glanced up at the device in the corner, but I could not tell if it was operational.

Straightening, I kept my voice steady and flat. "Recorders do not have friends."

Her forehead wrinkled. "Maybe not."

"Tia! Zeta?" Rodriguez called.

When she looked away, I allowed myself to tap my leg again before I hobbled around the corner. The young men waited at the wide double doors to the bridge.

"'Bout time," Eric said as we approached.

Tia's grip on her weapon tightened. "Will we find more of those things in there?"

"Without my drone or neural implant, I can no longer detect their presence. Between the three members of the Consortium sent to retrieve me, there were five drones. The Recorders each had one, and the Elder had three. I do not know if *Agamemnon* has a ship's Recorder, so not including the one I deactivated, there will be at least four more drones on the ship, beside those in storage."

They exchanged glances.

"Thirty-four on board." Rodriguez's tall frame slumped. "Twenty-one of us, eight staff, and five Consortium: the ship's Recorder, the two who accompanied the Elder, the Elder himself, and you. When the emergency lights activated, Captain Stirling commed us to tell us we should stay in our quarters. We didn't hear from anyone until Jenkins banged on our door, told us about the bridge not responding, and handed us weapons. No one answered us, either, so we don't know who—if anyone—is left."

Eric nodded down at his injured arm. "Due payment for ignoring captain's orders, I guess."

Tia patted his shoulder.

"Eric, you and Zeta stay back," Rodriguez said. "Ready, Tia?"

As Eric took his place at my side, Tia touched Rodriguez's forearm. Bursts of emergency red delineated his profile when he glanced down at her.

"We'll get through this, Cam. We're doing what needs to be done."

His jaw muscle jumped, and he raised the identification band on his wrist to the access panel. The doors slid apart, and he led us in.

## 03

Cameron Rodriguez stopped so abruptly that I bumped into his back. Beside me, Eric caught himself before he ran into Tia.

The lemony scent of disinfectant overlaid a subtle rancid odor and the acrid smell of urine and waste; the combination singed my nostrils. Eerie quiet competed with the continuously flashing red light.

Tia gagged. "I might throw up."

"No drones. We're clear, but Tia was right." Rodriguez glanced back at me. "We might need your help with the bodies."

Three motionless forms, arms folded neatly over their chests, lined the far wall below the Consortium recording device. The captain slumped, unmoving, in the navigator's chair, and a woman lay in a heap at his feet. My stomach knotted at the unfamiliar familiarity before me. I did not like death.

Eric leaned around me and held his identification bracelet against the panel next to the doors, and they slid shut. Rodriguez went to the captain and stood rigidly for five seconds before kneeling to check for a pulse.

The man straightened in the chair and grabbed Rodriguez's jacket. Eric jumped back, and Tia squeaked. My heart hammered painfully, and I bit my tongue to keep from crying out.

Rodriguez tried to jerk free. The captain's clutch only tightened, and he raised bloodshot eyes. Livid bruising marred his stubbled jaw.

"Off course," the captain growled like spoken static then released the sleeve to cough into his elbow. A dark stain smeared the deep green of his uniform.

Cameron Rodriguez moved back a meter and scrubbed his palm on his leg. "Captain Stirling, sir?"

The captain wiped a shaking hand over his eyes. "Turn back."

"We'll get you to the infirmary, sir."

"Codes—" The man's unfocused gaze scanned the bridge before he beckoned Rodriguez closer.

The young man glanced back at us before kneeling in front of the chair. The captain murmured something then broke into a wracking cough. Tia shifted closer to Eric as the captain slipped to the floor, his forehead shining in the red, flashing light.

"Help me." Rodriguez's whisper seemed to tear through the bridge. Tia balled her hand into a fist and started forward, but he snapped, "Not you."

Before Eric could volunteer, I motioned to the drone's tendril. "Nor you, Eric Thompson."

The captain's head lolled as Rodriguez and I hoisted him from the floor. His fever burned through his clothing.

"Must," he wheezed, "stay."

Rodriguez met my eyes over the captain's disheveled hair. I nodded. Despite the disparity in our heights, we half-carried, half-dragged the man to his chair, and I strapped the safety harness around him. The captain's breath rattled in his chest.

Eric passed us to kneel by the woman on the floor and check for a pulse. His lips pinched. "She's gone."

Silence snuck through the room, like shadows, until Rodriguez said, "I'll take comms."

Eric flexed his good hand and stepped over the woman to stand at the navigation control panel. "I got nav. Didn't grow up on a freighter for nothing."

"Voice entry will be offline," Rodriguez said.

"Course it is. Emergency protocol and all that." Eric huffed. "I can input data one-handed, but I can't do anything without those codes. You going to enter 'em or not?"

"I'll give it a try."

Tia made her way to a console behind the captain. "And I'll get the lights."

Rodriguez met my gaze, motioned to the other bodies, and said, "Please."

Bile rose in my throat. I had not wanted to touch the shriveled corpses on the research station last quarter, either. The very stillness of these three bespoke their state as clearly as a drone's readouts. My feet carried me to where they lay. Crouching next to the first one, I held my hand a centimeter above the woman's mouth and nose, but no air warmed my fingers. Neither the man nor the other woman, whose long black hair reminded me of Zhen DuBois's, breathed. Stale red-brown crusted the man's ears. I shuddered but lingered a moment to touch the hollow of the last woman's throat. Her skin was cold.

The room spun, and I fell backward.

Boots sounded, and Rodriguez hauled me up. "What's wrong?"

From the console across the room, Eric muttered, "And they say there's no such thing as a stupid question."

Rodriguez's inquiry might have been well intended, but I could not know. I centered my mass over my bare feet, scrunched my eyes to stave off the blurriness of fatigue and hunger, and frowned up at him.

"Will you be all right?" he asked.

Eric answered Rodriguez before I could. "None of us have much of a choice, eh?"

"I will be." The words stuck in my throat, but I said, "I shall move the other body."

Rodriguez studied me as if I were an unknown mathematical equation. "No, I'll get her. You don't look too steady, and she'll probably be difficult to move. Comms can wait a few minutes."

And so I stood under the light's steady pulse, hands tucked under my arms, while Eric adjusted *Agamemnon*'s course, Tia attempted to turn off the emergency lights, and Rodriguez tried to pick up the navigation officer. After several awkward attempts, he finally grabbed her ankles and backed across the room. Her uniformed shoulders rasped across the flooring, and her dark braids trailed behind her like tired snakes.

"Seriously?" Tia glowered at him. "You need to drag her like an old sack?"

I refrained from echoing Tia's protest.

"Easiest way," Eric said. "Saw it in a training vid."

Her glare switched to Eric, then a dull thud informed me Rodriguez had dropped the dead woman's legs. He rejoined Eric at the communication controls, touching my shoulder as he passed. I kept my hands tucked to prevent myself from scrubbing away any contact with the dead.

For five minutes, the only sound was the tapping of fingers on panels and the flipping of switches, then Tia uttered an imprecation and gave up her attempt to enter computer commands. She took a utility knife from her belt and pried open an access panel. The red emergency lights blinked once and went out. For three and a half seconds, we were enveloped in darkness as deep as space itself. Anxiety hit me like a wave, then dissipated when, with a buzzing flicker, full-spectrum light flooded the bridge.

"Thank the founders for that." Eric flopped back into the chair and closed his eyes.

"Good job, Tia." Rodriguez blinked at the light but kept his focus on the readouts spiraling before him.

"Got comms running yet, Cam?" Eric asked.

"Almost."

"Almost doesn't count." The panel snapped back in place, and Tia sprang lightly to her feet and joined Rodriguez. "Go on, Cam."

He edged aside, a slight blush coloring his cheeks.

"I'm faster with my fingers, and this isn't your forte"—her lips lifted slightly—"since it's not a book."

Eric rubbed his neck under his red-blond braid. "Who would've thought I'd rather be back in class than on a work tour?"

The crease reappeared between Rodriguez's eyebrows. "We'll make it."

When the captain's communication link chimed, I jumped.

Tia startled, as well, and whispered, "Should we answer?"

Rodriguez glanced at the closed double doors. "Maybe we should wait?"

"But what if someone needs our help?" she asked.

Eric's good hand paused in the middle of the datastream. "The best help we can give right now is getting *Agamemnon* back on course. After that, we'll get the captain help and find anyone else. Leslie's the medic, not us."

"I suppose," Rodriguez said, and the three of them fell quiet again.

Minutes dragged past while the students worked. Fatigue and

hunger caught up with me again, and I sank into an empty seat. Communication links pinged from the bodies behind me, and each time, I barely suppressed a jump. The chime sounded twice from Captain Stirling's chair, but he never answered it. Neither did he cover his face when he coughed the last time before subsiding from thick gasps to shallower respiration.

"We're in." Eric flicked some images aside, expanded others. He selected one and pointed to it. "We're drifting, all right. The nav officer hadn't activated autopilot before—"

"Void take it!" Tia slapped her palm down on the console, her eyes locked on the data in front of her. "We've been sending out a distress call for the past thirty-nine hours!"

"What?" Eric groaned. "Stars. *Agamemnon* doesn't even have basic defenses, and we're broadcasting 'loot me now' to the universe? We're spaced."

Rodriguez stepped over to Tia's side. "Has anyone responded?"

She enlarged a strand. The image remained steady while other data twisted past. "Someone from Lunar Twelve. They're closer, but, hold on . . ." Her fingers raced through the data. "I told them who we are. They want to know if we can get autopilot working so we can make it back to Lunar One, or if they need to send a ship to tow us. And about damage and losses."

"Doing our best," Eric grumbled. "Twelve is closer. Shouldn't we go there?"

"They said not to." Tia enlarged one piece of data and read, "'All vessels having had contact with Lunar One are to return. No exceptions.'"

Rodriguez's frown lent his young face more years than he had, and he glanced back at the bodies. "Lunar One, then. Tell them the captain is down and crew members are dead."

"And notify them of a probable biohazard," I added.

"Right."

A small cleaning bot detached from its alcove and scuttled across the floor toward the bodies. I resisted the urge to shoo it away, since in all likelihood, the bot's presence had kept the smell to a minimum.

Rodriguez's mouth clamped into a line. "We need to get them out of here."

"Getting them out of here isn't enough," Eric said, still intent on the data rising above the organized confusion of knobs, levers, switches, and screens on the navigation console. "We need to get them all into cold storage before they swell up."

"Perhaps—" I stood, but dizziness made the bridge appear to dip.

Rodriguez took several long strides in my direction then stopped. "You don't look too good, Zeta."

After an uneasy peek behind me, I finally admitted, "I have not eaten recently."

Eric paused in his work to pull a food bar from the pocket on his right thigh and tossed it in my direction. Rodriguez snatched it from the air, tore it open, and handed it to me with the quiet assertion that Eric could always be relied upon to carry snacks. Eric threw him a sidelong glance, then resumed his work. I took a small bite and chewed slowly.

Rodriguez frowned, his eyebrows a thick line. "When did you eat last?"

Worry? Max worried like that.

"It has been a while," I said, reluctant to reveal how long it had been.

"There." Eric straightened and exhaled. "Good as it gets. At full speed, we'll be back at Lunar One in, oh, day and a half?"

"Letting them know," Tia said. "They want any data the doctor pulled."

"All right. Infirmary next."

The captain's communication link chimed again, but the young people's uneasy glances were the only sign they heard it. Eric and Tia's voices continued in a dull blur while they secured the computers, but Rodriguez studied me silently.

At length, he pulled off his jacket. "Put that on." The other two fell quiet, and Rodriguez offered me a small smile. "You're shivering. Besides, we can't have Eric ogling you."

Eric's ears reddened. "I don't ogle."

"Take it," Rodriguez urged. "At least until we find you proper clothes."

I cleared my throat. "I should not wear . . . I have no desire to wear someone else's clothing."

For a minute, the only sounds were fans and the bot scrubbing the floor near Eric's feet, where the navigation officer had lain. The air circulation pumps made the absence of conversation louder.

"Put it on." Rodriguez's voice gentled. "You're cold. And, if you help us with them"—he indicated the bodies at the side of the room—"you'll need some protection. You're limping, too, but if borrowing my jacket bothers you, shoes from a two-day-old corpse would probably be worse."

I choked on the food bar's powdery crumbs.

Eric stomped over, snatched the jacket from Rodriguez's hand, and swung it over my shoulders. I winced when it hit the small cuts on my back.

"Wear it. Not because I ogle." He grimaced. "Because the idea of bare skin on shells turns my stomach."

"Shells?"

"Bodies, corpses, the dead. Fodder for recycling."

Tia rolled her eyes. "Don't be crass."

"Just wear the jacket."

His point was valid, so I slid my arms into the sleeves, steeling myself against the residual warmth, the seams, and the way it snagged on the cuts on my shoulder and back. The cuffs dangled past my fingertips, so I rolled them as precisely as I could. It took three attempts to match the left sleeve's length to the right.

"You're still shaking, Zeta," Rodriguez observed. "When *did* you eat last?"

I sighed quietly. "A Recorder brought me a small evening meal the day before yesterday."

Eric's eyes widened. "You can't be serious. They were starving you? What kind of psychotic—"

"Eric."

"Well, blast it, Cam. It's just wrong." Eric fumbled in his pocket again for another food bar. His injury made grasping the wrapper difficult, so he tore it open with his teeth and held it out.

My stomach growled, yet I did not accept the offering.

He shoved the bar at me. "Just take it."

Tia left her console and took the proffered food bar. "Zeta probably doesn't want your spit." Breaking off the exposed end, she extended the rest, still in the wrapper.

The bot scooted between us, eliminating crumbs.

"Withholding food is contrary to Consortium protocol. Even a rogue Recorder is reprimanded by traditional means, not by starvation, although the usual methods are lessened, to prevent possible damage before primary reclamation—" Once again, I had spoken too freely. "It is probable illness incapacitated the Recorders and prevented them from bringing me meals."

"Well, that's dross." Eric squinted at me. "How does a Recorder go rogue anyway? What'd you do? Kill someone or something?"

"Of course she didn't." Tia still held out the bar. "Please, Zeta."

"Legitimate question." Rodriguez crossed his arms. "What did you do?"

I adjusted the jacket to reduce the discomfort on my back. "I killed no one. My drone was destroyed in an accident. The ship's doctor saved my life, but I . . ."

A faint whir caught my attention, and I froze. The recording device across the bridge from the bodies had shifted.

Someone was watching.

I pulled my attention away. "Without a drone to maintain the integrity of the record, my judgment is not reliable. I deviated from my assignment."

"That's not your fault." Tia pressed the bar into my hand.

"I erred."

Rodriguez glowered. "That's ridiculous."

I turned my back to the device and gestured at the dead to redirect the conversation. "Should we move them? Or should we first attend to Eric Thompson's injury and relocate the captain?"

"I can wait, but maybe not everyone can." Eric's gaze shot from the man in the chair to the door. "Someone else was trying to ping the captain. They could be hurt. Now that we've contacted authorities and turned the ship, we should check."

The three of them exchanged looks once again, then Rodriguez said, "All right. Zeta, finish eating, then we'll head to the infirmary, run Eric through the medicomputer, and grab a few hoverbeds."

I swallowed a cautious bite of the bar. "To relocate the captain? And transport the bodies?"

Rodriguez rubbed his upper arm, which was as thin as the rest of him. "They're heavy."

"Dead weight," Eric said.

Tia groaned. "Eric, try to be sensitive."

"Where d'you think the term came from? And sensitive to who? It's not like I'll hurt their feelings, you know, since they're dead."

"Not the captain," Tia murmured.

We all glanced at him.

"We can't drag him all the way to the infirmary." Rodriguez knelt before the captain. "We're not abandoning you, sir."

A low moan was his only answer.

I made myself finish the food, but apples and oats had never been so unappealing. "Thank you, Portia Belisi. And for the food, Eric Thompson. And for the jacket, Cameron Rodriguez."

Tia inclined her head. "You're welcome."

"I'm Cam." A brief grin creased his face, and Cam rolled his thin shoulders. "All right, everyone, keep an eye out for the other drone."

The recording device followed him to the door, then returned its focus to me, and my stomach threatened to evacuate the food bars. "Should we chance upon the drone," I said, "remember to relax and allow it to investigate and comfort you."

"What?" Eric sputtered. "Like it comforted Jenkins?"

"Drones compel cooperation if they encounter resistance, but compliance will allow it to move on."

Cam scowled. "We're supposed to comply with something that'll kill us?"

"Yes. Remember to take slow breaths. Be still and focus on the tendrils' comfort—"

"Sure," Eric said under his breath.

"The drone will release you, as the other one released me."

Tia's attention flitted to the bodies lined up against the wall, then she hoisted her weapon. "All right. Let's go."

The doors slid apart, and the brightly lit halls seemed wider without the flashing emergency lights. We had not progressed more than three meters when Eric hesitated and turned to me.

"Zeta, you can call me Eric."

Despite the possibility of being recorded, a half-smile crept across my face. The young man, little more than a boy, raised an eyebrow.

"In my head, Eric," I said, "I already do."

Still alert for the other drone, we progressed down the hall toward the crew quarters, until the click of a disengaging lock caught our attention. Eric and Tia halted, and Cam, who was several paces ahead, spun back and raised his sidearm. The four of us stood together as the door to our right opened. A small, athletic woman with greying blonde braids strode out. She stopped, eyes darting from the students to their weapons.

"What are you kids doing?"

"Specialist Watkins." Cam lowered the weapon, but the tension in his shoulders did not abate. "Jenkins got us, since no one else answered his comms. He's dead."

"What?"

"A drone killed him, ma'am."

"Interfering, self-righteous . . . Serves him right." She did not elaborate, only put her hands on her hips. "But before anything else, you three will turn over those weapons. Founders' sakes. Children playing with knives."

Cam stiffened. "Yes, ma'am. We only—"

"I don't care why." Watkins snapped her fingers and held out her hand. "Now."

They complied. Watkins took Tia's first, easing the strap over her head and shortening it so the weapon did not thump against her leg, then secured Cam's holster around her hips. After a glance at Eric's sling, she eyed his rifle critically. "You broke it, Thompson?"

She did not clarify her antecedent.

Eric tensed, but Cam said, "We made it to the bridge and have *Agamemnon* heading back to Lunar One."

Her focus slid to me, from my hair, to Cam's jacket, over to Cam. "Why is she in your uniform?"

Tia and Eric edged in front of me like a human barricade, but I watched the older woman over their shoulders.

"She was locked up for a reason," Watkins continued. "They said she was a traitor to the Consortium. She was supposed to be in solitary until we reached Ceres and the Consortium took custody."

"Without food?" Eric growled. "For two spacing days?"

Watkins held up one hand. "Watch it, Thompson. Just look at her. No Recorder has hair like that. She betrayed her gifting, and—"

"She hasn't faced her superiors yet," Eric declared forcefully. When Tia bumped Eric's shoulder with her own, he ignored her. "What about 'innocent until proven guilty'?"

"Eric," Cam murmured.

The shorter young man fell silent.

Watkins narrowed her eyes. "So why is she out?"

Cam straightened to his full height. "I broke her out, ma'am. We needed her help. Like I said, a rogue drone killed Jenkins, but she took that one down by herself. We've seen at least one more, but there could be five left."

Eric added, "When the one that killed Jenkins came after us, Zeta—"

"Zeta?" Watkins fixed her blue-grey eyes on him. "You named it, Thompson? I know you're from the belt and things are less civilized there, and I know you're slow, but everyone knows if you feed it or name it, you have to take it home."

Slow? The young man, scarcely out of his teens, who had run at a drone to save me—a stranger and a Recorder—slow?

Eric's ears reddened, and I pushed my way between the students.

"My identification designation is Zeta4542910-9545E. Their use of Zeta as a distinguishing epithet is quite unexceptional, given my lack of drone and my unusual appearance." This was not precisely untrue. There was no protocol for a Recorder in my situation, and while I rejected the title among my friends, technicalities indicated I yet belonged with the Consortium. "As Eric Thompson indicated, I have not faced judgment. Despite my irregular appearance and whatever you as a citizen may believe of our procedures and protocol, I maintain status as a Recorder."

Watkins scoffed. "Without a drone, you can't record."

"No?" I gestured at the ceiling-mounted camera. If the devices were indeed tracking me, I could manipulate their focus. Watkins and the young trio glanced up and grew quite still when, as if on cue, the camera's lens extended, zooming in on us—on me. I enunciated each word with precision. "Are you certain?"

Watkins raised her chin.

"But beyond that," I said, "I will remember."

Her upper lip curled. "A Recorder wouldn't hide behind children like you did just now."

"I did not hide. If you, however, wish to discuss hiding and responsibilities, we can indeed do so."

Watkins flinched.

"For the record," I continued with deliberate emphasis, "you displayed prejudice when you belittled Eric Thompson. Moreover, you remained safely ensconced in your quarters and left the job of securing the ship to three university students on a work-study tour. It would seem that *you* have abandoned your responsibilities. Now, if we are finished exchanging"—it took me three seconds to remember the correct word—"pleasantries, the students wish to check for crew members before continuing to the infirmary. Eric Thompson's arm needs treatment, and we must retrieve a bed to transport the captain for medical care."

Watkins's nostrils flared. "Do it, then. I'll comm you with orders." She strode toward the bridge.

"Orders. She's a phycologist," Eric grumbled. "Only thing she's supposed to boss around is algae."

"And she did hide the whole time." Tia's forehead scrunched. "Unless Jenkins lied about no one answering."

Before Cam resumed knocking on the doors, however, three of them slid open, almost in unison. A petite brunette in her late twenties tripped over her doorsill and grabbed the frame for balance. Then, an angular man peered through the farthest door and edged his way out.

Confusion surged. Though I understood why the students had needed me, a Recorder, to deactivate the drone, why had these people not answered the call for help earlier? Surely they had not lacked the courage to emerge because of blinking emergency lights?

The petite woman focused on Cam. "What's the deal, doll? Watkins just commed me to say we've—" She broke off, staring at me. "Void it, who let *that* out?"

Before Cam could reply, two more people appeared, a broad, towering man with a loose tail of black hair and a tall woman, whose wavy hair hung in limp strands. When the man saw me, his jaw tensed. The woman sidled up to him, tucking a hand through his arm.

"We needed her help." Perhaps Cameron Rodriguez was as tired of repeating his reasoning as I was of hearing it. "There are rogue drones—"

"You break out a Consortium prisoner, you'll disappear. You think removal is a vacation on Ceres?" The tiny woman flicked her fingers at me. "You've just asked to be sentenced to the belt by breaking out someone they locked up." She lounged against the wall and added, "That's Thompson's home turf, though, so maybe it doesn't seem bad to him."

Red spread across Eric's face.

The towering man was staring at Eric's arm. "That a drone's tendril, kid?" When Eric nodded, the man's thick eyebrow raised. "You'll get in a cargo hold of trouble for damaging their stuff."

"I have accepted responsibility for damage done to Consortium property," I said. "The focus, however, should not be on the tendril but on his injury, treating those who might be ill, and acquiring the necessary equipment to remove the bodies."

The tall woman shuddered.

"This can't be everyone." The angular man looked to the towering one. "Who else is left?"

"Doug and I don't know." The tall, slender woman spoke up for the first time. "All we know is that Watkins said we need biohazard suits and hoverbeds before we—"

"I don't like the sound of that." The short woman lurched toward us, and I detected a dull, sour bitterness on her breath. "So who's doing what? And are the lifts working? We can't get the beds down here otherwise."

"I hope they're working." The lilt in Eric's voice grew stronger. "Gonna be hard to climb ladders like this, eh? And rigor mortis has set in, so moving the bodies'll be a challenge."

"Right." The short woman cupped her hands to her face and

shouted, "Come out, come out, wherever you are." She gave an abrupt, brittle laugh. "Happy now?"

The subsequent, uncomfortable silence was broken by a hacking cough, and an older woman wobbled into the hall from the last open door. The others took several paces back, and her glassy, reddened gaze wandered over them, then fastened on me. She coughed again, the harsh sound obscuring the circulation fans for seven and a half seconds. Her cheeks flushed, but somehow that only accentuated the branching red of broken capillaries which spread across her face like fine roots. She pointed at me.

When she spoke, her voice was ragged. "Consortium . . . Her fault—" Heavy wheezing doubled her in half, and she spat bloody phlegm on the floor then wiped her mouth with the back of her hand.

The thin woman cringed. "Stars, Kavanaugh."

I watched Kavanaugh for four more seconds, wishing I had a drone to ascertain her temperature. The sour smell of perspiration and illness pinched my nostrils. "If I am not mistaken, you require medical assistance."

The towering man crossed his arms, and the seams of his engineering jumpsuit strained over his biceps. "Then give it."

"We need suits." The tall woman touched his forearm. "Doug, maybe you and I should get them?"

He glanced down at her. "You and I are stopping at the infirmary first. Let Bryce and Foster get the suits." His gaze snapped up. "Just to be clear, I'm not touching shells."

The petite woman rolled her eyes. "Like anyone wants to, Hugo. But whatever. Foster, you and me'll get the suits."

"I'll take point," Cam said, "in case of another drone."

"No." Attempting to walk with confidence despite my limp, I blocked his path. "Should we encounter a drone, Cameron Rodriguez, I shall deal with it."

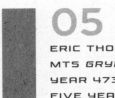

Things wouldn't be the same once Samara left for university, because they weren't even the same now. Sure, the living quarters on *Gryphon* might feel bigger without her bossing him and Blythe around, and sure, their little sister was excited about having quarters to herself, but now that he thought about it, maybe bigger wasn't that important after all.

Eric threw the ball against the painted bulkhead. It flew back at him fast enough to sting his hand, though on his next throw, the trajectory was off. He lunged to catch it, but it knocked over his water. With a short curse learned from Uncle Brian—one Dad would never approve of—Eric grabbed a dirty tunic off the floor and mopped up the puddle before it reached his school computer.

His commlink chimed, and he groaned.

"Eric?" Sam sounded irritated. "I can't even *think* with you crashing around like that. Founders' sakes, what are you doing?"

To be honest, he'd even miss Sam nagging him.

"Homework."

"Sure you are." His older sister's tone changed. "Blythe wants to know if, when you're done cleaning up whatever mess you made, and *if* you've finished your grammar, you want to join us in VVR?"

*Because who knows when we'll be able to again* hung in the air like one of those Recorder's drones.

"Ask Mum," Blythe suggested, her voice clear enough that Eric knew she was right at Sam's side. "When Dad was reviewing times tables with me before lunch, he and Uncle Brian were going on and on about having people for cargo."

The strangeness of having dozens of patients, attendants, and guards onboard pinged through Eric's mind again, and he glanced at the hatch. Transporting ore was better—well, maybe not better. Saving lives was better. But before, when Mum and Dad found out Sam had been accepted into the nursing program at Brisbane University, they'd promised to take her. They'd all get to stand on an actual planet, and he'd get to see his friend. Now with the hold full of dying miners to transfer to Krios's hospital platform, there wouldn't be time, and unless Mum and Dad managed to swing a hold of ore to transport directly to New Triton, visiting the inner planets would be next to impossible.

"She'll only agree if school is done," Sam said. "And that means *you*, Eric. We've already finished."

"Fine." He chimed off.

Sam was right, of course. He tossed the damp tunic at the laundry chute and restarted his school computer. Once he'd sent his response to Elliott's latest message, he opened his schoolwork. Grammar flashed up at him, though at least it was the end of the unit, and only the quiz was left. He skimmed the questions and randomly selected answers. Not waiting to see if he passed, he shut it down and zipped up the bright yellow suit he wore every time he left his quarters. After tucking his gloves and hood into the loop on one pantleg and a few snacks into a pocket, Eric palmed the panel, and the hatch retracted.

He stopped at his sisters' quarters, but there was no answer, so he jogged over to VVR. The activity light blinked green—they'd already started. He entered his code and stepped onto the forecastle of an ancient, ocean-going tall ship, with sails snapping and a black flag with a skull and crossbones fluttering overhead in a digital breeze. Blythe's favorite program.

"Catch!" Blythe tossed him a light wooden stick and a bandana.

He ignored the cloth but snatched the stick from the air and parried Blythe's immediate strike. The three of them battled until they were laughing and sweaty, but without warning, the program flickered off. Overhead, the light flashed orange then red. They all froze.

Their commlinks chimed simultaneously, though a delay in Blythe's gave Mum's voice a weird echo. "Kids, I've secured the hatch. Stay tight but don't worry—"

Dad interrupted. Eric didn't catch what he was saying before the commlinks cut out. The program did not resume.

"Maybe we ought to keep our sticks on hand," Eric managed. "Just in case."

"I don't want mine." Blythe's voice sounded tiny as she handed him hers. Sometimes he forgot she was only eleven. "What d'you think happened?"

"Probably something with the transports," Sam said.

The sound of a muffled pop penetrated the bulkheads. Blythe sidled close to their older sister and took her hand.

"We'll be fine, though." Sam's eyes fastened on the red light over the hatch, and she gave Blythe a sideways hug.

Eric swallowed. "Yeah."

Three more pops, in close succession, were followed by a deep thud and distant shouts.

"Everything will be fine," Sam said again.

No one spoke for a while. Blythe huddled on the floor in the back of the room with Sam's arm around her skinny shoulders. Eric paced, wooden sticks in hand, occasionally spinning them around. Another sharp crack made him jump.

Blythe sniffled.

"You're scaring her. Put those things down."

"*I'm* scaring her? She's smarter than that." Eric pointed one stick at Blythe, who tucked her head against Sam's shoulder. "She's not even looking at me. And at least it's something. If someone broke in—"

"A couple stupid pieces of wood won't mean anything against real weapons."

Blythe whimpered.

"And who's scaring her now?"

"Shut it, Eric!"

He glared at Sam, who looked away.

An eerie quiet overtook the pops, thuds, and shouts. Under the yellow suit and long-sleeved shirt, goosebumps rose on his arms, and it took a while to realize it wasn't nerves—the temperature had dropped. Eventually Eric joined with his sisters and shared the food bars from his pocket. They sat there, watching the light, waiting for the red to fade to orange.

When it did, their commlinks chimed, and the three of them jumped to their feet.

"Everything's fine, kids." Mum's voice was calm, as if she hadn't hung up on them earlier. "Uncle Brian is on his way to escort you to the common room. Samara, Dad needs you to check some coding. Blythe, sweetie, you can watch some of those vids we've been saving. Just stay tight until Dad or I tell you otherwise. Eric, Uncle Brian will need your help."

"Got it, Mum."

"And kids? It'll probably get chilly. Keep your suits on, even in the common room. We'll all stay in there tonight. Love you."

"Love you back," they said in unison.

Before the light turned green, the hatch slid open and Uncle Brian entered, a holster on his right thigh and a bandage around his left hand.

"Ready?" Instead of his usual booming voice, their uncle spoke softly, but he flashed them a tired smile.

"Yes, sir," Sam said.

"It's pirates, isn't it?" Blythe gnawed on her thumb. "But not the good kind."

"Pirates? No, kiddo, nothing like that." Uncle Brian rested his bandaged hand on her short red hair. "Just a situation with some of the patients." He glanced sideways. "Eric, leave the sticks here."

A thousand questions rose, but Eric shoved the sticks into the locker in the corner.

Uncle Brian limped as he led Eric and his sisters past the forward lift to the ladder, then down the main passageway, pausing outside the common room.

Sam finally asked what they all had been wondering: "What happened?"

"A couple of the guards needed guarding, is all," he replied lightly. "Your parents and I have it sorted. And your mother is the best shot on the ship, so no need to worry."

"Then why—"

He turned to Blythe, who watched them with round, brown eyes. "Honey, can you whip up some cookies? I think we could all use a treat."

Her face lit up. "I can do that!"

After Blythe trotted off to the small galley in the back, Uncle Brian said, "Your dad is patching up nav." His laugh seemed forced. "My sister can do many things, but making quick work of higher math isn't one of them. Since she can't do it, your dad needs you to double-check his work, Samara. And although life support is functional, climate control took a hit. That's one of the things you and I will be working on, Eric. The people who tried to gain control—"

Sam gasped. "But you said there weren't any pirates—"

"There weren't." Uncle Brian shook his head. "Mutineers, maybe. Turns out, a couple of the patients weren't actually sick, though that can't have been accidental. One of the guards helped them overpower the others and—" He stopped.

"But why?" Sam asked in an undertone.

Uncle Brian glanced at Blythe, who was pulling out mixing bowls and ingredients. "A lot of people don't like the powers that be. Some get caught and sentenced to the belt. Once in a while, they escape and try to take down the government or the Consortium all over again. But not on *our* ship. We stopped 'em, but they damaged some equipment. Used the deaths—"

"No!" Sam's hand flew to her mouth. "You killed them?"

"Of course not!" He ran his fingers through his curly hair, making it stand up in little horns all over his head. "A few patients died this morning, which wasn't anyone's fault, and those rotters took advantage of the timing. Poor dross won't need lung transplants, after all. The Consortium never sends enough anyway, so maybe it's just as well. We're not a priority out here." His expression softened. "Go solve for *x* or whatever it is you and your dad do, Samara, then help your sister. Eric and I have to find a way to heat a ship and chill some shells."

Sam nodded. "Right."

Uncle Brian turned her about like she was eight, not eighteen, and sent her off, securing the hatch behind her. "Come on, Eric. We've got a morgue to build."

Eric hadn't known how cold a cold locker for six people needed to be—the answer was *really cold*. Thankfully, the shells were already in body bags, so he hadn't seen anything. While he finished sealing the vents,

his mind wandered away from bundles of wires and stacked black bags
to the distance between their current heading and New Triton.

He closed the panel and sighed.

"All done?"

"Yeah. But it would've been nice if another ship had taken those
people to the hospital platform. I don't like this." Eric jabbed a thumb
toward the sealed room behind them.

Uncle Brian didn't look up from repacking his tools into the thick
canvas bag. "Neither do I."

Eric leaned against the metal-grey bulkhead with its blue and red
stripes. "Why'd those guards really try to take the ship?"

A frown tugged on features which usually smiled. "Not everyone
can wait out a long game."

"You mean the way it took two generations for our family to get
out of the mines and pay back the debt for being involved in designing
those nanites?"

"And another two to get *Gryphon*." Uncle Brian clicked the case
shut. "Not that I think it's fair to punish children for their parents'
crimes, even if those crimes did involve genetic cleansing. They got
what they deserved. We didn't. Point is, people like those mutineers
believe that working in the system for change is a waste. One of the
women was ranting about making them pay with blood when they
locked her up. I'm not a fan of the Consortium, myself, but that doesn't
mean they should all die."

"And now we have a room full of shells."

Uncle Brian studied him. "This isn't about making a cold
locker, is it?"

Eric only shrugged.

His uncle hefted the tool bag and set off down the passageway, his
limp more pronounced after several hours of squatting, climbing, and
sealing off vents. "It's about Sam, eh?"

"No . . . Fine," Eric admitted. "Void take it. I was excited for her
when she got the scholarship, but stars, I didn't think about what it
would mean here after she left. How stupid does that make me?"

His uncle shook his head. "You're not stupid, Eric. She's your sister
and your oldest friend."

"My only friend, really, other than Blythe and Elliott." Eric took a breath. "We'll have to send her on a transport from Krios, won't we?"

"'Fraid so."

"I wanted—No, never mind."

Uncle Brian set a hand on Eric's shoulder. "It's not selfish to want to stand on a planet. And it's not selfish to want to see a friend you haven't seen in five years, either."

It was seven years, but though he was right about Elliott, that wasn't the point. Time to dodge the subject.

"Being on a planet is probably just like standing here, only without the engines tickling my feet," Eric said. "And it isn't like we'd see stars from New Triton, just domes. I can see them from the viewing platforms around Krios, anyway."

When they reached the storage area, Uncle Brian entered a security code and palmed the panel, then tossed the bag into its locker. It landed with a metallic clatter.

"Your mum and dad are plenty smart, Eric." He shut the locker door. "Me, not so much, but this is a chance the three of us never had. Samara has to take it, just like you will if you manage a scholarship like hers. Can't cut her fuel lines to keep her here."

Eric huffed. "Like I'd do that?"

"She'll be okay, Eric." The two of them started back up the passageway. "Change is the way of things, but we all need something steady. A constant."

They reached the hatch before Eric managed past the knot in his throat, "I guess that's what family's for."

Uncle Brian gave Eric's shoulder a light punch. "It'll be all right."

A constant. Sam was his sister. That wouldn't change. He'd hold fast to that.

Deactivating the emergency system had allowed the lift to resume service. Cam and Tia accompanied Eric and the sick woman, but the others refused, insisting that they would use the ladder and that I go first. Despite the students' protests, I preceded everyone else up the ladder, and the harsh scent of medical-grade disinfectant grew stronger as I climbed. When I stepped cautiously onto the upper deck, the astringent odor burned my nostrils. No drone's microantigravity unit whirred over the stillness, and only the occasional chime of a medicomputer and the whisper of air in the vents broke the silence. I called down the ladderwell that the infirmary doors stood open and the hall was clear.

One by one, the crew members arrived: Hugo, the tall woman, then the angular man they had called Foster. When the lift arrived with a soft jolt, Hugo and the tall woman edged away from the shivering older woman. Last of all, Bryce pushed off the ladder and dusted her palms on her thighs.

Cam and I led the way to the infirmary, stopping at the threshold. Two cleaning bots scuttled across the smooth floor, while a round sanitizing bot climbed snail-like up the walls and over the counters, leaving shining trails that evaporated within seconds. As in Max's infirmary on *Thalassa*, soothing blues and greens tinted the walls, and data rose above the larger consoles in blinking amber, cyan, and red. The metallic doors of the closet-like medicomputer gleamed. If there had not been bodies on the two hoverbeds and one slumped in a chair in front of a computer, the familiarity would have been comforting. Given the differences, it was not.

Bryce rolled her eyes. "Guess we have a few things to move before we get those beds to Watkins."

Kavanaugh staggered through the doors to drop heavily into the closest chair, but Cam and I hesitated briefly before entering the brightly lit room. Then, while he checked the beds, I went to ascertain whether or not the grey-haired woman in pale-green scrubs lived. She did not. Her identification bracelet stated she was Dr. Amanda Smithson, but Cam's soft exclamation stopped me before I could inform the others that she had died.

"It's Leslie."

Eric uttered an oath.

"She can't—" Tia's voice broke. "But, Cam, she's going to be a doctor."

Cam shook his head. The bots' scuttling, the fans' steady thrum, and Kavanaugh's thick, burbling gasps filled the room.

Bryce barged through the infirmary and searched the cabinets. Without turning around, she asked, "Who's the other one?"

"Specialist Shen."

"Rust it," Foster grumbled. "I'm guessing Smithson's gone, too?"

"Yes," I said succinctly.

"We need biohazard suits," the tall woman said from the doorway.

"No point." Bryce pulled a box of jet injectors from the cabinet and shoved five into her jacket pocket. "We've already been exposed. Come on, Foster. Let's get those suits so Rain can celebrate her placebo effect."

Foster backed further into the hall.

"I shall go with you," I said.

"I don't think so." Bryce stabbed a finger at me. "I don't want some spacing unRecorder breathing down my neck. Not only do you have to stay here and"—she fluttered one hand—"record, but I don't need *you* anyway. It's not like there are insurgents crawling the hallways. Just germs."

"Germs are not the sole adversary. There is at least one rogue drone."

Hugo widened his stance, blocking the infirmary doors. "That a threat?"

"It's the truth." Cam's intervention drew their attention. "She stopped one, but the other's still out there."

Tia straightened her jacket. "I'll go."

Cam gave her a terse nod, but Eric frowned.

Though it was not my place to issue orders, I wished I could. I closed my eyes momentarily before asking, "Tia, should you encounter a drone, do you remember what to do?"

She swallowed and nodded.

At first, no one moved, but when Kavanaugh broke into a prolonged cough, Bryce startled, then darted to the hallway. After she and Foster trotted off, Tia followed them, and Eric watched her leave.

"The question is," Rain said, "where do we . . . I mean, what do we do with the bodies? A ship this size only has one cold locker."

Eric turned away from the door. "Not too hard to rig a temporary morgue. Since there's only the one main airlock—which was bad planning if you ask me—we'll have to use a room. Seal the vents, set the temperature low enough, pull out the humidity."

Hugo scowled down at him. "And you know that because?"

Eric pointed his thumb at his chest. "Freighter brat. MTS *Gryphon*. We had to improv a morgue, maybe six years back, on the way in from the outer belt when some of the medical transports died three ten-days from Krios."

Shoving past Eric, Hugo retrieved two analgesic jet injectors from the box Bryce had left on the counter. He depressed them into his arm before asking, "How many, Rain?"

"Just one," she whispered.

He tossed it to her, and she deftly caught it and popped it into the side of her neck. The tension on her face faded, but she did not dispose of the empty injector, only gripped it in a white-knuckled hand.

"Better?" Hugo asked quietly.

She nodded.

"If," I began, "someone could administer medication to Kavanaugh—"

"Do I look like a doctor to you?" The sneer returned to Hugo's face. "Just so it's clear, I'll say it again: I'm not touching shells."

"Fine." Cam's jaw muscle ticced. "Eric, Zeta? Is the medicomputer open?"

"The light is on, Cameron Rodriguez," I said. "It is occupied."

Rain glanced at the doctor's still form. "That scan should be done by now."

Eric wove between the hoverbeds and chairs to the medicomputer. I followed a meter behind. When he fumbled with the lever on the door, the scanner pinged once.

"Subject deceased," its gentle, programmed voice announced. "Calculations complete and transmitted to Dr. Smithson's computer."

Eric jerked away.

Silence swelled. Rain gnawed on her lower lip. She glanced down at the jet injector in her fist and tucked it into the pocket on her thigh. From the chair near the door, Kavanaugh moaned. She required treatment, though the bodies on the hoverbeds belied any hope for recovery.

Whatever the case, the medicomputer needed to be cleared, so I stepped around Eric and opened the door. Together, he and I pulled out one of the infirmary's hoverbeds, but I averted my eyes from the still form underneath the thin cotton blanket. Before Eric could enter, I closed the door and activated the self-cleaning cycle.

"But I—"

"You must wait, Eric Thompson." Clasping my hands behind my back to keep from tapping my leg, I explained, "Given the possibility of pathogens, sanitizing the system first is advisable."

"Good point," Cam agreed. "Who is it?"

Eric shifted the blanket aside to check the body's identification bracelet. "Alfred Butterfield."

Hugo snorted. "No loss there."

"Douglas," Rain protested.

"He's Consortium, Rain."

"He was staff, but he's a citizen now."

"Was." Hugo crossed his thick arms. "Past tense."

Cam frowned at him. "We should check Dr. Smithson's records. Are we the only ones left? If not, where are the others?"

Eric rubbed his left shoulder. "We're only two days out. If it's just these four and the ones on the bridge, maybe we don't need a makeshift morgue. They might fit in the galley freezer if we stack them."

Hugo grunted. "Don't be stupid, kid. I don't want a bunch of rotting shells in with my food."

Rain hugged herself as if she were chilled. "Dr. Smithson would have figured out where to put them."

When no one else moved, I returned to the doctor's desk and

reached over her to pull up files. The most recent were garbled and unintelligible, but the seventh one was almost coherent. I summarized, "Twenty-three hours ago, Joseph Shen, Alfred Butterfield, and Leslie Mendoza sealed off the storage room near the loading bay. Records indicate the remains of one crew member and five Consortium staff are stored there."

Eric grimaced and rubbed the back of his neck. "That'll work."

"Dr. Smithson's records do not indicate completion. Alfred Butterfield had been running a low-grade fever, but he knew the system best." I skimmed further. "When he collapsed, Shen and Mendoza carried him back. They both fell ill before he died."

Boots sounded from the corridor, and Eric's expression lightened when Tia entered the infirmary.

Bryce twirled a mask in her left hand, then tossed it and several more onto the counter. "Here you go, whether or not they help."

Foster set sealed packages next to the masks. "We only found seven—"

One of Kavanaugh's wracking coughs interrupted him. She doubled over, then slid to the floor. I started toward her, but Cam was already at her side, his fingertips on the hollow of her throat.

"She's alive, but her pulse is weak. Although, if the doctor couldn't save them"—he gestured at the bodies—"I don't see what we can do." He shifted back into a crouch. "Should we scan her?"

"I don't think scanning will help." Rain sidled closer to Hugo. "But she should be in bed."

Someone made a noncommittal hum.

Cam, face drawn, stood. "I'll make room."

He pushed the beds close together, and I studied my bare toes while he maneuvered Joseph Shen's unwieldy form next to Leslie Mendoza's. Cam finished and applied a handful of cleaning gel to his bare skin, once, then twice. Everyone withdrew as he slid his arms under Kavanaugh, grunting when he stood.

"Shouldn't you change the sheets?" Rain asked.

Hugo backed away from the bodies. "Why? Doesn't matter at this point. She's as good as dead."

Bryce, who had been watching Cam lower Kavanaugh onto the bed, spun on her heel and glared at Hugo. "Stars, man. She can hear you."

"You want me to lie, Bryce?" he sneered. "That never fixed anything."

The medicomputer chimed in, counterpoint to the low burble of both the medical tank and my anxiety. Eric opened its metal doors, and the odor of disinfectant billowed from the white interior. After the smell dissipated, I pushed a chair into the scanner.

Eric's eyes met mine. Their brown reminded me of tea, and though I could not say why, the thought made me miss my friends. He fingered the cool metal encircling his arm. "Do I need to take this off first?"

"No," I said gently, "but if it makes you uncomfortable, I shall remove it."

"That'd be good."

I unwrapped the tendril, coiling and stuffing it into the right jacket pocket to remain in possession of Consortium property.

Eric glanced over my shoulder, then back at me. "All set, I guess. Thanks."

The door swished shut, and I activated the scan.

A cabinet slammed. Startled, I spun around just as Foster flopped into a chair and dumped sanitizer onto his hands.

Bryce stopped sorting through the biohazard suits. "What?"

"We're out of body bags." He pinched the bridge of his nose.

"Body bags or not, we need to check out the temporary morgue," Cam said. "Once we store these three, we'll have a bed to transport the captain. Or we could double them up now and move him first."

Hugo scowled. "Why should we listen to you, kid? Even Bryce here outranks you."

"Don't be such a trog, Hugo. You two can compare testosterone levels later. Right now, we need to stow the shells before they swell up. And you don't have room to talk. You were hiding under Rain's bed." Ignoring both Rain's protest and Hugo's epithet, Bryce turned to Cam. "What're you thinking, doll?"

Pink suffused his cheeks. "We'll need to get the bodies secured in that storage room and make sure it's sealed up right. Anyone know about ventilation systems?"

"That'd be you, Hugo, *if* you can cooperate," Bryce said. "I don't think bags matter anymore, since—"

Everyone's communication links chimed simultaneously, and almost in unison, they answered.

Watkins's disembodied voice asked, "What's taking so long?"

"Got shells here, Watkins," Hugo said. "Four, including Smithson, but before she died, she had people rig a temp morgue on the deck above engineering. I'll head down there, check it out."

Indignation swept over me that Hugo would take credit for Cam's ideas.

"Get it done," Watkins ordered. "I want these shells off the bridge."

"And the captain to the infirmary," Cam added.

Watkins ignored his suggestion. "I need Gretchen. They're sending us all the way back to Lunar One, even though Twelve is closer, and she needs to throw her weight around."

Gretchen? I glanced at Bryce, then followed her gaze to the moaning woman.

Rain cleared her throat. "Gretchen Kavanaugh isn't going to make it."

Watkins cursed. "Then you get up here, Rain. You're our next best chance."

Hugo's frown deepened.

"It'll take a few trips to get everyone down to the lower deck." Bryce stuffed her hands into her tunic pockets. "Unless we double load the hoverbeds and dump Kavanaugh in the corner and use all three."

My hands curled into fists, and I forced them flat. "The living—both she and Captain Stirling—are the priority."

"The dying aren't," Watkins snapped. "Clear the bed, Hugo, then get them all to that morgue."

"The vents and seal on that room'll need checking, since she had Butterfield rig it." Hugo lowered his voice, but everyone heard him mutter, "*Consortium dross.*"

Rain glanced at me, then up at the recording device and tapped his arm. "Butterfield paid back the cost of his gifting. He earned his position."

Hugo's upper lip curled. "Better off if they didn't let staffers pretend to be citizens. Not like they're—"

"Bicker later." Watkins's voice seemed brittle. "Get the first load back to whatever storage they have, then get these out of here. We'll deal with the *living* after that."

"Not touching shells," Hugo repeated.

"Founders' sakes! Just get it done! And Bryce? Bring me a suit." Watkins cut the link.

As if on cue, the recording device's dull eye moved with a mechanical hum, but Hugo did not seem to notice—or if he had noticed, did not seem to care.

"Foster, Rodriguez," Hugo barked. "Get going."

Foster interlaced his fingers, palms out, and stretched his arms.

Cam's fists curled and uncurled. "But the captain—"

"You heard Watkins. Later." Bryce took a palmful of sanitizing gel and slathered it on her hands, shaking the excess onto the floor. A bot crawled at her feet, mopping it up. "Once the bodies are gone, Rain and I'll head to the bridge. Tia and the unRecorder can stay here with Kavanaugh and Thompson. Just"—she pointed at me—"don't leave *her* alone. She needs supervision."

Foster lowered the hoverbed and shoved the shivering woman back onto the floor. She groaned. Hugo snapped his fingers and pointed. Cam, his jaw set, helped Foster lift the doctor's awkward form, and the three men pushed the hoverbeds toward the door.

"Cam?" Tia called.

"Yeah?"

"Be careful."

We watched the doorway as the lift's chime sounded twice, taking first Cam and Butterfield, then Foster, Hugo, and the other two hoverbeds to the lower deck.

"They should have put on the biosuits first," Rain said.

"Yeah." Her eyes still trained on the dying woman, Bryce exhaled heavily. "Maybe you and Watkins have a point about those things."

She sorted through the suits, tossed one at Rain, and slathered mint-scented cleansing gel on her face, hands, and arms, then tugged off her boots. Rain proceeded to copy Bryce in stripping off her jacket, T-shirt, and pants. Both women tossed their clothes down the laundry chute and pulled on the orange jumpsuits. Bryce folded the pantlegs around her ankles, then shoved her feet back into her black boots.

I cleared my throat. "Proper decontamination procedure—"

"Shut it, *Zeta*." Bryce pulled up the hood and adjusted the clear facial shield and small respirator before she tugged on thin, black gloves. "If you're going to be like that, you don't even get one."

Rain paused, her hood halfway up. "I don't think—"

"We don't have spares anyway. Why waste one on her?"

I did not want a suit, but Tia protested, "That's not fair."

Bryce rounded on her. "Maybe you don't need one, either."

She snatched up the last five suits and masks, then stormed out of the infirmary. Rain hugged herself for a second but said nothing as she, too, donned a mask and gloves. She slowed at the door and looked back at us, her goggles glinting in the overhead lights. Tia glowered after the departing women.

Stressful situations could indeed bring out the worst in people, but at that moment, I admitted to myself that I did not like Bryce at all.

## 07

Without the hoverbeds filling the center of the room, the infirmary felt cavernous. Its quiet was only broken by Kavanaugh's moans and the occasional burble of the medical tank.

Apple-tainted bile rose in my throat. If the tank's nanodevices had begun their work . . . I pulled Cam's jacket closer around my torso, despite the discomfort when it snagged the small cuts.

"Zeta?" Tia's voice seemed to echo. "You went white as a sheet. What's wrong?"

"The medtank," I managed. "Nanodevices purify the medical gel like macrophages, eliminating dead material. If someone has died . . ." I could not finish my thought aloud.

"It's all right. I got it."

The medicomputer chimed, but I did not reach it before Eric's muffled voice came faintly from inside the machine. "Tried to use the emergency lever, but it's jammed. You gonna let me out?"

"I am coming."

I opened the medicomputer, and when he emerged from its red-lit interior, its pleasant tone announced that Eric's arm had sustained two occult fractures, then recommended the appropriate dose of specific nanodevices to knit the bones. I requested that he sit while I found the supplies, but Eric paid me no heed. I followed his gaze to Tia, who stood over the tank, unmoving.

"Tia?" he asked, his voice more hushed than I had yet heard.

"It's . . ." She gulped. "It's Lydia White."

"I'll take care of her."

"No." She offered a wan smile. "You take care of your arm. Zeta can find the injectors, and you'll be sorted in no time."

Eric's jaw tightened. "Just a splint."

His remark pulled her attention away from the dead woman, and her eyes narrowed in our direction. "You heard the medicomputer. Your arm's broken."

"No nanites. You can't know what's inside 'em." He turned to me. "Could you splint it again, without that drone's tentacle?"

Before I answered, Kavanaugh groaned from the bare floor in the corner. A flood of memories hit me: *Max, Edwards, Williams, all at my bedside; Nate with his mug of coffee; Kyleigh at the computer; and even Elliott slouched in a chair.*

A bot scooted around Kavanaugh, and Watkins's order to dump her from the bed, whether from fear or emotional distance, made my jaw clench.

"Yes. I will tend to Kavanaugh while you find the supplies."

Averting his eyes from the woman's thrashing, Eric turned to rummage through the cabinets one-handed and pulled out oral analgesics, a splint, and bandages.

I took a heated blanket from the cabinet, shook it open, then tucked it around Kavanaugh, who cringed away from me.

Her broken capillaries had leaked, staining both her cheeks and jawline with scarlet, and fine red lines traced down her neck. Bloodshot eyes stared wildly, and she choked out the words, "Not you . . ."

"No," I said, though I did not know what I meant. "Not I."

When she moaned and her forehead creased, I wished again for my drone and the ability to access records. Eric appeared at my side with the box Hugo had left on the counter. I took an analgesic jet injector, placed the narrower tip against Kavanaugh's neck, and hit the flattened end with my thumb. It popped, and almost immediately, her writhing slowed, and her eyelids fluttered shut. I could do nothing more to aid her.

"What's next?" Eric asked. "And where'd everyone go?"

Tia finished punching commands into the medical tank's panel, and with a chug, the liquid began to drain away. "Cam left with Hugo and Foster to check the temporary morgue. They took the bodies." She watched the tank. "Well, most of them."

I added, "We are to remain with Kavanaugh and you, Eric Thompson."

"Are we just supposed to wait, then?"

Tia shrugged.

He handed me the supplies, and while I wrapped his forearm, Tia contacted Watkins and gave her a brief summary of the situation.

"You should have pinged me before draining the tank," Watkins said. "Whatever state White is in, that'll have to wait. Have to get the bridge cleared. Get Thompson's arm treated, then get down here and help."

Rain's soft voice murmured in the background.

Watkins exhaled loudly. "Fine. One of you stay with Gretchen Kavanaugh, and the other get up here. Just keep an eye on that unRecorder." The link chimed as she signed off.

Eric's arm tensed under my hands, and I hastened to finish fastening his sling.

Pushing himself away from the counter, Eric wavered, then caught his balance, but the color drained from his face. Holding his injured arm close, he asked through clenched teeth, "How do you want to divvy this up, Tia?"

"Zeta and I will head down to the bridge," she said. "You stay here. Shut the door, in case of drones."

He glanced at Kavanaugh. "By myself?"

"Moons above, Eric," Tia snapped. "Yes. And if personal preference is a valid reason, I prefer not to be on a blasted plague ship at all."

An argument ensued, their voices falling in pitch while rising in intensity, but I kept my eyes on Kavanaugh, who drew a shuddering breath before she went completely still. The low murmur of their disagreement faded away when I knelt to check for a pulse and slowly pulled the blanket over her head.

Seconds ticked past, and no one spoke. Only the sanitizing bots moved, leaving iridescent trails of cleanliness.

"No need to stay now," Tia finally said. "You don't look good, Zeta. Maybe you should rest a bit before we leave."

"She needs to eat."

Tia's brown eyes widened at me. "Right! I can't believe I forgot."

Eric checked his pockets. "I'm out of food bars, but maybe I can dig some up."

I shook my head. "I have not been of much help with the bodies. I offer my assistance now to prepare both women for transportation to the lower deck."

"You've done more than you think." Eric pushed a chair toward me. "But you've got some cuts, and infection isn't a good thing, especially when you're on"—he stole a glance at Tia—"a plague ship."

"It is immaterial . . ." The memory of Max's disapproval when I had been injured and Nate carried me to the infirmary stopped my protest. Instead I sank into the chair. "I thank you, Eric. You are correct."

"You probably want the gel bandages, right?"

I nodded, and while he resumed pulling out supplies and setting them on the counter, Tia approached and held out her hand. I attempted to raise one eyebrow, but once again, I did not manage it.

"Take off the jacket."

Packaged, sanitized medical tools clattered to the floor. Eric knelt to gather them, then cleared his throat. "That should be everything. I think I'll head down to the bridge."

Tia spun to him. "No, you'll stay here so we all go together. That other drone is flying around somewhere."

"Nah, I'll be fine. I mean"—he glanced at me and away—"I faced one down already, so it isn't like I don't know what to do."

She pointed at his arm. "And that went so well."

"I'm not worried," he said as he headed to the door.

"Eric!"

He gave her an almost-smile. "Ping me, and I'll come back up to walk you down, if you want."

"Eric David Thompson, don't you dare—"

The door slid shut, and Tia let out a low string of imprecations.

"He knows what he must do," I assured her.

She sighed. "I suppose Eric is right, and there's really no point in inviting infection. Let's see to those cuts."

My hand rose to the tiny scabs and dried trails of blood on my neck. I removed the jacket and folded it neatly. The infirmary's chill crept over me, so I held the olive-green fabric against my bare abdomen.

She put on a pair of disposable gloves. "Tilt your head down."

I did, then closed my eyes. The sharp cold of antiseptic burned, and I winced at the small sparks of pain.

"Sorry about that. Got a sliver of metal—" The sound of a package tearing open interrupted her. "Eric found tweezers, so he anticipated fragments, even if I didn't." A sharp tug pinched my neck below my ear, and she dropped a fragment of metal and a pair of tweezers onto the countertop before me. "This happened when Cam shot out the lock?"

I gave a single, careful nod.

The icy sting disappeared into the soothing coolness of medgel as she affixed a bandage. "Let me see your shoulder, too. Cam and I probably shouldn't tease Eric about ogling. I guess it isn't really funny, but he's a little . . . skin shy. He had a hard time adjusting to the dorms. Evidently it was different on his parents' freighter. He didn't even share a room with his sisters. You'd think, with limited space and all, that it wouldn't matter, but I guess they also had a dress code and didn't even wear short sleeves." She chuckled. "He blushed so much first ten-day of class that I would've sworn he'd burned in the sunroom."

"Perhaps," I said, "they were concerned about propriety?"

"I guess." Tia began working on my shoulder and upper back. "Blast, Zeta. We should've treated this ages ago." She used the tweezers again. "You've got some pretty bad scarring here, too."

I grimaced. "Yes."

She exhaled. "Almost done." After a few seconds, she said in hushed tones, "Back when we met the first drone, it shocked you and Cam."

I stiffened.

"He thinks you're used to it. Is that . . ." She picked up the tweezers again, and a sharp pain shot through my back. "Sorry. Caught your skin."

"It is well," I managed. "I appreciate your help."

She pulled the sliver free and set it on the counter, and the cold sting of antiseptics replaced the trickle running down my back. "Do all Recorders—I mean, I've been thinking, running through things I've seen, but never understood. He isn't wrong, is he? Those drones punish you."

I did not answer.

"It really isn't related to the scarring?"

"The scars are from injuries sustained thirty-two days ago."

"What happened?"

"I was hit by burning debris." I did not explain further.

"When your friends carried you out?"

"As you say." At the thought of the recording device's solitary eye watching me, I tried to lie, "They were my teammates. Not . . ."

I could not say it, could not declare such a falsehood, but she did not inquire further, only hummed noncommittally. Three minutes ticked past. Then, for some reason, words came pouring out, whether because I was too tired to stop them or needed to share the story, I could not tell. "My assignment was to document a recovery team and retrieve Consortium property. We had found the medical stasis pods, when a—" The memory stopped me momentarily. Again, I saw with clarity the improbable, nearly two-meter insect crush the drone that had been by my side for years, aiding my work, comforting me in anxiety, reprimanding me when I made mistakes. "Something destroyed my drone, nearly incapacitating me. The team fought their way through. There was an explosion, and debris hit my back."

"Is that the same accident you told me about earlier?"

I should have been relieved that she did not remember that I had mentioned that Nate carried me to safety. Of course the story would have meant little to her, though to me . . . I did not trust my voice, so I merely nodded.

"Sounds rough." She applied more bandages to my back. "Did you . . . I mean . . . Zeta, what was it like, growing up at a Consortium training center?"

The question, which had no obvious reference point, confused me. I answered cautiously, "We are cared for. The gardens are peaceful."

"Do you stay in touch with the other kids from your cohort? Your friends?"

A short laugh broke from me, despite the bodies, recording device, and the virus. "Friends. Recorders cannot have friends, just as we cannot have names. We live to redeem our gifting, and personal involvement would betray that purpose."

"I didn't know." Her hands stilled, and her voice sounded small. "I toured a training center with my class when I was younger, and the kids were all studying quietly or playing in the gardens. They seemed happy."

"'Happiness,'" I quoted, "'is irrelevant.'"

"I don't agree," she said. "They say that gifting is an honor."

"So they say."

"That'll do it."

Relieved, I pulled the jacket back on. The bandages eased its chafing over the cuts. She deposited the tweezers in the small autoclave, then tossed the metal fragments, gauze, and her gloves into the trash receptacle. I fastened the jacket shut, and she found a nanodevice-saturated compression bandage for my ankle. While I bound it, a sanitizing bot crept up the cabinets and scoured the countertop, its trail drying quickly. I finished and stood cautiously, the pain subsiding as the devices penetrated my skin.

"Ever had the rug pulled out from under you?"

I stopped in the act of refolding the jacket's sleeves and turned my attention to Tia. "Is that an idiom?"

"Yes." She bit her lip. "It means to suddenly take back support or security. A betrayal." Her eyes darted from Kavanaugh's shrouded form to the Consortium device on the wall, and she shivered.

We were both silent for several moments before Tia said, "Maybe we should head down to the bridge."

"Indeed."

She started the decontamination cycle on the medicomputer and turned off the lights. Though one bot continued its duties, the other docked in its station. Again, she glanced at the silent medical tank.

"I don't know. Maybe losing your drone is something like that."

I checked both directions, but the hall was clear.

"That happened to me," she said quietly. "Not losing my drone, obviously, but I trusted someone. I . . . I thought we were in love. Then I was stuck."

Indignation and concern stopped me in the open doorway. "Stuck? Emotional or physical entrapment—"

"Oh, not that," she said quickly. "Just . . . consequences."

Sudden concern prompted me to say, "Cam or Eric—"

"What? No, not them. I mean, Cam isn't . . . And Eric?" She shook her head. "Either one would've been a better choice than that trog."

I did not scold her for language.

She gave me a sideways glance. "Do you . . . do you regret being gifted?"

The sudden shift in topics jarred me. "That is a deeply personal question."

She flushed.

We left the infirmary as clean as it could be on a virus-ridden ship and walked to the lift, and she slowed to match my uneven gait.

"I do not know that I can regret an action I did not take, but have I pondered what might have happened had I not been gifted? We all do."

"All of you?"

"I was inaccurate, but most do, at some point." Aware of the Consortium device trained on us, I waited for the lift to arrive, for us to step inside, and the doors to close. "To me, the fundamental value of each person is the true gifting, and that value must be the core of our relationships. Beyond that, I do not know."

Her eyes, wide and deep, stayed on mine. "Is life without affection or happiness worth living?"

"Do you speak of the individual who stole your rug?" I frowned. "If that person acted selfishly and dishonestly, that was not love."

A faint smile quirked her lips, then faded.

"Basing choices on emotion is not sound, but choosing to set oneself aside for the ones who are loved, that is beautiful in its sometimes-pain." I could not tell her my choice to surrender and not to run had kept Nate and my friends safe, and that was what mattered. That was all that mattered. And yet, it hurt. "To be loved like that, and to love like that, yes, it is worth a great deal."

"Maybe you're right." Tia's forehead puckered, and she looked away. "Blast it all."

The lift doors opened, and we were but meters from the bridge, with the Consortium devices again watching.

"Zeta?" she asked, without looking at me.

"Yes?"

"What do you do when someone betrays you?"

Julian Ross's face jumped to the forefront of my mind, followed by Elliott's, then Captain North's, but I only said, "I do not know."

"You know what I'd like?" Tia's alto seemed almost harsh. "I'd really like it if he suffered."

My jaw clenched, and the words clawed their way from my chest. "As would I."

She pivoted to face me, but when the camera whirred from across the hall, she clamped her mouth shut. We crossed to the bridge in silence.

Fatigue pulled at me in those last few meters to the bridge, and I limped several paces behind Tia, both of us still alert and checking for the other drone.

She opened the door as Rain was saying, "They picked up his body three days ago, floating outside Lunar One."

I stopped short. Tia looked back at me, wide-eyed.

"I served on *Thalassa* five years back and didn't like him at all." After a brief pause, Bryce added, "Still, no one deserves to be spaced."

While Bryce's reference to *Thalassa* surprised me and ejecting anyone into the void was a heinous crime, a rogue drone roamed the ship. Standing in the hall was inadvisable, so I entered and motioned for Tia to follow.

Only Eric, Rain, Watkins, and Bryce were on the bridge; the neither the bodies nor captain were present. My heart sank, for no one had brought the captain to the infirmary.

We were too late. He, too, was gone.

Watkins, who was leaning on the captain's vacant chair, straightened. "About time you got here. Get these cleaning bots out from underfoot and back in their charging stations, before I shoot the whole blasted lot."

Tia's attention, however, was on Bryce. "That's horrible! It's one of the worst ways to die! Who? Was he murdered?"

Bryce twirled around on the chair in front of the navigation console, running her gloved hands through the amber and green readout. "Captain Gregory North."

"What?" I asked before I thought not to.

Eric spoke, "*Thalassa*'s captain."

"Not anymore," Bryce said.

I settled back on my heels, tapping my thigh.

So. Captain North was dead, and I was not displeased by the news.

In truth, a surge of satisfied vindication was my immediate response. He had aligned himself with Julian Ross, who had no compunction about killing swaths of society, young or old, innocent or not. Captain North should not have been murdered, but "should not have been" had never, in all the course of history, been adequate to prevent anything—for good or ill.

"He wasn't murdered," Rain corrected from the communication officer's chair. "I told you the report said North was dead before he was spaced, though how they could tell after the fact—"

Bryce made an uncouth noise, then sprang from her chair and leaned over Rain to peer at the data. The taller woman moved from her seat, and Bryce took it. I edged closer.

"Ha!" Bryce enlarged a cyan image and jabbed at it with her index finger. "No cause of death listed, but see this? I know what killed him."

"Heart attack, again?" Watkins theorized. "About eight years back, I served on a freighter with his son. When he disappeared, North was livid, instigated inquiries. He raged about his son's disappearance until he had that attack and transplant, then the whole thing settled down." Her voice slowed. "Losing a kid changes people."

Bryce actually laughed, then, and my dislike for her grew. "I remember now. Good thing they never found out he blamed the Consortium. Would have cost him his job and more."

Rain's forehead creased. "Was his son removed, then?"

"Stars," Watkins hissed. "You can't say *that*. Not in public."

I glanced at the Consortium camera, but it remained still.

"Doesn't matter anyway, since they're both gone." Bryce stood, stretched, and sauntered back to the navigation console. "But I know what killed North."

Eric crossed his arms. "The report didn't say, so what makes you so sure?"

"They locked down the patrol ship that found his shell."

"So?"

"You're a voiding idiot, Thompson. They were quarantined, but the report says over half of them died so far." Bryce gestured at the door. "Same as here."

"Two-thirds," Rain murmured.

I tapped my thigh harder than usual. I did not wish to believe Captain North had been ill. That would be worse than murder, if it was not, indeed, the same thing. Perhaps he had met with a violent accident. Or his appendix had ruptured, and having deserted his post, he had not obtained medical assistance.

"I think you've all missed the most important thing." The overhead lighting gleamed on Bryce's face shield, obscuring her features, but she turned toward me. "North's ship is where the Consortium shuttle picked *her* up."

"What's your point, Bryce?" Eric demanded.

"Just wondering how many on *Thalassa* are dead."

My heart gave a painful jolt, and the hall around me seemed to spin.

Rain slid back into the communication seat, and her hands darted through the data. She leaned back with a sigh. "None."

*They were well.* Relief trickled through me, but it did not last long. If indeed this virus was Ross's bioweapon—and probability seemed high— it had escaped containment, and members of both the Consortium and the citizenry had fallen ill. If he had intended to destroy the Consortium, Ross had clearly erred. If he had loosed it, if it tore through the public as it had CTS *Agamemnon*, if . . . if . . . if . . .

A sudden chill raced through me, despite the warmth of Cam's jacket.

"That's not the case here, though, is it?" Bryce gave a brittle laugh. "Too bad you didn't get a suit, Tia. That unRecorder's probably a carrier."

I shrank from her words. Yet, as a disgraced Recorder, an aberration, was I not the perfect carrier? Ross had said as much.

"I don't think so," Tia said. "Or *Thalassa's* crew would've gotten sick as well."

"She's the commonality. Comes in contact with North, *boom*"— Bryce smacked a gloved fist into her palm—"he's dead. Comes here, and what? People die. Might be a good idea to space her, Watkins, before she gets us sick, too."

Eric spat out, "That's ridiculous."

"Sick or not, no one is getting spaced." Watkins set gloved fists on her waist. "She might be an unRecorder, Ursula Bryce, but that's murder."

Bryce shrugged.

"I don't . . ." Rain hesitated. "People were getting sick before they released her, so I don't think that's what happened. And, like I said before, footage shows Jenkins getting into the samples from *Thalassa*. He could have started it."

"Jenkins was an idiot." Watkins dropped into the captain's chair and relaxed into the black synthleather. "I wouldn't put it past him."

"We don't know—"

"Oh, let it alone, Bryce." Watkins lifted her chin at Tia and Eric. "You're scaring the children." She then snapped gloved fingers at me. "You. Do your job—start scanning records and verify that footage Rain found, and Rain, focus on comms. Bryce, see what you can find in the databases that'll help protect us. Vitamins, meds, face paint, or burning feathers. I don't care. Anything." As I moved to the nearest console to comply with Watkins's instructions, she addressed Tia. "Belisi, you going to follow orders, or are you just going to hover there like some sort of drone?"

Lips pinched, Tia shepherded the small bots to their alcoves.

Watkins then rounded on Eric. "Thompson, like I told you when you waltzed in here with your arm in that stupid, archaic sling, you can't afford to shun treatment when we're short-staffed."

Tia's face was even tighter as she locked the last bot down. "He has the right to refuse biotech, ma'am."

"Can't expect logic from belters, Watkins." Bryce laughed, though the humor escaped me. In truth, her frequent, harsh bursts of amusement grated on my nerves. Bryce spun her chair around twice, then added, "Not my problem, I suppose, if he wants to be such a waste of carbon. Don't know why they let you into university, Thompson, if you're that stupid. Just stay out of the way until we reach Lunar One."

Bryce's assessment was unjust, but I did not allow myself to utter the rash sentences forming in my head. Instead, I tried to focus on accessing relevant records.

"We're less than a skeleton crew here, Bryce. We can't afford to spare anyone," Watkins snapped. "Thompson understands nav and can take your station if necessary. Don't make me confine you to quarters."

"You? Send me? That's rich. You're a *phycologist*, Watkins. You work with algae. Being old doesn't give you the right to send me to my room like I'm twelve."

Watkins's communication link pinged, and when she tapped it, Hugo's voice bellowed, "Open the door! Now!"

Bryce leaped over and hit the panel to the doors' right. Boots thundered in the corridor.

A blur of biohazard orange skidded sideways onto the bridge as Foster plunged through the doors before they had opened fully, Hugo right behind him. Hugo slammed his gloved fist onto the control panel.

As the doors slid shut, a drone's hum vibrated through the air, silenced by the gentle click of the magnetic lock.

My breath caught. Only Hugo and Foster?

"Where's Cam?" Tia demanded.

Rapid exhalations fogged the inside of Foster's mask. "Spacing monstrosity nearly got us," he gasped. "Had to leave Rodriguez behind."

With a low cry, Eric lunged toward the doors, but Tia grabbed his uninjured arm. Though his cheeks flushed unevenly, he stopped. Fists clenched, Tia reiterated her demand for Cam's location. The men ignored her, and Watkins, no less rigid, repeated her question.

Hugo scowled. "Drone."

"So I gathered." Neither the baggy orange suit nor the mask muffled Watkins's intensity. "Where is Cameron?"

Hugo leaned against the communication console. "I don't know—"

"What?" Tia and Eric cried in unison.

My heart sputtered.

Watkins thrust a gloved finger at the men or the door; I could not tell which. "What happened?"

"We dumped the shells from the bridge, then Rodriguez led us to Jenkins. That blasted thing comes hurtling out of nowhere, so Foster starts running. I call for the stupid kid to hustle, but, no, he goes the wrong way, walks toward it, holding out his arms like it's a long-lost lover." Hugo cleared his throat, but his breath still wheezed. "We left the hoverbed in the hallway."

Silence swelled.

Finally, Watkins said, "Well?"

Hugo shrugged. "Last I saw, the drone was wrapping itself around his chest and trying to pull his arms off."

"And you left him? Space it, Hugo, he's not even out of school yet." Watkins turned her masked glare on Foster. "You have anything to add?"

"No."

If Cam had, indeed, imitated my actions, an undamaged drone would release him unharmed, as long as he did not attempt to access the panel to shut it off. Surely, Cameron Rodriguez would know not to do anything so foolish. Surely . . .

Rain groaned, but Bryce merely folded her arms and leaned back against the console. "Might as well have ejected the poor kid into space."

"What the void was I supposed to do?" Hugo shot back at Bryce. "Dance with it, too? Not after I saw what it did to Jenkins. Left *him* in the hall."

"He's not a pretty sight," Foster interjected.

Hugo guffawed. "He never was."

Bryce lashed out, "Like either of you have room to talk."

Watkins held up a gloved fist. "All of you shut it."

"But," Eric asked, his voice tight, "what about Cam?"

Hugo's massive shoulder rose and fell. "Nothing you can do, kid, not with a broken wing."

"But Cam . . ." Tia's wide eyes sought mine. "He'll be okay? It'll let him go?"

"Yes." Truthfully, I thought it would, but I also did not want to consider the alternatives. "It will if he remembered to remain calm."

"Let's hope," Watkins said curtly, and she swung to me. "Cameron said you deactivated a rogue earlier." I nodded once, and she pointed at the doors. "If you know what to do, get out there and do it."

"Watkins," Rain expostulated. Her mask gleamed under the overhead lighting as her head turned from the door to me. "You're sending her out there alone?"

"Yes. I am."

"What else is she good for?" Hugo scoffed. Then his tone changed, softened. "And you're not going out there with that thing on the loose, Rain."

Watkins remained focused on me. "After the drones are shut down, head back here."

"We have to find Cam." Tia's voice rose in pitch.

"And Zeta shouldn't go out by herself," Eric added.

"What do you care, Thompson?" Watkins rounded on him. "She's Consortium, not a citizen."

He glowered at her. "Yes, she's a Recorder, but she's—"

"On her way out. Everyone else, away from the door in case that drone is lurking." Watkins motioned me forward. "Don't bother with anything else, *Zeta*. Just shut it down and get back here."

Eric clenched his jaw. "Well, space that. I'm going with her. I'll find Cam myself."

"Oh no you're not!" Watkins shoved herself out of the captain's chair. "With Gretchen and the captain gone, the responsibility of getting you kids back to New Triton lands squarely on my shoulders. Mendoza's dead, who knows what happened to Cameron, and your arm is broken. You're staying here until the hallways are clear, Thompson."

"But I—"

"You argue, you'll get confined to quarters."

"Eric," I said as mildly as I could, "do not worry. Your assistance will not be necessary for what I must do. It will be well."

Hugo snorted again—the sound irritated me more each time he made it—and began a vulgar recitation of both Eric's failings and my own. Rain protested, and he fell silent.

Eric locked eyes with Tia, who quirked a brow and nodded at the door. He shook his head but then glanced at me, and his shoulders shifted. All expression fled Tia's face, though when she caught me watching her, her lips tilted upward for a fraction of a second.

Watkins again stabbed her finger at the door. "Move, unRecorder. Take that thing down."

As I crossed the bridge, Hugo and Foster stepped aside. My bare feet seemed loud in the sudden quiet. Though the doors were thick and doing so was pointless, I listened carefully before tapping the panel to open them. No drone waited. I left the bridge.

Footsteps hurried after me.

"What did I tell you, Thompson?" Watkins warned. "Stay where—blast! Hugo, grab that boy!"

I spun around.

Hugo lunged at Eric. With apparent disregard for his injury, the larger man picked him up by his upper arms. Eric yelped. While everyone focused on him and Hugo, Tia slipped around them. Watkins shouted her name.

Tia hit the access panel on her way out, and the doors slid shut, muffling the shouts to whispers. She grabbed my sleeve and pulled me down the port hallway. When no one followed us, we slowed.

"Well?"

I did not respond. She should not have joined me, but though it was likely she did so only to look for her friend, I was grateful for her presence. Even so, I did not admit it aloud.

"Where to? Do we take the forward lift, or ladder, or what?"

It would have been logical to search one level at a time, but the thought of Cam, alone and possibly injured, played over and over in my mind. "If he confronted the drone near the forward lift, it would be best to check there first."

She nodded.

I preceded Tia down the hall, and when I turned the corner, a single hoverbed drifted away from Jenkins. Cam was not present, but whether his absence was good or bad, I did not know. Averting my gaze, I sidled past the body on the floor. Tia, too, edged away from the remains. As I retrieved the equipment, the familiar whir of a drone caught my ear, and I released the hoverbed and spun around.

Tia gasped as it grabbed her. The slender tendrils snaked around her arms, one tapered end twisting about her wrist, accessing her identification bracelet. Another slithered around her chest and abdomen.

"Zeta—" The single, strangled word tore through the hall.

"Remain calm," I said, attempting to imitate Jordan's authoritative voice. "Breathe slowly. Allow your body to relax."

Her eyes closed, and a trickle of perspiration ran down her temple.

The drone released her abdomen and chest first, tapping her midsection, then lingering on her throat. Her breath shuddered audibly. Then it dropped her hands and flew toward me. She backed away.

Its appendages encircled my wrists and waist, but this time, I focused on memories of Nate, of his reassuring presence, his smile, his fingers entwined with mine. The undamaged drone released me, and without the interference of weapons' fire or concern for other people, I accessed the panel easily. The drone's thrumming quieted, and in only eighty-three seconds, it settled on the flooring, all tendrils and tentacles spooled inside, all arms folded in tidy rectangles underneath.

Tia approached cautiously and tapped the drone with her booted toe. "Is that all?"

"Yes."

"Would the other one have been like this? If we hadn't . . . if Jenkins hadn't . . ."

"Yes," I said, "and no. You are more fortunate in my presence than you might have guessed. I was trained for this. Most Recorders are not. That, however, is immaterial."

Her brow puckered, and she repeated, "Immaterial?"

A single word was an ineffective query, so I did not answer her. "I will relocate both drones to a secure room later. For now, I intend to search for Cam, despite Watkins's orders."

"I'm not going back without him. No matter what. Let's check the lower deck first."

"Lift, then, or ladder?"

She shuddered and tapped the lift's panel. "It flew at me out of the ladder."

The ride was short, and when a quick glance in the multipurpose room attached to the kitchen showed no sign of Cameron, we headed past the chemical backup and algae rooms, straight toward Butterfield's temporary morgue. At the corner, where the hall turned left, Tia paused for a fraction of a second, her face brightening.

Orange had replaced the olive-green and black of his uniform, but Cameron Rodriguez sat on the floor facing the aft lift, his back against the wall, elbows on his knees, head in his hands. His mask lay on the floor at his side.

"Cam!" Tia broke into a run, and I tried to keep pace, though my weak ankle slowed me.

At the sound of his name, Cameron's head came up, and he clambered to his feet. Tia threw her arms around him, knocking him slightly sideways, then released him and punched him hard in the arm. He winced.

"Moons above, Cameron! What do you mean, walking at that blasted drone, then not reporting back? Eric and I were worried sick."

He rubbed his upper arm. "Needed a moment."

Her face darkened as she scanned his person. "You're all right? Did that drone hurt you?"

"I'm fine. Zeta was right. It let me go once I relaxed. I just didn't want to chase after it and . . ." His voice faltered. "Tia, the captain didn't make it. I promised we wouldn't abandon him, but that's what we did." His gaze went to the closed door beside him.

"Oh." Tia was silent for three seconds. "Cam, there wasn't anything we could've done."

"There was not." I tugged at the jacket's hem and offered the tall young man a half-smile. "But I am glad you are well."

For approximately thirteen seconds, no one spoke, then Cam puffed out his cheeks in a slow exhalation. "The drone . . . I assume you took care of it?"

"Yes," I said. "Although I will need help, eventually, securing them in a locked room."

"If they're both off, they're not a threat."

"No, but they are Consortium property."

Three meters away, a cleaning bot detached from its recessed slot and scooted across the floor. We watched it meander down the hall.

Cam frowned. "Why aren't you in a suit, Tia?"

"Long story. Eric isn't, either, but that story is even longer. Should you put your hood up before we go back?"

"Why? When Foster handed me this one, the seal was already broken. I only put it on to make them happy."

"Conflict avoidance?" Tia raised an eyebrow. "Right. Well, no amount of that will get us out of trouble now. Should we head back and check on Eric? Make sure that spacing tr—" She stopped herself mid-word. "Make sure Hugo didn't bust his arm even more?"

Cam's eyes narrowed. "What did that minotaur do this time?"

She choked on a short laugh. "That's a better word for him, I guess. Well, Watkins wasn't going to let us leave with Zeta to look for you, so we sort of staged a diversion, but Hugo grabbed him by the arms."

His nostrils flared. "If I were bigger—"

"Then you wouldn't be Cam." Tia punched his arm again, though with visibly less force. "Why don't we let Watkins know it's clear?"

Cam nodded, tucked his mask under his arm, and the three of us walked abreast to the lift, the sound of their boots and my bare footfalls echoing in the forsaken corridors.

Cam held his identification bracelet to the scanner outside the bridge, but the doors did not move.

Tia swallowed. "You don't think—"

Cam raised a hand for quiet. "I hear arguing."

He was correct, for the indistinct murmur of masculine and feminine voices waxed and waned. Cam pounded on the metal and called for admittance. Although the muffled sounds came to an abrupt stop, the magnetic lock did not disengage.

While Tia also tried to open the doors, I rested my temple against the wall's beige paneling. Fatigue made each breath feel as if the air had thickened. Adrenaline's rush, which had supported me while facing the drone and searching for Cam, disappeared, and lethargy and a sense of dull resignation took its place.

Though Nate had repeatedly asserted that the loss of my drone was not my fault, the Eldest would disagree. Since my assignment on Pallas and then on *Thalassa*, I had acted instead of observing. I had already condemned myself, and whatever subsequent actions I took would do little to worsen my fate. Moving from the wall, I motioned both of them aside and input a simple Consortium access code, not even bothering to ask them to turn their backs. The doors parted.

Overhead lights glinted on Watkins's mask as she jolted from the captain's chair. Foster swiveled around from Rain's former seat at the communication console, and Bryce glowered from navigation. Rain now huddled next to Hugo, who shoved Eric back down when he sprang to his feet.

"You're all right!"

Cam nodded but kept narrowed eyes trained on Hugo's towering frame.

"Is it done?" Watkins demanded.

I assured her the drone had powered down.

"At least you did that right." Watkins turned away from me to throw a glance at Eric before advancing a step toward Tia. "Belisi, Thompson, if we were back on medieval Earth, you'd be flogged for a stunt like that. Both of you!" She angled toward Cam and spat out, "And don't think your behavior's gone unnoticed, Rodriguez. You disobeyed a superior, then failed to report back."

She continued her harangue until my growing anger finally compelled me to interrupt.

"That will suffice." Again, I tried to emulate Venetia Jordan and must have met with a modicum of success, for Watkins stopped mid-sentence. "Your complaint will be recorded, but I will again call attention to the fact that you, yourself, have not acted in the best interest of those around you. None of you have." A bot crept past me, following the base of the wall, turning right into the corridor beyond. "When Hugo and Foster abandoned Cameron Rodriguez to potential danger, you, Watkins, neither rebuked their cowardice nor searched for him."

Watkins put her hands on her hips. "A killer drone—one of your Consortium monstrosities—was running wild."

"Between that and whatever is killing people off, what else was there to do?" Bryce added. "We suit up and wait."

"And yet not everyone donned a biohazard suit." I could not quite modulate my voice; disgust adulterated my tone. "Though there is but one remaining, I see that Eric Thompson is still in his uniform. When you, Ursula Bryce, would not allow Portia Belisi to have one—"

"What?" Cam blurted.

"I didn't—"

"It's okay," Tia murmured. "I don't need one."

"And why give Thompson a suit?" Foster leaned back in the chair, crossing his arms. "He's—"

"Stow it, Foster," Watkins snapped.

"No, Watkins, no matter what rank you may hold, you have surrendered your moral authority. All of you have."

Hugo pushed forward. "You're not even a Recorder, so if you think—"

"If I *think*?" I strode across the room to stand with the Consortium recording device behind me, hoping the machine's mere presence would serve as a reminder of the organization to which I had belonged. The memory of citizens' reactions to Recorders' emotions prompted a slight smile to my face. I was not wrong. Rain sucked in a short breath, and the other orange-clad crew members stilled. "You err. I do not think. I *know*."

Whatever or whoever controlled the devices did not disappoint me, for at that moment, the lens whirred. I dropped the smile and fought back a tendril of fear when I realized that the camera could capture the reflection of my expression from their facial shields.

For three seconds, I held my breath. Then, in the relative quiet of *Agamemnon*'s bridge, I exhaled and met Watkins's eyes behind the reflection on her mask. She looked away.

"So what do we do now?" Foster asked.

"Finish collecting the shells." Bryce laughed again, and I forced away a scowl. I was heartily sick of her unending and senseless mirth. "Shell collecting means something else in vids."

Rain flinched. "Bryce, please don't."

Watkins held up both gloved hands. "Easy, now. We'll get through this all right."

"If you say so." Bryce flopped back against the synthleather chair. "Do we have everyone, or do we have to search for bodies?"

"There are nine of us. Then five bodies from the bridge"—Tia glanced at Cam—"the first four from the infirmary and then two more. And Jenkins. Nine, fourteen, eighteen, twenty-one, and six already there, that's twenty-seven."

Bryce smirked. "Very good, youngling. You can add."

Eric shot her a glare. "That just leaves three, plus the Recorders and the Elder, right?"

"It is likely that the Recorders and the Elder are in their quarters," I added.

"I'm not breaking into Consortium quarters to collect their rotted shells," Bryce flung out the words. "Send the unRecorder."

"No one's breaking into anything," Watkins said. "After all, it won't be breaking in if the unRecorder accesses Consortium space. She can do that once we get all our people into storage. Are the bodies tied down? We can't just throw them in there, unsecured."

"Doesn't matter as long as the vents are sealed and the temp is low enough," Hugo said. "They're just shells."

My jaw tightened. "Aside from your verbal disrespect for your former shipmates, any improper containment could damage remains and potentially obscure autopsy findings. It is imperative that their bodies remain intact for proper analysis, since—"

"They lock you up for talking too much?" Hugo advanced toward me, but when he passed her, Watkins put a hand on his arm. He angled his face shield down at the diminutive woman. "What?"

She jerked her head once in my direction, and he gave an indecipherable reply. Together, the two of them marched across the room, Rain trailing behind them. Hugo's height and solid bulk dwarfed Watkins, but they stood like mismatched twins on either side of the bridge's open doors. Their blank, reflective masks glinted like insectile eyes.

"We could secure them with netting from the storage bay," Foster said slowly.

"Do it." After a half-second, Watkins added, "And no matter what Bryce said, you should suit up, Tia."

Tia, however, did not move. "Putting on suits without decontaminating properly won't do a micron's worth of good. And what about Eric and Zeta?"

Watkins shrugged. "We only have one left."

"Thompson is being an idiot," Hugo added. "An idiot who shuns proper medical treatment. He'll get what he deserves."

"Doug," Rain protested.

Cam straightened. "He has the right—"

Hugo cut Cam's answer short. "Standing up for people like him only makes you look stupid, too."

"Antagonizing either boy won't fix anything," Watkins said. "Either Thompson will live with his decisions—or he won't. Who knows? Maybe he has a point."

"A point about being stupid," Foster muttered.

Tia's fists opened and closed, though she did not strike her thigh as I had often done.

"Don't worry about it, Tia," Eric said. "Suit up, if only to make me and Cam feel better."

Cam nodded in agreement, but Tia glowered at Watkins. "I'll pass."

"I know you planned to—" Cam's eyes skimmed over Tia. He glanced at me, then back at her, and his mouth compressed into a thin line. "Is that wise? Considering?"

"Considering what?" Watkins eyed them both sharply. "Something we should know?"

"Nothing that concerns you," Tia snapped. "Let's just get this over with. I'm tired—we all are—and I need something to eat. In spite of everything, I'm so hungry I'm queasy."

Hugo's mask was still trained on me. "What did *she* do to get in trouble with the Consortium?"

Rain touched his arm. "Does it matter?"

"It does if she designed a virus to kill people."

The injustice of his comment incensed me, but evading the inquiry was pointless. "My drone was destroyed in an accident."

"Destroyed?" Bryce cocked her head. "I don't buy it. Those things are tough."

Hugo's sneer was visible through his face shield. "And you somehow survived?"

"Let it go. We've got shells to deal with. Blood and bones, but this ship is a disaster. Not even worth reclaiming." Watkins shook her head, and reflections from the overhead lighting temporarily hid her face. "Since the drones are out of the way, we can split up. Someone needs to stay on the bridge, and the rest of you can search for the missing citizens."

"Look at you, so grown up and caring," Bryce mocked.

"Please," Rain pled, "just stop."

Watkins did not respond, though she must have heard the comment.

"Told you no shells," Hugo repeated.

Watkins pivoted toward him. "Don't give me that rubbish. Pushing a hoverbed won't require touching a single corpse."

Rain swayed a little, then leaned against Hugo.

"Need more meds?" he asked quietly.

She hesitated. "If you have any left, Bryce?"

Bryce's hand went to her hip, then smacked her forehead. "In my greens. Which I shoved down the infirmary laundry chute."

Rain's shoulders drooped. "At any rate, we don't know for sure what Jenkins did with those samples, not after the records go all staticky."

I tensed. Not here, too? I had dealt with damaged records on *Thalassa*, and the inherent dishonesty set my nerves on edge.

Watkins nodded. "Good point. Hugo, make sure that there isn't anything in the vents and in engineering that shouldn't be there. Looking around won't bring anyone back, but it might save our skins if we can find something like a source or anything suspicious. We'll get to Lunar One and let some ego-driven scientist figure it out while we sit in quarantine and catch up on vids."

Foster yawned and started for the doors. "I'll tie the shells down."

Watkins put her hands to her head, but when her gloves touched her hood, they dropped to her sides. "No, you stay here. As Bryce so generously pointed out, I'm the phycologist. I'd better check the algae tanks, then seal up the room. Can't have anyone messing with the oxygen-filtration system. Thompson and the unRecorder can help me, then search the lower deck and tie down the shells. Rain and Bryce, you take this deck, and Cameron and Tia can check the upper one."

"I'll need Rain if you want both ventilation and the mechanical systems checked." Hugo tipped his head at Foster. "Better send him, too, once you are back up here."

"I'm not searching a whole deck by myself," Bryce snapped.

"Fine. Cameron, go with her. Thompson can go with Tia. Everyone, back here in two hours."

Two hours with Watkins? Never had one hundred twenty minutes sounded so long.

"Wait here."

Watkins tried to block my view of the control panel while she input her personal code. Her attempt at security amused me. Locks were one of my favorite games, and even in my disgrace, I would be able to access the phycology room on a Consortium vessel.

"I don't need you underfoot. Just stay where I can see you."

The doors parted, and cold air spilled over my bare toes. As it always did, my nose wrinkled at the peculiar, musty yet sulfurous smell of algae.

Without another word, Watkins turned on the full-spectrum lights, which masked the algae's faint glow. Her liquid crystal computer was a newer model than the one in my laboratory on *Thalassa*, and the desire to play in its numbers and programs, to see how well and how quickly it functioned, tickled the back of my mind. I pushed the desire away.

Data projections rose in alternating amber and cyan planes. Watkins studied the information, then examined one of the massive tanks. Not wishing to further provoke antagonistic remarks, I remained at the door and watched her.

As she pulled up information and adjusted feedlines and temperature, her shoulders lost their sharp edge. She even hummed an off-key and repetitive tune. My own tension eased in response until the lift behind me opened, jerking my attention to the hallway. Watkins stopped humming. Eric and Tia hurried from the lift to the algae room's double doors.

"What is it?" Watkins demanded.

"We found three service staff in their quarters." Tia rubbed her arms. "We need the hoverbeds."

"Hugo left two down here. Since the other one is up with Jenkins, can you handle the shells by yourselves? No, with Thompson—" Watkins paused. "Take the beds up, and I'll send Foster to help, but since you two are already here, go ahead and search the quarters up near the galley. And while you're there, grab some food."

A divot appeared over Eric's nose. "But you said not to—"

"Of all the stupid—Did you search the whole upper deck?"

"Yes, ma'am."

"And you found three, which means there shouldn't be anyone left. And those three aren't going anywhere without help. Help you can't give, Thompson, not with only one arm. The sooner I am done here, the sooner I can send Foster up to assist you. The sooner I do that, the sooner I can send him to help Hugo and Rain, and the sooner that part of this mess is handled. Use your brain." She gestured at me. "The unRecorder can start on Butterfield's morgue while I finish up in here. When you turned off the emergency lights, you messed with the temperature. It's too warm, and I have to fix it. You two search the rest of the deck, and she can secure the shells. The whole process will go faster."

Both young people met my eyes before trotting down the port corridor.

"Very well." I set my shoulders. "I shall check the room first, then gather netting and supplies."

Watkins did not acknowledge me as she resumed her work, but somehow, the fact she no longer hummed was a loss.

Butterfield's room was unlocked. The single door slid into its pocket with only a tap on the panel, and after a quick check at the tie downs along the walls, I closed it again. It took three trips to bring the netting from the compartment in the loading bay, and my arms ached before I finished.

Eric and Tia returned without having found anyone else, as expected, though Tia carried a container of food bars. They waited in the hall until Watkins emerged from the algae room, the smell clinging to her orange suit. She and Tia stacked the two hoverbeds and took the lift, and I began implementing Foster's plan of securing the double rows of bodies.

My breath curled in tiny clouds, which dissipated almost at once. The bandage around my foot and ankle was inadequate protection, but at least it kept that sole from the burning cold. My toes ached, and I struggled to keep my teeth from chattering. The inherent contradictions in Watkins's behavior kept me from dwelling on the nature of my task. Why would she leave me alone with these bodies when she had been insisting that the students keep watch over everything I did?

Uneasiness pressed down on me, and I found myself counting the netting-covered shapes, over and over again. Fifteen, fifteen, and still fifteen.

Before anyone brought the bodies from the uppermost deck, Cam and Bryce arrived, pushing Jenkins on the hoverbed. Bryce refused to enter, and with a terse, "Whatever," she stomped back to the lift while Cam brought the bed inside, unloaded it, and silently helped me complete the task of tying down the remains. With his assistance, it went quickly, and when it was finished, and all sixteen were safely secured, he gave me a small bottle of sanitizer.

"I have to go back up to the bridge," he murmured. "You going to be okay?"

"Yes." I applied the disinfectant, then handed back the bottle. "It will be well. I will wait for the others. Go."

They left.

Before closing the room to wait in the hall, I stood on the threshold. Though fabric hid their features, I could not help but imagine these bodies as the people they had been. Had the citizens left family behind? Surely they had friends as well. Had the staff members sifted through databases for the right names and chosen obscure ones, as Alfred Butterfield had done?

All of them, citizen and staff alike, had laughed, talked, cried. My throat constricted, and I backed from the room and closed the doors. For a moment, I leaned against the dull beige paneling, but the lift chimed again, and I straightened.

Foster shoved out one laden hoverbed, then tugged two more into the hall and glowered at me. "Why the—what are you doing out here? Why's it shut up?"

"I—"

"You know, I really don't care." He pushed the beds in my direction. "Just get rid of these. I have to head down to engineering. Hugo needs my help." He strode back into the lift, which chimed once before descending yet again.

For one full minute, I stood alone with the three hoverbeds and five bodies, then I forced down the sob which threatened to erupt, summoned my resolve, and did what was required.

After all, what was there to do but to serve?

Finishing quickly, I adjusted the microantigravity to stack the beds and left the solemnity of the cold room.

No one was in the infirmary when I arrived, and the deserted room mocked my memories of *Thalassa*'s infirmary, which had become as homelike to me as any place I had been, if home meant familiarity and acceptance. Yet, I had no time to dwell on what could not be. Instead, I pushed all three beds into the medicomputer for a decontamination cycle. There was no point when whatever had killed the crew must have been airborne, but it was what Max would have done.

Had Bryce been correct that no one on *Thalassa* had fallen ill? There was nothing I could say, no one I could ask to check, not without betraying my personal investiture in their lives. Not knowing was as horrific as the roaches on Pallas had been. If Nate should fall ill . . . If he—

I tapped my thigh. "It will be well. All manner of things will be well."

The only answer was the whir of the recording device as it focused again on me.

So I washed my hands before limping back toward the lift, the bandage around my sprained ankle bunching uncomfortably at my instep. The entire ship was eerily quiet.

If only they had not released me from my holding cell, though if they had not, would the ship be heading back to Lunar One? It was an impossible question, and there was no answer.

Bryce's announcement about someone recovering Captain North from the void of space echoed again in my ears, and my satisfaction with the captain's death ebbed. Whatever his inclinations and acts had been, he was human after all, with the flaws and graces that attended that state. Perhaps there were mitigating circumstances. Perhaps he had been the one who had saved my life by prying me off the charging station on *Thalassa* when I had nearly killed myself in order to stop Julian Ross. Perhaps the captain had saved my life.

Then again, perhaps he had not.

"Zeta!"

I startled, then turned.

Eric jogged up from the starboard hall, his right hand holding his injured arm close to his chest. "Been looking for you. Watkins said you should've been back already. She's on a tear about you being unsupervised again, though it's her own fault, really."

"I am on my way."

His eyebrows knotted over tea-colored eyes. "You okay?"

"I . . ." But what was there to say?

He scrubbed his good hand over the patchy stubble on his jaw. "Just so you know, you've been vindicated. We all saw the records Rain pulled up. Turns out, Jenkins broke into the sealed room where they had your drones and some sort of samples—"

"He did indeed tamper with the evidence from *Thalassa*?" Anxiety shot tendrils as strong as a drone's around my heart.

"Seems so," Eric said. "Sealed up the room again, messed with the records, so no one knew."

"The records are damaged? But it cannot be true that no one observed . . . Surely the Elder or Recorders on *Agamemnon* bore witness?"

"Maybe. But wouldn't the Recorders have done something? I mean, don't they have permission to act on a Consortium transport? Anyway, it's a mess, and data's missing." He grimaced. "Rain reported that to Lunar One, and they said someone messed with *Thalassa*'s records, too, before North ran off and died."

If I understood literary terminology, it was with a degree of irony that I responded, "I know."

He threw a sidelong look at me before continuing, "Watkins had Foster seal off Jenkins's quarters. When we reach Lunar One tomorrow or the next day, the authorities'll sort through it. *If* they let us dock and let them on."

"If, indeed."

"Honestly, I'm . . ." He rubbed the back of his neck and growled, and for a second, I believed he growled at me. "Blast it, Jenkins is dead. That drone killed him, which is awful and everything, but if he was the one who set all this"—he waved his hand at the hallway—"in motion, he got what he deserved."

"Perhaps."

When we reached the lift, he tapped the panel. "Leslie is, or was—" he sighed "—a nursing student, so Dr. Smithson called for her pretty soon after the captain locked us down, but she . . . she never came back. Cam, Tia, and I hunkered down in our quarters, just waiting. Then, Jenkins showed up last night, about eleven. Handed us weapons, and said he needed to get to the bridge, 'cause they weren't responding. That blasted drone found us around midnight. I couldn't . . ."

"You would have needed considerably more firepower than you had to stop the drone, Eric Thompson," I said quietly.

He blew a loose orange-brown curl off his forehead. "If that's so, what destroyed yours?"

The lift arrived, and I selected the next level down. "It will not sound believable."

Eric flashed a half-grin. "Give it a try."

The door slid shut, and my stomach jolted with the lift's descent. Deciding it would not matter if I told him, I squared my shoulders and said, "A two-meter cockroach crushed it."

Eric's brows rose toward his hairline. "*What*?"

"We never discovered why the insects had grown to such a size, though based on the report of one survivor, there may have been experiments without proper—"

"*Animal* experiments?"

The lift settled, the door slid open, but neither of us moved.

"Yes." I tugged at Cam's jacket. "Sanctioned by both Parliament and the Consortium."

His brows drew together. "That's unethical. Doesn't seem likely."

"I am aware. Nonetheless, that is what destroyed my drone."

"Well." He exhaled loudly. "Must've been terrifying."

"It was."

"The universe can be such a mess."

He was correct, though I could not surrender the thought that either there was indeed order behind the chaos, or that the chaos itself had an order I could not grasp. Or was that the same?

"I don't know, Zeta. I just feel conflicted about Jenkins."

"I understand. Today, I feel conflicted about many things, as well."

In unison, Eric Thompson and I stepped into the empty hallway.

Tia's alto rose above the murmur of agitated voices from the bridge. When Watkins shouted, Eric dashed forward, and I limped after him as quickly as I could, wincing with each step. He skidded inside as I paused for breath, one hand on the frame.

Cam and Tia faced Hugo, and Watkins stood between them, arms wide, palms out. Tia's eyes blazed, and Cam's lips compressed to a thin, white line.

"You don't know that," Watkins asserted. "You'll stop antagonizing the boy and making unfounded claims against that unRecorder, Hugo, or I'll lock you up myself."

The overhead fixtures' reflections gleamed blue-white on Hugo's face shield. "Really?"

For a moment, it was as if the air in the room thickened, then Watkins moved aside. "Take something to eat and go to your quarters. Report back here at midnight."

Hugo grabbed a few sealed packages from a box near the captain's chair, but when he noticed me at the doorway, his fingers tightened around the food bars, and the noise crunched sharply in the room's sudden quiet.

"I still say we lock her up. Keep her virus from spreading."

My chin lifted. "It is not my virus."

Rain stood and gripped the back of the communication chair. Her voice sounded faint when she murmured, "Douglas?"

"Get some rest, Hugo." Watkins pointed past me. "You, too, Rain. I can't stay awake until we reach Lunar One, but someone needs to be on the bridge. I'll figure out a shift cycle that makes sense, but you'll need to take over later. For right now, Foster, Bryce, you're on nav and comms."

"Fine." Neither Hugo's posture nor the way he glowered at me changed. "Rain?"

She released her hold on the chair and took only one wavering step before collapsing.

Though he had been halfway across the bridge, Hugo reached her side before anyone else did. His back to me, he slid his hands under her shoulders, but when she gagged and began choking, he ripped off her mask and threw it aside. Red droplets splattered the floor.

Bryce and Foster lurched backward, and Watkins cursed. Tia's hand flew to her cheek, and Cam froze. I glanced at Eric, who shook his head, then made his way to Tia's side, and she turned her face to his shoulder. I followed him, stopping next to Cam, staring down at the shaking woman on the floor.

"Don't just stand there," Hugo barked. "A cloth, something—now!"

Foster managed a strangled, "Just a nosebleed, man. Take a damper."

"I thought lying didn't help anyone."

"Shut it, Bryce," Watkins said.

I removed Cam's jacket, then met his eyes. He nodded, and I handed it to Hugo, who took it without a glance in my direction. He held it to Rain's face, and the olive-green fabric darkened all too quickly.

Eric began, "Lean her forward—"

"No, back," Foster said.

Hugo murmured Rain's name. "Stars." His voice cracked. "You're burning up."

Rain coughed a little, and the sound, small though it was, rattled through the bridge. She gulped down air. "Maybe," her voice gurgled slightly, and she coughed again. "You should stay back, Doug."

I heard him whisper, "Not leaving you," before he raised his head and glared at Cam. "What are you staring at?"

Cam said nothing.

"Void it," Bryce muttered.

Eerie silence ate away at the room like aqua regia dissolving gold. I knew the sounds were there—the thrum of the ship's circulation fans, the ever-present base rumble of the engines—but their amplitude seemed to have dropped, rendering them nearly indiscernible.

Watkins said, very slowly, too slowly, too cautiously, "Hugo, take her to her quarters and seal the door. Rain, don't worry. Someone will bring you food and meds if you quarantine yourself."

Rain shrank back against Hugo, who straightened and glared at Watkins.

"I'm not going to toss Rain into her quarters and lock her in like a criminal. She needs treatment—"

"There is no treatment," Bryce put in.

Watkins kept her eyes on Hugo and Rain. "Not helping, Bryce. Look, at this point, all we can do is try to contain whatever it is. Focus on the living—"

"She is living, space you!"

"She's . . ." Watkins paused. "Hugo, I think you should quarantine, too."

"You aren't even an officer, Watkins," he snarled. "You don't have the authority, and even the spacing unRecorder knows it."

She stiffened. "Just do it."

He guided Rain's hand to hold the jacket over her nose, carefully lowered her to the floor, and stood, towering over all of us. "Who's going to make me? You and whose squadron?"

Watkins hit a button on the captain's chair, and a drawer popped out. She lifted a sidearm and aimed it at Hugo. Her expression unreadable, she ground out the words, "Me and this squadron. Don't force my hand."

Time stood still as panic surged inside me like a sine wave. I wanted to tell them to remain calm, to be reasonable, that we would all do what we could, but I could not find my voice.

Without a word, Hugo knelt again and lifted Rain as easily as if she were a child. The red-stained jacket fell to the floor, and he kicked it aside. Cam tugged me out of the towering man's way, and my bare foot crushed one of the food bars Hugo had dropped.

Cradling Rain in his arms, Hugo stopped on the threshold. "Void take you all."

He left, his bootsteps swallowed by the thrum of the fans.

For approximately two minutes, no one spoke, then Watkins said in a shaky imitation of her previous tone, "Bryce, Foster. We need to figure out a new rotation before we get any rest." She turned to the students. "In the meantime, you three liberated the unRecorder, and you three can take care of her. Grab something to eat and stay in your quarters. All of you."

We each collected some prepackaged food and water, and Cam led us out. By the time we reached their bunkroom, fatigue sat heavily on my chest, but I scanned the room for recording devices. Two narrow bunk beds nestled into the walls on opposite sides of the room, and two closets, each half a meter wide, stood on either side of the door, their pale beige a shade lighter than the walls' standard paneling. A single door at the back probably led to the water closet, but as I studied the ceiling, relief washed over me. For the first time since the Elder had taken me from my friends, I did not fear being observed.

Eric groaned and flopped backward onto the lower bunk to the right of the door, wincing and cradling his arm. "I'm gonna vote for today being the worst day ever."

"Yeah." Tia bit her lower lip and sighed. "How's your ankle, Zeta?"

"The pain has lessened." I forced a smile. "Though my name is not Zeta."

Eric sat up. "What do you want us to call you, then?"

"I have no preference. I merely wished you to know."

Tia sat on the opposite bunk and opened a food bar and a bottle of water. I followed suit. It took but one bar before my stomach protested, but Eric nagged until I forced down two more. Cam gathered the wrappers and disposed of them while Tia removed folded blankets and a pillow from the right-hand closet.

"Zeta, you'll take Leslie's bunk. The one you're sitting on." Her voice lacked its usual animation, but her meaning propelled me to my feet.

Cam was already in motion, pulling off the bedding and tossing a clean sheet over the mattress. I stood there, useless, while he made the bed.

Tia returned to the closet, took out a navy-blue tunic, leggings, and a small towel, then indicated the door in the back. "I know you don't like borrowing things, but these are mine and they're clean. You can wash up and change in the water closet—though you'll need to be careful with the bandages. There's soap and lotion in the cabinet."

When I emerged, the drone's tendril that had served as Eric's splint coiled in my hand and my three-centimeter hair damp from a quick rinse, Cam pointed at the laundry chute, and I deposited the dirty clothes. Eric handed me a clean bandage for my ankle. I sat on the freshly made bed to wrap it.

Tia tossed a pair of short, white, fuzzy socks in my direction. "It's not shoes, but it's something." She gathered an armful of clean clothes and disappeared to change.

Eric's sling was askew, which bothered me, though I did not offer to adjust it. Circles of exhaustion darkened his eyes. His fair skin seemed even paler than it had before. He shook two analgesics from a small white bottle, then swallowed them without a drink.

Cam tucked his loose hair behind his ear and settled on Eric's bunk, across from me. "While you were changing, they told me what happened today and about losing your drone and all that."

My cheeks heated at once again being the topic of gossip.

"Not that you need me bossing you around," Cam added, "but between what they and some of the others said, stay close. Not much we can do about a virus, but we can watch out for each other."

Eric grunted agreement, then opened the water bottle's lid with his teeth and chugged half the contents. When Tia exited from the water closet, she threw her dirty clothes in the laundry and began unraveling her two thick braids, combing her fingers through the long, sharp waves. She looked much younger with her hair down. Eric glanced over, and uneven pink color rushed to his face. He handed his water bottle to Cam and dodged around Tia to the door in the back.

Cam nodded to her, then put his elbows on his knees, water bottle clasped in his hands, and refocused on me. I set the tendril on my pillow. Our relative silence had little in common with the ship's eerie quiet, but I could not parse why. My eyelids grew heavy. I must have dozed while sitting upright, for when my eyes fluttered open, Eric again sat across from me.

"So what happens next?" The weight Eric added to his words, the heavy finality he placed on the syllables, confused me, so I did not reply.

After five seconds of silence, Tia prompted, "To you, Zeta, when you get back home?"

I had no home, but something kept me from admitting as much, even without a recording device monitoring my comments. "When I boarded, the Elder indicated that the severity of my violations had cost me a tribunal."

Cam's hazel eyes drilled into mine. "Tribunal?"

I studied the fuzzy white socks hiding my toes. "A tribunal consists of three High Elders who review nonconformities and sit in judgment."

"'Nonconformities' sounds like a fancy insult," Eric said quietly.

Tia folded her right leg underneath her and silently sank onto the bunk beside me.

Cam steepled his fingers, tapping the tips against his chin. "You don't get a trial?"

"I shall not." My arms folded tightly across my abdomen, like a shield. "Rather, the Eldest herself will sit in judgment. When the Elder informed me, he did not need to explain."

Tia's dark eyes narrowed. "Why not?"

The Hall of Reclamation at Consortium Center Alpha seemed to flash across my field of vision. "It is all I needed to know."

One of Eric's long curls snagged on short, reddish stubble. "That's rubbish. Is that some super-secret Consortium code for already being sentenced?"

I refused to answer.

"If it's Recorder related, she probably can't say, Eric." Cam rubbed his eyes and stretched. "Look. Don't break any more codes of conduct than you have, Zeta. Staying here with us is probably bad enough."

He was, of course, correct.

Tia twisted her hair into a loose braid and tied off the end, then studied the young man still sitting across from me. "Eric."

He glanced over, his attention resting on the single braid falling over her shoulder before refocusing on the ceiling. "Yeah?"

"You can't untie regulation synthleather one-handed. Do you want help?"

Even his ears grew pink as he stammered an incoherent answer.

Cam snickered, though I could not see the humor.

Tia rolled her eyes. "Just ignore him, Eric, but if you don't do something with your hair tonight, it'll be a mess in the morning. Curly hair—"

"Oh, those disordered curls," Cam said in a falsetto which dissolved into chuckles.

Scowling, Eric grabbed his pillow with his good hand and hurled it at Cam, who caught it and tossed it back as he made his way to the water closet.

"Knock it off, Cam." Tia plunked onto the bunk next to Eric. "Just ignore him."

Eric closed his eyes while Tia untied the binding and smoothed his hair, then plaited it and retied the end. Cheeks still suffused with color, he murmured his thanks, but when she stood, he rolled onto his right side and faced the wall. He did not turn back over until the bunk above me creaked and Tia settled under her blankets.

His cheeks clean shaven, Cam rejoined us, still grinning. He winked at Eric and ducked when Tia swatted at him as he passed her bunk on the way to the door.

"G'night," he said and turned off the lights.

Darkness welled up around me, swallowing me whole, erasing—

"Please," I croaked, without meaning to say anything at all.

Immediately, the lights flashed back on, and I blinked against the brightness.

Tia peered over the edge of her bunk, her braid dangling in front of me. "Are you all right?"

I could not manage a reply.

Eric's tea-brown gaze shifted from me to the door and back. "Like I said, Cam, today was just about the worst day ever. I vote for you leaving on the night-vision light. You know, in case Watkins needs us or something?"

Cam studied me, then nodded at Eric. "Good idea."

Full-spectrum light switched to a gentle red, then Cam hauled himself onto his bunk.

I sagged back onto the pillow. "Thank you."

"Not a problem."

Still upside down, Tia added, "Good night, Zeta."

"As I have said before, that is not my name. I have not found one yet." She flashed a smile. "Keep looking."

One by one, they fell asleep. As I lay in the dark and listened to their quiet breathing, some of the weight on my heart lifted. Even after seeing Rain collapse, even with Watkins's threats, and even though the captain was dead and I knew not what my future held, there in the dim, red light, fear loosened its grip.

Finally, I drifted into sleep.

# 13

I dreamed of Nate that night, though the dream did not comfort me upon waking. I had not dreamed of his touch nor the way he had asked me to stay. Not of the flecks of blue and brown in his green eyes, nor the intensity of his gaze as the Elder and Recorders escorted me off *Thalassa*. Not of the faint scent of pine on his neck, nor the taste of cinnamon on his breath. No, those things flooded my memory after I woke in the steady red glow of the light over the door.

In my dream, he walked beside me through *Thalassa*'s bland corridors. When we reached my computer laboratory, he leaned one shoulder against the doorframe, arms crossed, and winked, and the smile that showed his dimple grew until he laughed. Then, with no respect for sequence and logic, we sat in the dining commons, and he lounged in his chair, sipping coffee.

The deep ache which nudged me awake swallowed me whole, and the comfort of his dreamed presence fled. For several minutes, a flood of memories hid the bunkroom around me, and I fought my way through them before I drowned.

Tia shifted overhead. Across the room, a light snore came from Cam's bunk. Eric moaned in his sleep, and a frown etched lines on his young face. I slipped from my bed and tucked the blanket over him. His moans subsided.

I paced the room several times, but when Tia murmured nonsense on her bunk, I paused. While leaving the unobserved safety of their bunkroom did not appeal to me, they needed sleep, and my restlessness could disturb them.

Tea, however, did appeal to me, and the idea of a soothing tisane with steam twisting in faint tendrils over translucent, aromatic liquid pulled me to the door. Surely the ship's pantry would have a variety of tea. Determination to find some degree of comfort therein prompted me to input a Consortium general access code on the panel. The door slid open.

Full-spectrum light combined with unnatural quiet to magnify the ship's emptiness. For a moment, Cam's warning whispered in my mind, but the potential of lavender-mint whispered louder. I turned toward the bridge, the borrowed socks softening my steps.

As I walked, the pervasive stillness seemed to deepen. The fact that two-thirds of the crew lay in a storage room on the deck below heightened my perception of isolation. I decided to use the forward lift, to avoid emerging on the lower deck across from Alfred Butterfield's temporary morgue.

However, as I approached the bridge's open doors, Bryce's voice snapped as sharp as electricity in a plasma ball: "Where do you think you're going?"

I met her masked scowl and merely said, "The kitchen."

She did not reply, so I limped on.

When I turned down the starboard hallway, however, I faltered. The hall was empty. My focus had been first on reaching the bridge and later on clearing the bodies. I had forgotten to collect the drone, yet it no longer rested unevenly near the dented paneling where it had been. The short hair on my forearms stood on end.

Someone had taken it. Cam's warning to stay close to the three students tickled my memory. Regardless of whomever had moved it, whenever it had been taken, and to wherever it had been relocated, I would not search the ship alone. When we reached Lunar One, authorities would recover it.

When I approached the corner where Jenkins had lain, the second deactivated drone was gone, as well. Only a persistent bot scrubbed the stains in front of the lift. Avoiding the darkened flooring, I climbed down the ladder instead. Motion sensors triggered the lights, illuminating the halls as I emerged on the lower deck and turned toward the multipurpose room.

The sharp scent of artificial lemon indicated that the bots must have recently sanitized it, but none prowled the room. Lights clicked on as I passed between the long tables to the narrow kitchen. The metal door leading to its refrigeration unit gleamed on my left, but on my right, the pantry stood open, like a deep, dark hole. Logic told me nothing was amiss, that someone had merely forgotten to close it, but even so, a frisson of apprehension snaked down my spine.

Shaking off my concern, I manually activated a light and searched the shelves while the water heated. *Agamemnon*'s pantry held neither lavender-mint nor ginger-turmeric, only melon-green tea and a slightly less nauseating hibiscus blend. Selecting the least offensive of the two, I settled at a table facing the deserted room, intending to finish the tea before returning, but as I sat, uneasiness swelled. I thought I heard the lift's faint rumble and the swish of its doors, but no one joined me.

Discomfiting aloneness propelled me to my feet. I took my half-full mug with me, hibiscus notwithstanding. The camera over the door whirred, and stifling a sigh, I raised the mug to its single eye in acknowledgment.

I left the room weighing two undesirable options: choosing the lift which would bring me to the site where Jenkins had died or the lift opposite the temporary morgue. I chose the latter, since the persistent cleaning bot toiling over the stains saddened me. The prospect of passing my former holding cell also held little appeal, so I proceeded down the port hallway. The socks muffled my footfalls, and the ship's ventilation system continued its soft hiss, while the circulation fans' pulse grew louder.

When I passed the chemical backup system's control room, my grip on the rapidly cooling mug tightened, for the door stood open. I peered through the press of shadows but saw no one at the control panels' tidy rows of amber and cyan lights. An almost indefinable urge to hurry quickened my pace.

Before I turned the corner, the musty sulfur of algae assaulted me, and indeed, the room's double doors gaped, though it too was vacant. Without the overhead lights, the tanks' phosphorescent glow barely penetrated the room's farthest corners. The rhythmic thumps from the ship's giant circulation fans reverberated in my chest. Shivering in the cold air that crept through the doors, I limped over to close them before proceeding to the lift.

Down the short hall leading to the airlock, two more doors stood ajar. They had been shut when I closed the temporary morgue, hours before. I knew they had. Despite the warm tunic, a chill passed over me.

The desire to stand with my back to the wall and scan the empty hallway was like an itch, but unreasonable fears could not be allowed to dictate my actions. It was one thing to secure the algae room, since climate control was essential for the giant tanks, but another to close every door I saw. Setting my jaw, I tapped the button, watched the panel as the lift descended from the decks above, and took a sip of the tepid hibiscus blend.

A soft ping announced the lift's arrival, but simultaneously, footsteps thundered from the door to my right. I spun around, tea sloshing onto my borrowed tunic and the floor. The solid orange of a biohazard suit slammed into me. My knees buckled, my head smacked against the panel, and *Agamemnon*'s corridors disappeared.

My head throbbed. I struggled to parse why everything felt wrong, but when I opened my eyes, I saw nothing. It took only half a second for me to process why: my lashes scraped against a blindfold. I tried to speak, but a wad of material filled my mouth.

Heart thundering, I fought to rise. The backs of my hands banged against metal—my wrists and ankles were tied. Tugging against my bonds, my fingers wrapped around the cold railing of a hoverbed. I thrashed against the bindings to no avail.

As if from another room, a man's voice growled, broken by thick, rough coughs. I tried to call to him, but the gag served its purpose and muffled my pleas. Grabbing the railing, I threw my weight from side to side in an attempt to rock the hoverbed and tip it over, but the microantigravity held firm. The bed did not even dip.

More voices joined the man's, a woman's alto gaining clarity first. *Tia's voice.*

" . . . seen her?"

The man grumbled a reply.

"Well, she's missing." That was Cam. "Bryce said she was going to the kitchen, but she isn't there."

Why could Cam and Tia not see me?

"We found a broken mug by the lift next to the storage bay." Eric punched out his words. "Checked each deck and—"

A wrenching, prolonged cough interrupted him.

"Look, I don't care . . . if you kids want to play . . . Hide-and-Find with that Consortium reject." I finally recognized Hugo's voice. "Don't bother me with it."

"What're you doing here, anyway?" Tia asked, her voice closer than before. "You were quarantined."

"Scanning myself. Have to run a cleaning cycle first."

Their voices blurred again as panic choked me as verily as the gag, for I knew where I was.

I was in the medicomputer. Hugo must have bound me and placed me there. If he bypassed safety protocols and ran a sanitation cycle, there was no possibility of surviving the heat and chemicals. I screamed through the fabric until my throat was raw.

Eric asked, "You hear something?"

"No," Hugo snapped.

I kicked and jerked against my bindings, folding my thumbs to my palms, trying to slide my hands through.

There was a pause. Then Eric again. "Pretty sure I heard something."

The fabric tightened around my left wrist, and the loop which tied me to the railing seemed to stretch. I bit down on the material in my mouth and stilled my thrashing, all my focus on the act of freeing my left hand.

"Hugo, I've been—" Watkins's voice stopped as suddenly as it had appeared. "What are you three doing here?"

"Zeta's gone," Eric said.

"She didn't leave a note." Tia's alto sounded sharper than usual. "We talked to Bryce—"

"Well, she obviously isn't here. Look somewhere else." Then Watkins's tone lost its harshness, and her words became difficult to discern. I strained to hear her. "Scanning yourself isn't going to bring her back, Doug."

I pulled again. My thumb was almost through. Threads popped, but the fabric cinched tighter. The gag hid my moan of frustration.

"Too late," Hugo rasped. "Should have done this earlier . . . that Recorder's fault."

"No, it—" Cam began, but something slammed against the medicomputer's metal doors.

Hugo cursed.

Watkins snapped, "Hugo! Control!" Then she added as gently as a Caretaker speaking to an overtired novice, "Go back to your quarters. I can practically see your fever from here. And you three, find that unRecorder. She can't be left unsupervised, not when the Consortium locked her up. Comm me when you find her, and then, Cameron, report to the bridge. But founder's oath, you kids can't just wander the ship like this is a carnival. If you three take one step from your quarters again without permission, I'll lock you in the morgue."

I screamed again.

"I heard something that time," Tia said.

"I did, too," Cam said tersely. "Open the medicomputer."

I could not discern Hugo's response.

"Do it," Eric demanded. "I'm not leaving until I see inside that thing."

"Can't tell me—"

"Founders' sakes, just open the thing, Hugo," Watkins ordered. "If only to shut them up and get them out of here."

The possibility that they could not convince him drove me to pull harder. My fingers went numb.

Hugo's reply was punctuated by coughing. "I told you. Foster told you. Blasted Recorder, carrying her virus . . . killing . . . killing Rain . . ."

"Open the door, Hugo."

Fabric tightened painfully around my wrist, but the gap between my hand and the rail was finally large enough—I twisted my hand around and pulled it through. It fell free, slamming against the railing. Nerves prickled as blood rushed back to my fingertips, and I yanked off the gag, spat out the gauze, and screamed.

"Zeta," Tia cried. "That's Zeta!"

"Open that door," Watkins barked. "Foster, Bryce! Infirmary, now!"

Glass shattered, metal hit metal, and I heard a thud, like a body slamming into something solid. I frantically tugged my right hand free and bent to untie my ankles. My numb feet hit the floor, and I stumbled through the medicomputer's red light to the door, fumbling for the emergency release. It was jammed.

Foster shouted at Hugo, and while I wrestled with the lever, a woman screamed. All sounds of conflict stopped as if switched off.

Foster's voice broke the silence. "Let her go!"

Not Tia, please, not Tia—

I pushed harder on the unmoving metal.

"Get back," Hugo rasped.

"Put it down," Watkins ordered tersely.

"Have to . . . to kill the virus."

"Hugo!" Foster repeated. "Let her—"

A susurration of obscenities interrupted him, then silence again eclipsed sound.

I leaned against the lever. It moved—only a centimeter, but it moved.

"You have been instructed to release the woman," a new masculine voice said. The man's familiar, clear diction made me shiver. "Do so at once, and step away from the medicomputer."

"Killing germs." Hugo's tone lost its edge and held a hesitation I had not heard in it before. "Run a scan."

"You were warned."

A hideous duet of screams—Hugo's and a woman's—tore through the walls as though ripped from the depths of their beings.

My pulse painful in my throat, I threw all my weight on the metal bar, and that time, the lever slid left. The door opened with a click, and I fell forward into the infirmary's full-spectrum light, catching myself on hands and knees. Hugo's ragged breathing and a woman's whimpering were not the only sounds. The whir of a drone and the faint clicks of telescoping arms resounded in my ears. I froze.

Safe but pale as an infirmary blanket, Tia stared over Eric's shoulder, not at me but at the door. Eric's laryngeal prominence rose and fell. A woman in a biosuit flattened herself against the wall, and Foster shrank backward. To my left, Cam crouched over another orange-clad woman, who was curled into a ball. As Cam helped her to her feet, I recognized Bryce's features through the fogged mask. Cam kicked a metal screwdriver away from the medicomputer, toward Eric and Tia, then he scooped Bryce up, carrying her to Foster. Only a meter away, Hugo tried to push himself onto his hands and knees.

But Hugo did not matter. Neither did the drone which held his thick upper arms. Nor did the cold, thin tendrils snaking around my wrists like steel cuffs.

What mattered was the Elder.

He stood in the middle of the room, the solid grey of his eyes glinting behind the helmet's non-reflective faceplate. The mottled black of his lightly armored suit made him seem taller than his one hundred seventy-five centimeters, and his personal drone hovered above him, two tendrils encircling his torso. The tightness in my chest had nothing to do with my near escape.

Watkins whispered, "What did you do to them?"

An Elder's steady grey gaze had never seemed so foreboding. "I have prevented willful destruction of Consortium property."

I tried not to stiffen. I had escaped the medicomputer on my own. While the Elder's arrival might have kept Hugo from retaliating or caused him to release Bryce, the claim that he had prevented further incident and had saved me was incorrect. Moreover, though I might still be identified with the Consortium, I was not property.

"Destruction . . ." Watkins trailed off. "Bryce? Are you all right?"

Still gasping, Bryce shook her head.

Hugo coughed, and red droplets spattered the inside of his face shield. The slave drone tugged him to his feet, coiling its thicker appendages around his waist when he slumped.

Tia sidled around Eric, but he caught her arm, even as she called, "Zeta!"

The drone above me spread out its tentacles and yanked my arms up. Cam frowned.

The Elder's expression tightened. "Come."

No one spoke while he led the way out of the infirmary. Borrowed socks bunching around my ankles, I followed, and the drone's grip loosened and slid down to encircle my wrists.

When I reached the doors, Watkins called out, "Wait. What about Hugo?"

The Elder's voice was calm, almost monotonous. "Douglas Raymond Hugo attempted to murder a member of the Consortium. He will be tried."

Her voice rose. "He's sick, dying—"

"That is neither my problem nor my concern." He made an almost military turn and shot a grey laser-like glare at her. "You, however, Sarah Beth Watkins, will be held accountable for the behavior of the people under your command."

I glanced back. The overhead lights glinted off Watkins's mask, hiding her expression.

"But I'm not—"

"As this one indicated"—his personal drone pointed two tentacles at me and two at her—"your actions have been recorded. You yourself have borne witness."

She faltered back.

The Elder nodded once. "Compliance is beneficial." He tilted his head in my direction and repeated, "Come."

"Then what about Zeta?" Eric blurted.

The Elder focused his blank grey gaze on the young man, and sudden nausea writhed in my gut.

I pulled against the drone holding me. "Eric Thompson, be still."

The Elder's scrutiny whipped to me, and his right eyelid twitched. "Designation Zeta4542910-9545E has nothing to do with you. She will serve her purpose."

"But—"

"Eric Thompson, it is well. Do not worry. The Consortium," I lied, "does not reject its own."

The Elder's solid grey eyes narrowed. "You *will* desist."

I bowed my head. "Yes, Elder."

Another ragged cough shook Hugo, and when he tripped, the drone holding him dragged his bulk through the door. The Elder followed us to the lift, which seemed to shrink around the three of us and the three drones. Hugo braced a large hand against the wall and swayed to his feet. The lift's doors closed.

The man's harsh breathing all but covered the sound of our progress. When we reached Consortium quarters, the Elder commanded us to enter the apparently sterile, white room. I knew it was not as barren as it appeared to normal human senses. Though I could no longer see them, infrared and ultraviolet patterns twisted across the walls, and if subsonic music played, I could not detect it. The door slid shut, the magnetic lock clicking into place. The sound echoed in my heart like a citizen-judge's gavel.

Those who had only seen our outward calm might have found it difficult to reconcile the expression that flitted across the Elder's typically emotionless face. His features unwound into neutrality so quickly that I knew he had used neurochemicals to control his emotions. For a moment, I missed that as well.

"You will not face tribunal."

I bowed my head. "As you informed me when I boarded, Elder."

The drone released me and pulled two small retractable beds from the wall.

"Sleep," he ordered, and though his expression remained unchanged, his tone seemed subdued. "I will retrieve necessary medication for abrasions and the contusion on your forehead. You are tired. Other Elders are discussing your final end, but for now, the drone will guard you. The citizen who tried to harm you will face retribution."

"Elder, may I . . ." My words faltered. I steadied myself. "Unless I misinterpret his symptoms, Douglas Hugo is dying." Hugo raised reddened eyes at me. I turned my back on him before I lost the will to finish. "Would you grant him a chance to record a farewell to friends or family he might leave behind?"

It felt like the subsequent eleven seconds were eleven minutes, or even eleven hours before the Elder asked, "Why?"

"He is dying," I repeated.

"No citizen's life or death is your concern."

I bit back a protest.

"Please." Hugo's voice grated on my ears.

The Elder did not reply. Instead, his drone strained and lifted Hugo onto the bed. Hugo thrashed, but he could not escape its grip. The corner of the Elder's mouth lifted. He turned his back on the man, his nanodevice-veiled eyes fastened on me.

"Rest," he ordered.

While the Elder sat at his desk, straight as a plumb line, eyes closed, palms resting on his thighs, one of his drones tended my scraped wrists and contusions, administered an analgesic jet injector, and retreated to its charging station. Pain dissipated as nanodevices flooded me with the scents of lavender and pine. I collapsed onto the bed. Time lost meaning as I lay there, trying to collect my disordered thoughts, trying not to hear Hugo's protests that subsided into coughs and then into quiet, strangled breathing.

I rolled over to face the wall, and silent tears dampened the sheets.

# 15

Shadows blurred the distant corners of the Hall of Reclamation and pressed against the cool light from the recessed fixtures. The Recorder, who in defiance of his training called himself James, hesitated in the doorway, his back to the kilometers of long white corridors leading up to the main buildings and his cell. Rows upon rows of portable medical stasis tanks stretched before him into dimness, and the bass rhythm of the massive circulation fans throbbed in his ears. His drone hovered behind him, its four jointed legs folded up into tidy cubes.

He gritted his teeth, and the drone tightened a slender tendril around his neck, the pressure and its steady purr warning him against emotional reactions. As if that mattered anymore. Muting visual and auditory input below human standards, the Recorder walked the aisles, adjusting the tanks' requirements and confirming the viability of the units, living or dead. Thinking of them as donation units instead of deceased citizens and living Recorders made the job easier.

Medical processing notified him through his implant that the seventeenth unit in the twenty-ninth row contained a donor match for the patient now being prepared for surgery.

Life and death unto life.

He finished his task of increasing the amino acids in the secondary feedlines and made his way over to the requested unit. His drone plugged a long tendril into the port near the readout screen, and the amino acid feedlines retracted into the floor. The magnetic anchor clicked off, and he pulled the portable medical stasis tank from its mooring and maneuvered its bulk to the door to surgery, where a tall Recorder hooked it to a service bot.

James glanced down at the tank's window and stilled. It—she—was the woman he had helped, the woman who had died in his arms. Her long, greying curls were shorn—what little hair remained was dissolving away—and her silvery eyes were closed, but he recognized her.

She had claimed to be his mother.

"You must let go," the Recorder said quietly.

James could not make his fingers release the tank. His drone's thicker tentacles undulated through the air by his shoulder, wrapping around his neck before reprimanding him. He let go and leaned against the wall while the bot guided the woman's tank back to surgery.

Squinting at James through auburn lashes, the other Recorder shook his head. "It does not get easier."

James met his tan eyes. How long had he served here amidst the tanks? Yet, he knew better than to ask.

The other Recorder shrugged one shoulder, but his drone wrapped a tentacle around him. He flinched, then said through gritted teeth, "And yet we do what we must."

A warning from the administrator pinged James through his implant. With the barest of nods to the other man, James sent the administrator the appropriate notification of compliance before returning to the Hall, but his mind remained on the woman.

Had she been truthful? Her eyes had been the same unusual silver as his own, but eye color was not proof.

Without pausing to consider the ramifications, he accessed her medical files. She had indeed gifted twins—a boy and a girl—to the Consortium. He skimmed his own medical files and compared their DNA. It was conclusive.

She was indeed his mother.

He pivoted toward the closed surgery doors. The drone issued a mild reprimand, but when the buzzing jolt of pain subsided, the drone administered a dose of neurotransmitters. His near panic eased, and his heart rate slowed, until the impact of the information hit him.

Had he known his sister? Another search found an image—the girl with slate-grey eyes. She had been in his cohort but had received her drone shortly before he had. He looked deeper, but all he found was *Missing. Presumed Dead.* Unexpected loss pierced him.

His father, then? Did his father yet live? He needed to know. He needed his parents' names—

With a snap like a whip, the drone released him, and the Elders severed his connection with the Consortium network.

Even in his frustration, he recognized the validity of their action. They had done as they should.

As a Recorder, he knew better than to violate a citizen's privacy. The consequence for his action was isolation from the Consortium, from his people. Biology did not make him a citizen, not when his mother had disposed of him twenty-six years ago. Like blood from a deep wound, bitterness welled up. He closed his eyes and took slow breaths to steady himself.

It was unjust. He had already been sent to work in the nightmare of the Hall, knowing full well that after the Eldest reviewed his case, he would be sent to serve here permanently, inside a tank, parceled out piece by piece, saving lives by forfeiting his own.

His drone's long tentacles twitched. Apprehension edged out resentment, and he tensed, preparing himself for the reprimand. It did not come. The drone merely hovered behind him, humming at the same pitch as it always did. He wetted his lips and resumed his duties, but even then, he was not punished. Realization dawned, and James smiled.

Disconnection was not the punishment they intended.

James resumed checking the feedlines, adjusting the proper salinity of the medgel, and replacing the ozone filters. While he finished routine maintenance on the smaller units, he ranged through his memories without consequence. He relived the day he had disobeyed, saved the children, held his mother—*his mother*—in his arms, and consigned himself to service in the Hall.

A twinge of anger tainted the discovery of family. He paused to drive it down. Yes, she had gifted him, but she had also asked his forgiveness. And he had given it.

He would give it again, now that he knew she had spoken the truth. And again and again, if need be.

*Long, slow breaths. Relax the muscles.*

Waves of emotion faded to ripples, and he waited until his pulse calmed.

Her tank returned before his midday break, and when he slid it into its place, feedlines snaked up from the floor and reconnected. Her donation was not visible through the tank's sole window, and he closed his eyes in irrational relief. Though his drone hovered behind him like a great silver jellyfish, it did not seem to notice.

The image of her face in the tank swam before him long after he moved on to other tasks, her words echoing through his mind—

*"He wanted . . . to name you . . . James."*

Despite the rejection of gifting, he clung to the knowledge that he had a name, even if only he knew it. He would not surrender that identity. He was James, and he was free to think. He might play the part of a Recorder, but he had five days left until his adjudication. Five days to be. Five days would have to be enough, because that was all he had.

After his midday meal, his drone reconnected and wrapped around his neck, informing him that a shipment of new units from the Consortium donation center in Siena would arrive in thirty-six hours. Several of the Consortium tanks needed to be shifted. He sent an acknowledgment, and the drone released him.

The work was tiring but simple enough, though maintaining focus was always more difficult around the tanks holding the smallest units— not children, not infants, merely units. At least it was true that none of the little ones—no, he needed to remember to call them *units*—had been assigned to the Hall of Reclamation as punishment, as he had been. Most of them were sent to the tanks because their genetic flaws were egregious enough to prohibit development, or because their genetic material was too valuable to allow them to serve in any other way.

For a splintered second, he envied the ones who had never awakened, even though the selfishness of the thought appalled him. If the only thing he did in his life was to carry people to safety after a disaster, was that not purpose enough?

A soft chime told him his shift had ended, and he circumvented the section with his mother's remains, though he paused at a tank containing a younger unit with strong life signs. He peered through the window, through the slowly circulating green medical gel, at its—no, at *her* delicate face. His drone's tendril encircled his neck, repeating that his shift had ended. Ignoring its insistence, he placed a hand on the glass window, then manually plugged the tendril into the tank.

He called up his own memories of children laughing and chasing each other. Light shining golden, or splitting into the full spectrum as it passed through a prism. The sound of a viola. Boats made of lily leaves floating down a narrow brook under a riveted sky. The exhilaration of a long run. Moss, cool, damp, and soft.

The information flowed into the tank's processor, sending the memories to the child. Not a unit. A child, who should have had memories of her own. The drone did not pull free, only coiled a tentacle around his chest.

Her eyes flew open. The green of the medgel made her irises a faded brown. Her pupils dilated, then constricted, and when he leaned close, she seemed to meet his gaze. He held his breath. She blinked once, then her pale eyes closed again.

James exhaled slowly. The drone disengaged and uncurled from his neck and torso, and he turned his back to the rows of tanks. One long, grey tentacle tapped his cheek, almost as if it wished to comfort him, but punishment still did not come.

Given that impulsive act, it was no surprise that a silent Elder waited at the metal-sheathed doors. She beckoned him to accompany her, and James steeled himself for the inevitable. While he enjoyed neither his life nor the idea of service from inside a tank, he would never regret his attempt to share memories with a little girl. If it hastened his sentencing, so be it.

Determined to experience as much life as he could before his effectively ended, he paid close attention to the world around him. Once more, color left him in awe. People glowed, even those who lacked the symmetry commonly perceived as beauty. He reveled in the fans' deep rhythms, the mechanical systems' low pulse, and the drones' dissonant counterpoints. It was music to him, beautiful, cacophonous music. Surplus sensory input triggered anxiety, but James doused himself with neurotransmitters, choosing to drink in the world while he could.

The adjudication room's doors slid apart soundlessly, revealing three Elders seated on simple white stools. All three turned their opaque grey eyes to him. The Elder who had brought him nodded to the others with an appropriate level of respect, then left.

The shortest Elder, who had recommended clemency at James's tribunal, waved a hand toward the solitary chair facing them. "Sit."

James did, his shadow drone hovering behind him.

The sharp-nosed woman said, "Recorders who are unable to serve are not given opportunities to redeem themselves."

Given opportunity? Suppressing irrational hope, James only replied, "As it should be."

The shortest Elder leaned forward, his hands braced on his knees. "Why did you attempt to access the eight-year-old unit?"

Truthful. He must be truthful. "The unit . . . I wished to offer comfort, something more—" But what more was there? Grasping the only concept he could, he said, "I did not know if the unit was happy."

"We serve in whatever manner the Eldest sees fit. Additional experiences are irrelevant." She ended with the echo from childhood: "Happiness is irrelevant."

"No, he may be correct." The tall, lanky Elder's eyes twitched as if he accessed data through his implant. "Slaughterhouses providing stress-free butchering produce better quality—"

"I find your comparison repugnant," the woman snapped.

"It is, nonetheless, a valid point." His opaque eyes shifted. "I propose an official study comparing the success of transplants from units which have been given endorphins to approximate 'happiness' to transplants from traditionally maintained units. This experiment, however"—his head tilted toward James—"needs approval before implementation."

James dug his fingers into the chair's arms. "Yes, Elders."

The short Elder spoke next. "Five days remained until your adjudication."

Remained. Past tense.

His stomach tightened, but he refused to regret feeding memories to the child. James lifted his chin.

"Someone has created a bioweapon which targets the Consortium." The short Elder paused. "There have been fatalities."

James's dread overshadowed his anxiety, and his drone responded with the mildest of reprimands. "A virus?"

The female Elder gave a stilted nod. "Once contracted, the fatality rate for the children of the Consortium is one hundred percent."

"Reports indicate death is painful, though quick," the short Elder added, as if speed negated pain and certainty.

"Do we know who is responsible?"

The lanky Elder's blank expression morphed into a frown. "Terrorists infiltrated a station on one of Krios's moons, perverting approved medical research into a way to destroy the Consortium."

His first assignment had been to a station orbiting Krios. "Pallas?"

The short Elder's eyebrowless forehead creased. "Ah. Yes, I see. This is fortuitous. You have met two of the verified terrorists yourself."

Had he? James summoned his memories, reviewing the names and faces he had encountered during his year serving on CTS *Pegasus* as the ship shuttled passengers and supplies from the inner belt to various stations and waypoints orbiting Krios. Although several citizens had expressed bias against the Consortium, he found no conclusive proof.

"Julian and Elliott Ross," the short Elder clarified.

At once his drone isolated their images. Though ten years apart, the brothers' familial resemblance was strong. Blue eyes, long dark hair, tall—the older had been nearly thirteen centimeters taller than James. The younger, Elliott, had been shorter and thinner, but Julian had the overly solid bulk of a man who spent excessive time in weight training. Neither of them had held members of the Consortium in high regard, but as James reviewed his memories, another face and voice surfaced. *A teenager tossed her light-brown braids over her shoulder as she glowered at Julian Ross—*

He shunted that memory aside before the Elders noticed that he remembered something else.

"I detected nothing amiss other than standard distaste for Recorders," he said.

"No one did. We had a cryptic transmission regarding illegal activity from the station's Recorder before all communication with Pallas Station stopped."

A deep inhalation and a dose of neurotransmitters aided him in maintaining calm. "What happened?"

"Reports from the Recorder sent last quarter—"

"She is no longer one of us," the female Elder interrupted.

The lanky Elder shot her a grey, sidelong glance. "You overstep. That is for the Eldest to determine."

Her drone twined several tendrils around her neck and torso, and she rested her cheek against the smooth metal.

"Reports," the short Elder said, "state that the station's Recorder and all save four citizens died. That, however, is immaterial."

How could death be immaterial?

The memories he had suppressed returned. Kyleigh Rose Tristram. The girl with hazel eyes and long braids had defended him, a Recorder, against the oldest Ross brother's verbal barbs. Her father, Dr. Charles Elias Tristram, had offered greetings and a smile whenever they had met in *Pegasus*'s corridors. Had the girl still been on the station?

Were they gone? And why would that disturb him at all? Once the Elders dismissed him, whether or not he should, he would find a way to plug his drone back into the network to discover if either of them had survived.

"The ship which brought the terrorists and virus to Lunar One will return to Pallas Station." A slow, rare smile crept across the short Elder's face. "While researchers on New Triton work on an antivirus, a team will search for the bioweapon's origins. Recorders will accompany them to maintain the integrity of the situation."

"The Eldest offers you and several others this opportunity." The lanky Elder stood and smoothed his tunic. "Should you contract the virus, you will die, in which case, you will be incinerated and no part of you will be recycled."

Hope shot through James. In comparison to the certainty of the Hall, the possibility of a fast-acting virus was a smaller risk.

The female Elder pursed her lips. "Success will lead to reinstatement. Failure is its own punishment. Are you willing to redeem your errors?"

"You would leave now," continued the shortest Elder. "CTS *Thalassa* must reach the research station before orbit makes the trip unfeasible."

"I—" James steadied his voice. "I will go."

"As I thought you would," the Elder said, and his smile abruptly disappeared.

# 16

Douglas Hugo disappeared from his bunk in the Elder's quarters while I slept, and although the Elder remained silent about the man's fate, I knew. The knowledge saddened me, though perhaps it should not have done so.

I had no way of knowing what happened to the remaining people onboard *Agamemnon*, and while I rarely thought of the other crewmembers, concern for Cam, Eric, and Tia buzzed in my chest like the incessant but faint sound of the poorly installed lights overhead.

For the next day and a half, the Elder and I occupied the same room, but neither of us spoke, save when necessary. The first day, after Hugo disappeared, a drone left and retrieved my old Consortium uniform and boots—I recognized the uneven double stitching on the inside left sleeve and the scuff mark on the right instep. I used the water closet to change from the borrowed tunic and leggings, and the Elder nodded what I assumed to be approval, but he did not know my small act of rebellion. He did not check the crumpled, dirty tunic before I tossed it down the chute to the empty laundry facilities. When I emerged, fully dressed, he could not know that I wore Tia's socks under the grey ones the Consortium provided.

Though I never saw him remove his armored suit to eat, I had regular meals of packaged food. Restlessness prompted me to resume the katas I had learned as a child, and twice, the Elder joined me. It was not unpleasant, but I was not at peace. Despite the meals and the exercise and despite the quiet company of the Elder and the drones, time lagged.

Tia's voice sounded over the ship's communication system, stammering through the standard docking announcement. One of the Elder's drones left its station to act as my safety harness while artificial gravity switched off and the ship docked. Its metallic tendrils were nothing like the magnetic blanket I had left behind on *Thalassa*, but the drone kept me safer than I would have been otherwise.

There was nothing to do but wait, so my mind wandered. Had Lunar One's port authority set up a quarantine area, as Watkins anticipated? Had *Thalassa* remained at the station, or had my friends dispersed? Whether or not they had, their imagined proximity alternately encouraged and defeated me.

Gravity pulled me down again, and the ship began decontamination procedures—if such a possibility existed given the presence of the bioweapon. The drone unwrapped itself from my torso, though it maintained a loose hold on my wrist and allowed me to pace.

During my seventh circuit of the room, the Elder uttered a hoarse, "No!"

I turned to ask what I had done, but the words died on my lips.

His already pale face had blanched, and his lashless, grey-shrouded eyes were wide. He protested, "But you cannot mean—" When he shook his head, I realized he spoke not to me but to other Elders over the Consortium network. "What have I . . ." His voice rose in pitch. "May I not serve in the Halls instead? . . . Yes. We serve. I understand." He closed his eyes and inhaled deeply. "As the Eldest wishes."

In an attempt to avoid adding to his distress, I retreated to my bunk, but though his eyes remained closed, his head swiveled in my direction, and his scowl deepened.

"You will not be transferred to the Eldest for immediate review."

"Yes, Elder—"

"Instead," he spoke over my response, "you are to track the origins of the illness that has contaminated this ship and several others, and I am to accompany you."

Only training allowed me to keep my voice steady. "As you say, Elder."

"We will transfer to another ship to join others who have accepted the proffered assignment."

Others? I filtered through possibilities. Was it possible that my first friend—my one friend from childhood—would be spared the Hall of Reclamation? Hope that he escaped the medical tanks soared like a sine wave of unreasonable amplitude. "Elder, will other members of the Consortium accompany us?"

His eyes narrowed. "Your concern is immaterial."

Like cold water poured over my head, the realization I had spoken too freely drenched me. Fist clenched in an effort to keep from tapping my thigh, I said, "I have no drone. My current state could make others uncomfortable."

I counted to eleven before he nodded.

"The Eldest will not waste people and resources. You, one other Recorder, and I have been exposed. We are expendable. Sending us to maintain the records is an efficient choice. Finding its origin may conceivably assist researchers in combating the bioweapon's spread." He exhaled so forcefully that his faceplate fogged. "Other Recorders were offered the opportunity to serve on this assignment rather than enter the Halls. Two have accepted and wait on board CTS *Thalassa*."

For three seconds, I forgot to be concerned about either my friend or myself. Either joy or fear wrenched me, but the sensations' similarities overrode my ability to judge which emotion held predominance. I dropped to the bunk behind me and buried my head in my hands. The Elder fell quiet, but he could wait a thousand days, for I would not explain that the news was simultaneously a gift and a reprimand.

"We will board last." He paused until I looked up. "And go into quarantine."

"But—" I forced my voice under control. "Why *Thalassa*?"

"Why, indeed? It is the largest of the vessels affected by the virus and will be returning to Pallas. Do you propose that another ship, an unaffected ship, transport people to the bioweapon's origin? That Parliament waste resources in securing another vessel when most of *Thalassa*'s crew is willing to go rather than wait in quarantine on a smaller, crowded ship?"

"Elder, are the same people—" I stopped myself. I would not

inquire after Nate, Jordan, Kyleigh, and the others. "What of *Agamemnon*'s crew?"

"Enough." He set his palms on his desk and stood. "You are too concerned with the affairs of citizens. They are not *ours*. It is no surprise the Eldest herself will judge you. Lunar One's Port Authority will not allow anyone from *Agamemnon* onto the station. When the first transport arrives, in twenty-nine minutes, to take the citizens to a secure area, we shall remain behind. What becomes of them is not your concern, unless they accompany us to Pallas, but even then, their fates will be merely a matter of record."

While I nodded in acknowledgement, my heart dropped at the possibility that Cam, Eric, and Tia would be sent to the dark, dust-filled tunnels, to a place with an infestation so unnatural that even now it felt more like a nightmare than reality. The drone's grip on my wrist tightened in response to my elevated heartrate.

"I will document the removal of all bodies from *Agamemnon*, after which you and I will take a secured shuttle to *Thalassa*. There, we will remain in isolation until scans and bloodwork indicate there is no danger." If he had not been an Elder, I would have said he sighed. His head drooped. "It would seem that our service is more vital than our selves. We have no choice but to go."

I did not know if he meant to test me or if his concern and regret weighed on him as heavily as mine weighed on me. "So it has always been."

"Indeed. Our success is imperative. Not only members of the Consortium are falling ill, but over thirty citizens, including the captain who fled CTS *Thalassa*, have also died."

I had known this, but hearing the Elder confirm the information prompted me to say, "Elder, I do not understand. Julian Ross admitted to targeting the Consortium. Why are citizens dying?"

"Either he lied, or his bioweapon has malfunctioned."

I bit my lower lip. "Will not the virologists find a cure, an antivirus, or a vaccine before we return? The trip to Pallas will take three and a half ten-days, and even if we find the information quickly, the return will take longer, given Krios's orbit." Despite knowing that this reprieve was all I would have, the words spilled out. "Is going necessary?"

The drone's appendage slithered higher up my arm to my neck, and the Elder took three strides toward me. "Do you refuse?"

I forced my respiration into a steady pattern. "No, Elder, of course I do not."

Eyes shut, he tilted his face in my direction. When I had a drone, I had relied on it to feed me the smallest of details—heartbeat, temperature, pupil dilation—to evaluate physical well-being and honesty or deception. The thought struck me that his silence over the past day had been to develop a baseline.

"I do not believe you have been forthcoming." His voice echoed harshly in my ears. "What have you omitted?"

Though the drone merely held me, anxiety itself provided the reprimand. Necessity demanded I give the Elder a valid reason to view my friends with neutrality, if not generosity. I opened my eyes to search his face for clues, but nothing was there, no hint of leniency, no—

But then, the image of his apparent anger at Hugo rose to the forefront.

It was possible he might overlook Nate's culpability and the others' silence, if he saw their actions as defense of Consortium . . . property. Misdirection and prevarication through telling the truth was the only acceptable option, and after all, Elliott had aligned himself with the Consortium's enemies. He would be my sacrifice.

"You are aware that Julian Ross attempted to use me to spread his bioweapon, and that I stopped him."

The corner of the Elder's eyelid twitched, and the grey in his eyes grew more opaque. "Yes. You grabbed a charging station, and if no one had pulled you free, it would have worked. He would have been stopped. We would have been safe."

Ignoring the implication that I should have died, I confessed, "I did not include the other incident in my report."

"Other incident?" His drone rose above him, its arms and tentacles outstretched like roots or branches. "Explain."

The memory still stung. "Several days before you arrived, I was returning from reviewing records in VVR, and Elliott Ross . . . behaved badly."

"Clarify."

"Without my consent, he grabbed me, and . . ." I swallowed. "Nathaniel Timmons, who arrived in time to stop Elliott Ross, assured me that it was not kissing, although there was an exchange of saliva."

The drone released me and flew back to the Elder, whose face flushed. I did not see him stiffen in pain, so he must not have been reprimanded for any heightened emotion. I clenched my hands to keep from tapping my thigh.

"If the virus is spread via bodily fluids, why have you not succumbed?"

"As I reported, I suspect that there are two parts which must work in concert." I rubbed my hands on my legs, focusing on the fabric's texture against my palms. The distraction was insufficient. "If I have but half the virus, or if his—"

"Why did you not report this at once?" the Elder demanded softly, and his gentle tone set my nerves further on edge.

I did not answer immediately. After thirty-seven seconds, I finally said, "It seemed a small thing. He was young, and I did not believe it was in his character to repeat it. I made them promise not to tell."

"Them?"

He needed to condemn me, not my friends. Though Recorders did not gamble, I swallowed and took a chance. "Nathaniel Timmons and Venetia Jordan reported the incident. Elliott Ross was taken into custody but released because the records had been damaged. I asked Jordan and Timmons not to reveal the incident in their official reports, though my request seems to be immaterial as the entire ship's records were damaged later."

"You interfered with the records."

"Yes." Hoping my words would suffice, I said, "At the time, my thoughts were incoherent, and I was concerned that their defense of me would be taken amiss."

His shadow drone wrapped a small tendril around his torso, and his right hand rose to stroke the gleaming metal. "Many people knew, then, but did not report it, and Elliott Ross faced no penalty."

"He did not."

"That is a violation of all we believe." Though his face was oddly blank, even for an Elder, one eyelid twitched. "The exchange of saliva could be material to the investigation, yet you did not speak of it?"

Shame, both at the incident itself and my dishonest truthfulness, undulated through me. I lowered my gaze to the floor and waited for the reprimand. It never came. Eventually, I looked up, and the Elder's gaze held mine. His nanodevices spiraled back, revealing hazel irises. I held my breath.

Although his posture remained stiff, his voice was quiet. "I have recorded such incidents. You are ashamed but also have feelings of gratitude to this Nathaniel Timmons?"

My cheeks grew warm.

"Both shame and gratitude are typical for citizens. In your case, without the assistance of your drone to prevent the incident and your neural implant to aid in neurotransmitter administration, your reactions are reasonable. If this is verified, it will be added to the record, and Nathaniel Timmons will earn a commendation for defending a member of the Consortium. You will not be punished for the incident itself, though the incomplete records are another matter."

Had I done it, then? I blinked away sudden excess moisture.

The film of nanodevices covered the Elder's eyes again, and he placed his gloved hand on my shoulder. I flinched.

"Ah." He removed his hand and walked to the door, where he paused. "The transport shall arrive soon. Remain here. Do not be alarmed if citizens approach the door. It will be sealed, and the other drones will guard you. Life without . . ." His voice faded, and then, without turning around, he said, "I am, indeed, sorry for your losses."

The magnetic lock clicked shut behind him, though securing me in the room was unnecessary. I was going nowhere unless the Consortium sent me, whether it be Pallas or back to New Triton to the Hall of Reclamation. Hands folded on my lap, I settled on the bunk to wait.

Losses. He had no idea.

# 17

No one greeted us when we emerged from the shuttle, and I heard no announcement of our arrival, though in all probability, any such announcement was made before we docked. Uncertain of the direction to take, I waited for the Elder to step into the bland corridor. I followed, his three drones trailing behind me.

I had only his word that this was *Thalassa*. The beige paneling and the low, periodic benches covering the chemical backup system could have belonged to any ship of *Thalassa*'s class. Since I wore an older model of the Consortium's standard suit, the filtration system that hissed cool streams of purified air into my helmet carried no scent. Without a glimpse of anyone else, we walked down one hallway after another, hearing only our own footfalls and the whir of the drones.

While reason informed me the halls had been cleared to protect citizens, staff, and Recorders from whatever contagion we might carry, the emptiness was an unwelcome reminder of *Agamemnon* and Butterfield's temporary morgue. If the same fate awaited this crew, I did not want to witness it, and the static of uneasiness increased with each meter I walked. I would rather face anything than to see my friends succumb. Despite the flow of oxygen, breathing became difficult.

Perhaps it was not *Thalassa*. Perhaps this was an attempt to unsettle me, to trick me into relaying things I refused to admit. Perhaps the Elder had been misled.

We turned another corner, and I stopped. The overhead light shone on the ugly, one-meter-square, unframed canvas secured on the opposite wall. Familiar, uneven brush strokes swirled through the garish red paint, and despite everything else, my smile broke free.

"We are on CTS *Thalassa*."

"As I told you we would be." After three seconds, the Elder spoke again. "I would not call that art."

One of his drones joined me, and its outstretched tentacles wrapped around my arms. My smile dissolved into nothingness. "Neither would I."

"Come," the Elder said. "The halls will not be clear forever."

I turned my back on the painting before the Elder chose to discipline me, and we progressed through the port hallway. I closed my eyes, allowing the drone and my feet to guide me, but olfactory memories of my time on *Thalassa* randomly activated—*the peculiar combination of coffee and lemon, the sharp tang of burning computer fail-safes, the scent of pine and cinnamon.*

"Here."

My eyes flew open. We had passed my old quarters and stood before an unused room. The door slid open, revealing a step up into a vestibule with a bench, an open shower, a receptacle labeled with the clawed pentagon indicating biohazardous waste, and a closed inner door.

Another decontamination area—another holding cell. I wanted to tap my thigh, but I refrained.

"There is a fifteen-minute countdown before the inner door unlocks."

"I understand."

"Only a Consortium-approved medical technician will be allowed to enter. He will bring you meals twice a day when he arrives to monitor your health. After I have been cleared in a ten-day, I shall check on you as well. Unless the room is needed, you will remain here until we reach Pallas."

It was indeed another holding cell. Even though I yet stood in the hall, the walls seemed to close in about me, and the weight of isolation bore down like malfunctioning artificial gravity.

"You shall not have a drone."

His words surprised me. "I have not had one since last quarter."

The solid grey of his eyes focused on my eyebrows. "I had intended to leave a drone with you, but the room was not designed for Consortium personnel and has no charging station." His eyelid twitched. "However, the ship's Recorder has fitted it with observation devices, so you will be watched."

Again? I held back a sigh.

"I will tell you now that while I have a degree of sympathy for your situation, for the loss of your drone, and for the crime committed against you, the Eldest herself has charged me to maintain tight control over your behavior. Do you understand?"

An ember of resentment lit in my chest. Why would he burden me with the knowledge that the Eldest had tasked him with such a responsibility? Whether or not her command was fair, telling me was unnecessary. "Yes."

"It has been decided that you are not a suicide risk, so a change of clothing has been provided. They have generously allowed you access to review information on virology and the station's layout."

His drone released me into the vestibule, and the magnetic lock snapped shut.

I sank onto the small bench.

Unless this short period in the vestibule was counted, my ten-days of isolation would begin in fifteen minutes. But whether or not I was a Recorder, whether or not I would see my friends again, whether or not I had a future, there was work to do, and I would do it.

Even though the isolation itself was a reprimand.

The inner door closed behind me, sealing me into the bland room that already felt like a prison, and the Consortium recording device tracked every move I made. Hiding was impossible, which made ignoring the moisture burning my eyes and the tightness in my chest imperative. I told myself all would be well. I removed the Consortium suit and went to store it in the appropriate section of the closet, but a uniform hanging next to the cleaning unit caught my attention. I glanced from my wrinkled tunic to the water closet. Hope sparked.

Without pausing to consider whether or not I had time before we left dock, or when the Elder would next provide clean clothes, I snatched the grey uniform from its hanger and shut myself in the water closet where no camera watched. I leaned back against the white paneling, slid down to the floor, and hid my eyes with my palms, pressing until stars danced against the dark.

Time slipped past uncounted before I finally changed out of the wrinkled, sweat-stained tunic and leggings into the clean ones. For two and a half minutes, I held the dirty borrowed socks by the cuffs, simply staring at them, my mind simultaneously racing and blank. A growing sense of urgency pulled me back to the present. I could not afford to stay in the water closet much longer.

The socks—*my* socks now, for I could not return them to Tia—needed cleaning. Never having washed clothing before, I scrubbed them fiercely with soap and hoped three rinses sufficed. There was, however, nowhere to hang them to dry. I settled for laying them on the far side of the room, under the white sink, where the camera's angle would not allow it to document their presence. So occupied was I with the socks that I nearly forgot to provide an excuse for the length of time I had spent in the water closet. Surely the Elder had little experience with such matters and would believe that the time had been spent on my hair.

I exited the water closet and tossed my old uniform into the laundry container marked with the clawed biohazard symbol, but my timing was faulty. While my socks yet dried, the ship's communication system pinged.

Officer Smith's familiar nasal whine recited the standard announcement. "During departure, artificial gravity will be offline. Secure yourselves and any liquid or loose substances. Any damage incurred will be levied against your personal accounts. Meals will resume after artificial gravity is back online."

Given her obeisance to Captain North, I would have preferred she was not on *Thalassa*, but I settled into the chair and fastened the harness. As always, gravity gave a sharp tug, then weightlessness released it. I relaxed for only three seconds before the thought slammed into me: My socks were not secured.

They could very well drift up to the intake vent and block it, which would set off alarms. Or, when artificial gravity turned on, they could fall in front of the door, even tumble out.

And the Elder would know. He would take them away.

Surely oxygen had not been affected by the loss of gravity, but I could not catch my breath. My fears were irrational, so I tightened my fingers about the chair's arms to keep them from detaching the harness. I could not check on my socks. Would not.

Surely I could justify their presence in my possession, and should the Elder discover them, I could reasonably defend them by stating that my feet had been cold. The worst that would happen is that I would be disciplined.

No . . . that was not the worst.

The Elder could not—must not—be allowed to take them away.

When artificial gravity resumed, I would find a way to rescue them, and I would never risk them again, even if I had to wear them, hidden, until whatever end I faced befell me. The Elder could not have them.

Time crawled past, and I called on prime numbers for aid. Once again, I remembered Nate with his hand on my head. In my mind, he whispered with me, *"Two, three, five, seven, eleven, thirteen, seventeen, nineteen . . ."*

My breathing steadied, and somehow, I fell into restless dreams.

A bell-like chime woke me. The light over the metallic door flashed green. In a splintered second I realized I had overslept, that I had not retrieved my socks. I was too late.

My pulse hammering, I fumbled with the harness and stood in time to face the door as it slid open, but it was not the Elder. A man in an orange biohazard suit entered. The door closed behind him, and I sank back into the chair.

From under a receding hairline and sparse, ash-brown eyebrows, pale blue eyes widened. Max's lead medical assistant blinked twice, and a huge grin spread across his face.

"Hello."

"Edwards," I managed.

When I glanced from him up to the camera above the door, he stiffened, but that welcoming smile did not fade.

"I won't stay long." He placed a disposable bag on the bedside table and gestured at a steel cylinder by the door. "I brought you a hot meal and some packaged food for later. You will need to dispose of leftover food and trash in the metal bin. We have reactivated the incinerator, so once it is sealed, all pathogens will be destroyed." His tone softened. "You look well."

"I do not believe I am ill, Edwards."

He hummed an indeterminate answer and began a quick physical examination. A crease furrowed his forehead. "It has been a difficult few days, hasn't it?"

"Yes." Questions rose—was he well, who was on board, had Kyleigh taken care of the cats, was there news of Max and Jordan or Alec and Zhen? About Nate? I kept silent.

"Archimedes Genet was appointed captain," he said. "I suppose you knew that."

"I did not."

He asked about symptoms: cough, shortness of breath, achiness, on and on, then about contact with ill people on *Agamemnon*, and a myriad of other things. He took a blood sample and told me I would resume the treatment for the toxoplasmosis Max had prescribed before I had been taken away. I told him of what had happened to Rain, of Kavanaugh and the others, though I did not speak of Hugo and the medicomputer. While I answered he flashed a light in my eyes. I blinked away the afterimages.

His back to the recording device, he mouthed, *"Are you all right?"*

I did not know what to answer, so I dropped my gaze to my lap.

Edwards set an orange-gloved hand on my shoulder. "You have lost more weight. Please eat."

I peeked inside the bag. After the past ten-day, the amount of food seemed daunting. "This is too much."

"Do your best," he said quietly. "I will return in the morning."

Without another word, he left, and silence swelled around me. The sight of a friend and the subsequent loss of his company exacerbated the emptiness of the room. Afraid to call attention to my behavior, I made myself eat the soup and drink the hot tea—at least it was peppermint, not hibiscus or melon—before I opened the water closet door and darted inside.

Relief flooded me, for my socks lay on the floor under the intake vent, out of the camera's range. The fabric was crunchy and stiff. Either they had not dried well, or I had washed them poorly. It did not matter. I wore them anyway, the tall Consortium socks over them to conceal my defiance.

The remainder of my afternoon was spent reviewing the information on RNA replication and synthesis while I snacked on the packaged food. I left the soft red nightlight on when I crawled into bed, shivering slightly under the thin, useless blanket. Here in my temporary prison of a quarantine room, *Thalassa* was not the same, but I did not feel as alone. Edwards was onboard as well. And in their double layer of socks, my toes, at least, were warm.

My time in those quarters dragged on past one ten-day, past a second, past a third. While the Elder periodically inspected my quarters, he offered no explanation as to the protracted quarantine but he never found my socks.

On the morning of my thirty-first day on *Thalassa*, when Edwards entered my room, he did not wear a biohazard suit, and the sight lightened my heart. Surely, if he had been allowed to enter without protection, there must be no evidence of infection in my system. He left a clean steel bin by the door, then put the usual bag on my bedside table.

"I have two announcements. First, they have officially decided you are not contagious. Second, we will be in synchronous orbit over Pallas Station around midnight."

Surprise edged past relief. "I assumed it would take several days longer."

"So had I, but the marines are getting ready to shuttle down to the surface. They'll handle the infestation and make it as safe as they can before the researchers and security teams head down. VVR has been tied up with their scenarios since we left Lunar One, so they should be as prepared as they can be. Dr. Clarkson and the others heading up research have been unhappy."

"But why would they need—" I stopped before I could protest that Max was the best doctor in the system. After all, he was a medical doctor, not a researcher, and Parliament or whoever maintained control of the situation would send the people they deemed best. And though Edwards's presence gave me hope Max was on Thalassa, I did not know for certain.

Edwards raised one eyebrow at my truncated question. "They have simulations for deconstructing the virus, and they are anxious for their turn in Visual Records. Preliminary reports, of course, are a matter of gossip at this point, but Max wants the infirmary ready to handle injuries." He held up a hand. "And before you worry, the need for freeing up medical personnel has nothing to do with clearing you."

While Max's presence on *Thalassa* was a comfort, the prospect of anyone heading down to the intrusion-overrun research station was cause for concern. I said nothing. I did not even point out that *marines* seemed a misnomer, for it was highly improbable they had ever served on Ceres' oceans.

"The other people under observation were cleared last eighth-day, and as far as I can tell, the other Recorders are ready to go as well. We haven't seen them, of course. The Elder has been our contact, and he has kept them in quarantine in case the virus was onboard. That way, even if we got sick, there would be someone to represent the Consortium. They will remain in quarters as well until, well, until he sends you all somewhere else."

I merely nodded. "Do you know, then, what my assignment will be?"

"You should find out at the briefing tomorrow, at the latest." Edwards glanced up at the camera, then rolled his shoulders back and pulled a sealed packet of tea from his tunic pocket. "Lavender-peppermint to celebrate, which is your favorite, I think. There's a flask of hot water in the bag."

"Thank you."

"Since they've decided you're clear, there's no need for further examinations." His expression faltered, and he tipped his head toward the door behind him. "Though, *they* do not know you are *you*."

"Who?"

Edwards ran a hand over his short ash-brown braid. "I am the only one who knows you are here, although I believe Bustopher suspects."

"The cats remain aboard?" I blinked in confusion. "Edwards. A cat, no matter his intelligence, could not suspect anything, especially when he is contained in the storage room."

He grinned. "Ah. I did not tell you earlier. Archimedes Genet allowed the cats free range of the ship, declaring their presence 'good for morale.' I suspect he is correct, even if the kitchen staff is divided. Half of them sneak scraps for the cats, but the other half are incensed that Macavity has taken to stealing food."

"He and Bustopher frequently attempted to convince me their food supply was inadequate." I found myself smiling as well. "I am not surprised."

"At first, I thought Bustopher kept following me here simply because I had food, but I no longer believe that is the case. The past ten-day, he has been sitting outside your door, trying to get in. Twice I have had to pick him up and set him back in the hall. You might not recognize him. Bustopher is quite a handsome fellow since his fur has grown in." Edwards chuckled softly. "Even so, Max does not appreciate the captain's decision."

My smile grew. "I believe you. Max did not admire the cats at all." Without thinking the better of it, I asked, "How is he?"

"Max is well, though he is not quite himself. The past ten-days have been challenging, and losing—" He broke off, his posture stiffening as if he had been reprimanded. My fingers curled around the packet, and I tapped my thigh. Neither of us glanced up at the recording device. Edwards cleared his throat. "Enjoy your tea."

He collected the trash and left, but before beginning my morning studies, I set my tea to steep and took five minutes to review pictures of cats, verifying that tuxedo cats like Bustopher were indeed my favorite.

The morning and afternoon crept past. My mind kept returning to the marines and researchers heading to Pallas, my unknown assignment, and the destruction of my drone. If the infestation had not been eradicated and the Elder sent other Recorders down, the trip could very well be a death sentence. If one of the roaches crushed another drone, that Recorder's neural implant would trigger the programmed sequence of events, turning the Recorder's body against itself, ending life in an abyss of pain. With an Elder present, Max would not be allowed to operate and save someone whose drone had been crushed. Any Recorder who was sent to the station was in danger. And my friend—

If he was indeed onboard, I could not allow him to die such a painful death. His sister was already gone, swept away during a storm on Ceres. I would not allow him to be destroyed as well, for his sake and his father's. There had to be a way to shut down the neural implant and save him, to save them all.

None of the articles regarding the detection of recombination in viral sequences and its use in evaluating breakpoints made sense. Finally, I signed off my computer, so I could wash my socks again before Edwards arrived with my dinner. However, as I did, I lost track of the number of times I rinsed them. Instead, my mind raced through ideas, discarding each one: shut down the drone, shut down the implant, disconnect the system . . .

While I was laying the socks to dry on the floor under the sink, I heard the vestibule door open. Hastily drying my hands, I exited the water closet, but the greeting died on my lips.

Still in his lightly armored suit, the Elder stood in the middle of my room, hands behind his back and all three drones above him, their tendrils moving as if caught in a draft.

The room seemed to spin around the grey-eyed man in front of me.

Surely the Elder did not know. He could not have known I had been mulling over shutting off the neural implants. One fisted hand tapping my leg, I ran through all the articles I had read, trying to remember if I had somehow given away my thoughts.

"Elder," I finally managed. "Good evening."

He said nothing. His personal drone moved closer to him, snaking a long tendril about his torso. The other two began a circuit of the room. Pulse pounding, I leaned back and closed the water closet door.

The Elder's eyelid twitched.

His drones converged on me in front of the water closet and stopped to flank my left and right like prison guards. I swallowed.

Then, without a word, he exited, leaving one drone behind, but even with it hanging in the air like a threat, I backed against the door and slid to the floor, hiding my eyes with my hands.

He must not have known of my idea to disconnect the Recorders from their drones, or he would have punished me. But why had Edwards not brought my meal? Apprehension writhed inside me as I reviewed our conversation.

Edwards had brought me tea, had mentioned the cats. I had asked him about Max. If he had been disciplined for talking to me, the burden of guilt would be mine.

Or, duty could have kept him away. That would have been preferable, save that it might mean someone had been injured and Max needed Edwards's help.

Worse yet, were they wrong about me? Had I contaminated him after all, made him ill? The thought of Edwards suffering like Rain, Kavanaugh, or Hugo destroyed my appetite. I crawled into bed without changing or eating, and my feet were cold under the thin blanket.

With the drone hovering at my bedside, I did not sleep well that night.

# 19

I woke to a drone—tendrils withdrawn and arms folded—hovering above my head like a silver moon. There was no avoiding its attention, but to maintain a semblance of my regular routine, I ducked under it to the water closet, quickly closing the door behind me. I hurried through my ablutions, pulling on the dry socks as quickly as I could and the tall Consortium socks overtop. When I emerged, the drone entered the water closet and rotated slowly before resuming its place in the middle of the room. Trying to appear as if a drone's presence was expected, I nibbled on the packaged food from the day before, but in truth, I had adjusted to being alone since I had lost my own drone, over five tendays before.

It had not been thirteen minutes since I had opened my eyes to the drone's underbelly when the door slid into its pocket and the Elder stormed in.

"Where are they?"

It was as if the marrow in my bones iced through. I swallowed, and my food fell in dense clumps to my stomach.

Lashless lids narrowed around grey-veiled eyes. "I am not a fool. Do not make it necessary to take this room—or you—apart to find them."

The drone overhead unspooled its tendrils, unfolded its arms.

*He knew.* My resolve crumbled, and I capitulated. Balancing on one foot at a time, I pulled off the socks, laying both pairs side-by-side atop the thin cotton blanket. The antistatic flooring chilled my soles.

The drone reached down with two long jointed arms and took Tia's gift.

I did not need to ask the Elder's intent. My eyes closed, and my throat tightened as a sharp crack sounded. A flash of light penetrated my eyelids, heat made me flinch, and acrid smoke stung my nostrils.

Attempting to ignore the knot in my throat, I told myself they were only socks.

"I warned you." The words were crisp. "I informed you that our fates are tied, that the Eldest requires compliance. When Douglas Hugo attempted to murder you, I came to your defense, acted to prevent your destruction—"

My eyes flew open, and I scowled through the wisps of smoke. "I escaped the bonds and the medicomputer on my own."

"You have done *nothing* on your own." His nostrils flared behind his faceplate. "You have interfered with citizens and entangled yourself in their lives."

The fundamental truth in his words did not stop my rebuttal. "If I had not acted, would we not still be drifting through the void, lost and open to pirates and looters?"

His drone released the ashes and debris, and the remnants of Tia's gift floated gently onto the thin, white blanket.

"If you had not acted"—he enunciated each syllable carefully—"would we be going to our deaths on an abandoned station?"

His personal drone sent an arm around his neck, and he stiffened. I looked away as his face blanched.

At that moment, a cat's trill sounded in the hall, and one drone shot from the room. The cat hissed.

My jaw clenched. "You will not harm Bustopher."

His respiration uneven after his reprimand, the Elder slumped against the wall, but he narrowed his eyes. "You will not tell me what to do. Despite Captain Genet's claims, all cats will be returned to the Consortium to be disposed of as the Eldest sees fit. As will you. Do not forget it."

The Elder grasped the drone's dangling arms and pulled himself upright. The drones preceded him out the door, but he stopped in the open vestibule. His gloved hand clutched the doorframe, and he turned to me, that eyelid twitching again.

His voice was emotionless and empty as he hit the panel to close me in. "It seems you have killed us both. And I am through protecting you."

I waited, alone with the ashes of my socks. Little caring what the Elder thought, I scooped them up—soft and powdery on my skin—and dusted them into a disposable napkin. My tunic had no pocket, so after I had recited the first one hundred prime numbers, I laid the napkin carefully inside the stainless trash bin.

Soot blackened my fingers, but eventually, I washed my hands. Water divided over my palms and carried away the final particles to the filtration unit deep in *Thalassa*'s bowels. I settled in the chair and rested my head against the back.

They had only been socks, after all.

Time crawled past.

Over and over, I replayed the past twenty-nine hours. I should not have asked about Max. I should not have washed my socks. The Elder might have found something else for which to punish me, but the socks would still be mine. Over and over, I redirected my thoughts to the problem of finding a way to protect any Recorders from the roaches which would surely survive the marines' extermination procedures. If my friend had indeed accepted this assignment, I would not let him die as his sister had.

Her death—I stopped myself, for the exact wording mattered. Missing. She was only presumed dead. I closed my eyes and concentrated. During the storms on Ceres, drones would be a liability. The Consortium must have shut them down. It must be possible to not only disconnect from the network, but to power off the neural implant itself. If I had access— but I dared not ask now, dared not let them know—

The datapad.

My eyes flew open. I had loaded the access codes to my datapad before the Elder took me away from *Thalassa*.

The day the Elder had taken me to *Agamemnon*, my friends and I had sat in the dining commons, and I had entrusted my datapad to Zhen DuBois. If she had not done as I had requested, her frequently contrary behavior could give me the chance to save them all. Unable to sit still any longer, I began to pace, and the camera tracked my every move. Even if Zhen were still on *Thalassa*, the Elder watched. There would be no opportunity to—

With no warning, the door opened. A drone hovered and summoned me with one thick, jointed arm. Wordlessly, I followed it through vacant halls to a small meeting room, though it remained outside like a sentry as the door shut me in.

The Elder was not present, but three Recorders and their drones waited. The first Recorder sat stiffly on the edge of her seat, her drone close to her shoulder with a tendril encircling her left arm like a bracelet or a snake. Her lips twisted into an uneven line as she glared at me. The second lounged at the long, faux wooden table, his legs kicked out in front of him, his drone overhead, its appendages waving unevenly. The third Recorder stood with perfect posture, studying the mediocre oil painting over a low cabinet, his hands clasped behind his back.

When the door's lock clicked, the lounging Recorder's focus narrowed on me, and the one studying the painting turned. His silvery eyes widened.

Despite my concerns, I could not hide my smile. For, there he was— my first friend. The one who had taught me to make boats of lily leaves. He was not in a tank in the depths of the Hall of Reclamation, and though this assignment held the potential for an equally disastrous end, thankfulness at the reprieve washed over me.

I quickly schooled my features into neutrality, nodding first to him, then to the others. "Greetings."

The woman, who was approximately five years older than I, frowned. "Why do you wear our greys, when you are not . . ." Her eyes flickered over me. "You are *she*. As *Thalassa*'s Recorder, I have been warned about you. I did not expect—"

"So we could grow hair, if we lost our drones? I always wondered." A grin flashed over the lounging Recorder's face, but when his drone tapped his shoulder, the grin disappeared.

"Yes, we can," I said, then turned to my friend. "You are familiar to me, but I no longer have access to records." It was true, although the implication of uncertainty could have been considered false. I hoped the ambiguity of my statement allowed him the opportunity to process any recognition.

"Training Center Alpha," he said slowly, as if he measured each word. "You were several cohorts behind me." His silver gaze met mine. "I recognize you, despite your hair."

The woman at the table observed, "Your eyebrows are unsightly."

"Yes." I inclined my head. "I was damaged."

"Sounds painful." The lounging one shot a quick sideways glance at his drone. Though he kept an eye on its tentacles, he clearly said, "I'm sorry."

I tensed.

"Enough," snapped the woman. "Your slovenly grammar is appalling."

"Enough of what? What do you believe they will do? *I'm* here to avoid the Halls." He offered us an uneven smile. "They will no longer send me to serve there. And should I die of this bioweapon, isn't it a better end, a better service—"

"Perhaps," I interrupted, "it is not the end."

Please, I begged no one at all, may my calculations not have sent these to their deaths.

The talkative Recorder crossed his arms and leaned back against the chair.

"Indeed," my friend said.

His voice was as resonant as I remembered, though not as deep as Max's. The similarity between their profiles struck me. Surely no one else would notice? My intention had been to save him, not to bring either of them trouble.

The woman sniffed, but before she spoke, the door opened again. She stood abruptly. Even the lounging Recorder snapped to attention. Though the Elder still wore his lightly armored suit, he had removed his helmet and cap. One of his larger drones glided toward me and curled a delicate tendril around my shoulders.

Again, all the Elder said was, "Come."

We fell into step behind him and marched in unison down the hallway with the drones' soft noises providing a steady background. The Elder's slave drone tightened its grip, so I was careful to maintain the same pace as the Recorder beside me, even though her stride was shorter than mine. I wished to close my eyes, to release my anxiety, but the tendril touched the base of my throat. It became more difficult to ignore the tightness in my chest.

The halls grew increasingly recognizable. We passed the cabinet with the old analog clock and then the door to Jordan's office, and memories piled on memories, trying to smother me. I mentally listed prime numbers.

Archimedes Genet's steady baritone and the restless undercurrent of an audience drifted toward us before we reached the multipurpose room. My heart rate sped up. The Elder led us in, the woman at his heels. His drone tugged gently on my shoulders. I drew a breath and followed her, and the other two Recorders entered behind me.

" . . . assignments to your shuttles. The administration center and adjacent rooms must be secured before the primary research team arrives." Archimedes Genet fell silent when I entered.

Boots hit the floor, chairs scraped back, and whispers crescendoed, one voice or another occasionally rising above the rest, then ebbing back into a rush of murmured conversation. I kept my gaze on my boots until I could bear it no longer. Lifting my eyes, I scanned the packed room. Marines in blue uniforms stood in the back, their Recorder at the front, her drone behind them all. People I recognized. People I had never before seen, but not—

Oh, my heart—

He was here.

And though I knew I should look away, I could not. The voices faded as from across the sea of faces, Nate's green eyes locked onto mine. He paled, then flushed.

"Stop." The Elder's voice cracked my focus, but did not break it.

While I drank in the sight of my Nathaniel, I became peripherally aware of Jordan, her golden-brown eyes glancing rapidly between Nate and me. Alec stood on his other side, thick eyebrows raised, his right hand on Nate's arm, just below a band of green fabric. Zhen DuBois seemed to be struggling for breath, but her hair caught my attention. Though it still fell like a sheet of water, it was no longer black, but navy with electric blue tips. Kyleigh bounced on her toes at Jordan's other side. I did not see Max, and concern threaded through me.

"Stop," the Elder repeated.

One last glance.

The slight scar on Nate's cheekbone stood out as his color deepened.

The drone released my shoulders to twine around my neck instead.

I lowered my eyes. "Yes, Elder."

Voices tempted me to look up, so I flattened my hands against my legs and forced myself to remain still. On either side of me, large boots appeared. I peeked at my first friend, then at the talkative Recorder, whose eyes met mine. A crease appeared over his nose, and he shook his head ever so slightly.

Archimedes Genet's baritone rang out: "Everyone settle down."

The murmurs faded.

The Elder's voice was scratchy and sharp after the captain's. "The Eldest has sent us to maintain an accurate record of your attempt to track down information leading to an antivirus. Each shift of researchers will have increased security and one additional Recorder. This one"—the increased harshness in his tone raised my head, so I saw him motion toward me—"shall remain on the station to coordinate our efforts. The others will rotate from *Thalassa* to Pallas Station."

"What?" Was that Eric Thompson? I scanned the room and found him—arm no longer in a sling—standing with Tia and Cam at the back.

"That's not fair!" Kyleigh's exclamation jerked my attention to her. She glowered at the Elder. "You can't honestly expect her to work round the clock on the station with those . . . those creatures that destroyed her drone and nearly killed everyone?"

The Elder's face remained impassive. "It is so. She will redeem her errors."

"Simmer down, Kye," Jordan murmured, and Kyleigh subsided, her thin arms folded across her chest.

I turned to Archimedes Genet. "Having been to Pallas Station, I am the most logical choice of Consortium representatives to stay there. I have knowledge of the station's computer systems and the"—from the corner of my eye, I saw the Elder frown—"the particular infestation. I place myself at your disposal."

The Elder resumed his speech, but I could not focus on his words. The need to see them—to see *him*—churned inside me until I capitulated.

Nate had gone pale, but surely he could not have imagined the Elder would have allowed anything else. I tried to offer the hint of a smile.

"Enough," the Elder snapped, interrupting his own monologue.

The drone reprimanded me. The world roared and flashed until the jagged pain finally stopped, and I sagged. Its hold around my neck tightened. Hands caught me, and the pressure on my throat eased.

Dimly, through the ringing in my ears, voices began to separate from a general roar of protest, as if the entire room had cried out, although I could not follow the overlap or discern the speakers.

"Back off!"

"Get away from—"

"—not your concern—"

"Let her go!"

Nate? No, he must not—

I fought my way up from the still-buzzing pain.

"—Now! or I'll—"

"I am well." The words scraped from me, and I blinked against the sea of faces that seemed closer. My stomach heaved, and I closed my eyes again.

"She's lying, of course," said the talkative Recorder.

My friend's low rumble added, "She needs medical attention, since she does not have an implant to monitor functions."

"Her outbursts—and yours—are insupportable." The Elder's voice was like ice.

"She's not a Recorder." With every word Nate growled, anxiety grew.

I needed to speak up, needed to reassure him, but my body hurt and my nerves reverberated with static echoes of pain.

"She doesn't have a neural interface." Nate spat out the words. "And the drone trying to kill her isn't hers."

"Release her." Archimedes Genet's voice rose above the clamor. "The Prime Minister granted me full authority on this expedition with the Eldest's acknowledgment." He repeated, "Release her now."

I tried to count the seconds before the Elder answered, but the flashes in my vision and the way my nerves buzzed prohibited it. I clamped my eyes shut to block the spinning room.

The Elder's voice came out unevenly. "Very well."

The tendril slithered away. My breath snagged, and I coughed. The Recorders at my sides shifted their hold on my arms but still supported my weight.

"I'm with you." Nate sounded too close, and panic snaked up to replace the drone's strangling hold.

"No, Timmons. You're needed here." I had never heard Archimedes Genet speak so quickly. "Recorders, get her to the infirmary and keep her there. Timmons, back off. Edwards is completely capable—"

"I'll help," Kyleigh said in a rush. "I'll show you the way." Without waiting for a reply, she darted past us out the door.

The Recorders on either side turned me about, and the three of us followed Kyleigh Tristram down the hall. She was unusually quiet.

Each step, however, pounded the consequences of my folly further into my heart. Though it was not my doing, not my design, returning to *Thalassa* had endangered my friends. Neutralizing Julian Ross's bioweapon was a necessity, but I regretted boarding the ship that had once felt like home.

# 20

When the infirmary's double doors slid open, I was able to walk through them with very little support, but I halted just inside the threshold. The Recorders at my sides tightened their grips on my elbows as if to keep me from falling, but it was neither dizziness nor weakness that stopped my steps. Instead, the familiarity of Max's infirmary was like a whiff of oxygen. My anxiety ebbed, then surged again.

Kyleigh was already demanding, "Edwards, where's Max?"

"I made him leave to get something to eat, Kye. I'll be with you in a moment." Edwards pulled off his gloves, his focus still on a patient in the back of the room. "You need to return after dinner for another dose."

"Right." A skeletally thin young man pushed himself off the bed.

Surprise and recognition gripped me simultaneously.

Freddie? Yes, those were the angular features I had seen through the viscous green of medical gel, though his hair had begun to grow in. I bit my lip. He should have been transferred to Lunar One's hospital facilities. He needed specialized care. If the authorities had not allowed him to leave *Thalassa* because of Ross's bioweapon, they had placed his recovery at risk, and that distinct possibility angered me.

The welcoming smile he flashed at Kyleigh dissolved when his gaze found me and the Recorders. His jaw dropped. "Kye! That can't be—"

"It is." She held her arms tucked close, as if she were cold. "Edwards, please."

"One minute—"

"Edwards!"

He turned, paused for two seconds, then he was pulling on fresh gloves as he crossed to my side and bundled me onto a bed with a datapad built into the headboard. "What did you do this time? Kyleigh, warm blankets."

"I have it." Freddie was at the cabinet before Edwards began scanning my vital signs.

"She didn't do anything!" Kyleigh waved one arm expansively at the doors behind her. "Nothing at all."

"Not quite nothing," said the talkative Recorder. "I believe she smiled."

Freddie handed Edwards the blankets, but while Edwards accepted them, he kept his attention on the talkative Recorder at my side. "What do you mean?"

"She made eye contact with a citizen and smiled, thus angering the Elder. She was, therefore, punished."

"Blankets are unnecessary," I informed Edwards.

Ignoring my protest, he tucked them around me, his frown deepening. "You know very well that provoking the Elder is unwise, especially when he was unhappy to begin—" He broke off and glanced from the Recorders to their drones.

"As you say." The talkative Recorder actually shrugged. "Though, it is reasonable that he would not be 'happy' with this assignment. My understanding is that he, unlike the two of us"—he gestured to himself and my friend—"wasn't offered a choice."

Kyleigh drew closer to Freddie and slid her hand into his.

"Can you even say that, Recorder?" Freddie hesitated. "I mean, won't that get you in trouble?"

One corner of the talkative Recorder's mouth lifted for half a second. "My comment itself is indicative of my ability."

Even if he had accepted this assignment to avoid serving in the Hall, his behavior could very well summon the Elder's displeasure. My fingers rose to the welts left on my throat by the drone. The Elder's disapproval was nothing to mock.

"Another blanket, Kyleigh," Edwards said. "She's shivering."

I did not correct him, only glanced up at the recording device near the ceiling. Unlike those on *Agamemnon*, it did not move. Of course, with two drones present, the Consortium had no need for additional records.

While Kyleigh shook out another unnecessary blanket, Edwards studied the readouts scrolling over the headboard, then retrieved a jet injector, which hissed as he fired nanoparticles and medication into my arm. Again, lavender flooded my memory centers.

Kyleigh set a box of gel packs on the foot of the bed. Freddie, who was at least twelve centimeters taller than he had been before his time in the medical stasis pod, came up behind her. She leaned back against him, and he wrapped his arms around her.

She pointed. "Edwards . . . her neck."

He tilted my head to the side and frowned. "Yes, I see."

While Edwards began treating my neck, Kyleigh looked over at my friend, who stood like a sentinel at my bedside, and offered him a small smile. "Thank you for catching her. And, if I might add, it's good to see you again."

A smile almost formed on his face, but all expression fled his silvery grey eyes when his drone coiled a tendril around his arm. "Kyleigh Rose Tristram, I am pleased you survived. I wish to express sympathy for your father's death. He was a good man."

Freddie's eyes traveled from Kyleigh to my friend. He said nothing.

Edwards disposed of his gloves and the bandage wrappings, but when he turned around, his attention focused on my friend. Before I could find a way to warn him, the doors slid apart.

I heard Max's voice before I saw him.

"Edwards, you were right. With everyone in that meeting, I finally—"

And he came to a sudden stop in the door, his nut-brown eyes widening as his gaze landed on mine.

"Good afternoon, Max"—my voice croaked and I cleared my throat—"Dr. Maxwell." I snuck a glance at the drones. "Having spent an inordinate amount of time in the infirmary before, it seems appropriate that I have returned. Edwards has treated me already, and I anticipate a full recovery in very little time."

Eyes still on mine, Max took five long strides to my bed and extended a hand to Edwards, who gave him a linked datapad.

"You're staying here until Max releases you this time," Edwards said, his voice gruff.

"It is likely that the Elder will demand my presence before then."

Max skimmed the data, then looked up. "What happened to your neck?"

"Ah. Allow me," offered the talkative Recorder. His drone snaked one tendril through the air and connected with the datapad in Max's hand.

Edwards froze; Kyleigh and Freddie drew back; Max only nodded. He glanced from the talkative Recorder to me then back to the small screen. One long ribbon of data spiraled upward, and he frowned at it, then switched his gaze to the talkative Recorder as the drone retreated behind the man.

"He did this, then?" A muscle in his jaw ticced. "Edwards, we'll need a full scan to rule out internal damage. You get her in the medicomputer. I'll talk to Archimedes. That *Elder* cannot be allowed to torture her again." He touched the blanket over my boot, and when he spoke, his voice lost its harsh edge. "You're in my care now, and Edwards is right. You aren't leaving without my consent this time."

"You are then, as they say, in good hands," the talkative Recorder said to me as Max focused again on the bed's readout. "If you no longer require our service, he and I should report to our appointed locations. We did not, after all, have express permission to catch you."

"You must exhibit more caution," I told them both. "There will be consequences."

The talkative Recorder rubbed his jaw. "This assignment is sufficient consequence in and of itself. What else will the Elder do? He will not risk the ones sent to go down to the station, or he must travel in their stead." He headed to the door, then turned to me. "Recorder? I'm afraid that you are the one who must be cautious." His gaze scanned the others. "All of you must display more care, but do not worry for me. I shall do my best."

He left without clarifying which best he meant.

My friend's drone moved in and softly tapped his cheek, then drifted to the door, where it hovered just outside.

Before my friend followed it, I touched his arm. He glanced down at my hand but did not move away.

"Do you—" The eye of the recording device remained silent, and though it should have moved, the knowledge that the Elder had used them directly on *Agamemnon* would not leave me, and I could not risk my idea if he would see. But I had to know. I rushed through my words:

"Recorder, you should not leave. When I left *Thalassa*, the recording devices had been damaged. If new devices have not been installed, your drone's presence is necessary."

Kyleigh shrank back against Freddie as if I had struck her.

Edwards glanced up at the recording device and answered before my friend did. "There have been technical difficulties, and your replacement has not managed to repair more than the bridge, the quarantine rooms, and Consortium quarters."

Relief flowed through me.

"Then I must say thank you."

"You are welcome," my friend said.

"I have the medicomputer programmed," Max began. He set the datapad in its slot, but when he looked up, his attention caught on my friend for the first time. Max startled and grabbed the bedrail with both hands, gripping so tightly I had the fleeting thought he might bend it. Edwards put a steadying hand on his back.

A half-smile reminiscent of Max's flitted over my friend's lips, and he inclined his head. "Good day."

The door slid shut behind him, and I shoved the blankets aside and scooted to the foot of the hoverbed. Kneeling before Max, I put one hand over his and whispered, "I did what I could to keep him safe. I know this is dangerous, but please believe it is better. And Max, he does not know."

He tore his gaze from the door to me. "You knew?" His voice shook. "Is this what you meant, before you left, when you said you had something to do?"

"In part, yes. I did not wish to tell you. You would have worried for him."

He shook his head, and his long, dark cords of hair whispered on his shoulders. "I worried anyway. He has—they have—been on my mind for twenty-six years." He set his other hand on mine. "And I had someone else to worry about, too."

I did not allow myself to wonder who else he worried for, not when I felt the need to justify putting my friend in danger. "He had already faced tribunal. The risk here is smaller than primary reclamation."

Edwards's sparse eyebrows rose. "He faced reclamation? Why?"

"What's a tribunal?" Kyleigh asked.

Neither Edwards nor I answered her question.

"I could not let that happen. When I had the opportunity, I planted suggestions, and they grew." I bit my lip. "But . . . Max?"

He squeezed my hand.

I forged ahead. "When I searched the records before I left, I also found her."

He stilled. "Is she . . ."

"Missing." I should have added *presumed dead*, but I could not, not when his cheeks went ashen. "She disappeared on Ceres during storm season while on patrol and was never found."

Max inhaled sharply and took a step back.

"I do not wish to cause you additional pain. I am aware that this assignment is not safe, not with the roaches and the virus, but there is more hope here than in facing the Eldest, for she does not tolerate aberrations. He would be sent to the Hall of Reclamation, and anything is better than facing service in the Hall."

"That is true," Edwards stated.

Kyleigh folded her arms and looked around before settling on Max. "Would somebody explain what's going on?"

"That young man . . . that Recorder . . ." Max did not finish.

"Yes, he's the one from the ship when I traveled out with my dad."

"The one you told me about?" Freddie asked.

"He is my friend," I managed.

Kyleigh gasped. "What? He's the one who made boats with you when you were a little girl at the training center? Your friend was my Recorder?"

"Yes," I said, still watching Max.

His brown eyes held mine. "You're sure, absolutely sure, it's true?"

"I verified the records."

Max carefully straightened the blankets then turned back to the door, his eyes fixed on the blank metal as if it held secrets. "Then I just met my son."

# 21

PERSONAL RECORD: DESIGNATION ZETA4542910-9545E

CTS *THALASSA*
478.2.5.05

Edwards, Kyleigh, and Freddie's exclamations rushed over and around us, but Max's attention remained on the door through which his son—my friend—had left.

I took Max's hand and said his name, because somehow, I understood.

The others' words evaporated when Max turned to me.

"This both hurts and heals, does it not?"

His eyes closed momentarily, but he did not answer.

"You should be proud of him. He is good, Max, and always has been. And yes, being here, he faces danger, but this future is far better than what he would face on New Triton." I shifted to look at Edwards. "You should have no part in the explanation. You have risked enough already."

"I'm not leaving the room now, not unless someone escorts me out." Edwards shook his head. "The Elder already informed me that my behavior yesterday has added to the debt I owe the Consortium. It isn't as if I am a Recorder and have no escape. What is another few years' service?"

"Yesterday?" Kyleigh blurted. "You knew she was here?"

Edwards nodded once.

"This whole time?" When he nodded again, tears filled her eyes. "You knew and didn't tell us when we were all worried sick? Didn't tell me—didn't tell *Timmons*?"

He rubbed the back of his neck. "I could not."

"So that's why you weren't surprised when we brought her in." She rounded on Max. "Did you know?"

"Easy, Kye," Freddie murmured. "Everyone saw that he didn't."

She dashed the tears from her cheeks with the inside of her sleeve. "What else are you not telling us?"

"Do not blame him, Kyleigh, for fulfilling his duty. Though he is not a Recorder, he, too, was raised by the Consortium." The tightness in my throat had nothing to do with the earlier reprimand. The Elder's words rang in my mind: *returned to the Consortium.* "He is theirs, even as I am."

"No one owns you," she said, her words firing like a weapon's burst. "Or him—"

"This is true and not," I conceded, though perhaps she did not see it as a concession at all. "But that does bring to the forefront the problem with my friend."

"What problem?" Max asked too quietly.

"To begin with . . ." I paused. Max had saved my life, had told me that I was not nothing. I had to tell him, for he should know why his son was here, in danger. "My friend—your son—he had been assigned to monitor the situation in a tenement neighborhood in Albany City on New Triton."

Max stiffened. "That's where . . ." He shook his head. "Go on."

"The district had experienced civil unrest, so authorities had been slow to replace seismic sensors. An earthquake struck, and several buildings collapsed. At first, my friend only observed and recorded, as he had been instructed, but when a citizen called for help, he defied our directive. He and the woman who called to him saved nine people, all of whom survived. The woman, however, did not." I hesitated. The probability would seem astronomical. "I do not pretend to understand the complexities of relationships, but I am sorry. Her words were recorded, and I viewed the verified file. While she held his hand, she told him who she was and that his father wanted to name him James."

The normal pastel blue and green of the infirmary had not changed, and the white of the blanket under my knees remained the same, all as if I had said nothing out of the ordinary. Max seemed to have stopped breathing. In my peripheral vision, Kyleigh reached toward him, then fisted her hand and leaned back against Freddie.

"You must know that he disobeyed a direct order when he came to her assistance and saved those people. After his review, he faced a tribunal, but their verdict was inconclusive. He was assigned to serve in the Hall of Reclamation until his case was reviewed by the Eldest herself."

Max's angled eyebrows met over his nose.

"I still don't know what a tribunal is." Kyleigh's voice wavered. "Nor whatever the Hall of Reclamation does."

"Neither do I," Max said, nut-brown eyes on mine.

I glanced at Edwards, who gave me a nod, but the direct question hit me like a blow. All desire to explain fled. I tugged a blanket around my shoulders, but its heat was gone.

"I could tell them," Edwards offered quietly.

Cowardice almost made me acquiesce, but I had capitulated earlier, when the Elder destroyed my socks. I would not allow it victory twice in one day.

"No." I gathered myself and began, "A tribunal of High Elders reviews cases of aberration, and their verdict must be unanimous. For my first friend, the opinion was split, two for removal and one for restoration. He received a ten-day reprieve while awaiting the Eldest's judgment. I hold no confidence in her verdict, for she does not suffer deviations."

Freddie approached with another heated blanket and slung it over my shoulders. "Deviations? Like what you did? And him, in disobeying orders?"

"Yes." How could I explain the Eldest's burden, show them the weight she bore? Air scraped my throat like sand, but I needed to explain, so I wetted my lips. "To care for and direct the vastness of the Consortium, no Eldest can afford leniency. If he faces the Eldest, he will serve permanently in the Hall of Reclamation." I looked at Max who stood still as a stone. "I would—and will—do all I can to prevent that."

"Will you just tell me what that is?" Kyleigh's whisper was almost lost in the infirmary's noises.

Edwards answered for me, quoting from the Consortium's Central Tenets, "'The gifted must serve to redeem their gifting.'"

"When we cannot serve through our actions," I explained, "we serve with our *selves*."

Kyleigh frowned. "That's a rubbish answer."

I inhaled for the count of three, held my breath for five, then exhaled slowly for seven. "From inside stasis tanks."

Max's jaw muscle ticced, and he said slowly, "Do you mean what I think you mean?"

"As I do not know what you think, Max," I said with a degree of hesitancy, "I cannot tell."

Edwards cleared his throat. "From the Halls, Recorders who have been deemed aberrations serve in parts. Physically."

"Organ donation?" Max choked out the words. "Alive?"

All I could manage was, "Yes."

"You mean—no!" Kyleigh's hands flew up to cover her mouth. "But I dreamed in the tank!"

"I did, too, and the nightmares . . ." Freddie's voice faltered. "My eyes? The transplant I had when I was a kid—is that why . . . why I can see ultraviolet? Are my eyes . . . Did they belong to an Elder?"

Kyleigh caught his arm. "Even if they did, that Elder could have died in an accident or something. It has to be unusual." She looked at me for confirmation. "Right?"

My attention dropped to my hands.

"But it's true, isn't it? And the doctors knew." Freddie's rate of respiration increased. "That's the reason they knew the colors would deteriorate, that residual effects would fade, but not why."

Freddie's increasing distress overrode training to keep Consortium secrets from citizens.

"I cannot know with all certainty, Freddie, but if you can indeed perceive ultraviolet and infrared, it is likely that you have a high concentration of nanodevices embedded in your retinas and optic nerves, which would indicate the donor was an Elder."

"They *lied* to me." Max's voice shook. "They said transplants were willed by citizens. If I had known . . . How many times have I—" He stopped abruptly.

Kyleigh buried her face against Freddie's thin chest with a strangled sob, and he held her close.

Max growled a curse, the uncharacteristic language harsh in my ears. He punched his fist on the bed's railing, but the microantigravity held it steady. "They will not have him. Not my son. Not anyone's child."

In the corner, the centrifuge still clicked. Overhead, air whispered through the vents, but Max's infirmary no longer felt like home. Instead, it felt as alien and cold and unwelcoming as the infirmary on *Agamemnon*. I had destroyed that peace somehow, and the loss pinched my heart.

"Max . . . I have done my best. He was offered this assignment as an alternative to that review. I suspect that he, like the others, was offered absolution and a second chance, should the assignment succeed."

"It will," Kyleigh said with emphasis. "We will make it succeed, and he will never go back. Neither will you. We'll see to it."

I blinked back sudden moisture. The memory of my friends had both sustained and undermined me while I was gone, but I knew what I needed to say. "I missed you all. But you must stay away. After today, the Elder's focus on me will only intensify—"

Max interrupted me with another growl, and Edwards said something under his breath.

"I have already given myself away. Be cautious. And, Kyleigh, I need my datapad."

She raised puffy eyes from Freddie's now tear-stained tunic. "Your datapad? The blue one you told Zhen to destroy? Why?"

"If Zhen DuBois did not listen, which would not surprise me, I have some programming to do."

"No work. You need to rest and heal," Edwards said.

Max, however, searched my face.

"This is important. A roach destroyed my drone, and even the best of marines cannot eradicate them all. If there is anything I can do to prevent your son and the other Recorders from meeting a similar fate, I must do it. I must find a way to shut down the implants."

"Is that possible?" Max asked.

"Theoretically." Edwards tapped his chin. "Shutting down the implant is how Recorders survive storm seasons on Ceres—" His lips pinched, and he shot a glance at Max.

"Stars!" Kyleigh wiped her cheeks with her sleeve again. "I'll go find Zhen right now."

"Kyleigh!" I called after her before the doors slid open, but when she turned, my voice would not cooperate.

She studied me for another eleven seconds, her light brown eyebrows lowering as if she concentrated, then she ran down the hallway and the doors closed behind her.

Freddie leaned on the hoverbed's railing. "Recorder, can you really do that?"

"Of course she can," Edwards said with a huff.

"I believe so." Max offered me a half-smile. "I've seen what she can do."

Though I did not flinch when he touched my shoulder, his assertion did not lift the fear twining through me.

"I hope so." Freddie straightened, but his balance was off, and he wobbled. "I think . . . maybe I should rest."

Edwards began, "Do you need—"

"I'll manage." The young man squared frail shoulders. "I have to. It's that or give up." He nodded to each of us, walked carefully to the door, and turned left.

"He does not seem well," I said.

When Max gave a noncommittal answer, a flush of guilt for asking inappropriate questions washed over me, but an even less appropriate question tumbled out: "Max, why did you gift them?"

Edwards shook his head, and my guilt increased.

But Max met my eyes squarely. "We didn't have a contract. I fought it, but she was determined to gift them both once the doctors told her that he was defective—"

"That is false," I snapped, incensed. "He is not defective."

Max gave a hollow laugh. "We're all defective."

I wanted to ask how we could all be defective when he himself had told me that whether we were stardust or creation, we were each valuable, but I did not.

After thirty-seven seconds of silence, Edwards spoke up, "You had chosen a name for your son. Did you choose one for your daughter as well?"

Max's attempt at a smile was not convincing. "We couldn't agree. I wanted to call her Hope, but their mother found that name archaic."

Again, I wished to tap my thigh, but sitting on the hoverbed covered with blankets made doing so awkward.

"You should," Edwards murmured. "Now that you know, name her and allow yourself to mourn."

"I thought I already had." Max's gaze seemed unfocused. "I searched for twenty-six years but never found them."

"He will be well." I choked out the words. "We shall get through this, and he will be well."

"'Well' isn't enough." His words came out in staccato bursts, and he strode to a computer. Using more force than usual, he yanked back his chair and pulled up a new datastream. "I still want my son."

My own chest ached. "I am sorry, Max."

His back to me, he said, "Don't be. You've given me more than I had. I have seen him, talked to him, and you've spared him a death in"—the bass in his voice deepened—"in a tank."

"It is not done yet. But I will do my best."

He glanced over his shoulder at me, and a fraction of his usual warmth slid back into his expression. "I know. Even if Zhen destroyed that datapad, you'll find a way. But we'll worry about that later. Right now, we need to make sure that Elder didn't damage your heart. Edwards, get her in the medicomputer."

Suddenly, I could not breathe, and the infirmary swirled around me. I could not go in again—

Before I realized he had moved, Max was at my bedside, and Edwards tapped my arm.

Reason told me that I was safe, that neither of them would harm me. Still, I asked, "Does the release lever work?"

Edwards watched me closely. "Of course."

"Then it is well," I managed.

Max sat down on the end of my bed, as he used to. "Something happened." His tone gentled. "What?"

They waited, but that was a story too long to tell. I avoided their questions by removing my boots, and the grey socks mocked me. "Perhaps later. For now, I am ready."

Their eyes met over my bed.

"Later, then." Edwards pushed the hoverbed into the medicomputer, pausing to cover my toes with the blankets.

"Stop—" burst from my lips, and they both turned at the open door.

"Please, would you be so kind as to speak to each other while I am in here, so I know I am not alone? I do not care what you say, so long as I hear your voices."

Some unspoken emotion flitted over both their faces, but as the door shut, neither said a word, only watched me with furrowed brows, as opposite but as similar as any two people could be.

The medicomputer's red light surrounded me, and I fell back against the pillows. When the uneven clicks and thuds and gentle hums began, the music of their conversation resumed.

All I could do was wait.

Not for the first time, color distracted Freddie, and he forgot about the science project he and Elliott had come to the lab to work on. Kyleigh and Elliott's voices faded into the background, as did the scratchy sounds from the bugs' terrariums.

Their carapaces' deep, rich brown—what would he use? Burnt umber, burnt sienna. Naples yellow or yellow ochre and . . . cadmium red medium. Maybe some Prussian blue or cobalt for shading? No . . . that'd make the bugs sort of green. They didn't glow, not like the scorpions he'd seen a few years back or some of the plants in hydroponics, so he didn't have to worry about catching ultraviolet in ordinary, visible light. Though, that might not matter much longer.

The colors were fading. Infrared used to be as vivid as the visible spectrum. Losing it had hurt almost physically. And ultraviolet had already dimmed a little, like turning down volume on a vid. He hadn't figured out yet the right way to make its beauty real to others. Digital renderings didn't have the same soul, and watercolors were inadequate. Maybe acrylics or oils or—

"Freddie's thinking in paint again." Elliott's voice wrenched him out of his thoughts.

Blinking rapidly, Freddie turned. "What?"

A grin wreathed his friend's face. "You get this expression, halfway between vacant and sick to your stomach."

"True." Kye nudged Freddie's shoulder.

His heart flipped whenever she looked at him like that. Like she understood somehow, even though math and microscopic robots didn't seem to have much in common with art. She insisted that there was a rhythm and pattern to them, like there was to poetry. He didn't see it.

The beads in her pale braids clicked. "I still can't believe your dad took your art supplies."

Freddie studied Kyleigh's profile as she glared at the open doorway. She'd said something once about being plain and monochromatic, but she didn't know the flecks of sap green in her hazel eyes glowed. Or the uniqueness of her freckles, which he'd been memorizing.

Last time he'd drawn her portrait, he'd shown Elliott first, like always, and Elliott protested that she didn't have blotches. But then, he hadn't known that Julian had them, either. If freckles really only were visible in ultraviolet, and he lost that, too, well . . . sun damage from living on Ceres or not, he'd miss Kye's freckles. They suited her.

He cleared his throat. "Yeah, well, he's letting me earn them back with this project. And I did borrow the paint without asking."

"It's my fault, really," Elliott said.

"Your idea, maybe, but my decision to act on it." Freddie pulled his attention from Kye's eyes to his best friend. "*You're* not the vandal who borrowed the UV paint or painted murals in the hall."

Elliott groaned. "Just the accomplice."

Sympathy twisted in Freddie's gut. Elliott hated disappointing his brother even more than he hated letting Dad down. Julian Ross never made mistakes, and Elliott Ross never forgot it. "Told him, did you?"

Elliott nodded glumly. "Julian's right—"

"No, he's not," Kye interrupted. "He's obnoxious."

Elliott's brows snapped together over a nose that could have been printed from the same file as Julian's. "He gave up nearly everything for me when Dad died."

"But that doesn't mean he owns you."

Elliott leaned back in his chair and repeated the facts he'd told Freddie a dozen times or more. "His girlfriend left him, and he'd been saving up for a contract, and so he lost her and his internship. Julian risked his education—his whole future—to bring me back from the belt. Had to take that one job. Well, it might not matter to you, but I'm not going to forget it."

Kyleigh slumped back against the cupboard and absently chewed a bead. For a few heartbeats, the only sound was the stupid bugs in their glass boxes. Freddie sighed and punched his security code into the entry pad on the cupboard near the door.

"It's ridiculous that Johnson and SahnVeer made me get clearance for this stuff." He pulled on his gloves and gathered the food and the growth hormones. "Like the whole base doesn't have security codes?"

"No, it makes sense," Elliott said. "The little kids get into all kinds of things."

The idea of a little one getting into these supplies stilled Freddie's hands for a moment. He hadn't thought of that.

"Exactly." Kye shoved off the counter and landed with a thud out of proportion to her tiny frame. "Little Allison started climbing things last ten-day. It's only a matter of time before she escapes the nursery and wreaks havoc."

Freddie carried the supplies over to the two largest terrariums to Elliott's left. While he measured and mixed the food and growth hormone, Kye chattered. Her rambling reminded him of birdsong back on Ceres, rising and falling almost musically. That was when sound had been the only magic—in the dark years before his transplant.

Elliott's voice broke into Freddie's thoughts. "Kids from belt schools aren't accepted at universities unless they have really good marks. Julian had to pull some strings to get me in. But Freddie's dad and Dr. SahnVeer think if we do well with this, they can get me an exemption. Maybe even a scholarship."

Freddie gave himself a shake. His friend earning a scholarship was more important than his paints. "And we'll be amazing."

"I hope so. You know," Elliott mused, "Julian's never once reminded me that at my age, he'd already won a full scholarship and was in his second year. Tells me to do my best, and he'll back me up. That I'll find my purpose."

What would that be like? To not be pushed into something awful like electrical engineering? Freddie sighed.

"And you'll be splendid at whatever it is," Kye said, "whenever you figure it out." She threw an uneasy glance at the terrariums lining the wall and shuddered. "But I still can't believe Dr. Johnson's letting you mess with her precious insects."

Elliott pushed the chair back from his desk. "Well, Dr. Johnson says the idea of biological search and rescue—"

"You mean Christine?" Kyleigh batted her lashes. "Don't you get to call her that since she and your brother are together?"

"Her being friends with Julian has nothing to do with being able to use the roaches."

"Friends, is it? I don't think your brother has eaten dinner with you in the past couple ten-days."

Kye was probably right that Elliott's brother was behind Dr. Johnson agreeing to let them have some of her bugs. And Julian had been spending more and more time with her, though that was probably the way things went.

"It's more fun to hang out, just the three of us." Freddie glanced at Kye, who smirked at a glowering Elliott. "Well, when you two aren't sniping at each other, anyway."

But . . . his brain glitched. What if Kye and Elliott quarreled because they liked each other? Well. Even if they did—he swallowed—he had his paints and a goal. He might be the only one who could show people the beauty of a world beyond their sight. He should concentrate on that.

"Maybe we can stop arguing and try to design these things?" Freddie asked, more sharply than he should have. "We can both get scholarships, and I'll get my paints back, and things can be normal again."

Elliott's gaze fell to his shoes, and he shuffled back to his worktable, the box of electronics in hand.

Irritated at himself for snapping, Freddie pulled out a scale, weighed out the precise number of grams for each tank, added the premeasured hormone to one food supply and the placebo to the other. He removed the first terrarium's heavy glass top, but before he scooped the food into each compartment, he checked his identification band for the time, reached for his datapad, and—

"Did you forget something?" Kye sounded as smug as a cat.

He glanced over his shoulder. She was grinning.

"Maybe your datapad?" Kye handed it to him but threw an uneasy glance at the terrariums. Her grin disappeared. "Bigger roaches are disgusting. Roaches are disgusting, period."

"It's not like I'm doing anything unusual," he protested. "Your mom's work with isopods—"

"Designing more efficient methods for farming larger isopods for food is *completely* different from making them into living batteries and cyborgs! Roach cyborgs? That's . . . ." She made a face. "And even if they are roaches, I didn't like it at all when you wired that electrode thing into their antennae and made them go places against their will."

"Do they even have a will, Kye? They're bugs—"

"They aren't bugs." Elliott didn't look up from sorting through the box and pulling out some wires. "Insects, yes. Wrong order. Blattodea, not Hemiptera."

"Bugs or not," Freddie pointed out, "we've been over this before."

Elliott's baritone was barely audible. "I know. But I've thought about it long and hard, and I don't really like it, either."

"Should have said something earlier. It's too late to back out now," Freddie snapped.

"Freddie!" Kye protested.

Remorse hit him at the expression that flitted across Elliott's face. The reproach in Kye's voice didn't help. Freddie groaned. "I didn't mean . . . It's just that if this works—I mean, *when* this works—things will be fine."

If the experiment went well, they'd both be done with school and head off to university. Freddie would have to juggle studies and art, and Elliott could finally start his own life. Loyalty to Elliott kept him from saying it out loud, but as good a brother as Julian was, heading out on one's own was when life really started. Freddie refocused his attention and put the food in the compartments, logging the amounts and the times. The insects scrambled over each other, tiny mandibles grinding at the moistened pellets.

Kyleigh started to speak, but Elliott stopped her. "No, it's okay, Kye. He's right. When Dad's mining tunnel collapsed, drones couldn't get past the debris. Something has to be done to help miners. And nobody on New Triton cares. They're not even looking for a solution. If the mining platforms in the inner belt had something like bioelectrically powered and controlled search and rescue, maybe cave-ins wouldn't kill everyone."

Freddie closed his eyes, but the dark didn't block out the loss in his friend's voice.

Kye's boots tapped out a quick rhythm as she moved quickly to Elliott's side and laid a hand on his arm.

Elliott shrugged one shoulder. "It's okay. It's just how I make peace with turning the stupid, living"—he glanced at Freddie—"*bugs* into cyborgs."

"Insects." Freddie tried to smile. "Pax?"

"Pax."

A comfortable silence filled the room, and Freddie pulled out a stylus and started sketching the bugs on the datapad. Drawing wasn't really disobeying if it was for science.

"They're really good, Freddie," Kye said.

He slid the stylus into its slot and set the datapad behind him. "What are good?"

Kye smiled a little sheepishly. "The murals."

"Since when can you see ultraviolet?"

Her smile turned into a grin. "Since yesterday, when I swiped my dad's goggles—the ones he wears to track the tagged items between labs—and went to take a look."

Elliott choked back a laugh. "Kye, no!"

"I put them back. Don't worry. I just wanted to see it." Her eyes twinkled. "If your dad finds out you made Dr. SahnVeer into Medusa, you'll be in so much trouble."

Freddie's cheeks heated. "Medusa had to be beautiful if Poseidon—"

"You didn't!" Elliott laughed so hard he had to wipe his eyes. "Maybe I'll borrow Julian's goggles, just to see that."

"You'd better not," Kyleigh warned. "Actually, it might be best if both of you avoided that hallway for a while."

Her dancing eyes met Freddie's, and he promptly forgot what he'd meant to say.

Kyleigh's commlink chimed, but instead of answering it, she stifled an exclamation. "Oh, stars! I was supposed to observe Dr. SahnVeer this afternoon! Dad'll be so disappointed I forgot."

She scooped up her satchel, and Freddie moved to try to block her view of the roaches. His heart thumped painfully when she stopped and took his hand, and even the names of the colors of the flecks in Kyleigh's eyes fled his mind.

"I might not like your experiment, but I'm sure you can get them to grow big enough to run the camera and the rest of it. They might just save people's lives. Plus, you'll get your paints back. I know you will."

She gave his hand a squeeze . . . then she let go and darted over to Elliott and gave him a quick sideways hug.

Freddie's chest constricted.

"Elliott, I shouldn't pick on you about Julian. He does his best. That's all any of us can do."

She dashed out of the lab.

After a moment, Elliott stood. He looked a little dazed. "I think I'll work on this in my room, unless you want the company."

"I'm done. Have to work on some math later."

Elliott flashed him a sideways smile. "Well, I won't be of much help with that, but you know where to find me." He gathered the supplies into the box and slung the satchel over his shoulder. "I'll see you at dinner?"

Freddie forced a smile back. "Yeah. Like I said, it's fun, just the three of us."

Elliott shambled out, and once he was gone, Freddie watched the roaches skittering in their glass boxes. Dad's lectures about setting aside childish things and serving others and being salt and light—like Dad even understood what light was—echoed in his mind.

This project would definitely get Elliott and him into university. Give them both a chance to help others and then chart their own courses. And the sooner it was over, the better. He set his jaw, checked over his shoulder, then added an extra dose of the growth hormone to the food supply and secured the terrariums' lids.

All those years back, the doctors had told him and his parents that the occasional ability to see beyond visible light would fade over time. But those colors had carried him through losing Mother, then the move across the system to this rock. They would carry him through whatever came next.

Until they were gone, too.

The terrarium lights switched on when Freddie turned off the overhead lighting. He shut the door behind him and stared down the vacant hallway.

Nothing glowed.

With the first shuttles to Pallas scheduled to leave in the morning, a steady flow of people wended through Max's infirmary that evening, ostensibly to synchronize their armored suits' monitors and medpacks with the ship's medical computer. However, after the first score and a half of them either darted glances in my direction or stared blatantly, I began to feel like an exhibit, rather than a patient.

Even the marines' Recorder watched me as they filed past, though they all acknowledged her with a nod or a smile before staring at me. Her drone remained by the door, all appendages tucked inside, and she stood at parade rest, eyebrowless forehead wrinkled and sepia-brown eyes narrowed in my direction. The last of the marines filtered out, and still she lingered, despite the fact that Max had completed any adjustments to her monitor and medpack.

Finally, I could no longer abide her silent scrutiny and sat up on my bed. "Recorder. I wish you and your marines safety and success."

"*My* marines? Indeed." Her full lips pursed, and she quoted, "'Wishes are either cheap or beyond measure.'"

"True," I agreed. "But I wish beyond measure."

"Yes." Her gaze darted to the door where her drone unspooled tendrils, but she did not lower her voice. "As do I."

She pivoted on her boot heel and strode out. Though her drone unsettled me, I wished she could have stayed.

The dull ache in my chest at my friends' absence was illogical. Edwards's and Max's distracted presence compensated for the loss I had fully expected—almost hoped for—but had dreaded.

Soon after dinner, Freddie returned, Kyleigh at his side. She did not bring the datapad, did not even talk to me. The one time she met my eyes, all she offered me was the slightest shake of her head.

The soup I had eaten for dinner seemed to congeal in my stomach.

Zhen must not have kept the device, and without it, accessing the information I needed without the Consortium codes seemed improbable at best. The futility of attempting to shut off the neural implants without that device eclipsed all hope, and I sagged against the pillows and studied the lights in the ceiling until afterimages flashed when I closed my eyes.

The evening crept on as the afternoon had, and I chafed at the forced inactivity and lack of knowledge. Edwards checked the bandage around my neck and announced that the immediate application of bandages might prevent further scarring. I had, he said, enough scars already.

Scars, however, did not concern me as much as the Elder's continued absence did. It was not that I wished to see him again, but the afternoon's incident might impact my assigned trip to Pallas. I could not depart until the marines returned, and that timeframe might impact my ability to figure out a new way to save James and the others, since Kyleigh had not procured my datapad.

Williams arrived for the evening shift with a large cloth satchel over her shoulder, but though she offered me a smile, she did not return my greeting. As she tucked her bag under a desk, Edwards reminded her that she had but to call him should his presence be necessary, bade me good night, and left. Max waved goodbye without looking away from the data twisting above his desk.

Williams cleared her throat, and when he glanced over, she said, "You need to eat and rest, my friend. I can call Edwards, should the need arise."

He hid a yawn. "I know."

"The shuttles leave at nine and ten, this time," she said. "The round trip is three hours, and who knows how long it will take them to clear the station. Rest in the calm before the storm." She inspected a few boxes, then pulled out an injector. "Exhaustion makes a poor surgeon, and the probability that we need your skills on the morrow is high."

He grunted a response, tidied his workstation and stretched. When he passed my bed, he paused. "I'm glad you're here again. We'll do our best to keep you safe."

Safety.

The idea distracted me from bidding him good night, though perhaps he did not mind.

Soon after he left, the lights dimmed slightly, though the doors stayed open. Williams puttered about, straightening boxes of supplies, placing clean blankets in the warmer, and smoothing the sheets on the other hoverbeds. Then, she brought her bag over, pulled up a chair, and perched on the edge.

As if it had not been nearly four ten-days since we last spoke, she said, "I am very glad to see you. It will be safer for you to remain in Consortium grey. I gathered a clean set from the laundry, but Jordan sent this." She held out neatly folded greys, on top of which rested a russet sleep shirt.

My heart lifted at the splash of color on the grey, and I swung my legs over the side of the bed and took it. "Is this Jordan's?"

"It's yours." She eyed me critically. "You like lavender, yes?"

"I do enjoy lavender-peppermint tea," I answered cautiously, "and the color is not unpleasant."

Smiling, she set two small bottles of cleanser and lotion on top of the sleep shirt, then nodded at the infirmary water closet. "Go change. I'll get you up in the morning so you can change back into Consortium grey."

The socks' ashes pushed through my memories, and I glanced at the open doors before handing the smooth russet fabric back to her. "You should not tempt me."

Her smile fell. "At least feel free to wash your hair? I will change your bandages when you are done."

And that was why my hair smelled like lavender when Zhen breezed in through the open doors an hour before midnight, her knitting satchel over her shoulder and a band of white and spring green around her upper arm. Citizen tradition associated such armbands with mourning. She, Alec, and Nate had worn them earlier, as well. Worry nagged me. Whom had they lost?

After a cursory glance around the room—one which seemed to skip over me—Zhen slung her bag onto the bed next to mine and addressed Williams.

"Good. No one's here. I was going to say I had a headache."

I was not 'no one,' but then, this was Zhen, and somehow her apparent rudeness was not unwelcome.

Williams set down her personal datapad and picked up a portable scanner. "Do you have a headache?"

"Of course I do." Zhen crossed to the sink, filled a disposable cup with water, and drained it in a matter of five seconds. "That should take care of it. Haven't had anything to drink since the disaster earlier."

I glanced at the open doors, concern rippling through me.

"Since you came for medical treatment," Williams informed her as she began a quick scan, "you will submit to it."

Zhen rolled her eyes. "Is this really necessary? I just needed a valid reason to be here."

"Well, you've done a stellar job of it." Williams set the scanner on its charging station and put her hands on her hips. "Have another glass of water. And I recommend an analgesic."

"Only if you need to chart it."

"Of course I must chart it. And I'll have to take you off tomorrow's roster." Williams paused. "Though, it is not that I believe you could not perform adequately."

"I know. New protocol because of Julian-Spacing-Ross's virus."

Williams nodded and fetched a jet injector. The medical device popped, Zhen closed her eyes for a moment, then drank another glass of water and filled the glass a third time.

"Your hair's a little longer now." She squinted at me. "But you look awful."

"I am well."

"That is not strictly true," Williams said softly. "You should not attempt to deceive your friend."

Zhen frowned at Williams's word choice, but the appellation did not displease me.

"Max insists that the mild damage from earlier today is enough to keep me here, though I suspect he has exaggerated the severity—"

"Not blasted likely. We all saw what that voided trog—"

"Zhen," Williams protested mildly.

"—did. He ought to be spaced, that poisonous . . ." Her nostrils flared. "Strangling you with his drone. Hanging is illegal. So is torture. Somebody ought to torture *him*."

"Indeed," Williams agreed. "Which is why you will stay here until Max clears you and until Archimedes smooths things out with the Elder."

Zhen gulped more water, then brought her knitting bag onto my bed. She pushed aside the delicate work—a deep variegated navy blue, not the orange of several ten-days ago—and my heart skipped a beat as she pulled out a datapad, which she tossed onto my lap. With a swift glance at the open door, I snatched it up and ran my fingers over the smooth blue surface. Yes, it looked like mine.

"Of course I didn't wipe it. I'm not stupid. But I wouldn't let Kyleigh bring it."

"Why not?"

She shook her head, and her long hair rippled over her shoulder. "She might be in and out of here a couple times a day with Freddie, but Kyleigh can't afford to draw any more of that dross-Elder's attention. She also gave us your message. Stay away? Really? Like we aren't clever enough to come up with work-arounds?" Her eyes darted to the bandages around my neck. "Are you just going to sit there and say nothing?"

I should have thanked her, told her that I was glad she was well, warned her to be more cautious with the doors wide open. Instead, what I managed was, "Your hair is blue."

Zhen raised an eyebrow. "And why wouldn't it be?"

"It's her war paint."

At that tenor voice, my heart stopped, then jolted. The monitor behind me beeped.

Zhen spun to face the open door. "You're supposed to let me handle this, Tim."

My gaze followed hers. There, as in my memories—though his usual black attire was broken by that band of white and green—Nate lounged against the doorframe. His overly long, blond bangs fell over his cheekbone and hid one eyebrow, but no dimple peeked at me. While seeing him was a greater gift than I deserved, I found I needed him to smile.

"Nathaniel, you should not have come."

I was unaware I had reached for him until he was there, his fingertips tracing my cheekbone for a second, then catching my hand. "Try keeping me away this time."

Zhen's voice broke in, "While I'm sure that's an admirable sentiment—"

"Not up for debate."

One of my hands held his, the other the datapad. I knew I had to choose between my future and my duty, though I knew which one I wanted, but oh, how I wished I could say anything else. I found my voice and managed, "It must be."

"Not if what Kye told us is true." He ran his thumb over my knuckles. "And I suspect it was, since you were so closed-mouthed about it. Was the Elder taking you to face a tribunal?"

I glanced away, but my fingers tightened around his.

"Hey," he whispered. "Look at me?"

The desire to turn my head, to say, *I am looking,* pulled at me like a gravitational well, so I bit my lip to keep silent.

"I was wrong to let you go." His voice dropped in pitch. "And it won't happen again."

Zhen's communication link chimed three times, and she quickly kicked off her half boots and sprang over the railing to settle atop the blanket. "Moons and stars," she hissed. "It's too late to leave, but at least hide that thing."

Nate took the datapad from my hand and tucked it under my pillow just as boots sounded in the hall. I tugged my hand from his, but he did not leave. Instead, he bent and placed a soft kiss on my forehead, then straightened and faced the door.

"Please go, Nate." The words choked me, and as the pain in my chest increased, the hoverbed's alarm chimed. Williams circled to the other side of the bed to study the readout. "Zhen? Williams?" I pled. "Please, make him leave."

He set his jaw.

Williams shot us both a look, and her lips tightened into a white line. She hesitated a splintered second, then pulled a jet injector from her pocket and adjusted its dial. I pushed back against the pillows, and when the datapad dug into my spine, my mouth went dry. If she dosed me, I would not be able to use my limited time to find a way to save them. I shook my head.

The sound of drones came from the hallway.

She hesitated then slid the injector in her pocket. Nate shifted, putting himself between me and the doors, and widened his stance.

Two drones entered to hover like sentinels on either side of the doors, and the Elder's personal drone preceded him into the infirmary.

The Elder's blank grey glare surveyed the infirmary and fastened onto Nate. "Why are you here?"

I could not draw sufficient oxygen.

Williams cleared her throat. "I am afraid that is my question to ask of you, Elder."

His voice whipped through the air. "There is no reason for these two—"

"I beg pardon," Williams snapped, and part of me panicked. Had she actually interrupted an Elder? She stepped around Nate over to Zhen's bed. "DuBois had a headache, and per protocol, she came to be evaluated. Scans do not indicate anything serious, but she is under observation. I already reported that she won't be going to the surface tomorrow."

"And I came to check on DuBois," Nate said smoothly. "Her partner told me she wasn't feeling good. Figured I might as well stop by before I turned in. I was about to comm Alec—"

"I know who you are, Nathaniel Timmons. You are the reason she was reprimanded earlier." The Elder's words were like a blade of ice to my heart, and his personal drone left his side and moved toward us.

Behind me, the vital signs monitor's chimes accelerated. My own body was betraying me, and fear swallowed me whole, preventing me from rebutting the Elder's words, from lying, from—

"Move." Williams's green scrubs replaced Nate's black shirt in front of me, and her hands adjusted the monitor's noise, smoothed my blanket. "Elder, whatever your reason for being here, you are agitating her. I must ask you to leave if you are not a patient. Which," she added sharply over her shoulder, "you are not."

The Elder did not leave. "Nathaniel Timmons, I have verified that you are the one who prevented Elliott Ross's attack."

My pulse thundered so loudly in my ears that I could not tell if the Elder's tone had gentled. The drone drifted closer.

"She feels an obligation to you, as citizens often do toward rescuers. I have requested a commendation, for your efforts. However, you are balancing on a thin line, for while you protected a member of the Consortium, in not reporting the incident, you also interfered with the records, and her reaction now could be construed as loss of neutrality. Therefore, I will retract my request, should you stay. Your presence here complicates the situation. Go."

"No." Nate's tenor lost its smooth edge. "You think I'll leave her for you and your drones to torture again? I don't think so."

"You violate Consortium regulations. She is neither your property nor your concern."

More footsteps approached in the hall, a lighter but rapid beat, but Nate paid them no heed. "Not your property, either." His hand fisted. "Didn't interfere with one attack to let a worse one take its place."

Zhen breathed, "Tim . . ."

A baritone asked, "Who is under attack?"

"No one is," the Elder said. "This citizen, however, is defying a direct order."

Archimedes Genet strode into the middle of the room, his dark hair free from its regulation braid, the shadow of a beard darkening his jaw, and his jacket unbuttoned. "Elder, you surpass your mandate. You have no right to command a citizen to do anything."

"I am charged to watch over the Recorders." The whir of a drone sounded, and a tendril snaked across my field of vision, reaching for me—

Nate's arm flew up. He caught it, and the silver metal twisted and twined its way up to his shoulder.

Panic eclipsed reason. All I saw was the metal spooled about his arm, and I threw back the covers, grabbing his hand and the smooth tendril. I could not pry it off.

The Elder said, "I suspected as much."

"Let go. She is not a true Recorder." Archimedes Genet's voice was measured and calm. "As was pointed out earlier, she has no neural implant, no drone. And you will release them both now."

I heard the Elder speak, but the drone did not punish us, did not even entangle itself around my hands. Instead, it went still.

Seconds ticked past.

"Let it go," Archimedes Genet ordered. "Both of you."

What other choice was there? I sank back onto the bed, and Nate released the tendril, which slithered free. Williams exhaled loudly.

"His actions have been documented." The Elder's arms fell stiffly at his sides. I knew that with his drones, he saw me, saw us all, but his gaze centered on Nathaniel. "He should be placed under—"

"No, he shouldn't," Zhen interrupted. "Tim is the best pilot we have."

"He has corrupted the integrity of the records and should face consequences in the courts. She must accept responsibility for her actions as well."

Archimedes Genet's expression betrayed nothing. "Elder, we'll sort this out later, but short term we need him to transport the marines down to clear out the intrusion. I believe your emotions are betraying you. I'll be filing a formal complaint of bias."

Zhen drew an audible breath. Williams turned off the hoverbed's medical alarm, leaving the white noise of the vents and the whir of the drones the only mechanical sounds.

"That will be all." When no one moved, Archimedes Genet said, "Everyone is dismissed to quarters."

The drone over my bed rotated slowly in midair, then floated to the Elder's side. He stormed from the infirmary, but the two large drones remained by the doors.

Williams wetted her lips and spoke, as if the words were difficult to form, "I can't have those things blocking the entrance. They . . . they are in violation of safety regulations."

"Elder," Archimedes Genet said, "I know you heard that request. Recall them."

Appendages writhing, both drones followed the Elder down the hall, and Archimedes Genet closed the infirmary doors.

Williams sat heavily on the end of my bed.

Zhen slumped back onto her pillow, but her black brows met over her nose. "That was stupid, Tim. You're going to get her reclaimed and yourself removed."

He did not answer her. Instead, he took my hand, and his eyes—greener than I had remembered—searched mine. "You all right?"

"Zhen is not wrong, Nate. Please do not endanger yourself."

Had I thought on it, I would have expected him to be cross, as he had been when I left those ten-days ago, but he only lowered the hoverbed's railing to sit beside me.

"Recorder, while it's good to see you again, the circumstances are less than ideal." Archimedes Genet approached the foot of my bed. "And a formal complaint won't slow him for long."

"Less than ideal?" Zhen's usually melodic soprano cracked. "Archimedes, do you know what she faces if they take her away again? What being here saved her from?"

"Discipline. I would assume—"

"No," Nate growled. "They'll kill her."

It seemed as if a cloud descended over Archimedes Genet's face. "You'll need to explain that later."

Nate threaded his fingers through mine. "She's not going back."

"There is nothing you can do, my heart." The knowledge settled heavily in my chest, but I had known my time was limited. "Two purposes remain: to aid in tracking down the origins of Ross's bioweapon, and to keep you and my first friend—and the other Recorders—safe. That is all I can hope for."

"Hope is bigger than that," Williams murmured.

Archimedes Genet set a hand on Nate's shoulder. "There's nothing you can do tonight, and tomorrow"—he checked his identification band—"*today* will have enough worries of its own. We aren't giving up that easily, Recorder." For a split second, the smile that creased his stubbled cheeks reached his eyes, and then he left.

Once the doors closed again, Zhen blew a strand of blue hair off her face. "Go on, Tim. I'll be staying with her tonight."

"I'm not leaving."

Zhen folded her arms. "Yes, you will. If you stay here, you won't sleep a wink."

His fingers tightened around mine. "You underestimate me again."

She rolled her eyes. "Moons and stars, Timmons. Alec will still be in the hall, worrying, especially with that dross-Elder storming around.

Get out of here. Tell him we're fine, but I'm staying here tonight, then get some sleep. You can't fly anything if you're dead of exhaustion."

"Ping Alec yourself," Nate said. "You'd stay, if things were reversed."

Williams opened her mouth, then closed it.

One of Zhen's rare smiles flickered. "True enough." She tapped her communication link. "Alec?"

"What's going on?" A *click-click-click* sounded in the background, summoning the visual memory of him flipping olive wood beads over his fingers. "First the Elder stormed past, followed by Archimedes, who must've just thrown his clothes on. I've never seen an Elder look *angry* before. Then they passed me again."

"We're—I mean, I'm fine. Williams says it's just a dehydration headache." She cleared her throat and glanced at me. "But I'll be staying here tonight. Williams took me off the flight tomorrow, though."

"We?" The beads stopped clicking. "Who all is there?"

"Williams, of course, and that Recorder." Zhen quirked a brow at me. "Tim hasn't left yet."

"Tim is there?" Alec's voice dropped. "Is everything all right?"

"We're fine, Alec. All of us are." Nate traced his thumb over the back of my hand. "Just thought I'd check on Zhen before I went to bed. I'll see you at the shuttle in a few hours."

"Right." Alec made an indeterminate sound, then said, "Good night, babe. I'll stop by in the morning before we leave."

The link chimed as Zhen signed off. Nate covered a yawn.

"Nathaniel, please," I said, and he looked down at me. "You must not risk yourself and the lives of the others."

Holding up a hand to forestall his reply, Williams pushed a chair to my bedside. "Before you begin any more indignant protests, Timmons, sit." But her expression softened. "You have managed this before. Should I ever . . . Well, I understand."

I glanced at the door again, which effectively stopped me from pulling the datapad from under my pillow. "I shall not be sleeping."

Zhen burrowed down into her pillows. "*I* will."

Nate only stretched out his long legs, and his dimple finally peeked at me. "And I'll be right here."

Nate sprawled in the chair, only a meter away, and his chest rose and fell evenly. Zhen slept, curled on her side in the bed next to mine, while Williams read. I closed my eyes and imagined that it was five ten-days ago, and an Elder had not said Nate had interfered with the records. That Ross's virus was not active. That Recorders were not endangered by behemoth insects. That I faced neither the Halls nor returning to Pallas Station.

Yet while I imagined, the datapad pulled at me, and my concern that the Elder would return chiseled at the comfort I found in the presence of my friends.

"You need to work your magic, don't you?" Williams asked.

"My magic?"

"Blocking those implants. I know you: you won't let Max's son suffer as you did." Her head tilted. "But you haven't started yet."

"If the Elder returned—"

"Of course." She slapped a palm on her forehead. "You need a cover, in case anyone shows up. Well, I'll set the door to chime before it opens, and you can borrow my book and swap the datapads if it does. I'll study instead of reading, which I suppose I ought to do anyway." Color came to her cheeks as she pulled her violet datapad from a deep pocket and clutched it over her heart. "Just . . . please don't tell anyone."

"Do not tell . . . " Concern edged out my fear of the Elder's return. "Williams, if you are reading banned material, utilizing your datapad will serve neither of us."

If her face had been pink before, it neared scarlet then. "Not that! It's historical."

"There is nothing wrong with history—"

"It is a love story," she whispered in a rush. She glanced at Nate and Zhen, but still they slept. "It is not banned or even rated orange—only somewhere between green and blue, so it shouldn't make you uncomfortable. It's . . . I couldn't bear people knowing."

I waited.

"I can dream." The faintest of smiles touched her lips, but it fell away. "I am forty-one, you know. I have quite a few years before I finish paying back my gifting, and that's assuming we make it out of here and Ross's bioweapon doesn't end my chance. When I finally get to choose my name, to be my own person, it will be too late. I'll be older, and starting with nearly nothing. What future I have will be small, though that hope of freedom beckons. The one man I—" She stopped to adjust the datapad's screen, then extended it. "Here. I started it over."

I accepted the datapad wordlessly.

Williams fingered the hem of her mint-green scrubs. "It's a second-chance story, where she refuses him years ago, but her sea captain returns and courts someone else at first, because he's angry she refused him, though he says it's because he finds her 'much changed.' But in the end, he realizes that she is still the woman he loves."

The inconsistency in the sea captain's behavior bothered me, but I only said, "I will only explain if necessary and in no way seek to diminish you, Williams."

She walked to the door and began to recode the chime. The words she had spoken grew in importance, and determination surged. If I could do anything to keep Edwards and Williams safe, I would do it. I would keep the Elder from reporting Nate—or any of the others. And I would keep my first friend safe.

These thoughts swirling in my head, I skimmed the first chapter of Williams's novel, in case the Elder returned and questioned me, then pulled out my datapad and entered the password. For half a second, I smiled, but my flash of happiness evaporated quickly. The memory of the conversation that had prompted my choice and the image the word conjured still gave me hope, but the password needed to be changed. Though I had hoped that Zhen would deduce it, if she needed to protect the others, it was a foolish choice, too simplistic. First, however, I had other work to do.

Hours alternately crawled and sped past as I managed to connect the datapad to the Consortium network without alerting anyone, then puzzled out a way to shut down the neural implants. Only twice did the door chime. My respiration quickened, and I hid the one datapad and picked up the other. One of the staff, Consortium trained as Williams was, entered to bring her a simple hot meal, and later, another one needed treatment for a mild steam burn. I attempted to be interested in Williams's novel while the second young woman set a mug of hot chocolate on my bedside table. She watched me for a moment before saying someone else had been right and she was glad I was back. Then she spun and nearly fled the infirmary.

Not long afterward, while Williams yawned and Nate shifted again in his chair, I isolated the frequency, and the solution presented itself. I blinked at the datapad. Could it be that simple? All that remained was to uncover the universal access code. Finding and breaking codes had always been enjoyable, but even as that burden of uncertainty lifted, fatigue settled in like a weight. I rubbed my eyes, saved my work once more, and slid the datapad back under my pillow. I set Williams's book on the small bedside table, then resting my cheek on my hands, settled on my side to study my Nathaniel.

Stubble a shade or three richer than blond covered his jaw and made his cheekbones stronger. His bangs still fell straight, but the hair on the nape of his neck had grown long enough that the curl I remembered was more of a wave, and though I would have thought I would miss the curl, the wave suited him, too. I could see no new scars, no injuries, though even in repose, his face seemed shadowed. I did not count the minutes I watched before his green eyes blinked open, and once they focused on me, a smile traced its way across his face.

"Morning." He rubbed a hand across his jaw and grimaced. "Guess I need a shave."

"No," I said. "I need to memorize this, too."

He stretched, then extended his hand. I took it. My eyelids drooped, and while I held Nate's hand, sleep found me.

Sudden weight on my feet startled me awake, then padded up my legs to settle on my shoulder until whiskers tickled my ear. A trill asked a question that I did, yet did not, understand. Yellow eyes blinked, and I snuffled back at Bustopher, who butted his head against my chin. Edwards was wrong: I knew the cat at once, despite his full coat. He settled on my chest, his limbs tucked as efficiently underneath him as any drone's spooled appendages, and his purr vibrated like happiness.

"I promise," Zhen was saying in an undertone, "we won't leave her."

"You can't guarantee that, and you know it," Nate said in a repressed whisper.

My temporary contentment fled. I caught the black-and-white cat in my arms and pushed myself up against the pillows. Bustopher glared up at me, then nestled back down as I stroked his head.

Alec, still wearing the white-and-green armband denoting mourning, had joined Nate, Zhen, and Williams, where they clustered near the doors.

"There's nothing you can do, Tim." Zhen's hands were on her hips. "If you don't go fly that thing, you'll wind up in the brig until that voided Elder can send you wherever they toss people they don't like. And Eric Thompson's shadowing the first flight. He might be from the belt, but he's a good kid. If you aren't piloting, Archimedes will send Osmund in your place, and that man's a bigot and a bully."

Surely Eric was not going down with the marines? Bustopher nudged my hand until I resumed rubbing his ears.

Nate's perfect brows descended. "If I leave—"

"You can do nothing more here than we can," Williams interrupted.

A muscle in his jaw jumped, and Zhen jabbed a finger at his chest. "You think your performance helped? Risking her life to make yourself feel better won't help anyone."

"I am not—"

"She has a point, Tim." Alec raised a hand, forestalling Nate's comments. "I get it. You've been on edge since they took her away, and finding out what that they were going to do? That makes us all angry. But staying endangers her. It's selfish."

Williams set a hand on Nate's forearm. "Timmons, please. Think. What would *she* say? If you refuse to leave, that Elder will rip her away, and—no, listen," she said hastily when he began to protest. "And whether or not he's within his rights, he is frightened, and frightened people act irrationally."

"Frightened?" Zhen spat out. "I hadn't heard that euphemism for downright evil before."

Tucking a lock of light brown hair behind her ear, Williams explained, "He was only to retrieve her and take her to her tribunal. This sickness has claimed every member of the Consortium who has been exposed, and it is likely he views this assignment as his death sentence. Of course he is frightened."

"Not every member," Alec put in, and all of them glanced back at me.

Anxiety lashed inside me, like a frightened hatchling snake, finally free from its egg, striking at the unknown. No matter what I wanted to be true, they were correct. However, I remembered the proper social etiquette and managed a small, "Good morning."

"Good morning, yourself." For a second, a smile lit Alec's eyes, then his thick brows drew down. "You look exhausted. You need more sleep."

Before I could either agree or disagree, a communication link chimed.

"Go, Tim," Zhen said more softly than I would have expected, given her previous tone. "Archimedes will be sending someone to watch over her."

"We'll do all we can to keep her safe," Williams added.

Instead, Nate approached my bedside and sat so close that our legs almost touched. Again, he took hold of one hand, while his other cupped my cheek. Leaning in, his lips brushed mine, the stubble on his face scratchy but not unwelcome, and though I wanted nothing more than his arms around me, I only whispered, "Be safe, my heart."

No dimple appeared, and I felt hollow at its absence. Nate should have smiled, for that smile was part of who he was. His eyes closed, and he tipped his forehead against mine.

His communication link sounded again.

Nate stood, and our fingers trailed apart. He took a backward step, then turned to the doors, which chimed and opened before he reached them. He nearly ran into a slightly taller but thinner man, who dropped his gaze with a murmured apology. Nate had vanished down the hall before I realized the thin young man was Cam.

Cameron Rodriguez tugged his standard work-study olive-green jacket straight. "Williams, ma'am, I've been assigned to watch over the Recorder this morning."

"Morning, Cam," Alec said. "Archimedes told me at breakfast, especially since Zhen has to report to the bridge this afternoon."

"I'd rather stay here, but no, Smith wants her beauty sleep." Zhen said something under her breath. Alec raised an eyebrow but did not reply.

Cam turned to me and surreptitiously wiped his palm on his pant leg. "Until yesterday, we didn't know . . ." He started again. "It's good to see you, Zeta—"

"Moons and stars." Zhen stalked toward him and stabbed a finger at his chest. "That isn't her name, Cam. I've lost track of how many times I've told you that." She paused and spun to me. "Unless it is? Don't tell me you picked a ridiculous name like Zeta instead of Chrysanthemum."

My voice, which seemed to have left with Nate, returned. "I did not. In fact, I—but no, I do not mind, Zhen. Cameron, you should not have come."

"The captain ordered—"

"Don't be slow, Cam." Zhen narrowed her eyes. "She means *Thalassa*, not the infirmary."

"It was this or quarantine with Foster, Watkins, and Bryce," Cam said, "so the three of us petitioned. Evidently, the situation's bad enough that they even need *me*." He took a breath, and a half smile wavered. "Besides, if I had to be stuck on another ship with only that awful tea again, I wouldn't make it."

Alec rubbed the back of his neck. "That's your motivation? Tea?"

The memory of boxes of melon tea propelled me to defend Cam's reasoning. "It was truly an egregious selection, Alec."

Cam added, "Melon tea was Watkins's favorite."

Williams wrinkled her nose, and a grin flashed across Cam's thin face.

"Nevertheless," I said, "I would rather you were safer."

"And I'd rather none of this was real, that no one died, that . . ." He cleared his throat, glanced at the others. "I would rather you didn't have some Elder trying to murder you."

Zhen's expression softened. "We can agree on that."

"I think we all can." Alec slid an arm around her and kissed her cheek. "I'll see you tomorrow, babe."

"Be safe."

"With J and Tim along, we'll be fine. I might have it easier down there with the bugs than you do up here with the drones." He nodded at each of us. "Be careful. Don't let them isolate you. And, take care of my Zhen, Recorder-that-isn't. Don't let her do anything too impulsive."

Zhen snorted.

"To the best of my ability, though I have yet to see my words carry much influence over her behavior. And you and Jordan will do the same for Nathaniel?"

He held out a fist, and this time, I remembered to tap it with my own. A smile broke across his face, and despite the Elder, the virus, and the roaches, my own smile answered his.

"That's what friends do."

Zhen tossed her hair over her shoulder, and when she spoke, her words were solid and confident. "Of course that's what we do."

Alec left, and Cam settled stiffly in Nate's chair, focused on the doors. Williams tidied the already pristine counters. Zhen pulled out her knitting, and the needles ticked softly as the variegated yarn danced from one to the other.

They *must* be safe. Nate, Jordan, Alec, and the marines would do their best to clear out the intrusion, but James and the others needed protection from those insects. The task loomed insurmountable, but I had found the first clues. A sliver of fear stabbed me, but I breathed through the memories of rows of tanks stretching back into the furthest reaches. There was no hope for me, not this time. I had surrendered it when I had faced Julian Ross alone.

But I had *now*. Now had to be enough.

I had my friends, and I would protect them.

My primary concern was, of course, that code. I knew I could find it. I leaned back against the pillows, Bustopher on my lap, my datapad at my back, and though I could not explain why, for the first time since the flash of recognition for the ugly red painting, a ray of hope shone past my fears. Not for myself. For them.

Perhaps—just perhaps—my friends could survive this after all.

I slept unevenly after Zhen and Williams left. Cam still sat near my bed, and despite Max's misgivings, Bustopher curled on my feet. Max's low voice and Edwards's mild replies ebbed and flowed in the background. I had not yet found the way to protect the Recorders, and that knowledge tumbled into dreams of tunnels, roaches, and the destruction of my drone.

When Tia brought us lunch, I pushed myself up and rubbed bleary eyes. Max rumbled appreciation, but he did not touch his food, only sat, a small transmitter fastened over his left ear, carefully observing the marines' medical readouts, which flashed in amber and shades of blue. Edwards finished the decontamination cycle on the medicomputer and attacked his meal as if he had not eaten since the day before. Tia set the tray with the remaining two sandwiches on the bedside table.

Like Cam, she still wore her greens, but unlike her practice on *Agamemnon*, her jacket was unfastened and her shirt untucked and tight. Last quarter, however, Jordan had implied that personal observations about weight were impolite, so I refrained from commenting. Cam handed me a mug of tea then separated our meals, but Tia simply stood in the middle of the infirmary, her bottom lip caught between her teeth.

I took a fortifying swallow of peppermint, set my mug down, and began, "Tia—"

"I've been thinking." Tears spilled over her cheeks. "I'm sorry I ever even considered—" She pulled a wadded tissue from her jacket pocket and scrubbed at her face.

Max turned his head from the display at her words, and his angled brows met in a thick line.

"Tia . . ." But Cam faltered.

"No." She held up a hand to keep him at a distance and released her breath in a slow stream. "Zeta, yesterday when that Elder . . . what he did frightened me. I thought he'd killed you. Even after all you said on *Agamemnon* and all we saw the Elder do, I thought—oh, I don't know what I thought."

I closed my eyes to push down anxiety. Bustopher curled up on my lap again, as if he knew that the pressure would calm me. I focused on his weight. "You have done nothing for which you need to apologize."

"You have no idea." She blew her nose, then tucked the tissue back into her pocket. "I feel like I ought to thank you for keeping me from making the second worst mistake of my life." She hiccoughed. "I take that back. The worst one."

The muscle in Max's jaw twitched, and though his nut-brown eyes fastened on Tia, he remained silent.

"I'm sorry, Zeta," Tia said. "No one should be treated like that."

The infirmary descended into silence. Even the centrifuge fell quiet.

Edwards started a partial fill in the three medical tanks in the back and smoothed the clean sheets on the other bed. On his way back to his workstation, he reached up to place his hand on Cam's shoulder. "Eat. There will be plenty of time in your future to curtail the input of calories, but you aren't there yet."

Cam stammered an inarticulate response.

Max crossed his arms and looked at me. "That goes for you, too." He cleared his throat. "Tia, you had a solid lunch as well, didn't you?"

She seemed to hold her breath, but when Max only raised one eyebrow, her shoulders relaxed. "Well, yes, I did. I probably ate too much, but I've been ravenous lately. I didn't know that ships could actually serve good food. You have better cooks than the staff on *Agamemnon* or in the dorms." Her nose wrinkled. "Although those reconstituted vegetables last night weren't my favorite."

"Mine, either," Edwards said.

"I believe—" Max stiffened, and his eyes narrowed. Tapping his earpiece, he spun back to his terminal.

Tia threw him an indiscernible look, then flopped into a chair. "Edwards is right, Cam. Eat."

I cut my sandwich into even triangles while Cam devoured his. With Edwards watching to be certain I ate enough, I suppressed the urge to make Cam take the other half of mine as well.

"No!"

Max's exclamation startled me, and I nearly dropped my half-eaten sandwich.

"Get her in that tank." Max's fingers flew through the data stream. "As soon as you reach the closest shuttle . . . I don't care about orders. Medical directive be spaced!"

*Her?* No—not Jordan! Please . . .

I could not breathe, and the monitor behind me sounded as my respiration grew ragged. Ignoring my bed's alerts, Edwards dashed across the room to the second terminal and tucked his earpiece in place as the display shot amber, red, and navy into the air. Neither student moved.

Edwards groaned.

"The tank, Venetia," Max ordered. "You know the consequences."

Relief flooded me when he addressed Jordan by her given name but was quickly overridden when what was either a prayer or a curse became a low, inarticulate growl.

"Belay that. Get Adams in the tank. His signs are faltering. She'll have to wait."

"We're ready here," Edwards said.

Max nodded. "Keep the others down there, and I'll send Edwards once we have these stabilized . . . Right . . . Stay with her, Venetia, no matter what anyone says. You're the only one . . . Yes! As much as you can for her weight. ETA?"

*Thalassa's* klaxon rang once, and the emergency light flashed red, then faded to a steady orange.

"Too long." He leaned back in the chair and pinched the bridge of his nose. "Edwards, we'll need Williams. She hasn't had enough sleep, but she was right. We'll need a third set of hands, and I'll need her in here after you shuttle down. Blast it all. I told them we needed more medics."

His eyes on the rotating strands of information, Edwards only said, "It could be worse."

Max grunted and turned back to the display, his fingers speeding through strands of amber, red, cyan, and a deeper blue.

They would require the beds. I needed to leave, though I had nowhere to go.

Before I could think of a destination, the vivid image of the conflagration in the hangar played in my mind's eye. The roar of insectile feet and flames drowned the everyday sounds of the infirmary. I forced back the memories, handed Bustopher to Cam, swung my feet over the side of the bed, and pulled on my boots. A yawn slowed me as I stripped the blanket and top sheet, but when I picked up the pillow to remove the casing, navy blue contrasted sharply with the white fabric. I stilled. I had no way either to carry or conceal it. For the first time I envied others' uniform pants. They had pockets. Leggings were completely ineffective. Nevertheless, I picked it up, and the smooth surface was cool on my palm.

Cam's eyebrows knotted. "Where are you going?"

"The marines." I indicated my rumpled blankets. "Max will need beds for the injured."

"Oh." His gaze fell to the datapad. "And that?"

"I need this."

He held out his hand. "I'll take it."

"It is dangerous—too damaging."

"No one will know." The smile on his face seemed too old for him. "I've got pockets."

He was correct, so I summoned the courage to give it to him. He shifted the cat to his left arm and tucked my datapad into the pocket on his right leg. I handed the bed linens to Tia, who dropped them down the laundry chute, then helped me remake the bed.

Max continued to select and move parts of the data, but after I had smoothed the sheets and a clean white blanket over the hoverbed, he turned around. "Thank you."

"You are welcome."

He angled his brows. "One more reason to not like all this is letting you out. You're not officially released, though you probably deduced that you don't really need care at this point. Lock up that blasted cat and take the trays to the dining commons. You'll need to stay out of the way until we figure out how to keep you safe from that Elder." He turned to Cam and Tia. "Keep an eye on her."

Tia gathered the trays, leaving Max's untouched meal on the counter near his elbow, though I suspected he would not eat. I picked up the violet datapad Williams had left as cover and handed that to Cam as well, and he placed Bustopher back in my arms. Whiskers tickled my neck when Bustopher tucked his head under my chin. Truthfully, the cat's welcome compliance surprised me.

I led the way to the storage room where the cats had been kept and deposited Bustopher inside. Somehow, though I had spent less time in that small room, it was home as much as Max's infirmary had been. Bustopher and Macavity circled my legs as I refilled their food bowls, though Hunter turned up her nose at the dried fish. I could not blame her. If I liked fish—which I did not—I also would have preferred fresh tilapia.

Tia held the stacked trays before her like a shield while Cam gently shooed away the brown mackerel tabby whose name I had forgotten. Jelly? That could not have been correct.

"Cam?" Her voice was small. "Do you think Eric is all right?"

"The pilots were supposed to stay back, ready for a quick takeoff, so he's probably fine," Cam assured her. "And he's a good shot."

Hunter approached her again, and she edged toward Cam, who scooped up the cat and deposited it near the food bowls across the room, then washed his hands. He joined Tia again, leaning down to whisper in her ear. She shook her head.

The door slid open, and Kyleigh and Freddie entered with the last cat.

"Oh good! You found Bustopher! That's all five then," Kyleigh said once the door was shut. She touched my arm briefly. "Why aren't you in the infirmary?'

"Max and Edwards are preparing for incoming wounded."

Her eyes grew round. "Do you know who—no, you wouldn't. Are there a lot?"

"I do not know that, either."

"Then how are you—" Kyleigh's eyes grew rounder. "Did you get the datapad?"

Cam tapped his pocket, and she relaxed. For a full ninety seconds, no one spoke, though there with the cats and the young people, the pause in conversation did not bother me.

When Freddie's stomach rumbled loudly, he flushed. "Anyone else up for a snack?"

Tia held up the trays. "That's our next stop."

"After visiting the dining commons," I said, "I might return here to work on . . . to read Williams's book."

"That's a good idea." Kyleigh seemed to choose her words with great delicacy. "I have a little more work to do with Dr. Clarkson, but I'll join you later."

Freddie cleared his throat, and she glanced up at him. "Jordan said to stay . . ."

She sighed loudly. "I forgot. Well, grabbing some snacks is a good idea. Last time the orange light came on, we had to clear the hall for a couple hours."

Tia's identification bracelet chimed, and she handed the trays to Cam. "That's the alarm I set. Can you grab something for me, Kye? I'm shadowing Zhen on comms."

Kyleigh dried her hands on a clean towel and dropped it into a bin. "Yogurt?"

Tia nodded. "But no apples this time. They're all grainy." She ducked out the door.

"It isn't that she dislikes the cats," Kyleigh explained as she took the trays so I could also wash my hands. "Max gave everyone a lecture about the cats and parasites, and she hasn't touched them since. I was hoping they would win Max over, though no luck yet. But! It is so good to have you back. How's your throat?"

Cam added, "You still sound a little hoarse."

My voice sounded no different to me. "I had not noticed. Edwards informed me that the surface injuries are healing very quickly and I should not scar." After seeking a proper conversational remark, I said to Kyleigh, "Your hair is growing in nicely."

"Isn't it?" Freddie beamed. "I loved her braids, but she doesn't need them. Kye has such a beautifully shaped head."

Cam choked back a laugh while Kyleigh blushed, but since Freddie was indeed correct, I concurred. She hid her face until we were in the hall again, walking four abreast. Even though the midday meal should have ended before we reached the dining commons, the murmur of conversation, familiar clink of flatware on dishes, and scraping of chair legs drifted into the hall. The noise died away when we entered, but although several unfamiliar people frowned in my direction, a small knot of crewmembers in engineering blue beamed at me as they passed us on their way to the door.

On our first trip to Pallas, I had my drone to remind me of names, but while I recalled their faces, the names had fled. The man with thick box braids pulled back into a thicker tail stopped in front of me. He extended his fist and waited until I tapped it.

"Welcome back, Recorder. Or . . ." His head tilted. "What should we call you?"

"Recorder shall suffice."

"But you're not," the woman barely Kyleigh's height protested.

"Spanos calls her Recorder-that-isn't." The man with sparse ginger hair crossed his arms. "Though that Elder might go after her for that."

The first man's gaze shifted from me to his companions. "We have to call her something."

The tiny woman scowled. "Well, whatever that monster does—"

"Please." Almost involuntarily, my hand rose to forestall her. Cam moved close, as if his tall, thin form could be a shield. "Do not say something which could endanger your safety if you are overheard."

The tiny woman pursed her lips, but the first man glanced over his shoulder at the people watching us from the quiet dining commons.

"I'll say what I like, and Elders be spaced. It isn't—"

"Isn't!" The ginger-haired man's eyes widened, and he snapped his middle finger against his palm.

"Isn't what?" the woman asked.

"Recorder-that-isn't." He grinned at me. "Isn't. We'll call her Izzy. That Elder won't have a clue."

The first man quirked a smile. "That'll do." He tapped my shoulder with a closed fist. "We have to head back to work, Izzy, but we're on your side."

A chuckle burbled from the tiny woman. "Izzy. I like that. And while we aren't precisely happy about all this"—she waved a hand vaguely behind her—"you were the only one who caught on about those voided Ross brothers and their attempts to kill off the system." She lowered her voice. "Just want you to know that we all—or most of us—believe you can figure this out, too. Stay safe."

Without another word, the trio left.

Kyleigh had looked down at the mention of the young man, Elliott Ross, who had been her friend. But the reminder of either Ross brother was not what bothered me. Instead, it was the errant thought that I knew the remaining crew of *Agamemnon* better than *Thalassa*'s. That lack of knowledge felt like a betrayal.

The four of us walked to the passthrough. Staff handed us small bags filled with snacks and bottles of water, and we returned to the hall, where warning lights bathed us in faint orange. I knew this part of the ship better than the halls from the shuttle to my holding cell, and my eyes were drawn to familiar scuff marks, small snags in the antistatic flooring, a long scratch on a ceiling tile. We moved aside when a cluster of security personnel passed us, their boots striking the grey-flecked antistatic flooring in unison. Freddie followed them with his eyes and kept an arm around Kyleigh.

We left her at the quarters she now shared with Tia, then Freddie, Cam, and I proceeded to Ross and Elliott's old room, which Freddie now shared with Cam and Eric. Freddie's face had gone ashen by the time we reached it. Unsure of propriety's demands, I intended to wait in the hall while Cam made sure that Freddie was well, but when I peeked through the open door, the walls pulled me inside.

Monochromatic paintings on scraps of paper had been affixed above the narrow beds: Kyleigh, flowers, the surface of Pallas, an ocean, and a detailed, almost scientific rendering of a cockroach, all in shades of brown. Elliott Ross's image peeked from under a stack of paper on the small table where several homemade brushes rested next to a mug of stale coffee. What made me catch my breath, however, was the half-completed portrait affixed to the wall above the table. John Westruther, Freddie's father.

Freddie had captured the minute twist at the corners of his father's eyes. I had seen that look in the records, in the last moment before Freddie went into the medical stasis pod that saved his life, when John Westruther had told his son that he loved him.

"No, Cam, I'll be fine," Freddie was saying.

I slipped from the room before either of them noticed my uninvited presence.

But while I waited, I realized that unlike these young men, I had nowhere to store my food and packets of tea. And my nowhere went further than that. I had no room, no place. Nothing.

Cam emerged, and the door swished shut. The corners of his mouth pinched. "I don't like it. He's stronger than when Captain Genet assigned Eric and me here, but he still gets so tired. Tia says Kyleigh is worried, too, even if she tries to hide it. He doesn't sleep well, either. We leave the red light on, but I think he wakes up in the middle of the night and paints because he has nightmares. Though how he paints in the dark, I have no idea."

*Thalassa*'s general communication system chimed once, and the Elder's voice flooded the hallways. "Recorder Designation Zeta4542910-9545E will report at once to the hangar."

The system chimed again and fell silent. At that one simple order, trepidation overcame my relative calm.

"He can't do that." The emphasis with which Cam spoke and the way his brows gathered into a straight line bespoke . . . anger?

"He is an Elder."

"But the captain told me—"

Cam's communication link chimed, and Zhen DuBois confirmed the Elder's orders, though she did not clarify his reasoning, adding a request that I hurry.

He squared his thin shoulders. "I guess we head to the hangar, then."

I nodded once and handed him the bag of food, and we strode down the hall.

It would seem that no matter what Archimedes Genet insisted, the Elder still maintained his authority. And even if my status within the Consortium was questionable, I was bound to obey.

# 27

The whir of AAVA equipment announced the Elder's approach before he rounded the corner, drones trailing behind him. Once again, his helmet hid the clean shape of his bald head. Cam ceased pacing and moved to my side, tension showing in his thin shoulders and the set of his jaw.

The Elder locked his dull grey gaze on the young man. "Cameron Rodriguez, you are dismissed—"

"No, Elder." Cam raised his chin. "Sir."

I placed my hand on his arm, then withdrew it.

Cam kept his eyes on the Elder. "Begging your pardon, sir, but Captain Genet ordered me to remain at her side until he himself told me otherwise."

The Elder's solid grey eyes closed for a moment. His personal drone dropped to hover directly at his shoulder, and it seemed to me that he leaned against it for five seconds. Then, his head cocked to the left, and he spun around to face the hallway behind him. Cam glanced down at me, but I only shook my head. Without a drone or access to the network, I could not tell what the Elder had heard, but in less than twenty-three seconds, the talkative Recorder appeared, wearing a mottled black-and-charcoal armored suit with the Consortium's triangular eye on his shoulder and carrying a helmet in the crook of his arm. He inclined his head to me, then to Cam, then to the Elder, but this time, he made no quip.

"Do not disconnect," the Elder ordered, "even while the drone charges. Is this understood?"

The talkative Recorder replied succinctly, "Yes, Elder."

"You shall remain on the shuttle until it lands."

The Recorder nodded.

More boots sounded, and security personnel accompanied Max

down the hall, though neither Edwards nor Williams was with them. His attention jumped straight to me. I felt that, once more, he was asking a silent question, and once more, I did not understand what the inquiry was. My gaze dropped to the floor, though a sound immediately pulled it back up.

Both the Recorder and the Elder pivoted to face the doors. Cam grabbed my arm and pulled me out of the way as a maelstrom of activity blurred past. Marines in blue armor rushed the shuttle's portable medical tank down the hall, then came six hover gurneys, carrying bandaged men and women. A security team jogged after them, but Max's eyes remained fixed on the double doors.

Venetia Jordan and a tall marine I recognized from the day before brought out the last hover gurney, on which lay a writhing figure in the mottled grey and black of a Consortium suit. My heart seemed to pump ice, for no drone followed them.

*I was too late.*

My failure to find the code might cost this Recorder her life.

Max moved toward them, but the Elder sent one of his larger drones to block him. It grabbed Max by the wrist, and though he tried to shake it off, his focus never left the Recorder with whom I had spoken only the day before.

"Get this machine out of my way," he demanded.

"You are not to interfere." The Elder's monotone rose above the Recorder's moans. "This is not your concern."

"She needs surgery—"

"No." The finality in that one word reverberated in my chest like a physical blow.

"If you don't let me get that chip out of her head, she'll die."

"This is not your concern," the Elder repeated.

"What?"

"You have no right to impose your particular moralities on the Consortium. We will care for our own."

"Care?" the tall marine repeated, his voice tumbling like falling rocks. "Crush you, you voided hypocrite. If you don't treat Parker, that's as good as murder."

My breath caught. *Parker?* The injured Recorder reached for the man at her side, but his steel-grey eyes were trained on the Elder's filmed ones.

The Elder's frown carved lines on his face. "If she has been named, that issue will be addressed later, as necessary. Where is her drone?"

"We left it where that spacing bug crushed it."

At the marine's blunt words, the memory of my own drone's destruction surged like a solar flare. For a fractured moment, the universe seemed to spin, and the argument both faded and echoed. I staggered into Cam, who grabbed me to prevent me from falling, and Max took hold of my other arm. He spoke into my ear, his indiscernible words recentering me in the hallway's orange light.

" . . . will retrieve the drone once the area is clear," the talkative Recorder was saying.

"For pity's sake." Cam's voice nearly cracked. "Stop her pain. If you're not going to help her, if you aren't going to try to save her, and if you're going to leave her to die, at least stop her pain."

The Elder exhaled so rapidly that condensation ghosted his faceplate. His eyebrowless forehead puckered. "As you say, Cameron Rodriguez."

A drone pulled one jointed arm inside its belly, then unfolded it to jab a jet injector at the woman's bare neck. She shuddered, then stilled, her respiration shallow but even. My gaze went to Jordan, who had set a hand on the Recorder's shoulder, and the woman's still-gloved hand clutched Jordan's wrist.

"Blast you!" Max thundered. "You can't just medicate her when you don't know what she's already been given—"

"It does not matter." Ignoring Max's protests, the Elder turned to me. "Zeta4542910-9545E." He waited until I forced an acknowledgment. "You will accompany her to the quarantine room where you were held. There she will remain until—"

"Until what? She dies?" The marine left the Recorder's gurney to tower over the Elder. "I demand you treat our Recorder. She's injured—"

"By her own choice." The Elder seemed unaware that a man nearly eleven centimeters taller than he and a third heavier loomed over him.

"Choice?" Despite the marine's gravelly voice dropping in volume, the words filled the hallway. "When Adams went down and that bug got to him, she sent her drone at the thing. We got him to the tank before he lost too much blood. She saved his life. And you're telling me—"

"I was linked to her drone. I bore witness," the Elder said. "Knowing the consequences, she elected to send it."

Red crept up the marine's neck, and a vein pulsed in his temple. "She—"

"She needs to be in the infirmary," Max intervened, his voice sharp. "Even if you won't let me save her, at least let me manage her pain."

"Her situation will be monitored."

As a drone latched onto the gurney and began to tow it down the hall, the marine grabbed the Elder's arm. "Treat her, space you!"

The Elder did not move, but two drones converged on the marine, who seemed unfazed by the tendrils snaking around him.

In five long strides, Jordan stood before them both. "Easy, Jackson."

Even three meters away, I could hear his breath rushing in and out. Though she eyed the drones, Jordan set a hand on the marine's— Jackson's—shoulder. The tall man's arms dropped to his sides, and the drones released him.

"I am sending an undamaged one to replace her." The Elder gestured to the talkative Recorder, then without a move in my direction, he ordered, "Zeta4542910-9545E, go."

For a split second, Venetia Jordan's golden-brown eyes met mine. Her delicate eyebrows gathered, but she said nothing. I nodded to her, then followed the drones down the hall. The Recorder on the gurney lifted a weak hand, and Cam moved quickly to take it. Her fingers curled around his. Behind us, the heated discussion continued.

"We're out here to save your sorry hides. The least you can do is save her."

"Jackson," Jordan said, her alto pitched lower than usual.

"She condemned herself." The Elder's calm rebuttal was swallowed by *Thalassa*'s halls.

Orange light pulsed three times as we walked, after which it faded, and ordinary, full-spectrum light resumed. When we reached the room, the drone ushered me and the gurney inside but barred Cam's entrance and shut the door. Cam pounded on the polished metal, calling for me to let him in. The drone wrapped all appendages around the Recorder called Parker and carefully lifted her to the bed. When she moaned, it administered another jet injector, and her eyes drifted shut.

Eventually, Cam ceased yelling. Though I had not—could not—answer, I felt the loss, for I should have said goodbye.

Ten minutes after Cam's demands ceased, the drone left, closing the door behind it, but the camera's eye watched my every move.

# 28

PERSONAL RECORD: DESIGNATION ZETA4542910-9545E

CTS *THALASSA*
478.2.5.06

The Recorder's respiration grew ragged, and when her back arched, the memory of pain blistered through me. I pulled my too-thin blanket over her, then fetched the spare tunic from the closet and tucked it around her, as well.

She writhed again. Her arm shot up and connected with my jaw. For several seconds—I could not count them due to the starfield that appeared before my eyes—I only blinked against the points of light. When I refocused on her, surprisingly coherent, deep-brown eyes met mine.

"How many?" she demanded and grabbed my sleeve. "How many have I lost?"

"I do not know."

"Adams was badly hurt—was in the medtank. He is barely an adult. For the sake of honesty and the record, tell me he lives."

At that moment, I considered lying, assuring her that the young man who had been carried from the shuttle in the portable medical tank was well. That he was sitting up, laughing, joking with the others about their escape from the dividing line between life and death.

But she deserved the truth. "I do not know. I only know that Dr. Maxwell is one of the system's best, and he is fighting for your Adams."

"*My* Adams." Her hand dropped back onto the white blanket. "Yes. They are all mine."

We lapsed into silence. Not knowing what else to do, I went to the small sink and filled a glass of water, but before I returned to her bedside, the door slid open, and a drone flew at me, snatching the glass without spilling a drop, and the Elder's brisk footfalls followed. Anger coursed through me.

He was barely a meter into the room when I found my voice. "You do not allow Max to save her, and yet you deny her even a sip—"

"Enough." His shadow drone encircled his torso with one whiplike tendril, and he placed himself between me and the injured Recorder. "You will not harm her."

"I? Harm her?" My hands clenched at his accusation. "When you will not spare her a drink of water?"

Without reprimanding me, the drone set the glass down on the small table, but whether or not the lack of punishment was due to Archimedes Genet's order, I did not know. On her bed, the Recorder shrank back against the flat pillow as the drone left my side to hover directly over her. As the Elder approached, she tugged her sleeve down over her wrist, and her chest rose and fell, sharply and unevenly. The third drone remained by the doorway.

"Recorder Theta4492807-3571R." The Elder's nostrils flared, then his face relaxed as if he had again released neurotransmitters, which did not seem fair when she and I no longer had that capability. He continued in a monotone, "You accepted the assignment to accompany the marines to clear the station, well aware of the risks."

"Yes, Elder," she managed.

"Your acceptance is counted as bravery. I have reviewed the records, and it is not your doing that the marines named you. Sending your drone to protect the young man, however, endangered that record. I have not yet filed my report and will delay it as long as I can to avoid any penalties."

Acid rose in my mouth. The only meaningful penalty now would be to withhold pain medication.

"You will have ascertained that your drone's destruction has damaged your neural implant. You were too long without—" Again he pulled back the nanodevices, revealing the hazel I had seen before. "Even if we had Consortium medical staff nearby, it would be too late."

Her back arched again, and tears seeped from the corners of her eyes and hung like dying stars on her short lashes. My own gut twisted in sympathy.

Syllables broken by gasps for air, she somehow managed, "I understand."

But while I might understand, I could not accept his pronouncement. Their verdict did not surprise me, not after last quarter when Max told me that damaging my implant had activated a program that began to destroy me. The unfairness of such planning—no, the *evil* of it—boiled in my chest, and although I had been taught not to judge, anger pulsed when the Elder pulled back the grey veiling his eyes, as if he spoke honestly. My fist drummed my thigh.

"There is little I can do but ease your pain."

"Then do it," I snapped. "You will not allow me to offer a drink of water, and yet—"

He turned to me, lashless eyes narrowing and filming over again. "Anything by mouth will rip her apart internally. I suspect you already know the process cannot be stopped, not now. That drink of water would have led to agony."

I had forgotten, and pain sharp as a reprimand tore at my chest. Max's voice sounded in my memory: *"But your small intestines nearly ruptured. We've patched them up, but you still need to be careful."* Guilt rose to suffocate me, and I staggered backward.

The pounding of running boots echoed from the hall through the door the Elder had left open, but he ignored the noise.

Instead, the Elder's grey-shrouded eyes blinked at the Recorder. "Whether or not you believe me, you have my condolences—"

Cam barreled through the open door, the tall marine, Jackson, at his side. Though the Elder did not otherwise move, his gloved hand rose as if to stop them both, and the larger drone left the Recorder and rose to hover by the camera. The outer door slid shut.

"She is indeed dying, and there is nothing that can be done. But before you speak, Kyle Geoffrey Jackson, I will present you with two choices. Recorder Theta4492807-3571R's final hours rest on your shoulders."

Jackson's jaw tightened. "What do you want?"

The Elder's expression gave nothing away. The drone near the camera seemed to shut it off and descended to hover, impassive and unyielding, with the other drone near the door. Although I knew the Elder saw everything through his feeds, he seemed to study the wall fifty centimeters above the Recorder's headboard.

"Jackson. If you and the other marines will sign nondisclosure contracts, I will refrain from filing a report against this Recorder until later."

"Paperwork? You're holding paperwork over my head while you let her suffer? She's dying—" His voice broke on the word, and color drained from his craggy face. "You wouldn't withhold pain medication, as well as treatment?"

The Recorder whimpered and pulled her legs up to her chest again. The Elder did not speak.

When the Recorder moaned again, Jackson stiffened and thrust out his hand. "I'll do it." His steel-grey eyes seemed as frightening as any Elder's. "We all will."

The Elder's personal drone pulled a datapad from an interior cavity. Jackson gave the screen a cursory skim and applied his thumbprint.

A drone from the doorway deposited a single jet injector and twenty cartridges on the table next to the bed. "Use it whenever the pain grows too severe. Zeta4542910-9545E may finish it, should the need arise."

Horror dawned, and the words squeezed from my chest. "Surely, Elder, you do not mean . . ."

A subtle shift in his expression stopped me. "As you say."

"Thank you," the Recorder breathed, her hand already fumbling for the injector.

I loaded a cartridge and discharged it into her neck, and her whole body relaxed.

The Elder's drones preceded him into the vestibule, but he lingered. "I have turned off the recording device. Kyle Geoffrey Jackson, you may stay as long as your duties permit. Your farewells, and those of your team who also agree to nondisclosure agreements, will not be documented. This, then, shall be her sole memorial, for given the potential of viral contagion, she cannot live on through reclamation or recycling. Instead, she will be properly incinerated." He closed his eyes, then exhaled. "In the end, we all die."

I wanted to protest that this could not be the end, but what else was there? It seemed as if a chasm suddenly appeared to swallow the Recorder, to swallow us all, and Max's claim of our value—whether we were indeed stardust or creation—mocked me. Of what value were our lives if they led to nothing?

The drones opened the outer door, and the Elder looked squarely at the woman. "I am not unfeeling. Recorder Theta4492807-3571R, it will not matter to the tribunal, but I will recommend posthumous clemency."

He left, closing the door behind him.

"Geoff." The Recorder's voice had thinned to a strand of what it had been the day before.

"Parker."

Her unfocused brown eyes drifted to the marine's. "Adams?"

"Stable. He's still in the medtank, but Maxwell says he'll pull through."

The faintest of smiles tilted her lips, and her dark eyes closed. "Good."

He moved to her bedside. "You saved him."

"What else could I do? I could not lose Adams."

Jackson removed his jacket and draped it over her shivering form. "We don't want to lose you, either."

She did not answer for fifty-three seconds, but then she startled and clutched his arm. "Keep them safe."

"I'll do my best—" he cleared his throat "—but that's Michaelson's job, mostly."

Despite her pain, her faint smile reappeared. "Liar."

"That's harsh, Park."

"It rests not only on leadership but is instead each one's responsibility. Citizen and Recorder alike."

"True enough." Jackson sat carefully on the edge of the bed and gently clasped her wrist.

I jumped when Cam set a hand on my shoulder. I had forgotten he was present. He edged close.

"This is what you meant, isn't it?" he asked in an undertone, and I glanced up at the camera. "What Kyleigh said you were hoping to prevent?"

That recording device . . . why had the Elder deactivated it, if he had indeed done so? I put my back to the door and mouthed, *Not here*.

"Zeta4542 . . . I cannot recall," the Recorder said, "bear witness."

I moved next to Jackson, and once my shoulders blocked the recording device, she exhaled, as if in relief. Apparently, I was not alone in my distrust of the Elder's word. When I was in place, she dropped Jackson's wrist and pushed back her sleeve, revealing a hand-plaited bracelet of russet, brown, and black hair. She rolled it over her wrist and palm and held it tightly. Jackson's attention, however, was riveted on her face, only turning briefly to her closed fingers when she placed her fist in his larger hand.

"Keep it, until you can give it to the next one," she whispered. "Fight for them, Geoff. Do not . . . do not let them die."

She opened her fist, and the bracelet fell onto his palm. His eyes widened.

"Tell them I have not forgotten, that this is not a burden but a memory, not to weigh them down but to propel each further. I do not regret what I have done, for you and I are the same."

"Is this—"

"My promise. And I have kept it, as the one who came before me had." Her respiration increased, and perspiration beaded on her forehead. She shifted under the thin blanket. "Each marine we lost is here in memory. Not in guilt."

Cam sat heavily into the chair. "You—I didn't know."

Her brown eyes left Jackson and went to Cam. "You are not meant to know. No one is, save the one that comes next, if he or she is worthy of the knowledge. Each marine we lost"—she touched the braided hair Jackson now held—"from each I rewove this, adding to the memory I was given by the one who came before me."

Jackson traced the auburn strand and breathed a name I did not hear.

Her bald head turned on the pillow. "Yes. The Elder cannot have this, cannot know."

"Parker—"

"He will send a replacement. Watch over him or her, but do not trust immediately. If he or she is worthy, wait till the drone disconnects and charges, then explain and pass this on. It is our calling, and we shall uphold it. But if the new one is not worthy, remember for me?"

The empty eye of the recording device seemed to burn like a laser through my back.

"I will." Jackson cleared his throat. "He's sending one on the shuttle tonight."

"Which one?"

His lips quirked, even though his forehead remained furrowed. "Tall fellow. Bald. No eyebrows."

The Recorder's brief chuckle turned to a groan. She dropped his hand and jerked back, curling into a ball. Cam's knuckles whitened as he gripped the chair arms.

The marine blanched.

"Geoff," she said so faintly that I would have doubted she had spoken at all, had I not been watching her closely. "Will you stay with me?"

"As long as I can."

Had I the option, I would not have left, either.

The Recorder called Parker drifted in and out of pain and nightmares as nine other marines visited that afternoon and into the evening. Jackson stayed until summoned to Archimedes Genet's office, and as soon as the door closed behind him, she moaned again and rolled onto her side, pulling her knees to her chest, then arching away from them. Cam glanced up at the camera over the door before joining me where I stood at the foot of her bed.

"She's a lot like you."

"No," I said. "I would not survive an assignment to the military. I did not meet their standards."

He shook his head, but I discerned no anger or frustration on his face. "You're a lot tougher than you think, but that isn't what I meant." His stomach grumbled, and his cheeks grew pink. "Sorry. I left our snacks in the infirmary where I found Jackson, but even if I hadn't, I couldn't eat in front of Parker."

Somehow, Cam calling her by the name was a sliver of light.

"I believe she would not mind." I kept my attention on the woman before me, her restlessness prompting me to prepare another dose. "You should go to the dining commons and have dinner. Could you bring me some tea?"

"I'm not supposed to leave you."

"I will not be alone."

In my peripheral vision, he rubbed his palm on his pant leg. His words rushed out, as if dumped from a bottle. "I didn't keep my word to Captain Stirling on *Agamemnon*, and he died. Then Captain Genet told me to stay with you, but the Elder shut me out. What if—"

"Cameron."

His hand stilled.

"You cannot live on *what if*." Though he had never cringed away from me, I could not bring myself to touch his arm and so settled for a small smile, instead. "What happened to Andrew Stirling was not your fault, and neither was the Elder's actions. You must not judge yourself for either. Reach out to Archimedes Genet, if you must, but first you need to eat."

"It's not right."

The Recorder shifted under the thin blanket and spare tunic. Jackson had left his jacket, but it might not be warm enough.

"I believe she is chilled. I often was, with only that cover. If you gathered several heated blankets from the infirmary, you could also collect our food, if it is still there. Go." I hoped he understood the command was gentle.

He walked backward to the door, his tired eyes on me. "I'll be back as fast as I can."

Once the door slid shut, I gave the Recorder her thirteenth dose, and she relaxed against the pillow. I settled restlessly in the chair, and my fingers twined and untwined.

"Should I ask forgiveness?"

I blinked at her question. "For saving Adams?"

"Never that." Her eyes locked onto mine as she whispered, "For jealousy."

I pulled the chair closer to her bed. "I do not know that jealousy is something one must confess, even to the Elders, and even at the end of things." For a moment, the thought of Kyleigh's unquantifiable God gave me pause. "Unless there is something larger than this life, after all."

She held out her hand, and not knowing what else to do, I took it. Her fingers were limp in mine. "I was jealous of you."

"Of me?" Briefly, the question of whether or not the Elder had truly disconnected the recording device seared through me, but in the end, it did not matter. She would die, and I could only do my best to prevent more deaths before I myself served in the Hall. "Then I say it is well."

"I watched you. And before I watched you, I read your story." Her hand tightened slightly in my own. "You must have meant to run—it is the only thing that makes sense. But you stayed."

My heart clenched. If she knew, surely the Elders did as well, and if they believed that Nate intended to run with me, he would be removed. "I did not—"

She drew a ragged breath. "Do not lie to me. I might not have a drone, but I can still see a lie." Her deep-brown eyes watered. "You stayed to keep them safe, and they love you. I . . . I would have liked to have been loved."

"You are. Do not doubt it." I tucked Jackson's jacket around her with my free hand. "You might know, or not, my specialty?" When she did not answer, I continued, "I was meant to become an Elder and was sent to Pallas Station to uncover what had become of the Recorder assigned there. She had died long before and was afforded but a footnote in their records. And that is the way the worlds are. The Consortium is not valued by citizens. But your marines care. They name you. They visit you. And beyond that . . ."

The Elder's words about the finality of life battled with Max's claim that each of us held value. My heart pinched, for somehow, I knew the Elder was wrong, even if I knew nothing more.

"You are valuable and unique. Not only as a Recorder. As you." I leaned forward in the chair. "Did you or did they choose the name?"

"I did not."

"Have you dreamed of one?"

A shudder swept through her again, but not enough time had passed for another dose. Torn between wanting to help her and fear of overmedicating, I bit my lip.

"I have," she whispered.

"Tell me."

Seconds crept past.

"Rose."

Whether or not it was appropriate, my smile blossomed. "Then, it is well, Rose Parker."

Her tension eased, but the moment disappeared as her face contorted. Her fingers twisted around the thin blanket, so I caught her hand, held it, and did not let go.

Before time came for the next dose, Rose Parker's fingers went limp in mine, and her features relaxed for the last time.

# 29

Time must have passed before the gentle whoosh of the door brought my attention from Rose Parker's still fingers. Two security personnel entered, pushing a hoverbed. When they untucked the lower sheet to slide her from one bed to the other, I let go and picked up Jackson's jacket. The taller woman pulled a sheet over Parker's face.

As they moved the bed out, I said, "Stop."

Both women turned to me.

I held up the jacket. "This belongs to the marine named Kyle Geoffrey Jackson. Could you return it?"

"Yes." The tall woman tossed it on Parker's form. "We'll have to clean it first, so it might not be finished before they leave. I'll take it down myself after we burn the shell."

*Burn the shell.*

The marines needed to know.

"I do not have a communication link. Would you please notify Jackson and the other marines that . . ." I could not finish the sentence.

She cocked her head. "Why? She's just a Recorder."

The shorter woman set her hands on her hips. "Space it, Frankie, she's 'just a Recorder,' too." She turned to me. "Don't mind her. She hasn't really known many Recorders before, and the one who replaced you, well, she's a prize and a half. As bad as that Elder." Her cheeks puffed as she exhaled. "All right. I'll let them know."

Frankie rubbed her hand over her upper arm. "I didn't mean to be offensive, Recorder. I'm new this trip."

My defender glared at her. "I'm getting tired of that excuse. You've been on *Thalassa* long enough to know her story."

"It is well," I said.

The shorter woman tapped her forehead like a salute and gave her end of the hoverbed a tug, towing it into the hallway. Since the door remained open, I heard her contact Jackson and his gravelly reply that they would join her at the lift.

I followed the security personnel into the vestibule, intending to accompany them to the lift and relay my sympathies. As I stepped through the door, however, a thought hit me: *No one should have known.*

I had contacted no one. If the Consortium recording device was indeed inoperable, I should have been the only person aware of Parker's death. The Elder had not come himself, had sent no drone to ascertain her status. The women had arrived with the hoverbed without being called. The recording device must have been functional, which meant the Elder had lied.

Alternating waves of heat and cold swept over me, the anger and fear propelling me forward. I ran, no destination in mind, my boots pounding the antistatic flooring.

I dodged around crewmembers, hurdled cleaning bots. My feet led me to what had been my computer laboratory, then around past my quarters, but when they brought me near the infirmary, I swerved. Max, Edwards, and Williams had enough to do without my worries, without a lying Elder who watched my every move.

A stitch in my side brought me to a halt, and my lungs burned as if I had inhaled clouds tainted by sulfuric acid instead of oxygen-laden air. While I leaned against the wall, panting, my mind raced through the conversations held while Rose Parker was dying. The bracelet of hair, the names, the tears her visitors had shed piled together with the memory of Cam's concern for me and of his questions.

*"This is what you meant, isn't it? What Kyleigh said you were hoping to prevent?"*

My eyes burned with unshed tears, for I had allowed Cam, who did not understand, to betray himself and Kyleigh. If something happened to either of them, such a lapse could never be forgiven.

Once the blood thundering in my ears and my frantic gasps for oxygen subsided, the unexpected sound of singing drew my head up. The slightly cacophonous melody leaked faintly down the hall. I followed the sound of men's and women's voices raised in disjointed harmony to a knot of security personnel, crewmembers, and marines standing near the lift that led to engineering and the incinerator.

The marines were all bald.

Every single one, man or woman.

And every single one wore the green-and-white mourning band around his or her left arm.

With no invitation, I would not intrude. I backed away, then pivoted and wandered through the bland corridors before dropping onto one of the benches created by the chemical backup system's housing. A Consortium recording device aimed down the way from which I had walked, and I eyed it warily. Once suspicion took hold, it would not let go, and doubt swirled that anywhere was safe.

I sagged as the realization hit. With no way to work in secrecy, I would not be able to create the device and transmit the signal. More Recorders would die. The talkative Recorder would take Parker's place. The ship's Recorder, whose drone wrapped around her arm like a snake's embrace, might remain on *Thalassa*, but there was no guarantee. The Elder—I refused to worry about the man who had left Parker to die.

But, my friend. James. Max could not watch his son die like Parker had.

Neither could I.

There had to be a way. My thoughts jumped to Cameron Rodriguez, who had the datapad and Williams's novel. I needed them back, but I could not ask without implicating him. In addition, transporting them would be difficult without satchels or pockets.

Very well.

It seemed I had no choice but to defy Consortium tradition and risk further consequences. What more could they do than send me to the Hall?

I wiped my cheeks dry, pushed myself to my feet, and made my way to the laundry.

# 30

Twenty-nine minutes later, I straightened the waistband of my black, pocketed pants. Once acquainted with what I needed, the staff had found a pair in my size from a stash of spare clothing, but when I emerged from the water closet, the younger of the two men, who had been pacing back and forth, shoved a folded black jacket at me.

"Needs to match," he urged, though he did not meet my eyes when I accepted it. He only backed away, his hands fluttering at his sides. "Needs to be a set."

I did not want the jacket. In the face of the Elder's constant disapproval, the black pants already seemed a greater act of defiance than was wise.

The young man's obvious agitation ate away at my tenuous calm, yet something in his distress resonated with me. Sets should not be separated. Having mismatched clothing should have seemed trivial in comparison to why I needed pants with pockets, but taking the jacket was a small thing. After all, what was a jacket compared with what I meant to do? And even should I wear it, would it worsen my fate?

I managed a smile for him. "If you insist."

The younger's tension abated, and the older man rested his hand on the younger's shoulder. "Thank you, Recorder."

Adrienne Smith's nasal whine sounded over the ship-wide system, informing all of *Thalassa* that I needed to report to the hangar again.

"You had better go," the older man said. "But take care."

"And you." I tried to catch the young man's eye, but he stared past my head. "Both of you."

The laundry's single door clicked behind me, and clutching the jacket to my chest, I considered searching for Cam before heading to the hangar. The datapads were essential, but without any idea of where to look, searching would mean a delay in obeying orders which surely were endorsed by Archimedes Genet, if Smith announced them.

The pants' loose fabric shushed as I walked, and I tried to ignore the constant sound. At least I had left my Consortium grey leggings on underneath the coarser fabric. I might overheat, but the seams did not chafe.

Vague worry edged its way past discomfort. Smith had given no reason for my summons, and Jackson had told Parker the Elder would send the replacement this evening. I had not heard that the shuttle had left, but even if it had, surely there had not been enough time for the talkative Recorder's drone to be destroyed as well. And, just as surely, my sole purpose would not be to sit beside a fellow Recorder while life ebbed away under the observation of a dishonest Elder. If my time was spent under close watch, holding the hands of the dying, how could I save the living?

Glaring up at the unmoving camera on the ceiling instead of watching where I walked, I turned the corner toward the hangar, and Kyleigh's exclamation brought me to a halt. Jordan and Zhen, both in their grey-and-black lightly armored suits, turned to face me. Cam pushed away from the wall as Kyleigh threw her arms around me, the quick embrace made all the more awkward by the armored suit she, too, wore.

"I probably should've asked first, but stars, you up and disappeared and made us worry all over again." Kyleigh moved back. "Are you all right? That's a decent bruise on your jaw."

My fingertips rose to my face where Rose Parker had struck me. "It was unintentional."

Kyleigh arched an eyebrow. "If you say so."

"That's rubbish." Zhen pushed past her and took my chin in her gloved hand, gently turning my head to study the bruise. "Who hit you? That voided Elder?"

"No." I glanced behind me before reluctantly adding, "Parker. She did not mean to, but . . . she thrashed."

"Oh." Zhen released me. "I remember. You thrashed pretty hard, yourself. Do you need a gelpack?"

"It does not matter."

Zhen's gaze skimmed over me. "I'm not saying that you should wear Consortium grey, but why are you wearing those pants? I thought you said you didn't want to provoke that Elder."

"More to the point," Jordan said, "why aren't you suited up?"

"I wanted pockets, and there is no reason to wear a suit." My gaze went briefly to Jordan's, then Zhen's empty weapons straps. "Cam also wears no suit."

"He's not heading down to the moon."

"Am I?"

"Didn't that dross-Elder tell you anything? Of course you are."

"Zhen, you should guard your language." I started to tap my thigh, but the additional fabric of the pocket's buttoned flap was unfamiliar enough to prevent a second tap. "I was not informed."

She only rolled her shoulders in response.

"I went back," Cam said, "but you weren't there. No one was, and I was worried the Elder might've locked you away somewhere—like on the trip from Lunar One. I started looking, but when Officer Smith made her announcement, I headed this way." He held out a plain sack. "I brought you something to eat."

I took the brown paper bag, which was heavier and bulkier than I recalled.

"I heard about Parker," Jordan said quietly. "I liked her."

The bag crinkled loudly when my hands tightened around it. I whispered, "Her death is not all that bothers me. The Elder knew."

Jordan's delicate brows drew down. "Explain."

So I did, lowering my voice in what would surely be a pointless effort if the recording devices functioned after all. Kyleigh's hand covered her mouth, and Cam's face went pale.

"Space him," Zhen hissed under her breath.

Jordan's golden-brown glare shot to the device at the corner. "I didn't think you lot could lie."

"'Dishonesty and infidelity are abominations,'" I quoted. "But we are human, Jordan. Of course we can lie, though untruthfulness damages the record, and consequences for purposeful inaccuracies are severe. His drone, however, would have reprimanded him had it detected falsehood, and I have no way of verifying my accusation. He might have told the truth."

"A functioning camera seems the best explanation for security showing up right after she died." Jordan stared down the hall, though no one was there. "Archimedes needs to know, but comms *will* be recorded, so it's best not to trust them. If we didn't need you on Pallas Station's computers, Zhen, I'd ask you to check."

"That'd be a great idea: just climb a ladder and mess with a Consortium device while that Elder spies on me? Not a thing wrong with that." Zhen fingered her thick navy-blue plait. "I could run down to let Archimedes know. We probably have time, since not everyone's here yet."

"No, ma'am." Cam straightened. "I'll do it."

Jordan nodded, and her braids' music almost made me smile. I had missed it. "Good man. Just make sure the Elder doesn't have cause to go after you for speaking out of turn. You'll have to be careful."

"I will."

She turned back to me. "That still doesn't address getting you a suit, monitor, and medpack. I don't want people down there without a reliable air source and some form of protection, especially with those bugs. Michaelson's marines are excellent at their jobs, but they won't get them all. Not that armor has helped so far anyway." She activated her communication link, asking for Max.

Something in me relaxed as they discussed locating an appropriately sized suit and related equipment. The kindness of their concern surpassed the meaning of the words themselves. I had little doubt the Elder meant it for ill, but if I had to go down to the moon below, I knew Nate, Jordan, and Max would not abandon me.

Williams's name, however, brought my errant thoughts back. "Is not Edwards going to the station?"

Jordan glanced at me, and said, "Change of plans," before continuing her conversation with Max.

My sliver of contentment faded, and I held the bag to my chest.

Earlier, Williams had challenged the Elder, but Edwards, too, had displeased him. It seemed unlikely the Elder would interfere with Max's authority in the infirmary. Moreover, Archimedes Genet would not permit the Elder to override Max's decisions. The doctor himself must have reassigned his staff, which meant it must have been more dangerous for Williams to remain on *Thalassa* or else more dangerous for Edwards to risk the intrusion on Pallas.

Williams already believed freedom would come too late for her dreams, that those dreams could only be met in books. The possibility that the Consortium might add time to her debt increased my need to protect her and Edwards.

"Nothing on that rock works properly." Zhen bared her teeth in a smile. "It might be the best place for both of you, despite the bugs, especially if you plan on doing *extra* work."

She was correct. At least on the station, only the talkative Recorder would be documenting events. I could not work efficiently under close watch on *Thalassa*, but on Pallas Station, with its tunnels and damaged recording devices, surely I would have an opportunity to find the code. Determination overpowered my concern that the camera down the hall could be recording our conversation.

"Cam. Would you be able to retrieve my—*Williams's*—datapad for me?" When Zhen quirked one eyebrow, I offered the incomplete explanation: "She had allowed me to read a novel."

Zhen snorted. "*You* were reading a novel?"

"I didn't know you read for fun!" Kyleigh beamed. "Books are some of my favorite things. What was it about?"

My cheeks heated, but my promise to Williams kept me silent.

"You're blushing." A glint came to Zhen's eyes. "It was a romance novel, wasn't it?"

"I . . ."

Zhen's laughter rang out, and Kyleigh rapped her on the arm. Cam shifted his weight and pointed to the bag in my arms, but I did not understand his meaning. Jordan signed off the link with Max, her deep frown cutting through Zhen's amusement.

"Williams is on her way. That . . ." She exhaled forcefully through her nose. "That *Elder* has your suit locked up and refuses to fetch it. All Max can gather last minute is a monitor."

"Only a monitor?" Zhen's hands clenched so tightly they shook.

Kyleigh gasped. "That's not right!"

"Nevertheless," I interjected. My gaze flickered away as I lied, "I am sure that it will suffice. We shall not be walking on Pallas's surface. I shall, no doubt, be warm enough."

"You're not going without proper equipment." Jordan raised her chin, though there was no need. Zhen, Kyleigh, and I were all much shorter than she. "Not if I have anything to say about it."

My shoulders fell when I understood her point. "I will, once again, be a liability."

Her expression softened, though she spoke firmly. "You've always been an asset, my friend, albeit one that needs to stop winding up in the infirmary."

I managed a weak smile. "That final assessment has my complete agreement."

"Is there a way she can stay? Although, if she does . . ." Kyleigh faltered, then brightened. "I know! If I am not here, someone has to take care of the cats." She whispered, "No recording device in that room."

"The Elder will be sure to keep close watch on me. But staying or leaving, however, is beside the point if I do not have the datapad with the . . . novel to read."

Cam cracked his neck to the side. After a quick look down the hall, he said a little too loudly, "I added some things to the bag you'd left behind. I thought you might need a few more snacks, so I took it to the mess, and one of the staff made you a sandwich. She gave me a bunch of tea, too, since she said mint and ginger were your favorites and who knows if they have tea on Pallas. And, since there was room, I put Williams's datapad in there."

I peeked in. The carefully packaged sandwich, several protein bars, and approximately twenty packages of tea almost hid two datapads in transparent covers. Relief washed over me, and I smiled up at him.

At the sound of footsteps, I folded the bag shut. Nearly twenty people filed down the hall. Now in white suits with engineering-blue circles on the upper arms, the trio who had stopped to talk to me outside the dining commons nodded at me as they passed. The bald marines who accompanied them still wore green-and-white armbands. Jackson paused beside Jordan. She held out her hand, and they clasped wrists briefly before he followed the others.

Once more, the five of us stood in the hall. Zhen picked up a helmet and tossed it to Jordan, who caught it one-handed.

"I don't usually condone disobeying orders, but there are exceptions." Jordan tucked her helmet under her right arm. "Stick close to Cam. Archimedes can put you in my quarters. I'll comm him and let him know."

"I'll be sure to talk to Captain Genet and let Max know about . . ." Cam paused. "About everything."

Jordan clapped him on the shoulder, but when she spoke, her tone was gentle. "You'll do well, Cameron. Be steady, and stay out of that Elder's way as best you can."

"Yes, ma'am."

She offered him a brief smile. "Call me Jordan. Everyone else does." She tilted her head toward the door. "Go ahead and buckle up, Kye. I'll wait for Williams. Zhen, let Johansen and Osmund know she's—"

The sound of drones interrupted her. I spun around, placing myself between my friends and the oncoming Consortium equipment. Four drones swung around the corner, dangling a wall of two-meter tendrils. Behind them stood the Elder and *Thalassa*'s Recorder, both in suits and helmets.

"Go." The drones amplified the Elder's voice, and the single word reverberated through the hall.

Jordan was at my side in an instant, her eyes flashing. Zhen, Cam, and Kyleigh were close behind.

I set a hand on Jordan's arm. "It will be well. I shall go." I began to say that she was not responsible for me, but Parker's words to Jackson replayed in my mind, and I could not lie. I was responsible for the Recorders and my friend, but could that apply in reverse?

Once again, I turned my back on the beige hallway and passed through the door. Zhen and Kyleigh sat on either side of me in the back row, leaving two seats for Jordan and Williams. I buckled the safety harness and kept the black jacket and the bag on my lap.

The first time I had walked from *Thalassa* to a shuttle, I lost my drone. The second time, I transferred to *Agamemnon*. Both had been less than fortunate. This time had to be different.

It had to be.

# 31

Although his new drone had accompanied him for the past quarter, nothing had prepared the boy for the wonderful explosion of colors splashing across his visual cortex and overlaying the familiar world.

Under the energy-efficient lighting, tendril-like scrolls covered previously sterile white tile work. Delicate geometric designs laced the ceiling in hues the naked human eye could not detect, and the grid work for the radiant heating in the floor glowed. His shadow drone's new connections clarified what had seemed to be imperfections, and when he closed his eyes, colors beyond the visible spectrum remained. Footage of infrared and ultraviolet had only approximated either the glow or the blotchy absence of light, not the delicate range of shades he could now perceive. With this new activation of the drone's connection with his neural implant, for the first time, the drone did not spark resentment. It was not a burden, but a gift.

The novice Recorder relaxed back into his chair without opening his hazel eyes. "The world is beautiful."

"Yes." The Elder radiated heat, and her drone hovered behind her, coruscating in waves of ultraviolet. "It is."

"You are also beautiful, Elder," said the boy. "Is everything so very different when we see the truth?"

The Elder's primary slave drone rose to the ceiling, its long tendrils extending from its spherical body like tree roots, and she smiled gently, though her unusual facial expression did not seem out of place in this new world.

"I am not so old that I have forgotten what it is like in the cohorts," she said. "I know you lay awake in the dormitory, wondering what it would have been like had you not been gifted to us."

Anxiety spiked momentarily. The boy held his breath and did not deny the statement.

The Elder nodded. "Never lie. We can see the lies."

He closed his eyes and called up memories of the tilapia ponds to mask his discomfort. "Yes, Elder."

The Elder knelt in front of the boy's chair so they were face-to-face, even though his eyes remained shut. "It is a normal developmental stage to wonder and theorize about one's donors. It is time now for you to leave those musings behind. Our gifting saves our lives. It is the most moral choice our biological parents made."

The Elder paused, and the boy hung his head. His wish for family and friends felt more shameful than ever before.

"When citizens reject us, when we are gifted, our compensations exceed anything citizens cling to. The Consortium becomes our family: the Eldest, our parent; Recorders and Elders, our siblings; the others, a precious responsibility. While we must strive to maintain the purity of the records, we ourselves are gifted tools citizens can never understand. Our lives"—she gestured around the room to the glorious colors—"contain wonders they cannot see, hear, taste, or touch."

"Yes, Elder," he said obediently.

She continued with even greater gravity, "We are given more than they can ever comprehend: the truth about the universe and the beauty in all things. Do not envy them the petty interactions that constrain them."

The boy held out his hand as he lifted his head. "I cannot say that I never will envy them, but this, all this . . ."

"It alters the balance, does it not?" Humor and understanding laced her voice. "You now behold the way the Founders sought to mitigate our supposed losses. They sought to ensure we would do our duty and record only the truth. They do not understand, even now, that their superficial and temporary associations are insignificant compared to what we have. They cannot comprehend how our far-reaching associations within the Consortium exceed their petty lives. This is our true gifting, and it is an honor we must work hard to redeem."

He bowed his head again in acknowledgment. "I see the truth in your words, Elder. How is it I can see truth?"

"If you can already perceive my truthfulness, you are indeed well chosen for your calling." She smiled. "Bodies do not like to lie. They will tell you when the evil in a person's heart becomes apparent through their speech. You will learn. Now: tell the drone to remove the other spectrums."

"I do not wish to do so." Nevertheless, he complied.

The Elder hummed in approval.

The boy sat in the isolating dark for only four and a half seconds before opening his eyes. The loss of the new world resonated deep in his bones, and though he had only had the additional information for a few minutes, he craved more. Now that he had a glimpse, he no longer wanted to understand the world without it.

"Be sure to pay close attention to your shadow drone. For the first few ten-days, utilize the feed only with permission from and in the presence of an instructor. Novice Recorders frequently find it difficult to believe, but the additional information will confuse your ability to perceive and interpret data. You must acclimate to the new input before other senses like hearing are enhanced."

Sudden anxiety seized him. "But, Elder, what if—"

"What if you never acclimate?"

She had known? Had he already failed a test and shown signs of failure? He choked out the single word, "Yes."

The Elder smiled, fine lines wrinkling around her filmy grey eyes. "I am not concerned, Recorder. If you can already discern truth, I have confidence you will have no trouble adjusting to the additional input."

There was no hint of a lie in the Elder's words, and the boy relaxed until another unsettling question intruded. But he had to know.

"Are there those who cannot adjust?"

"Yes."

"What happens to them?"

When she did not answer right away, the Recorder switched on his feed, and as colors rushed back, he saw the Elder's skin temperature fluctuate. An uncomfortable suspicion rose: had the Elder not been forthcoming? Had she herself possibly lied?

Surely an Elder would not lie.

"They are reassigned." Her neutral expression was more alarming than a scowl would have been. "If the feeds are overwhelming, they are removed. There are many positions within our Consortium. Do not allow your success to give you a false sense of superiority. Only the Eldest is above us all."

"And the Elders over the Recorders."

At this, her tone softened. "Only through experience. As we rely more and more on our drones, they allow us to change. Eventually, we rely on them completely, and our slave drones see for us, so that we can be aware at all times, with or without our eyes. But, I grow verbose. You must train. Switch on your drone."

"I have."

Instantly, the Elder and all three of her drones focused on him with the precision of a laser. "When?"

A frisson of fear went through him, but the boy said truthfully, "While you were explaining about adjusting to the new information from the drones."

The Elder closed her eyes, and they darted back and forth like in REM sleep. "When you were afraid of acclimation?"

"Yes, Elder."

The lines seemed grey on her face. "You were analyzing what I said."

"Yes, Elder." He did not add that he was also analyzing the Elder herself. He must only speak the truth, if he meant to redirect her attention, so he added, "There is much to process, and I am concerned about being able to adapt."

This was, undeniably, true.

Long minutes passed. The boy waited. Like all novices, he excelled at waiting.

"Very well," the Elder said at last. "One final time, I will remind you to abide by the words of the Elders. Until you have completed your training, you will only utilize your drone's feed with authorization. You will improperly construe the information without instruction."

"Yes, Elder."

She peered sharply at him. "I see and understand your concern, but your actions just now have necessitated a final step. Although this does occur for all novices at some point, few reach it so soon and continue to advance. You must guard your mind carefully. Choose wisely. Again, you have brought it on yourself when you activated the input without guidance."

The boy stilled. In a flash as clear as the world in full spectrum, the added colors were inadequate recompense for the acquisition of a drone, and though he remained determined not to fail, the desire to run shot through him. He slid his hands under his legs to keep them steady.

"This is not what I wish," the Elder said. "But unauthorized activation requires a penalty."

"I will refrain from doing so in the future," he whispered.

"Yes." The Elder turned away. "You will."

His drone draped a tentacle across his shoulders, and he ground his teeth to suppress a scream. The new connection did not merely enhance color.

After the pain subsided, the Elder handed him a paper tissue and wrapped her arms around her waist while he scrubbed his cheeks dry.

"You have had an eventful day," she said softly. "It is best for you to return to your quarters and disconnect while your drone charges for the evening. Use your datapad rather than the network to complete any schoolwork."

The boy deactivated the connection to color beyond sight and wadded the tissue into a ball inside his fist. "If I disconnect, I shall not be able to complete my research assignment for tomorrow."

Her drone descended to entwine tendrils around her torso, and her arms relaxed. "You may stop at the Scriptorium and gather necessary materials."

The boy's legs shook when he stood, and although his drone steadied him, he flinched in its gentle grip.

The Elder laid a hand on his shoulder. "Recorder."

Yes. That was who he was—no longer a novice, no longer merely a boy—but the title had never sounded so much like a reprimand. He slowly raised his gaze to her grey-filmed eyes, and his respiration evened, until he breathed as one with her—in, out; in, out.

"You have done well. Do not take the discipline to heart. It is but a natural consequence, meant to inspire you to work harder. The other Elders and I see your potential."

He nodded once more and left the activation room.

In the Scriptorium, he collected a datacube. When he approached the front desk to sign for the cube, the Recorder serving as curator leaned on the counter.

"A datacube? You are not going to utilize your drone?" She cocked her head. "Or did you receive your colors today?"

"Yes."

A slight divot appeared over her nose. "That can indeed be overwhelming."

"I erred." He could not call back the incomplete confession.

The Recorder's lips pressed into a flat line. She placed her palms on the counter and straightened. "Then you will need recovery time. I shall return."

She spun on her heels so quickly her grey tunic flared.

He waited while she palmed an access panel, then hunted through what appeared to be printed and bound books. His heart beat a little faster at the thought. Novices were rarely allowed to handle books once they graduated from the nursery.

She returned and slid a decaying volume across the counter. "The book is slotted for destruction, and as it has already been replaced, do not feel pressured to return it soon. When you disconnect, this will provide company."

He counted to ten, hoping the hesitation would mask his desire to take it. Her drone scanned the datacube, and he picked up both the cube and the book.

"What is it?"

"Earth history and legends. You have read it before on your datapad." She flashed him a tight smile. "Yes, my drone checked your reading logs. Take your time, if you must; we can destroy the book when you are finished."

For a moment, he stood, nonplussed, but she shooed him away and returned to stacking discarded materials. Determined not to alert anyone or anything of his anticipation, he returned to his quarters, where his drone went straight to its alcove while he settled into his studies. A bot brought his dinner, and he ate alone.

Finally, he finished the assignment, powered down everything except his lights, and opened the book, turning each leaf carefully, enjoying the feel of thin paper between his fingers and the soft *shush* the pages made. After a while, he leaned back and closed his eyes, seeing nothing, except the mental images the words had summoned. Monarchy, freedom, mountains, seas, and flags snapping in a breeze, red against a cerulean sky. A *blue* sky. How very strange. He had only seen domes and rivets, but he knew Ceres' sky was lavender.

Still, the color of the heavens was not the strangest thing.

Freedom.

Members of the Consortium were to serve the citizens. Redemption meant duty, protection, service . . .

But, what was it like to be free? To not fear punishment at every turn?

The black ink on the pages was so plain, so simple, so . . . ordinary. Nothing at all like the glories of invisible light.

Yet somehow—

Somehow he could see more through those letters than anything his drone had shown him, and the promise of life in the Consortium felt like a mockery.

He reread the chapter and closed the book, his mind returning to a footnote.

Once, there had been a prince named Lorik.

That was all he knew. Not whether or not the prince had led wisely or well. Not whether or not he was loved or feared, or even if love and fear meant two different things.

The note said that *Lorik* meant *freedom*.

The young Recorder centered the book carefully in the middle of his desk across from where the drone lurked in its alcove like a prison guard, ready to condemn him. He would never escape. Never.

And yet, that drone had given him sight.

The Consortium was all there was. No Recorder ever left, ever rejoined the society that did not want him or her in the first place.

The boy stood and tucked his chair neatly under the desk.

He would make the best of what he had been given. With or without the drone, there was freedom in small things, in everyday choices. He would find that freedom. He would repay his gifting and serve the citizens who had thrown him away, and in doing so, he would serve his brothers and sisters and keep them safe.

The boy turned off his light and stretched out on his bed, without bothering to change or even pull off his boots. His right arm tucked under his head, he stared up at the shadowed ceiling.

What would it have been like to have the best of both worlds? To have color without pain and the freedom to choose . . . anything. What to do, read, think, or feel. What to believe.

Freedom.

If he had a secret name hidden in his heart, he would choose Lorik.

Irrational disappointment lurked as Johansen smoothly landed the shuttle in the cavernous hangar. The marines had secured it when they struck at the heart of the roaches' intrusion, and there was no need to land on Pallas's surface.

I did not see the stars.

All we had to do was wait for the damaged doors to creep shut and seal us inside the moon, so we sat in the same oppressive silence in which we had traveled. I leaned my head against the blue seatback and closed my eyes, the bag of food and datapads clutched to my chest. Memories of my drone's destruction and of Parker's death played through my mind's eye in an endless cycle, alternating with visions of my friend and Max, side by side in the infirmary.

Without a passive link to the Consortium like the one I had on *Thalassa*, the task of blocking the connection between a Recorder and a drone seemed insurmountable. And I was tired.

Jackson's voice broke into my thoughts. "No one's going to steal your lunch."

I yanked my mind back from the hypothetical to the present. His eyebrows bunched over his nose, but his face almost seemed gentle, otherwise. Someone laughed, and heat rose to my cheeks.

Before I answered, though, a young woman with untreated razor knicks over her right ear said, "My head's cold."

The man beside her grunted and turned to the talkative Recorder. "Hey. Your head ever get cold?"

The Recorder shrugged, though he did so with more fluidity than I typically managed. "It does, indeed."

"Stupid question, Lars." The woman rapped her gloved knuckles on the questioner's armored knee.

A grin creased the talkative Recorder's face. "Hair is an insulator. His inquiry was valid."

After he spoke, however, everyone fell silent. I glanced at the sealed bag which held the monitor Williams had brought onboard, and envy for the others' armored suits replaced my restless thoughts. The light on the ceiling flashed green, and the rustle and clatter of unbuckled harnesses replaced temporary stillness as Jackson and the others stood.

I unfastened my seat's harness and retrieved my monitor. The low murmur of voices disappeared as the marines' helmets clicked in place. Without a link of my own, I was isolated from their conversation. I activated the monitor, fastened it around my wrist, then slid on my black jacket, but my sleeves bunched up around my forearm. I pulled it off, shook it out, and gripped my cuff as I had seen others do, then donned it. The stiff material made movement uncomfortable, but I fastened the front, then waited, cradling the paper bag with my food and datapads.

"You shouldn't bring that." The woman who had complained about being cold paused, her helmet in both hands, her attention on my bag. "They'll smell it. Those bugs can probably smell it through the shuttle doors."

My breath caught, though it was not due to fear of the roaches. If I had to leave the food behind, I would, but I could not leave the datapads. Inwardly berating myself for not transferring them to my pockets beforehand, I clutched them tighter.

Zhen tucked her blue plait into her cap. "Really? Like the lot of us don't already smell like a buffet dinner?"

The woman's reply was forestalled when Johansen's voice rang throughout the cabin, warning us the pressure had equalized, and the doors would be opening. Zhen and the last marines donned their helmets and retrieved their weapons from the aft lockers. All other conversation disappeared, and Kyleigh edged close beside me, her armored shoulder touching my jacket sleeve. I was left with only the sounds of boots, buckles, and occasional clicks of people bumping into each other. The cabin's muffled quiet seemed loud.

With a crack and a hiss, the hatch opened. Frigid air seeped past the marines as they filed out, and a sharp acidic scent combined with burned carbon and electronics flooded the shuttle. I gagged. Williams and the other personnel exited, then Kyleigh and I followed them, Zhen at our heels. The odors and chill grew sharper.

The burned-out hangar, thick with ash, was larger than I remembered, even with both shuttles side by side, and its very size increased my uneasiness. Instead of the orange light of fire, the cold light of a dozen large portable lamps illuminated the center, and smoke had left dismal residue on the unlit fixtures hanging from the jagged ceiling. The dull film of soot had settled over everything else, from the stalactites jutting like uneven canine teeth overhead, to the singed places where pale ovals of insectile eggs had once clustered around the perimeter of the hangar. Armed guards stood near the doors and open garage, while a lumbering industrial bot relentlessly plowed through piles of half-burned carapaces.

A deep metallic groan grew into a grating roar as the circulation fans started up. Shortly afterward, dim, ashen lights sputtered to life in the tunnels and overhead, lending the hangar a sickly hue. Even the four-meter cleaning bot appeared hollow in that light.

Accompanied by a score of marines, the talkative Recorder and the engineers departed through a set of double doors to our left. The engineers waved, though the ginger-haired man's face was much paler than it had been on *Thalassa*. Immediately upon their exit, regret caught me. I should have wished them luck.

The towering industrial bot's steady, creeping journey drew my attention, and my breath caught.

There, on the other side of the shuttles in the bot's path, unnoticed by anyone else, lay what remained of the drone that had exploded and injured Jordan and me. Hope sparked. That was the solution to finding the code. If enough of it was intact, I could pull it apart and create the device to block the link for the other Recorders. I handed Kyleigh my bag and dashed across the hangar.

Silty ash billowed around my feet as I ran, and acrid air burned my lungs. I slid to a halt as the towering industrial bot reached the damaged drone first and a metallic crunch vanquished my flare of hope. Scraping the floor clean, the bot swept over the blackened tendrils and misshapen oval body. Only a darker blotch on the concrete marked where the drone had been.

I was too late. Again.

Breathing heavily, Kyleigh trotted up and tapped a button on her neck. Her voice came, slightly delayed and tinny through the helmet's inadequate speaker. "Please—they say it's safer if we stay out of the way, over near the wall."

She cast a sideways look at a carapace and shuddered. My shoulders fell, and I accepted my bag again. Together, we walked to where Jordan spoke to a group of marines. I could not discern their words, but Kyleigh stumbled over nothing and came to a halt before we reached them. Her pupils constricted even as her eyes widened.

Jordan beckoned to us.

"I . . . Yes, I will be," Kyleigh answered a voice I could not hear. "But you need to contact Freddie. Please don't—" Her breath hitched. "Don't deny him a farewell. If he can have the chance, please let him take it."

When we reached the others, Jordan switched on her exterior speaker. "You have to believe me, Kye. This is worse." She tipped her head toward me. "Just ask. We saw them both last quarter." She pursed her lips, then clarified for my sake, "They cleared the control room and found Westruther and SahnVeer, both still giving off radiation signatures."

I glanced over at a pile of carapaces. "Were they . . . whole?"

Even in the pallid light, Kyleigh blanched, and Jordan quickly added, "Yes. They're untouched."

Kyleigh sagged against my arm.

The marine with sandy eyebrows said something before he turned on his speaker as well. "Recorder-that-isn't, the station Recorder's chambers are sealed. The Consortium wants us to access them and retrieve her and her drone."

Oddly, the opportunity to complete my original assignment felt more like a gift than an additional burden. I said, "I will do so."

Another marine, whose jawline was darkened with grey-touched stubble, hit the switch so I could hear him. I appreciated his courtesy. "Like I was saying, Michaelson, their security measures have us locked out. The computer issued a warning that one more try could trigger unspecified fail-safes, but the engineers need to get geothermal power back online. Our generators are enough to run the fans, but they sap too much power. If we have to be here long term, we can't burn out our resources."

"I'll go." Kyleigh's voice wavered at first but grew stronger as she spoke. "I know the access codes, and the computer knows me."

The small knot of marines turned toward her.

"The halls aren't all clear," the sandy-eyebrowed marine said. "It'll take a while to eliminate the bugs. At this point, Tristram, it's better if you tell us so we can—"

"It knows my retinas." Kyleigh's lips quirked. "And to be honest, Michaelson, I'd rather not let you take those without me."

"Sound enough reason," Michaelson said. "Jordan, go with her. Take Jackson."

"Right." Jordan turned to me. "An escort will take you to a secured room. Stick with Zhen until they get here."

"It's spacing stupid, sending civilians at this point. Too early." The dark-bearded marine eyed me. "And not even suited up?"

"Leave her be," Jordan snapped. "You heard what happened."

The man's expression was unreadable, but his voice softened. "They're my daughters' ages, Jordan. I'd never let my girls in a place like this." He looked at Kyleigh. "Stay close, Tristram. Jordan and Jackson will keep you safe enough."

Kyleigh merely nodded, and in the strange light, her short, light brown lashes and brows were nearly invisible, again making her appear almost like a very young, hazel-eyed Elder.

The dark-bearded man's agate brown eyes drilled into me next. "Like Jordan said, not-Recorder, Mike called for someone to take you down to the rooms across from where we rigged an infirmary. Got some pretty powerful air filters working double time, so breathing will be a little easier. Had some bots clean up the surfaces, too. We reinforced the ventilation system, set up laser alarms, so nothing should get in without warning."

"That's good to know," Kyleigh said quietly.

Zhen and Jackson joined us, and before Kyleigh had time to say more than, "Take care," she, Jordan, and Jackson were gone.

Michaelson clicked off his speaker, pivoted abruptly, and strode away, leaving me with Zhen and the bearded marine. When a sharp creak echoed in the hangar, the bearded marine switched off his speaker and jogged over to help manually crank open another garage. Zhen and I waited by the wall as the door crept upward, revealing the base of another industrial bot. Time passed in ever-slowing seconds, and fatigue pulled at my eyelids until Zhen's smooth voice startled me awake.

A half-smile graced her face. "Your escort's here."

I turned to the door through which my friends had left, and my heart lightened when a man of average height entered, a taller figure behind him.

"Hey, babe," Alec said.

"Hey, yourself," Zhen replied softly.

He looked at me. "Ready?"

All I managed was a small nod as Nate's green eyes swept over my black attire, then up to my cheek. His face tightened. But he only tapped his speaker as his gaze met mine, and he raised one perfect brow. "Welcome back to Pallas. We'll get you somewhere you can get some rest, if you're ready to come with me?"

Though I could not find my voice, I had never been so willing to say yes.

Nate, Alec, and I left Zhen to whatever task Michaelson had assigned her. Silent yet alert, neither man spoke as we walked through dust-filled corridors, the overhead lighting showing the dust's grimness, not its former mysterious beauty. The halls, which had been smoothed from ancient lava tubes, rarely followed proper ninety-degree angles but meandered like a twisting maze. When we reached double doors, which opened into a clean and mercifully straight corridor, the sight prodded my memories.

"Nate?"

He glanced over.

"Is this the hall with Freddie's murals?"

He nodded.

A hint of sadness touched me. I would have traded neither my short stint of freedom nor my friends for bondage to a drone, but I missed invisible light. When we passed a single door on our right, my feet slowed, and both men did as well.

"You okay?" Alec asked.

"Yes." I tapped my thigh. "I left the main AAVA drone in the control room. Does it remain?"

Alec shrugged. "Probably. It was there twelve hours ago."

"I should check. It was my duty to secure it." The explanation was inadequate, but uncertain if our conversation would be recorded through the men's communication assemblies, I would not chance revealing my goal of finding that code.

"We shouldn't dawdle. Alec still hates those bugs." Nate threw him an incomplete grin. "Not that I'm enamored with them, myself, but we need to get you somewhere safe, so you can get some food and rest."

"His distaste is shared," I said.

"Besides," Alec added, "not your job anymore, is it? Shouldn't the new Recorder take care of that, since he has a drone and all?"

I did not answer him. Nate's eyebrows rose.

The men slowed to match my pace as we continued down to the hall's end and turned left. Three meters in, dust motes flashed and disappeared in a web of red beams that wove across the dead-end hall, and beyond them stood an armed guard. She clicked a button on the wall, and the light-triggers disappeared.

Nate led us past the first two doors, opening the third. With a flourish, he waved for me to enter. Most of the furniture had been pushed to the perimeter of the room, but several desks had been shoved together, making a larger surface area near the front. Two sealed metal receptacles, like the one in the quarantine room on *Thalassa*, stood near the door. A dozen folding cots formed two rows down the middle. Seven were in use, and six marines, still in their suits, though without helmets, slept quietly. One arm dangling over the side, Eric Thompson snored lightly on the cot closest to the door.

"Eric is well?"

"Shh." Alec held a finger to his faceplate. "Of course he is."

Once the door closed, Nate pulled off his helmet and cap. His bangs flopped down over his eye, and he ran a gloved hand through his hair to push it back.

"It's safe enough." Alec pointed at the tall, cylindrical filter humming in the center of the room. "They brought the heavy-duty stuff this time."

Nate's gloved fingers brushed my bruised cheek. "What happened, sweetheart?"

I caught his hand and held it like an anchor. "It was but an accident." He frowned.

"It's chilly in here," Alec said. "Plus, it's after midnight, and you look exhausted. You won't sleep well, though, if you're shivering the whole time. Too bad they didn't bring more heaters. I'll check to see if anyone has a spare blanket." He paused. "Zhen said you had food?"

Setting my bag on the table, I pulled out the datapads and the sandwich, which had been smashed into an unappealing mess.

"Enjoy it while you can. Next time you have a decent meal will be back on *Thalassa*. We're stuck with packaged stuff down here. I'll be right back."

Nate motioned for me to sit, though I first tucked the datapads into the pockets on my thighs, where they tapped like a fist with each step. He handed me a bottle of water from a container in the center of the table, then spun a chair on one leg and settled next to me.

"It's good to see you," he said softly. "So. What have I missed?"

I glanced at the sleeping people on the other side of the room and left my unappetizing sandwich untouched on the table. "I cannot know what you have missed." I rested my unbruised cheek on his shoulder and exhaled with contentment as his arm slid around me. "But I have missed you."

No one had seen roaches since the marines had burned out the hangar the day before. Kyleigh hypothesized that they had scurried into ventilation shafts and crevices, as their smaller relatives were wont to do. Between the explosions designed to block exits, the self-destruct sequence, and Captain North's order to seal off specific entrances instead of destroying the base altogether, fissures had opened in the rock, so I suspected that Kyleigh was correct.

Since she had the knowledge—and as she said, the retinas—to access secured areas, Kyleigh left with Zhen and several marines shortly after a quick breakfast. I did not know where Jordan was, but Nate, Alec, and Eric Thompson had taken one of the shuttles back to *Thalassa*, bearing with them a marine who had been injured when a passage had collapsed. Williams had done her best, but he needed a higher level of care than was available in the small emergency infirmary. They were due to return shortly after noon, bringing Freddie to attend his father's cremation.

After they left, Michaelson and I ventured out to retrieve the station's Recorder and her drone. Given that there had been cave-ins, I followed Eric's example and brought sealed food bars with me, but despite both the contents of my jacket pockets and the marine's warning the day before, Michaelson and I encountered no invertebrates of any size.

The trip, however, proved fruitless. The Consortium security device on her door had malfunctioned. I needed a drone. Once again, frustration at not being able to fulfill my duties chiseled at me. As Michaelson and I returned through the silent, oily-scented halls, however, my disquiet shifted to apprehension. The odor, the darkness, and our echoing footfalls grew unnerving. I began counting strides to steady myself.

Six hundred ninety-seven steps later, we reached the control room.

Zhen and Kyleigh's grey-and-black suits stood out among the marines' blue. They were working at a terminal near the AAVA drone, which yet remained attached to the main computer with only slightly dusty black cabling. The control room was brighter than it had been, and two hoverbeds with sealed black bags rested in the corner. Several marines had accessed other terminals, but except for the dull roar of the circulation fans, the room was quiet until Kyleigh saw us and tapped the button at her throat. Zhen and Michaelson followed suit.

"There you are." Kyleigh's usually effervescent voice sounded flat, though the effect might have been due to the speaker. "*Thalassa*'s engineers managed to restart geothermal power, so they will be doubling up the fans. Plus, we'll be a little warmer. Smaller rooms should be back up to twenty degrees by tomorrow morning."

The marine on her left must have asked a question, for Zhen pivoted toward him. "No, Lars. Twenty degrees Kelvin." She snorted. "Of course she means Celsius. Don't be ridiculous."

Kyleigh continued, "At the moment, the scrubbers are working well, oxygen levels look good, and particulates are going down. It might take a while to clear out that musty smell, though, and the dust could clog up the scrubbers before then. Which isn't good since access to spare scrubbers is blocked by a rockfall. And on top of that, half of the algae tanks that maintained the carbon dioxide to oxygen ratio were damaged by the"—Kyleigh winced—"the roaches. They ate through the tubing to get to the algae."

Michaelson frowned past her at the computer console. "What about the possibility of airborne nanites?"

"I haven't found any. The only thing I've seen in the scans are—well, it's disgusting, but the dust around here is mostly decomposed roaches."

I almost gagged, and Zhen patted my shoulder.

"So far, none of the samples have had anything but the roaches' biological residue, smoke particulates, and a little rock dust." Kyleigh glanced at me. "And I think I know which nanodevices to look for."

Zhen leaned against the desk behind her. "Is what killed the people here the same thing that killed off the people on *Agamemnon* and those other ships? Or was it something else?"

"I don't know." Kyleigh studied her gloved fingers. "I sent the autopsy reports up to Max and Dr. Clarkson, but I haven't heard back. I guess Max hasn't had the chance to go over them yet, since he and Edwards are rather busy saving Miller. Dr. Johnson was the virologist, so she might have known, but I can't access her files. My passwords let me access most of Georgette's—Dr. SahnVeer's—records, since I was working with her at the end." Her attention shot over to the body bags at the edge of the room. "But . . . that doesn't help us now."

"We're thinking that maybe the AAVA drone could get in," Zhen suggested. "The thing never shut off, so it's still Consortium enabled. I can't get in now any more than I could last time, but"—she turned to me—"could you access deep storage?"

Her observation about the AAVA drone was correct. Even sixty-seven days later, it still siphoned power from the computer system to which I had attached it. The panels glowed in the same dull teal, and the cables were exactly as I had left them, albeit covered with fine dust. It was both familiar and strange, as if I had returned to a childhood dormitory and the sights and smells were no longer as I recalled them.

At that second, I realized that all the information necessary to block the neural link to the drones was here, live and active. No digging, no searching. I could retrieve any information still in the station's computers, then create a jamming device, and Michaelson would not know. The talkative Recorder was not present with his drone to observe. I would not even need my datapad, and I could protect them all. My fingers flexed in anticipation. It would be simple—

I stopped myself. Not simple. It would be foolish.

The drone was linked to *Thalassa*, and the Elder would know what I was doing. Despite the black jacket, I shivered. If I attempted to use this drone to save the Recorders from Parker's fate, the Elder would stop me.

For the first time, the drone seemed less like an elegant jelly. In my mind, it grew more spider-like. It waited like an arachnid, still and silent, until its oblivious prey wandered into its web. I backed away, and in my peripheral vision, Zhen's eyebrows soared.

I would not use it, not to enter the Recorder's quarters, not to access storage, not for anything. And I certainly would not disconnect it.

Michaelson shook his head. "Not right now. We need that drone to retrieve the station Recorder."

"I believe leaving this drone attached to retransmit information to *Thalassa* might be a better choice," I said hastily. "Instead, we should ask the Recorder sent to document the marines' activity for assistance."

The man's sandy eyebrows pulled together. He studied me for ten seconds, then, with a nod, he hit the switch and started a conversation I could not hear.

Zhen glanced at Kyleigh. "Do you need to take a break?"

I expected Kyleigh to refute the suggestion, but she only reached through the streaming data to pick up something on the other side. Cyan and amber swirled around her hand, the images freezing for a fraction of a second, then pixelating into nothing, then reforming. She studied the small datacube's blank sides.

"I suppose I should thank you, Zhen," Kyleigh murmured, "but having this back isn't as important as I'd thought." She looked up, her hazel eyes shining with unshed tears, and explained, "Zhen went with me to Dad's old office since that hall has been cleared. I meant to get some things, but this was the only thing left. Time can be so strange. It's been over two years, but it hasn't. Days flow differently when you're half-asleep in a tank. I thought going there would be healing."

Zhen moved shoulder to shoulder with Kyleigh and spoke so quietly I could barely hear her. "Healing takes time."

Kyleigh turned the cube over and over in her gloved fingers. "I know." She set it back down, scattering the colors above the console.

"The shuttle should be here in a few hours." Zhen touched Kyleigh's arm. "Is there anything that you or Freddie need? He can use my armband. I'll make a new one when we get back to *Thalassa*."

"That would be nice." Tiny droplets flicked from Kyleigh's short lashes onto the interior of her faceplate. She heaved a sigh. "Zhen, he's too thin. Your armband shouldn't fit him, and I'm afraid it will."

The fleeting thought that I eavesdropped discomfited me, but they were well aware of my presence. I had not acted surreptitiously.

The main doors slid apart, and the talkative Recorder entered, his drone two meters behind and above him, tentacles writhing underneath it. Two marines flanked him, and the group headed toward us.

Michaelson tapped his speaker. "We've got a little more than two more hours before the shuttle gets back. That should be plenty of time to get that Recorder's shell and her drone. The Elder wants her shell destroyed, but the drone will go back up with the next shuttle."

"Even so." The Recorder's eyes went to me. "Zeta4542910—"

"That's not her name," Zhen snapped.

"Of course it's not her name." A grin lit his tawny eyes. "But she hasn't told me yet what she wants to be called, and her identification number is convenient. The point is," the Recorder continued, "I have been *volunteered* to help access the sealed Consortium quarters. And if we are going to return in time to meet the shuttle, I suggest we leave now."

Again, we arrived without incident, and despite the eerie fissures at the second turning, the talkative Recorder conversed easily with Michaelson, who accepted his unusual behavior without hesitation.

His drone connected with the security seal, and we had no problem breaking it and entering her small quarters.

Michaelson motioned us back and checked the room while we stood in the hall. The smile that frequently wreathed the talkative Recorder's lean face vanished as he and Michaelson pushed the medical pod from the silent quarters.

Once they had quit the small room, I entered to retrieve her drone. Other than a thin layer of dust, the room was tidy and bland, as Consortium quarters often appeared to citizens. The drone itself was yet in its charging alcove, but while I could enter the emergency stop codes manually, after two years of inactivity, I needed another drone to turn it on. The talkative Recorder graciously lent me his. It reached jointed arms into the charging alcove, and in less than thirty seconds, the other drone rose in the air like a silver moon and followed the pod out the door.

That silver moon would grant me the opportunity to save the others, but for a moment, I stood in the empty room, and again my heart pinched that the former occupant had been afforded nothing but a footnote. Surely someone had mourned her. Though there was no need, I did a quick inspection of the room. Wishing to make some small gesture, I plumped her dusty pillow and smoothed the blanket on her bed. My knuckles bumped something hard.

A peek over my shoulder confirmed I was alone. Michaelson and the Recorder had pushed the pod further down the hall, and both drones had followed. I lifted her pillow. A single piece of paper rested on top of a brilliantly green datapad. Careful to keep the food bars' wrappers from crinkling and drawing attention, I slid both items into the pocket on my left thigh.

"Recorder-that-isn't-Zeta?" Michaelson called from the corridor. "Planning on joining us?"

I complied, and the door whispered shut behind me.

Both drones hovered by the pod, long jointed arms hooked onto the front. Michaelson and the Recorder waited patiently, but I felt compelled to offer a partial explanation. "Nothing is out of order. No remembrances were left. No one missed her."

The talkative Recorder's forehead furrowed.

Michaelson gave a single nod. "Probably not, though no one deserves that." He scowled down the hall. "Except whatever dross released the virus that set all this in motion."

The talkative Recorder exhaled abruptly. "I will not argue with your statement."

Though I had no fondness for either Ross brother, part of me disagreed. If we all held value, would that not also extend to those who did wrong? Still, I only asked the Recorder to have his drone seal the quarters yet again.

We resumed the trek in silence, heading toward the control room on our way to the incinerator, where the Recorder would document the woman's disposal. We walked three abreast, and from time to time, I glanced at Michaelson and the Recorder, whose frown etched deep lines under his high cheekbones.

Numbering my steps offered some reassurance, but we had taken only three hundred forty when the overhead lights flickered out.

I could not breathe.

Michaelson's voice sounded in the dark: "Easy, Zeta."

His weapon's targeting beam brightened narrow sections of the hall before us, and the contrast made the shadows even darker. I blinked against the sharp light. Behind us, the Recorder's drone pulsed, then emitted a dull glow, which touched the backs of Michaelson's blue helmet and the Recorder's charcoal-and-black one with eerie green. Michaelson pulled a torch from his equipment belt. He clicked on the red light and extended the cylinder to me.

"I need you to hold this steady so my hands are free."

I suspected he lied or at least exaggerated, for I had seen Jordan and Nate carry both lights and weapons, but it was a kind offer. I inhaled as deeply as I could and held out my hand.

"Good. Keep it focused ahead."

As I did so, he turned to check behind us.

"We're clear," Michaelson said. "Recorder, your drone have better lights?"

The green light cast uneven shadows through the faceplate onto the Recorder's features. "The Elders deactivated those when I was sentenced."

Michaelson uttered a curse, then he paused before he said, "No."

My pulse stuttered at the terse word.

"Not so far, just the lights went out," he said, and I realized he was speaking to someone over the communications assembly. Anger at the Elder pinched at me, for he had denied me communication in the dark. The decision was unfair, unsafe, and isolating. Michaelson glanced at me. "Tristram thinks the bugs've been chewing on the wires. They're working on the emergency lighting. Keep the torch focused straight ahead so we can see where we're going."

I did. On my left, the talkative Recorder offered me a grimace, which might have been intended as a smile. I had already counted three hundred forty steps, so we had nearly reached the halfway point. It would not be long, since but two turns remained until we reached the control room. Then, we passed the split wall, and only one turn awaited us. After another fifty-seven strides, the blue emergency lights along the baseboards pulsed and brightened. They did not do much to alleviate the darkness, but at least we could see where we walked. Michaelson's targeting beam swept the hall, but neither it nor the green light reached the ceiling.

Above and ahead, something moved.

I froze.

Moons and stars. We should have been watching the ceiling.

For the fraction of a second before I raised the torch's beam to the arched ceiling, the drone's pale green glow reflected from multi-faceted eyes and hinted at a smooth carapace extending back into the shadows. That fleeting glimpse sufficed to yank my attention and hand up, and red light swept up to the unnatural insect watching us from above.

The men stopped abruptly, and the drones' forward momentum carried them into our backs.

Michaelson cursed under his breath. "Don't move."

The Recorder set a gloved hand on my arm, holding me steady. "We will not."

For three seconds, my lungs did not function. The roach's antennae twitched as it cocked its head, and it gripped the thick fire-suppression piping as easily as if it had been grasping a twig. I told myself that the scratchy sounds behind us were echoes, that there was only one.

The Recorder, however, jerked around, his back to the roach on the ceiling. Its head turned, and its eyes followed his movement.

"Michaelson." The Recorder's voice cracked. "It is not alone."

"Keep the light on that thing." The marine pivoted, then inhaled audibly over the tinny speaker. "And I thought *one* was bad."

The Recorder said, "We have, evidently, passed under many. Walking under one more will not present a challenge."

Had we?

While Michaelson called for backup, the scratching noises grew too loud to ignore. Despite his command, I spun around. My heart stopped, then slammed back into beating as the torchlight illuminated the hall past the pod.

"Moons and stars," I whispered.

Green and red glinted from distant eyes, eyes which grew closer in quick, uneven spurts. Dark carapaces gleamed from above in the torch's light, and the glowing blue baseboards lit underbellies below. Behind the closest ones, dim outlines of more coalesced in the shadows. My boots seemed welded to the floor, and I could not move. I would not be able to escape. Walking under a known threat was surely preferable to walking under the unseen many, but I could not do it. I knew I could not. Memory transplanted images over the hall before me—*forelegs snatching my drone from the air—mandibles crushing it*—I blinked rapidly.

A scratching thud spun me around to the first roach. It had finished its descent down the wall, and though its bulk did not fill the entire hallway, it blocked our passage. I staggered sideways and bumped the dead Recorder's drone. The pod it pulled shot backward several meters, and behind me, insectile feet scraped faintly on the floor.

Michaelson's targeting beam swung to the behemoth before me, and it reared up, forelegs curled in the air, mammoth head hardly a meter from the ceiling. I ducked as the weapon's percussive crack echoed up and down the stone and concrete hall.

A thud behind me—

The pod shot forward and knocked me to my knees. The Recorder hauled me to my feet, jerked me away from the pod, and shoved me behind him and against the wall. I dropped the torch, which rolled to a stop, spilling a pool of red light over tarsi on the concrete floor. I could not breathe, could not even count the legs—*why could I not count that high?*

I peeked from behind the Recorder at the roach that had sprung onto the pod. As if my attention summoned it, the insect jumped down. Jointed feet landed on the floor, the thicker clawed legs bending under the weight of a smoothly ridged abdomen. Forelegs touched down almost delicately.

The Recorder remained like a barrier between me and the pod, and to my right, Michaelson's weapon fired. Then twice more.

A second roach sprang onto the pod with unnatural ease, and its compound eyes seemed fixed on the Recorder's glowing drone. Its movement snapped me out of fear's paralysis.

It would *not* destroy his drone.

I would not let that happen again.

Not after Parker.

The memory of deactivating drones on *Agamemnon* surfaced. All at once, I saw what I had done wrong when mine was destroyed.

I pushed away from where I had been cowering against the wall. Ignoring the Recorder's sharp protests, I dodged around him. The massive insect rose on its hind legs as I dashed to the dead Recorder's drone and hit the access panel. The roach lowered its head when its antennae touched the ceiling.

My fingertips flew over the keys—*restraint and containment at all costs*—just as the roach dropped to all six legs and advanced on spiked feet toward the end of the pod. Behind me, the Recorder called out again, but the blood pounding in my ears and another percussive shot drowned his words.

*Faster.* I needed to be faster.

The drone released the pod.

I pulled the food bars from my pocket, tore the wrappers open, and threw them down the hall with all the force I could muster. At least three roaches turned to skitter after the scent of oats and blueberries, but the two nearest us advanced.

The dead Recorder's drone rose into the air, and both insects paused, eyes intent on the glowing drone.

All twelve of the drone's appendages extended out like a squid's tentacles, then it hurled itself straight into the creature perched on its former Recorder's medical pod. Tendrils twisted around the two-meter roach, knocking it down and into the other one. The jointed arms shot out like spears, and tentacles imprisoned both insects as their frantic kicks scraped the concrete floor. I stumbled backward into the talkative Recorder, who caught my arm, but his dilated eyes remained fixed on the battle before us.

Michaelson screamed, but the cry came to a gurgling halt, and something crashed behind me. For a split second I froze, but the Recorder released me, dove past my ankles, and snatched the torch from under the pod, barely out of reach of the writhing tangle of metal and exoskeletons. I spun around as the first roach bit down on Michaelson's arm, and the fact that he did not cry out terrified me further.

Fueled by adrenaline, I raced toward the marine, but the Recorder was faster than I. He charged past me and hurled himself against the roach's thorax, swinging the torch down like a knife at the insect's multifaceted eye.

It released Michaelson and jerked back. I dodged around the Recorder and grabbed the marine's legs, dragging him behind me over the cold concrete as I ran up the hall. From around the final corner, boots thundered toward us, but I did not stop until someone caught me by the shoulders.

Jordan.

Relief washed over me like a wave.

Zhen caught my other arm.

Two marines lifted Michaelson from my grasp and ran back up the hall while men and women in blue armored suits tore past us. One returned, half carrying the talkative Recorder. Unharmed, obedient, and still towing the pod, his drone followed at his heels. Seconds ran together into something immeasurable. An explosion shook the floor, and as the pressure wave hit, I nearly dropped to my knees. Jordan urged us on. Zhen never let go of my arm, but I glanced back.

Dust and ash billowed down the hall, and the last of the marines emerged from the cloud, like beings spawned from myths.

It was not until that moment that I realized I was crying.

Once more, stringent disinfectant pinched at my nose.

I stood by the door of the temporary infirmary while Williams and a field medic worked on stabilizing Michaelson and treating the talkative Recorder. I still did not know whether or not Michaelson would live nor the extent of the Recorder's injuries when Zhen quietly escorted me to a room down the hall.

I saw Jordan first. She stopped drumming long fingers on the table and focused golden-brown eyes on me.

Enlarged images of nanodevices rotated above Kyleigh's computer terminal, but she sprang to her feet. "Are you all right?"

"I am well."

"That's what that medic said, at least." Zhen dropped her helmet and cap on the chair next to Jordan and shook her blue plait free. "Though she barely checked."

"Others are more at risk." A clear flash of memory—*Michaelson, the roach*—and I shuddered.

Jordan stood, and as before, the armored suit added to her height. "Are you really all right?"

I started to tap my thigh but refrained when Zhen noticed and narrowed her eyes. "Nothing is wrong with me."

"You . . ." Kyleigh hesitated. "You look like something's wrong."

Of course something was wrong. Michaelson might be dying, and the talkative Recorder was injured. My words formed and tumbled and disappeared like steam.

"That was a mess, back there, with those roaches. It's nothing unusual if you had flashbacks." Jordan eyed me closely. "Are you sure you're all right?"

"No. Or rather, yes." I dodged Zhen, who paced the room, but how I felt was not entirely the point. "Williams hovers over Michaelson like a Caretaker over a suffering novice. His arm . . . Jordan, his arm." My words splintered. I slid into a chair and closed my eyes to calm my thoughts, but all I saw was that creature savaging him again and again. I could not let that image triumph over me, not when I had work to do.

"Max will be on his way shortly." Jordan's delicate brows drew down. "The announcement was made over commlinks, so don't worry about knowing something you shouldn't. The shuttle is preparing to leave *Thalassa*, so they're loading specialized equipment. Tim will get it here as soon as he can, probably around noon. Jackson has people setting up laser triggers and patrolling to make sure there isn't a repeat of this morning."

"Jordan," I protested, "Max's infirmary is better prepared to handle such injuries."

Zhen's pacing slowed. "True, but it would have taken more time to bundle Michaelson into the other shuttle, fire up the engines, and send him up, even if safety regs allowed both shuttles to leave at once. Which they don't. Moving him is dicey."

"And the Recorder? He . . . When I ran for Michaelson, he charged at . . ." I forced the image away. "I know Williams is busy with Michaelson, but the Recorder only had a field medic caring for him. She would not tell me how he fares."

Zhen spat out, "Without that dross-Elder—"

"Zhen." Jordan's beads made tired music when she shook her head.

"I'm not wrong, J, and you know it." She pulled out the chair next to mine and perched on the edge. "Although that Elder would have to march through Williams and every single marine on Pallas if he wanted this Recorder to die. Especially after Parker and after today." She growled something indecipherable. "My point is, without that Elder around, Williams was able to help him. Not that he needed much. Just a few cracked ribs and a gash where his suit was punctured. Not a bite, at least." She grimaced. "I knew that Williams wouldn't be able to tell me anything, so I eavesdropped."

"You should not have done so."

Zhen bared her teeth, almost like a smile, and nodded at me. "Learned from the best."

"His drone was transmitting to the control room," Kyleigh murmured. "We saw what you did."

"It was either brave or stupid, but since it worked, we'll go with brave." Zhen set her elbows on the table. "Still, I don't understand."

I attempted to raise one eyebrow in response, but instead, they jumped simultaneously.

"Why didn't the roaches smash the drone, like the other one did yours?"

My shoulders sagged. "Because I erred previously."

Kyleigh touched my arm.

I could not escape my errors, so I focused on the red lasers the marines had affixed over the ventilation grate. "When Nate and I first saw the roach, I panicked. I yanked my drone off the computer console and hurled it at the insect without addressing the previous programming. Neither did I transmit instructions via my neural implant. The drone tried to send me biological terminology about mandibles in an attempt to interpret the action through its data search of moments before. Foolish panic." Deflated pride tugged at me. "Never before had I dealt with something so entirely unexpected."

Jordan made a small noise of assent. "None of us had."

"Nevertheless, I erred."

"Well." Zhen rested her chin on her clasped fist. "I'm glad your voided drone is gone."

I shifted in my chair. "Additionally, this time I had the experience of dealing with rogue drones on *Agamemnon*."

"Tia told me about that," Kyleigh said. "About how you shut it down after it broke Eric's arm."

"Yes, and that encounter was the clue I lacked. I simply issued an appropriate command and keyed in the code for restraint and containment."

"And it worked." Jordan tapped the table with her index finger. "When the situation arose, you met the challenge."

"And saved both of them," Kyleigh added.

"I did not. It was the other Recorder who dove at the insect and—"

"You did well," Jordan said quietly. "I'm proud of you."

Her assertion brought my initial comments to a stop. No one had ever told me so before. When Zhen and Kyleigh echoed her statement, however, I shook my head.

"Although Michaelson and the Recorder as yet survive, I did not find a way to block the neural connection. My delay on *Thalassa* cost Parker her life."

Jordan drummed her fingers on her arms. "We'd already left before you had the chance, and you can't function without rest. Be reasonable."

"Even so, if my first friend, if James—" I sighed. "I cannot allow that. I must find that code. I have missed several opportunities so far, and I fear the station Recorder's drone is beyond use."

Zhen huffed. "If *beyond use* means on the other side of a pile of rocks, which are crawling with gigantic roaches, yes, I'd say *beyond use* is about right."

The roaches had gone after the drones, and that fixation put Recorders even more at risk. Without a drone myself, I could not succeed, but that knowledge confirmed what I needed to do. "And that is why I must leave before the Recorder is released from Williams's infirmary."

Kyleigh's faint eyebrows flew upward. "Leave for where?"

The last place I wanted to go. "The medical stasis bay."

Zhen shot to her feet, but Jordan merely cocked her head, gold-brown eyes trained on my face. Both Zhen and Kyleigh began speaking at once, but Jordan raised her hands, and they subsided.

"I need my drone."

"*Your* drone?" Zhen exclaimed. "You want to go back to the place where we first encountered those monsters and get the vile thing that controlled and punished you?"

I nodded.

"Drones are downright evil." Zhen spat the words. "And that place is probably crawling with bugs."

"Simmer down." Jordan leaned back infinitesimally and addressed me again. "Why?"

"I need a Consortium device to find a code that applies universally to Recorders and drones. The industrial cleaning bot collected and crushed the drone in the hangar—the one that injured both of us when it exploded, Jordan—before I reached it. I cannot utilize the one still connected to the control room's computers without the Elder knowing. The dead Recorder's drone is gone now, as Zhen says."

"And Parker's was destroyed," Jordan said. "But, yours was destroyed, as well."

"Yes, it was damaged, but it remains my best chance."

"Oh, stars above," Kyleigh whispered. "You can't."

"I must. It should not prove too difficult," I said, hoping that it was true. "I will need to find a way to bring it back here and to secure a private laboratory to work on it. We cannot allow the other Recorders—the talkative one and my friend James—to be endangered."

"You're right. We can't." Jordan's face tightened. "Max is the best man in the system, and he's been through enough, as if this"—she waved one gloved hand at the room—"bug-ridden moon and that virus aren't too much already. We can't let his son die. We have to keep James safe and then break both of you free."

I did not point out the futility of running from the Consortium, so the conversation lapsed into silence. After the count of thirty-seven, I stood.

"Right." Kyleigh straightened to her tallest, which was still fourteen centimeters shorter than Zhen. "I'll go with you."

"You will remain here." I did my best to imitate Jordan's authoritative manner. The attempt must have worked, for Kyleigh's expression fell, and she sank back into her chair. My voice softened. "I believe Freddie is coming on the shuttle." Could it have been only an hour ago that Michaelson announced the shuttle's arrival around noon? "And he will need you here."

"She's right, Kye," Jordan said. "Freddie doesn't have much left now."

"And we don't know how long it'll take, either," Zhen added. "You can't miss the ceremony."

I cleared my throat. "I remember the way. Once I reach the control room—"

"You can't go by yourself!" Kyleigh protested.

"I will not risk anyone else."

Jordan pressed her palms flat on the table. "Too bad. I'm going with you."

Injudicious relief swept over me. "Then you and I shall leave—"

"Oh no, you don't." Zhen tugged on her cap, straightened the communications assembly over her ear, and checked her weapon straps. "Where you go, I go."

"Zhen, there is no need—"

"Need? Of course there is. I let you out of my sight three times before." She ticked off her points on gloved fingers. "The first time, that dross-ridden Elder carted you off to a plague ship. The second time, he locked you up and made you watch someone die. The third time, you wandered off with Michaelson and barely escaped being bug food. That is *not* going to happen again."

"While your presence is not unwelcome—"

"I don't really care what you think." Her eyebrows quirked. "I let you die, and Nate will kill me. Then Alec will kill him, and then where will we be?"

A smile snuck across Jordan's face. "I'll have to kill Alec, and you'll all be gone. There will be nothing left to do but take everyone's credits and retire on an island on Ceres." Her smile melted away. "Kye, we'll escort you to the control room first." Her gaze swept from Zhen to me. "We have an errand to run."

Massive stalactites hung like crooked teeth over the nearly empty control room. I tried to ignore their presence and tightened my grip on the small duffel bag we had taken from a maintenance closet. Inside it, the borrowed microantigravity devices and tool kits jangled. Jordan, Zhen, and I walked Kyleigh over to where Jackson and two others stood at a secondary console, well away from the AAVA drone.

The dark-bearded marine from the hangar offered us a short smile before resuming his perusal of the readouts. The marine they called Lars, however, beamed and clapped me on the shoulder, nearly knocking me off my feet, then for no discernible reason, his face flamed to fuchsia.

"Going somewhere?" Jackson's rough voice was oddly hollow over his helmet's speaker, and his eyes swept from the bag over my shoulder to Kyleigh, Zhen, and Jordan.

"Not all of us." Kyleigh's voice sounded small. "They're leaving me here to meet Freddie Westruther for . . . you know."

He shot a look at Jordan, who directly met his eyes—she was a centimeter taller than he. She pointed her chin at the AAVA drone, then at me. One of his thick brows shot up.

"I must address Consortium affairs," I interjected, drawing everyone's attention. It was, after all, a version of the truth. Jackson's expression darkened, and I added, again, with more hopefulness than honesty, "It should not take long."

For eleven uneven seconds, Jackson studied me, then nodded once.

Lars thumped his chest with a gloved fist. "We'll get everything squared and see to your girl, here. It's a right good thing Maxwell will be here for Mike." He heaved a sigh. "It's all too bad. Really puts a damper on Westruther's reclamation service."

Zhen glared at him before striding to the side door, but Jordan stopped before Kyleigh.

"Stay safe, Kye. We'll try to be back before the shuttle gets here."

"That'd be good." Kyleigh swallowed. "I'll just...wait here with Jackson and everyone."

Uncertain of what to say, I lingered for half a minute until Kyleigh offered me a weak wave. Jordan and I left to join Zhen, and the door shut us out of the cavernous control room. A cleaning bot scuttled out of our way, and the smoothly shaped hall stretched on before us, now clear of dust and no longer enshrouded in darkness. I missed the murals, which brought another pang of loss for the beauty of invisible light. As we walked, however, my gaze continuously flitted over our surroundings—the walls and ceilings, before and behind us. The dread of the place I had lost my drone replaced any longing for ultraviolet.

By the time we reached the medical bay's double doors, all saliva had evaporated from my mouth. I tried to swallow anyway.

"Ready?" Jordan asked.

Zhen hefted her weapon. "Do we leave the doors open or closed? Closed, nothing gets past us. Open, we can, theoretically, make a run for it."

"Closed," I said before Jordan could answer. "For the safety of others."

I keyed in the access code. As the metal-sheathed panels slid smoothly apart, Jordan motioned for me to get behind her, and then she and Zhen moved forward. I shut the doors, and the sound of the magnetic seal clicking shut echoed in my head.

If my first excursion into the bay had seemed eerie, the second was worse. The bay—what we could see of it—was empty, though I knew my drone should lay beyond the curve. With the station's power restored, the pods and their control panels glowed, although I refused even a single glimpse at what remains might lie behind their windows. I had watched the recordings when the station's inhabitants had entered the pods, and some of their faces remained in my memory. I did not wish their images to be supplanted by glimpses of death.

Of all the things I missed, the ability to self-administer neurotransmitters eclipsed both knowledge and invisible light.

The hall-like bay with its rows of retractable pods angled gently to the right, and as we rounded that bend, I released the breath I had unknowingly held. A single door was missing at the end of the hall, and we could not see past the darkness lurking beyond the doorframe. Only my drone and the roach's carcass were visible.

"I'll watch the door," Jordan said. "You help her, Zhen."

Zhen stepped past the dead insect, then over the snake-like metallic tendrils to the drone. Averting my eyes, I skirted the dried stains on the floor while she tried to lift my drone's mangled remains one-handed.

"It will be heavy," I cautioned her.

"You think so?" She rolled her eyes. "You think a *giant chunk of metal* could be heavy?"

"Zhen," Jordan said.

I glanced at the dried exoskeleton, and bile burned my throat. Something had been eating it. "If we position the microantigravity devices first, when we lift the edges, I can slide them underneath quickly."

In response, Zhen moved to the opposite side of the drone and held out her hand. I pulled the devices from the bag, and we placed them at regular intervals around my drone's crushed edges, avoiding the sharper points across from the access panel where the roach had bitten it. Both of us shot a quick look at the doorway before Zhen squatted next to me. We slid our hands underneath and heaved. My arms burned with the effort. When the drone rose slightly, I let go with one hand and pushed the device underneath—

"Slipping!"

I yanked my hand back before I could activate the magnetic clamp, and the drone fell, nearly crushing my fingers.

"Did it get you?" Zhen demanded.

Wordlessly, I held my hand up.

Without taking her eyes from the door, Jordan demanded, "What happened?"

Zhen settled into a crouch. "J, I can't hold it up long enough for her to attach the devices. I nearly smashed her hand."

"I sustained no injury," I said to alleviate any concern, "although neither did I secure the device."

Jordan glanced at us then. "Let's hope dropping a drone on it didn't damage it. If we can't get those microantigrav devices working, that thing stays here."

"Leaving the drone is not an option. Without it, I cannot save the others." I held Zhen's gaze. "I need your help. I cannot—will not—fail this time."

Zhen's mouth pulled to the side. Without looking away, she said, "J, you could probably lift this even without my help."

Jordan chuckled softly. "Maybe not, but hint taken."

She joined us, and the two tucked their weapons out of the way and lifted the drone. I slid microantigravity devices underneath it one at a time. We all kept looking over at the door's dark hole, but when it came time to attach the final device, there was no choice but to turn our backs.

It clicked on, and I pivoted to face the gaping door before they set my drone down.

Nothing.

Relief rushed over me in a nearly physical wave. I activated the devices, and the small units buzzed as they slowly lifted my old drone a meter from the floor, though the side with the damaged unit wobbled.

For three and a half seconds, I waited for the drone to follow me. Of course it did not. My chest tightened, though I could not parse why.

"Well?" Zhen's soprano emerged harshly over her speaker. "Can we leave now?"

"Yes," I said aloud, though mental images fired in rapid succession.

My first glimpse of invisible light—long tentacles embracing me when anxiety took hold—a blanket tucked about my shoulder when I was ill—anonymous conversations over the Consortium network. Then, overpowering those memories, others surfaced. The drone's irregular reprimands—fear that I had erred and would be punished, though I dared not call it that—loneliness in my quarters while the drone guarded the door—Nate crying out as he was hurt for trying to help me—and pain. Always the threat of pain.

Two of my drone's thin tendrils lay near me, so I stooped to gather them in shaking, reluctant hands.

"Are you going to be all right with this?" Jordan's question snapped me to my feet.

"I shall be." The drone's sharp, crushed casing drew my focus again. "It is but a shell. The absence of its nonlife—"

"Can we chat later?" Zhen blurted. "We need to get out of here."

She was correct, of course.

I looped the duffel bag's handles over my shoulder. Steeling myself, I coiled the limp tendrils around my wrists and gave an experimental tug. The drone moved slowly, as if the air were thick, and its appendages scraped the floor, setting my teeth on edge.

I forgot to look when I shifted my weight backward. One of the roach's legs crackled under my boot, and in my haste to move away from it, I lost my balance and landed on the floor a mere decimeter from the exoskeleton. Concrete jarred my backbone, and the fall drove the air from my lungs. Tools clattered inside the bag. I dropped the tendrils and scooted away from the dried carcass, acid burning my throat again. Its eyeless, damaged head seemed to stare at me, which was nonsense, and I knew it.

Zhen hauled me up and gathered the duffel bag, but I could not look away from the creature that had changed my life.

"Focus." Her voice echoed in my ears. "We need to get out of here and hide that thing before the Recorder is up and documenting again."

Thing? Oh. Yes, the drone.

I tore my attention from the insect.

Behind her faceplate, Zhen's eyes seemed to measure mine. "Good." She held out the duffel bag, and while I placed it back over my shoulder, she snatched up all four tendrils from the floor, shoving two into my hands. My fingers gripped the whip-like metal, but even with her assistance, we were slow. We trudged toward the doors, towing the drone behind us.

Jordan walked backward on my other side, her focus still on the darkened door at the end of the hall. "Can't you go faster?"

"The devices do not propel the drone, only lift it, and those forces make forward momentum difficult."

"It's like we're pulling it through sludge, J."

Jordan hummed a noncommittal response, but as we approached the curve, she said, "I see movement."

Zhen released her tendrils and spun around, her weapon raised.

The drone dipped, and its forward momentum slowed. Her helmet's speaker amplified her exclamation. "Moons and stars!"

"Zhen," Jordan said quietly, "get her out of here."

Zhen grabbed my arm, but I shook off her hand.

"Not without my drone."

"Zhen! Now! I'll hold them off, but get her out."

I should not have, but I turned then. My fingers tightened on the tendrils as I stared over the damaged drone, past the dead roach to the dark rectangular doorframe, where low shapes crept in stops and starts. Leaving the drone was not an option. I wound the tendrils around my arms three times and threw my weight backward, eyes on Jordan's tall form, which stood between me and the dark opening. The tool kits slammed against my hip as the drone lurched toward me.

Gloved hands pulled at my arm.

Another glimpse of movement down the hall.

"You heard J!"

"Zhen—" I lunged backward again, and the drone moved a tad faster. I gritted my teeth. "I will not leave this."

"Move," she demanded. "We'll come back for it later!"

I yanked on the drone.

"I don't hear you leaving," Jordan said tersely.

"She's not—"

"Then help her, but get her out!"

Light flashed as she fired, and the weapon's report echoed through the hall, pummeling my eardrums. Afterimages hid the dark shapes. I could not simultaneously cover my ears and pull the drone.

With a growl, Zhen grabbed a tentacle and counted to three. In unison, we threw our weight backward, over and over. The hall blurred as perspiration dripped into my eyes. Jordan fired again, the echo masking the number of times—two? Seven? More?

Zhen and I rounded the corner. The drone's appendages scraped the concrete in grating counterpoint to the weapon's echoing percussion.

We could not see Jordan. I wanted to call out, to tell her to back up, to come with us. I yanked on the drone instead.

Light brightened from around the hall's curve as Jordan shot at the insects again.

Zhen said something about running out of rounds, and my stomach clenched. If Jordan stood between us and the insects—

I could not bear it if this decision, however necessary, cost me my friends.

*Please no.* The thought—or prayer—pounded with my pulse as I focused on moving one foot at a time, on the tugging and the breathing.

Zhen dropped her tendrils and disappeared.

She left me.

As her boots pounded away, the air in the medbay seemed to grow too thin. Then, dimly, I heard doors slide apart. She had only left to open them. We were almost out. Zhen returned, and together we pulled. My arms burned. Another sharp crack echoed, and Jordan's footfalls grew louder. I backed over the threshold, the drone following me through the door. Zhen cursed, let go, and raised her weapon.

Jordan thundered past me as Zhen hit the control panel. A shape charged at us.

Zhen fired, and the shape fell.

The doors' magnetic seal clicked shut.

I dropped the tendrils and leaned back to slide down the wall, my breath rasping in my chest.

"Well." Zhen exhaled loudly. "That was much closer than I like."

Jordan's eyes burned into me like golden lasers. "When I say get out, you need to get out."

"No."

Her nostrils flared.

"Not this time." Using the wall to brace myself, I stood. "Death awaits without this drone. Death for the talkative Recorder. Death for James." I did not add that it was also death for me, if the Elder discovered my intent.

For three seconds, she glowered, then closed her eyes. "I know." But that was all she said.

Despite Zhen's disapproval, I tapped my thigh over and over. "And yet, we did escape. If I can make this work, you have helped me save lives."

For a full, eternal minute, no one spoke, then Jordan said, "Next time—"

I placed my hand on her arm. "Next time, I—we—will again do what is necessary."

Jordan began to speak, then cocked her head to the side. She stiffened.

Zhen groaned. She turned to me and explained. "They're almost here. Williams released the other Recorder to document everything. We'd better hide this piece of rubbish before that dross-Elder finds out about it."

Again, we grabbed the dangling appendages, although Jordan and Zhen only grabbed one each, keeping their other hands on their weapons. No one spoke for forty-three steps, then Jordan ground out, "I don't like bugs."

I did not feel the need to assert that I did not, either.

Chilled perspiration made me shiver. I tucked my hands under my arms, but Zhen stood alert, her gaze sweeping the corridor's walls and ceilings, while Jordan inspected a conference room off the central hallway.

"It's clear. No roaches," Jordan said as she emerged. "I don't like setting up your makeshift lab so close to the control room and all its traffic, but it's this or chance another run-in with the bugs." She waved toward the doorway. "In you go."

Zhen and I towed in the drone and centered it over the long rectangular table, and I deactivated the microantigravity devices. The drone plummeted with such force that cracks shot like fault lines across the table's black surface. The appendages poured onto the floor. Avoiding them, I placed the duffel bag on the closest chair.

The warmth of incandescent lights made the room slightly more welcoming. Pale, faux-wooden cabinetry ran above and below the fabricated countertop, which extended along the wall to the left of the door, ending in a small sink. Floor to ceiling artwork in black, white, and shades of grey covered every wall in the room, and while I suspected the art was Freddie's, the subjects lacked the depth of his ultraviolet murals and resembled instead the flat figures on ancient Earth pottery.

A creak of the door's old-fashioned hinges brought my attention back to Jordan. With a metallic click, the latch slid into place.

She frowned. "We should have lubricated the hinges first. I didn't think of that."

"Well, at least with those old-fashioned things, you don't have sensors in the pockets," Zhen said. "Unless they rigged something in the frame."

Fear welled up.

While they inspected the door, I checked the ceiling for Consortium equipment. There. Paint camouflaged the device embedded in the corner at the far end of the room, above the running man and woman—

"I didn't see anything." Jordan said.

While they discussed sensors, I pushed a chair underneath the camera's single eye and climbed up, but even when I stood on my toes, my fingertips barely grazed the casing. I jumped down. Both women fell silent.

"I cannot reach it."

Jordan wove around the table to my side. "Is it working?"

Zhen snorted. "If it is, we're all spaced."

Jordan narrowed her eyes at the recording device. "That's been true since we first set foot on this rock."

"Or maybe since we signed that contract and boarded *Thalassa* in the first place."

Pushing aside a pointless suspicion that I had been the true cause of misfortune, I focused on the device itself. "I do not believe it is active." I pointed up at the indicator light. "The Elder managed to watch Parker die though he had disconnected the camera light on *Thalassa*, but doing so here on Pallas without physical access would take a level of sophistication . . ."

"What level?" Jordan prompted after my words faltered to a stop.

I backed up three paces, searching for further evidence the device was inactive. "When the station went dark, the documentation equipment powered down. I found no recordings on file after Westruther and SahnVeer activated the self-destruct. However, the AAVA drone is still plugged in, and the Elder might be able to access that feed. I do not know if the connection is strong enough for him to be able to—"

The camera exploded, and the noise reverberated in my bones. I stumbled back, hands over my ears.

Jordan caught my arm to keep me from falling. She pivoted toward Zhen. "Good stars above!"

Zhen lowered her weapon. "Nobody's using that camera now."

"Indeed," I managed, though my voice squeaked.

Jordan dusted off my shoulders and glared at Zhen.

Zhen, however, smirked. "That was the most satisfactory thing I've done in ages."

"That blast could have drawn attention—"

"I doubt it," Zhen said. "No one's around."

"If the device was recording, it is just as well," I managed. "Once I find the code to protect the others, I shall check the system to see if the Elder had access and transmitted the records to the Consortium."

"If he did, he did." Zhen's smirk disappeared. "If he has been spying, there's nothing that can be done about it, but I stand with you either way."

"Zhen, how many times—" Jordan paused, cocked her head to the side, and pursed her lips. Flipping open a small panel inside her left wrist, she clicked a button. "On our way." She clicked it again and turned to me. "Marines met the shuttle. They escorted Max to Michaelson, and Freddie to the . . ." Jordan rarely faltered, but she did then. "To his father's service. Kye's asked us to join them."

Zhen stared past Jordan to where the painted man and woman hid behind broad-leafed plants. "We should get moving."

"We can't lock the door, but there's nowhere else to leave that thing." Jordan motioned to the drone. "I'll go first and make sure the corridor is clear. Wait for confirmation."

"I cannot leave."

Zhen's eyebrows met over her nose. "Why?"

"This is, most likely, my only opportunity. Do you not see? With the Recorder occupied, the control room emptier than usual, and with less traffic in the hallways, this is the safest time."

Jordan shook her head. "You can't stay here alone. The room is cleared now, but there's no way to be sure those bugs can't get in through the air vents. And you need to give that drone a chance to power up—"

"Wait." Zhen's gaze shifted from me to the crushed ovoid shape on the table. "Powering that up is probably a bad plan, right? The Consortium would know."

I nodded.

Jordan breathed in a mild epithet. "Then why on any moon or planet did we just risk our lives to fetch it out of that infested medbay?"

Zhen nudged one limp tentacle with the toe of her boot. "You're planning to pull it apart and connect whatever pieces you need to your datapad, aren't you?"

Feeling like a child's marionette, I nodded again.

Jordan cocked her head. "So that's why you grabbed those tool kits."

"Indeed."

"Well, I am ever so sorry," Zhen drawled, "but we're not letting you stay here alone."

"Not showing up at the service will look suspicious." Jordan drummed her fingers on the butt of her weapon. "I don't like this. We don't have laser triggers inside the ventilation grids. Most of those bugs look too big to get through, but they certainly squeezed through a small enough fissure this morning."

"I cannot neglect this."

"Fine," Zhen snapped. "Fine. J, I'll stay here. Make some excuse about her needing to rest or something. After this morning, it wouldn't surprise anyone if she's not feeling good. Just tell Alec so he won't worry. And Tim, too. You'd better get going."

"No!" Sharp fear ricocheted through me at the thought of Jordan walking alone through the corridors when her ammunition might be depleted.

One of her delicate eyebrows rose.

I hit my thigh, but only once. "You will not go alone. You will not put yourself at such risk." In eight rapid strides, I stood before the door, arms outspread. "If you do not go together, you will not go at all. I will not allow it."

They exchanged glances, and the absurdity of my statement hit me. I, a rogue Recorder, had commanded two armored and armed citizens to stop, but the fear entangling my heart like a drone's tendrils prevented me from backing down.

"Please." The word hissed its way from my chest like steam from a leaking pipe. "Do not go alone. Take Zhen with you."

"You're saying that either we all go, or we all stay," Jordan stated.

"I shall be fine. You should leave. I cannot allow a repetition of Parker's death. I cannot allow other drones to be destroyed as mine was, not when the Elder refuses to allow Max to save the Recorders."

Zhen heaved a sigh. "As much as I hate the idea of letting Kyleigh down, if this is our one shot, we have to take it."

Keeping her eyes on mine, Jordan again flipped open her wrist panel. "Jackson, the Recorder-who-isn't-Zeta needs to rest . . . No injuries for any of us, or . . . Yes, we'll miss the services . . . After she rests, yes." She flinched and punched something else on the panel. "Tim. You heard that, did you? . . . We're fine . . . *She's* fine . . . Corridor next to the control room. Kye told us about it . . . If you can." She tapped her wrist and exhaled. "So what's next?"

Zhen flashed me a smile. "Learning how to disassemble a drone."

Although part of me still did not wish to reveal Consortium technology and secrets, there was no denying that she was correct.

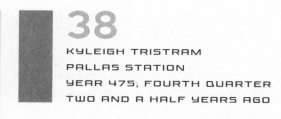

The clatter of utensils and the murmur of conversation filled the cafeteria as Kyleigh pushed sautéed spinach across her plate. "Someone should have noticed."

Freddie watched her, his earring twinkling though his eyes were serious, but Elliott asked, "Noticed what?" before shoving a forkful of vegetables into his mouth.

She glared at him. On top of not knowing the answer, it was irritating, really, that he could eat and eat and eat and still be lean.

"That the Recorder was gone," Freddie answered.

"And, Elliott Eugene Ross, if you say 'she's just a Recorder' again, I—I will do something *drastic*!"

Freddie's lips twitched. "Like what?"

"I'll think of something."

Unintimidated, Elliott only shrugged and took another bite.

She gave up on the spinach and reached for her chocolate pudding.

"She wasn't a bad sort." Freddie finished his coffee and set the mug down on his tray. "When Gideon called me and Elliott in after the mural incident, and Dad lectured us both, she was more than fair. Then, she stopped me a few ten-days later to tell me the murals were well done." His cheeks pinked. "Though she did point out some technicalities I hadn't noticed—"

"Which was rude," Elliott finished.

"Legitimate criticism is helpful, if not precisely enjoyable. It's not like a lot of people around here know much about art." Freddie stacked his dishes. "We talked some, a few ten-days back. She told me her assignments after university were at a bank, an art gallery, and then Albany City's Museum of Fine Art. She checked for forgeries and stuff."

"There were a couple Recorders in Julian's classes."

Kyleigh snuck a peek over her shoulder at Elliott's brother, who was eating with Christine again. Julian Ross had been with Dr. Christine Johnson for a couple quarters now, and some days, Kyleigh felt it was almost as if Christine set out to drive the brothers apart. She was obnoxiously condescending to Elliott, but only behind Ross's back, which was probably why she escaped the snide remarks Elliott's brother flung at other people. The whole situation set Kyleigh's teeth on edge.

Just then Christine laughed, tossing her long, honey-brown hair over her shoulder. Cheeks flushing, Ross leaned back and frowned.

Despite her occasional dislike for Elliott's older brother, Kyleigh felt a frisson of sympathy. She hated being laughed at, too. *Thinks she's the brightest star in the galaxy. She's not even much older than we are. Unless she takes nanotech supplements.*

Freddie slid his dessert in her direction. "She talked about that, too."

Kyleigh set her spoon down. "Who talked about what?"

He raised an eyebrow. "The Recorder. About being a student. The morning she stopped me in the hall to crit my mural, she mentioned something about the pressure to outperform citizens. She bit off her words pretty quick and shot a *look* at her drone."

"Recorders are just there to spy. They probably cheat. I mean, they can't take a test fair and square when they're hooked up to a flying encyclopedia."

"Regardless," Kyleigh intervened, not wanting to start down that road again with Elliott ranting about the Consortium. "I wonder if she ever felt lonely."

Freddie tucked a stray braid behind her ear, then placed his hand over hers. "I hope not."

Elliott choked, then tossed back the last of his water. "Maybe she did. I mean, I sometimes do, and I have you guys." He practically jumped to his feet. "I have to run more numbers on those cameras. And you know me and math."

Kyleigh shuddered. She'd been avoiding their lab for solid reasons. The insects had been as long as her forearm last time, and that was enough to give her nightmares. "So you're close, then?"

"I think so." Elliott's dark brows gathered over his nose. "They're growing much faster than we'd expected, and so far, the bioelectrically powered cameras hold up, unless the roaches run too fast. It's a good thing their speed doesn't scale up all the way. When they're small, they're about fifty body lengths per second, but there isn't a one-to-one correspondence, or they'd be running at who knows how many kilometers a minute."

Freddie withdrew his hand and turned his mug around and around. He cleared his throat. "Same with their weight. If we aren't careful with that, they might wind up being too heavy to cling to the ceiling."

"Freddie," Kyleigh protested. Maybe she shouldn't have eaten all that pudding. Not if they were going to talk bugs again.

Elliott stacked their trays on his. "Shouldn't be a problem on asteroids, with all the rough surfaces."

"Not when they can cling to—what did Dr. Johnson call them?" Freddie's pale green eyes focused on the ceiling. "Nano-somethings?"

"Almost. 'Micro-rough' surfaces, really, and with that adhesion-mediating stuff they secrete—"

Kyleigh clapped her palms over her ears. "You will *not* talk about this at dinner!"

Freddie tapped her shoulder, and she cautiously removed one hand.

"Dinner's over. But we'll stop, if you want."

"Sorry, Kye," Elliott mumbled.

He shuffled off, weaving between the tables to return the trays. When he passed his brother, Ross said something, and Elliott shook his head. A crease appeared between his older brother's brows, and Ross turned icy blue eyes on Kyleigh and Freddie. She raised her chin in response, and Ross's thick eyebrows drew down.

"So, to respond to your original statement, yes."

She turned back to Freddie. "What?"

"Someone should have noticed." He sighed. "She didn't show up for two days. It shouldn't have taken that long before they found her. Does Dr. Allen know what happened?"

"Dad was talking to him this morning, and I overheard." She glanced around, then whispered, "Heart attack."

Freddie's forehead creased. "But she was in good shape, though I guess that doesn't always matter. She couldn't have been more than, what, thirty-five?"

"Thirty-three. Dr. Allen was talking to Dad about potassium

solutions, but when he noticed me, he stopped and then said that being a Recorder was hard on internal organs, though he didn't say how." She chewed on her lip. "You remember, right? That I could have been one?"

His eyes fastened on hers. "Yes. Your aunt gave you to your mum and dad instead of to the Consortium, like most college students do."

"I can't help putting myself in the Recorder's place. She must've been so lonely here. And no one was with her in the end." Tears made her blink. "Dying all alone after a life with no family and friends?"

Freddie touched her cheek and then hugged her in front of everyone in the cafeteria. Together, they walked to the quarters she and Dad shared and sat on the floor in the hall, fingers intertwined. Alicia Brisbane hurried past, trying to hush little Allison, who was wailing loudly in her arms. Allison always cried at bedtime.

Kyleigh rested her cheek on Freddie's shoulder, and he kissed the top of her head.

"I wrote her notes."

Kyleigh sat upright so quickly that her head knocked his.

"Sorry," she said, touching his chin with her other hand. "You wrote to the Recorder? Why?"

"Yeah." He rolled his jaw experimentally. "I thought I was being all sneaky, but she knew." A sheepish grin spread across his face. "Of course she knew. She is—was—a Recorder. But when I thought about you and your parents and everything, I figured a few notes to tell her that she wasn't alone would be all right."

"Did she ever say anything?"

Freddie stared blankly at the ductwork overhead. "That was the strange thing, really. I was working with the insects late a couple ten-days ago, which wasn't as fun as it sounds, because they kept charging at me instead of scurrying away like they used to. Not even Christine Johnson knows why they're so aggressive now. Anyway, the Recorder just walked right into the lab without her drone."

"But—" Kyleigh hesitated. "That thing goes with her everywhere."

"I know. She set my notes on the counter and said she couldn't keep them but I'd made my point. Then she recommended I don't sound like a stalker if I write anonymous notes in the future. It seems anonymous notes that say *I see you* can have unintended meanings."

Kyleigh chuckled and nudged his shoulder. "She's not wrong."

He grimaced. "Point. But, I don't think I'll ever forget what she said next. 'Desist for your safety and my own. Leaving while my drone charges is not acceptable behavior, though worth the risk this time. But I thank you.' Then she actually smiled at me and left." Freddie straightened and pulled his small, older datapad from the cargo pocket on his left leg. "I drew this. This is her, when she smiled."

The device flashed, but instead of the three-dimensional display the newer ones had, the pictures remained flat. Nevertheless, the detail of the shadows and lines made it seem almost real. The station's Recorder smiled softly in grey and black, the gentle expression almost rendering her face unrecognizable.

Kyleigh traced it with her fingertips, and sudden moisture in her eyes made the image blur. "I wonder what she would have looked like as a citizen."

Freddie cleared his throat. "To tell the truth, I looked up similar faces on a few databases and started some drawings, but after a few tries, it felt disrespectful. Like I was making her into someone she wasn't. I deleted them, but I kept this."

Kyleigh closed her eyes for a moment and recalled the first time she'd seen the Recorder on the trip from New Triton to Pallas. Guilt pinched at her for thinking of her as a female instead of a woman, especially when she'd thought of the other one as a young man who could have been her friend, if the worlds were different.

This Recorder had always moved briskly, her drone at her side, tendrils snaking up her arm like vines. But in Freddie's portrait, the rigidity of her posture softened.

"I wish she could have seen this." A knot grew in her throat. "I wish I had seen her like you did."

"I didn't want to show anyone before." He held out his hand, and she passed the datapad back to him. "If my notes could've got her in trouble, someone finding this could have been worse."

"I hope they didn't, but there was no one here for her to be in trouble with."

"There was her drone." He leaned back against the wall. "She stopped by two other times, just didn't say anything. I don't think she was checking on me, more like she was looking for something or someone else."

"Maybe she just needed to escape her drone?"

"Maybe."

Their conversation lapsed, but the subsequent quiet lacked the usual calm that anchored her. He took her hand again, rubbing his thumb over hers. Slowly her missing peace returned, though it wasn't the same. They both stood, and he tipped her chin up to search her eyes. He wasn't too much taller than she was, but if she stood up on her toes—

The door next to them flew open. They both startled and moved apart, but Freddie kept hold of her hand. With his hair standing upright like a dim halo from old-Earth hagiography, her dad blinked near-sightedly at them. His glasses perched atop his head, as usual, half-hidden in the wild grey.

Dad peered at them. "Kyleigh? I've been—you didn't have dinner?"

"Of course we did," she began. "You didn't miss much this time, except—"

"No, no!" He blanched, then shook his head, and his hair grew even wilder. "Or . . . maybe it's all fine. I don't know yet."

She looked at Freddie. He shrugged.

"What do you mean, Dad?"

Her father ran a hand over his hair, knocking the glasses to the floor. Kyleigh picked them up before he stepped on this pair, too.

"Something is off, and I can't say what. She sent—" He shook his head. "Ah, never mind. I'm jumping to conclusions, though why she would've . . ."

"Dad?" Kyleigh asked. "Are you all right?"

Sometimes, Dad seemed lost in his own world, like he was unaware of anything other than the numbers he liked to play with, but this time, his eyes zeroed in on hers. "I don't know yet. I'll tell you when I know something, but for now, Kyleigh Rose, you be careful." He glanced at Freddie. "And you, young man. Be very aware of your surroundings. Go nowhere alone. Stick with packaged food, if you can."

Uneasiness prickled down her spine like insect legs. "That isn't funny."

He straightened to his full height, only a few centimeters taller than hers. "I've never been so serious in all my life."

Kyleigh looked at Freddie, who nodded solemnly at her father.

"We'll walk you home, then, Frederick."

She couldn't suppress a groan. "Dad."

"What do you think 'not alone' means, Kye?" He patted his pockets and ran his hand over his head. "I'll just need to find my glasses first. I can't very well be alert when I can't see."

Wordlessly, she held them out.

"Ah, yes, thank you, sweetie." He closed the door and locked it. "Come along, Frederick."

The three of them turned right and made their way up the halls. When they reached the Westruthers' quarters, Dad waved his arm expansively.

"You two say good night. I'll wait a minute." Dad's eyebrows waggled, and his usual soft grin returned.

"Dad!" Kyleigh's cheeks heated enough to glow in the dark.

"I was young once, too, even if I don't look it." And with that, he turned to face the hallway, like he was on guard duty. "Timer's going."

Kyleigh rolled her eyes and gave Freddie a quick hug. "Good night."

"You'll be careful?" Freddie brushed his knuckles down her cheek. "Your dad's plenty smart. Wait for me tomorrow before heading to class or the lab, all right? And message me later?"

When she nodded, Freddie placed a light kiss on her forehead, said good night, and closed the door behind him.

Kyleigh and her father returned to their quarters, their boots clicking in the quiet, but somehow, Pallas Station's grey halls no longer felt like home.

Jordan leaned against the counter to my right, while I reattached the drone's access panel and Zhen put away the tools. Williams's purple datapad charged on the black counter, since it had run down over the past thirty-seven hours.

Had it only been that long?

A sigh rippled through me.

I patted the pocket where the datapad I had snuck from under the Recorder's pillow remained safely hidden. The paper I had found with it crinkled, but neither Jordan nor Zhen noticed. I had yet to unfold it to see what possible secret the Recorder had tucked away, though there was no good explanation for my reluctance. Surely Jordan and Zhen would not be too inquisitive.

My stomach grumbled.

"You, too?" Zhen clicked the second toolbox shut and placed both back into the duffel bag. "Moons and stars, breakfast was far too long ago. J, can you ask Alec and Tim to bring us something to eat?"

"I don't want to disturb the service, but if it comes to that, we'll go find something." Jordan glanced at me. "How are you doing with that thing?"

"Incomplete." There was naught to do but wait, so I leaned back against the counter and surveyed the murals again, averting my eyes from the remains of my drone.

To my left, immediately across from the door, the outlines of a man and woman rested in a lush garden, surrounded by animals. The wall opposite the cabinets showed the same man and woman eating fruit, juice running in black rivulets down their chins, then they hid behind broad-leafed plants. On the last wall, no longer hand in hand, they fled, clad in furs, toward the room's door, which was framed by two monstrously large, four-winged humanoids, flaming swords in hand. The gatekeepers wept scalding, white tears but stood resolute and stern.

I disliked it. It was not reassuring, and I understood neither the images nor why anyone would choose to paint it. Perhaps Freddie— if he indeed had been the artist—had not asked permission for this mural, either. Perhaps he had painted mural after mural without official approval.

Tearing my gaze from the uncomfortable images, I asked Jordan, "Is there any news on Michaelson?"

She puffed out a breath. "Not yet, but that doesn't mean anything. Whether or not they're supposed to say, someone will let us know when he's clear." She cocked her head. After twenty-three seconds, she added, "Services ended. They'll be here shortly."

She neither clarified who might provide information about Michaelson nor who would be joining us.

Minutes crept past, and my datapad remained silent. Anxiety raced up my spine on skeletal tiptoes. With nothing to do but wait, I began coiling the drone's long appendages and placing them under the table. Zhen joined me, though her booted kicks made the tendrils skitter across the concrete floor like living things, occasionally knocking over the ones I had neatly rolled. Once that task was finished and without verbally coordinating our actions, the three of us took up positions to block the line of sight from the door to the defunct drone.

I tapped my thigh.

Zhen caught my hand, though her dark eyes were gentle. "Don't."

The door latch clicked. Jordan and Zhen raised their weapons.

When it swung open, Nate entered. Relief washed over me. His gaze swept the room, then fastened on mine, but when he ushered in Eric, Kyleigh, and Freddie, who wore Zhen's green-and-white band around his upper arm, my relief evaporated. Alec shut the door behind them.

"Zeta!" Eric exclaimed. "Founders' sakes, but I'm glad you're okay."

Zhen tensed.

Before she could again protest the appellation, I turned to Nathaniel and Alec. "Why? Why bring them here, where the knowledge of what we are doing could endanger them?"

Nate frowned, but Alec answered, "Can't leave them in the infirmary, and there was a roach incursion on the way to the secured area. Marines are cleaning that up right now. Should be safe, soon enough."

Horror replaced my concern. Attempting to school my face into neutrality, I merely nodded.

Without a word, Nate reached into a pocket on his belt, extracted a communication link, and placed it in my gloveless hand.

"Archimedes sent it," Alec offered in explanation. "You were supposed to have it yesterday, but then, you weren't supposed to wind up on this rock."

Zhen glared at me. "Don't fry this one."

My fingers tightened around the link. "Such was never my intention."

"We know," Alec said. "Smith supposedly patched it into our commlinks, but it ought to be checked first. She was too much North's sycophant for me to trust her, no matter what Archimedes says."

I placed the communication link in my outside pocket, then caught Nate's gloved hand in mine. It was not the same, holding gloves rather than his fingers.

Zhen cleared her throat. "Freddie . . . I'm sorry."

The lines of tension on Jordan's face changed subtly. "I'm sorry, too. I wanted to be there."

"It's all right." His pale green gaze fell to his booted feet. "A bunch of the marines came, though maybe they had to, and Jackson said a few words. That Recorder documented it, so I'll have an official datachip when we get back to *Thalassa*."

Kyleigh rested her helmeted head on his shoulder, but her gaze settled on me. "We understand."

Freddie raised his eyes from the floor. "No one else should die. Bad enough already." He looked up at the unfinished, cave-like ceiling and blinked rapidly. "When Dad said goodbye, I knew I wouldn't see him again. I thought I'd processed all that in dreams, but"—his throat worked—"being there is different."

"I understand. Losing a parent . . ." Alec trailed off, and he laid a hand on Freddie's shoulder. "It was an honor to be present."

In an instant, Zhen was at Alec's side, and he pulled her into a short hug. Zhen's movement, however, gave Kyleigh her first glimpse of the mangled Consortium equipment on the table.

She gasped. "That monster did a number on your drone. I haven't seen a live roach yet, and I really don't want to."

"I don't want you to, either," Freddie said. "You didn't like them when they were small. Now that they're gigantic . . . Plus, well, it's not safe."

Still eying the drone, Kyleigh asked, "Did you have any trouble getting that thing?"

I caught my lip between my teeth, but before I could tell the truth, Zhen spoke up. "Not much, though J's low on incendiary rounds now."

Nate scowled at her. "I'm pretty sure part of that is a lie."

"An understatement." Zhen shrugged. "Let's just say that we should avoid the medical storage bay."

Alec's frown rivalled Nate's. "Zhen—"

"She's not even in a suit." Nate's glare switched from her to Jordan. "That's—"

My datapad chimed, and I pulled away from Nate to check it. He followed me, and I wished suddenly for hot chocolate, the safety of my computer laboratory on *Thalassa*, and just Nate. No one else.

"Is it finished?" Jordan asked.

The station Recorder's green datapad thumped my leg when I turned. "It is still incomplete."

"What's next, then?" Eric asked.

Freddie spoke before I could answer. "It's my fault."

We all turned to him.

Behind the faceplate, Eric's red-brown brows drew down. "For what?"

"That." Freddie pointed to my drone. "For everyone dying. For the whole spacing, void-ridden mess."

Kyleigh dropped into a chair. Behind me, the datapad chirped again, but I only gave it a cursory glance.

"I doubt it." Jordan folded her arms. "How on any known planet are those monsters your doing?"

Freddie's words tumbled out haphazardly as he described losing his art supplies in punishment for painting the murals and confessed to adding additional hormones to their experiment to speed the roaches' growth so he could earn back his paints sooner. His face flushed further after a quick glance at Kyleigh, and his chronology grew even more muddled.

"I can't let Freddie take all the blame," Kyleigh interjected. "I was supposed to kill them. I saved the cats and tried to save the rats, but I didn't kill the insects. They were big and disgusting, and I couldn't do it."

"That wouldn't have mattered if I hadn't cheated."

Jordan studied them both, her fingers tapping an uneven rhythm on her suit's upper arm.

After nineteen seconds of quiet, Zhen dragged a chair next to Kyleigh's and perched gracefully on the edge. "There wouldn't have been any bugs here if not for that experiment, but do you blame Freddie?"

Kyleigh sniffled. "Of course not!"

"Try extending some of that mercy to yourself," Alec said gently.

Freddie turned to face the wall across from the cabinets, his back to the rest of us.

"My uncle Brian says emotions are tools," Eric added. "So, guilt's like, say, an arc welder."

Freddie looked back at him. "What?"

Eric's cheeks grew pink. "Or maybe a wrench. I mean, a wrench isn't a bad thing at all. Just can't go around walloping yourself, friends, and random strangers with it, instead of using it to torque loose bolts. You'd get sentenced for that, eh? You have to use it to fix the right things."

"Maybe." Freddie turned away.

I attempted to visualize emotions as wrenches and arc welders but failed, so it was a relief when my datapad chimed twice more. Nate removed his helmet, though not his cap, and remained at my side, almost close enough that our arms touched. The ebb and flow of conversation washed past, but Nate's presence steadied me while I worked. At last, a pattern emerged under my fingers.

"I think I have something," I whispered to him.

He leaned his elbows on the counter and watched the data move. "You know this isn't my forte, sweetheart. Tell me what I'm seeing."

I moved to point out the progress, then fisted my hand. "I should not."

He chuckled, and the sound warmed my heart like hot chocolate. "I'd say it's a little late to leave me in the dark. In kind of deep now. Question is, will it work?"

"I will not know for certain until we try it. If it is successful, it will disrupt Consortium neural implants within a five-meter radius, effectively turning them off. Beyond that range, implants will switch back on." I paused. "It is insufficient and will not protect Recorders more permanently."

"A short-range off switch? On this datapad?" He touched the elaborate web of cables and equipment spread across the countertop. "Or will you need all this?"

"If it works, no. If it does not, they will remain at risk."

"Hey. Look at me." When I again refused to answer him and meet his eyes, Nate gently turned me to face him. Though dark-blond stubble outlined his jaw and fatigue shadowed his eyes, his expression softened. "I have faith in you."

My cheeks heated, so I ducked away and began disconnecting the thin cables.

"You're done?" Alec asked.

Nate straightened. "We've got a prototype."

"Knew it!" Eric whooped. "So, we can set the other Recorders free now?"

"It is not that simple. There is no degree of certainty that this will succeed."

"I'll test it." Jordan held out her hand. "It's already running?"

I cradled the datapad to my chest. "This is my responsibility."

"If I take it and it works, you won't be there when the implants turn off, which might keep you safer from the Elder. If it doesn't work, it won't matter. Additionally, Jackson is expecting me, and chances are that the other Recorder will be with him."

"Let J take it," Nate urged me. "She'll be fine."

Despite the magnitude of my personal trepidation, I handed her the datapad. Jordan snapped it into the pocket on her right leg.

Eric jumped to his feet. "Right, then. I'm ready."

Zhen raised one eyebrow, and Alec's mouth twitched.

"No," Jordan said. "Zhen and Alec, you're with me. We'll find the Recorder to check the datapad's efficacy and warn Jackson of the intrusion in the medbay, then track down some food. Eric, you and Tim stay here. I'm not comfortable leaving these three"—she nodded at Kyleigh and Freddie, then me—"here without protection, and *she* won't leave that lump of metal behind." Her eyes smiled. "But I've seen you shoot, Eric. With you and Nate here, I won't worry."

The young man's jaw dropped. He simply stood watching Jordan while Zhen checked her weapon.

On the way past Eric, Alec clapped him on the shoulder. "We trust you."

The door clicked shut, and Eric glanced at Nate. "Did she mean that?"

"Zhen might exaggerate from time to time"—Nate's dimple appeared—"but J doesn't lie."

Eric beamed. "Nice."

I paced the room, my mind racing through outcomes for trying out that device. My fist tapped my leg, and I could almost feel Nate watching me. I stopped again, staring at the door.

"It's some of my earlier stuff." Freddie seemed to have materialized at my side.

Temporarily confused, my gaze switched from him to the murals. "Your paintings? If it is a story, I neither recognize it nor find it pleasant."

"It isn't meant to be." His gaze slid to the fleeing man and woman and the guardians at the doorway. "It makes more sense in invisible light."

"I would not know," I said.

Nate walked up behind me. I leaned back against his chest, wishing that he need not wear armor, so I could feel his heartbeat. Quietly, he asked, "Do you miss it?"

I nodded.

Freddie raised his eyes to the ceiling, and the diamonds in his ears winked. "Losing infrared gradually was hard. Having all that light ripped away at once must've been awful."

I swallowed past the lump in my throat. "I survived. You will as well."

Freddie shook his head. "I thought I'd already lost UV when I woke up and couldn't see Kye's freckles."

"What?" Kyleigh bolted upright. "I don't have freckles."

"You did," he asserted. Her hands rose to the sides of her helmet, and he offered her a lopsided smile. "Sun damage, but the tank healed it. Your face is still perfect"—he stammered for two seconds—"perfectly smooth."

Her gaze fell, then met his through her short lashes, and color tinged her cheeks.

My own cheeks warmed when once more my stomach protested aloud. Behind me, a pocket snapped and something crackled.

"Hey, Zeta."

Nate and I turned as one.

Eric grinned. "Catch."

This time, I snatched the food bar from the air myself. Cinnamon and peach.

"We got you," Eric said.

Nate's dimple peeked at me. "Always."

# 40

In the holding cell on *Agamemnon*, I had imagined spending the afternoon with my Nathaniel. I had not, however, envisioned doing so under the unspoken threats of insectile behemoths and an erratic Elder. Three other people had not been present, either, nor had my destroyed, disemboweled-then-reassembled drone, which crouched on the table behind me.

Nevertheless, Nate's presence at the counter steadied me. My hands did not shake as I placed the thin cables and equipment from the cabinets into the duffel bag. It would not do to abandon equipment, should we be required to leave precipitously, and it was simple enough to unpack everything if I could continue to use the room. Williams's violet datapad finished charging. I slid the station Recorder's green one from my pocket onto the charging station, turned my back to the room, and pulled out her paper. Only a decimeter long, it been folded into thirds. I lifted the top flap.

*I see you.*

A chill swept up and down my arms. Was it a threat or an observation? I hastily unfolded the last third, where the same flowing script read, *You have value, and you are not alone.*

Relief supplanted concern. Someone had seen her, and she had known. The message must have held value as well, since she had dared discovery to keep it, but the note was not meant for me. I folded it quickly and shoved it back into my pocket. It should have been cremated with her. Guilt, regret, and something like longing washed over me.

"You okay?" Nate asked quietly.

Right then, I wanted nothing more than to rest against him, to hear his heart, to linger there. Instead, I said, "It is . . . not nothing, but I am well."

The pause before his answer lifted my gaze. "We'll get out of this. And we'll find a way to set you free."

"That is not . . ." But it was, indeed, the crux of the matter, and saying otherwise would be to tell a lie I could not bear. Not to Nate.

His voice softened, drawing me closer. "Whatever it takes, sweetheart."

I leaned against his arm, and oh, I wanted to believe him. Before I could say anything, however, his communication link chimed. The others' subdued conversation ceased.

He did not shift away from me, but his voice returned to a normal pitch. "Timmons, here."

"I have mixed news." Jordan's transmitted words were clearer than they had been over her helmet's speaker. "The good is that Michaelson is stable. The bad is that he's lost his arm. Max and Williams are going to watch him tonight and send him up to *Thalassa* tomorrow morning with Johansen. Some marines pulled the portable medtank from the other shuttle, and Max has been programming it as best he can to get the nanites to repair nerve damage both so his arm won't ghost and to stave off any infection."

My early relief that he was stable fled, and I choked down a half-sob.

Nate set a gloved hand on my shoulder. "Anything else, J?"

"Yes." Her tone shifted. "Tim, I found Jackson and caught him up. That Recorder was there, too, and—"

Footfalls interrupted her. Her channel clicked off, as if she had paused the link. Nate's perfect eyebrows drew down, but when the link resumed, Jordan was chuckling, which seemed highly inappropriate.

"I'll fill you in once we find some food. Don't let our girl fall over before then."

"Eric shared a snack," I offered to alleviate any concern.

"Good. We'll be back in about twenty, and we'll have company." She signed off.

Eric grinned. "Bet that means it worked."

"I hope so," Kyleigh said. "But if it did, what's next?"

"If it did indeed protect the Recorder, I must increase its effective radius and create additional devices." After quickly reviewing all I had and lacked, I frowned. "I do not have the materials I require."

Freddie's smile shone as brightly as his diamonds. "I'm supposed to go back up to *Thalassa* tomorrow morning. I'm not much use here, and I know it." He waved off Kyleigh's protestation. "It's true, Kye. Up there, I can gather supplies and send them down to you, though that'll be a day at least."

"I can bring 'em," Eric offered, "and no one will even blink if I have a large bag of things. They'll just think I have extra snacks."

"That's not soon enough to keep the Recorder safe, though." Kyleigh stood, her focus on the drone.

Freddie gestured toward the locked cabinets. "You might find more stuff in those."

"It is where we found the cables," I admitted. "Though I did not see much else."

"That's strange. It had all of Elliott's electronics in it. I was with him when he stowed it all, before we went into the tanks." Freddie opened random cabinet doors and frowned at the empty shelves. "This was one of our study rooms. Elliott could've made the jammer, you know. He was good with puzzles and tinkering with small things."

"Don't you talk about him." Kyleigh's face grew taut. "After what he did—"

Freddie said quietly, "You told me he said he didn't mean to hurt her, only to stop her."

Before they could resolve their dispute, the latch clicked. Kyleigh, Freddie, and I froze, but in the time it took for the handle to rotate, Nate moved between me and the door, and he and Eric raised their weapons. The door swung open. My flash of concern that Eric would act impetuously as he had on *Agamemnon* was unmerited, for he remained calm, even when a man demanded, "Where is she?"

I peeked around Nate.

A grin split the talkative Recorder's face. "Ah! You!" He started toward me, and when I cringed back, he stopped and held up gloved hands. "How did you do it?"

The room grew too small again when Jordan, Alec, and Zhen followed him in and shut the door. Nate lowered his weapon.

No drone had followed the Recorder. Had it worked?

"I don't even care if that voided Elder is going to burn me for this."

The Recorder threw back his head and laughed, then his hand went to his ribcage, and he exhaled slowly. "They were going to space me anyway, but do you know—for the first time since they gave me that monstrosity—I can *think*!"

"Then . . . you do not mind?" I said tentatively.

The smile remained in his eyes. "Not all Recorders would be pleased, but if this means what I think it does, I might be safer this way, and I thank you."

Some of my tension dissolved like salt in warm water, dispersing invisibly. "Indeed. Then I have more work to do. Nate?"

One perfect eyebrow rose. "Yes?"

"Are we secure? Dare I spend more time creating additional devices?"

"We'll make the time."

I unzipped the duffel bag and began removing the cabling. "I shall need more materials to complete the task."

"More datapads?" Jordan asked.

"I have this." Kyleigh pulled a tiny, flowered one from a pocket and placed it in my hands. "I know where more are—or were."

The flowery datapad was not inconspicuous, but the green datapad was not fully charged, and I would not erase any records it held until I had viewed them.

Kyleigh glanced at the drone, then the vent near the ceiling. "Someone could go with me. Not you, Freddie," she said quickly, "because if we have to run, you'd be in trouble."

Alec motioned to the door. "You three need to eat. Tim, Eric, want to help me and Kye track down some datapads?"

Nate was already fastening on his helmet. His gloved fingers brushed my arm, and though he did not say goodbye, his eyes met mine before he turned to leave, and somehow, that sufficed.

Jordan and Zhen set prepackaged foods on the far end of the table, away from my drone.

"If you will excuse me," I said, "I have work to do."

"Right." The talkative Recorder unfastened his helmet and pulled off his gloves. "Where do we start?"

My previous behavior had already condemned me, but had it not, showing the talkative Recorder how to reconfigure Kyleigh's flowered datapad into what Freddie called a jamming device would surely have sent both of us to the Hall of Reclamation.

Jordan, Zhen, and Freddie ate quietly at the far end of the table, their helmets piled around my blue datapad, while I showed the Recorder codes, frequencies, and how to create the signal. When we finished, Zhen brought me the navy datapad. Feeling as if I were balancing on a knife's blade, I shut it down. Jordan, Zhen, Freddie, and I held our collective breaths and turned to the Recorder.

For three seconds, the talkative Recorder was silent, then he slumped back against the counter. His eyes closed, and a smile wreathed his face. "I still can't feel a thing. The second datapad works, too. It's as if there had never been a drone at all."

He sprang upright, snatched the flowered datapad, and managed to stuff it inside his mottled grey Consortium suit.

Still, I frowned. "This is insufficient. No charge holds forever, and we have no idea how rapidly this will drain power. Additionally, its range is too small."

Zhen tossed me a bottle of water and asked, "So what do we need to do?"

"We need uninterrupted power and a range that would cover the entire station."

The talkative Recorder whistled. "You do not ask much, do you?"

"I only ask what is necessary."

The green datapad chimed, and I took it from the charger and attempted circumspection by tucking it into my pocket.

"If we are in dire need of supplies, why didn't you use that one?"

I stiffened at Zhen's question.

"I understand why you don't want to give away yours with all the information you stuffed onto it, but that green one is new. You didn't have it on *Thalassa*. And given the cause, Williams probably wouldn't mind if you overwrote that romance novel you were reading."

"I was not—"

"The station Recorder used to have a green one like that." Freddie's comment covered my protest. "Never saw it during the day, but she carried it around when she was wandering the halls at night."

Jordan pivoted in her chair to face him. "Without her drone?"

The talkative Recorder tilted his head to the left. "It's unusual for any of us to leave quarters without a drone. It is, indeed, one of the things that provoked my sentencing."

Zhen's dark eyes shifted between me and the Recorder at my side. "Maybe Recorders are more unusual than we used to think."

Jordan studied me. "So where did you get that one?"

My mouth opened and closed, but I could not find the words.

She leaned forward, elbows on the table and gloved fingers interlaced. "Is it hers?"

"Yes." I exhaled. "I found it hidden in her quarters."

"What's on it?"

"I have not yet looked, Jordan, and I do not know if she had passwords preventing access."

"Go ahead, then." She leaned back against the chair. "Take a look. If nothing's on it, make a backup jammer."

They all gathered around me, their attention riveted on the green datapad in my hands. Reluctantly, I initialized it, and to my surprise, it opened with no difficulty at all.

"No passcode?" Zhen arched an eyebrow. "That seems rash."

"Indeed," I said, skimming a short entry. "But she believed that the only people who would find this were Consortium, so it was pointless to create a password they would break with little effort."

With a quick chirp, a small image appeared.

"That's her," Freddie exclaimed, but Zhen shushed him.

The Recorder's tiny, translucent projection stood rigid and stiff. "I am creating this to document my concerns and evaluate them before beginning a formal investigation. My drone has evidence that someone has been tampering with the records for several laboratories, but not wishing to act based on prejudicial assumptions, I am pursuing investigation alone while it charges. I have seen enough manipulations of the record and do not wish to continue that legacy by jumping to conclusions and unfairly damaging the reputation of potentially innocent citizens.

"I grow more and more convinced that Parliament's concern of industrial espionage only touches on the tip of the potential disaster. Someone is using the laboratories on the southern wings to create what I believe to be a bioweapon aimed at the Consortium. Again, this is supposition. I leave this—and subsequent—records on the slim probability that I am correct and do not make my case in time, and they indeed act in violation of the law."

Her image fell silent, and an index appeared. For the next ten minutes, we reviewed summaries. Apparently the disappearances of potassium chloride, agar plates, and other supplies had not provided sufficient proof. She had suspected criminal activity but, as a Recorder, had not notified Gideon Lorde, the head of security. Her sole thought had been tracking down documentation, though whether or not she intended to do anything other than report to the Consortium itself remained unclear.

A chill swept over me. She had been right. I was surprised that she did not name particular offenders, but indeed, the uncomfortable distrust between Consortium and citizen might have played a role in her death. She should have told John Westruther and Gideon Lorde.

Moisture filmed Freddie's eyes. "She wasn't a bad sort, and this must have been what Kye's dad was going on about when he said that we needed to be careful."

"Potassium chloride," Jordan said slowly. "That's used in surgery to stop the heart."

Freddie's pale eyes went wide. "Dr. Allen said she'd had a heart attack."

"That doesn't mean that was the cause of death," Zhen stated, "though it's probably too late to tell now."

"Indeed." The talkative Recorder crossed his arms, and his browless forehead creased. "But the likelihood is that someone stopped her investigation, especially given what we know of Charles Tristram's death and the development of the virus. This Recorder was correct in her theories."

"So, someone killed her, like they killed Kye's dad." Freddie's eyes went to me. "You'll find out who, won't you?"

"I bet it was Julian Voided Ross," Zhen growled.

Supposition was not fact, and since Ross had denied harming Charles Tristram while confessing to the virus, I did not comment on her assertion.

A divot appeared over the talkative Recorder's nose. "You cannot base an accusation on personal distaste—"

"That philosophy worked really well for her," Zhen retorted. "Didn't it?"

Jordan's communication link chimed, and when she answered it, Jackson's disembodied voice said, "We have an emergency request for transport to *Thalassa*."

"What now?" she said in an undertone before adding more loudly, "Does Archimedes need us? Or is it medical?"

"Neither," Jackson growled. "It's that Elder."

I glanced at the talkative Recorder, who had gone still.

Zhen leaned forward. "What does he want?"

"He seems to think Parker's replacement went missing. I told him the Recorder was still here and reminded him that Johansen is taking Michaelson up in the morning, but that isn't good enough. It's a waste of fuel and time, but Johansen and Osmund just left."

I shivered. It seemed I had not thought my plan all the way through.

Jordan clicked her communication link again and stared at the cabinets behind me. "Well. You have a little over three hours to fix your master jammer."

"Right." The talkative Recorder snatched up his helmet and gloves.

Jordan eyed him. "Are you going somewhere?"

He fastened his helmet with a click. "Of course I am."

"It is not safe," I protested. "You should go nowhere without armed escort."

He pulled on his gloves. "I won't go far. Your jammer works well enough that the Elder thinks I've disappeared, but as you said, we don't have a permanent solution. We need a station-wide device, or at least one with a broader reach. And my guess is that my drone can provide that. I left it in the control room, where it is now probably scaring people, the way it just hovers there, unattended." He paused before turning the door's handle and grinned at us all. "I'll be right back."

# 41

Frigid air billowed past me as the hangar's massive doors ground shut, and the change in pressure made my ears pop. I covered my mouth and yawned.

Only the talkative Recorder and I had joined the three marines who met the shuttle. The Recorder was breathing more heavily than usual, and his skin had paled.

Jordan and Nate had wanted to accompany me, but I had convinced them to remain behind. There was no need to escalate the situation by placing emotional connections on display. Thus, only Jackson, Lars, and the marine whose stubble had thickened to a grizzled beard stood behind the talkative Recorder and me.

No one spoke while we waited. Even the talkative Recorder fell silent. No hint of emotion showed on his face, and his drone hummed obediently behind him, as I had programmed it to do. We had not managed to create a station-wide jamming device but had increased the range of another dozen reconfigured datapads, which we tucked inconspicuously in chargers throughout the station to run unobtrusively. Only patches of the commonly used areas and some of the hallways were uncovered, and as long as he kept one or the other—the flowered device or the plain black one—charged and tucked into his suit, he should be safe.

The Elder, too, would be safe if he did not stray from common paths. Though, truthfully, at that moment, shivering in the hangar with no thermoregulatory suit and no respirator, my breath hanging in white clouds, I did not rank his security among my priorities.

The shuttle's hatch opened, and a man in the mottled grey of a Consortium suit descended. A separate chill shook me, and my self-righteous anger vanished, for he had but one drone.

*James.*

For three seconds, I could not breathe.

My friend made his way across the open concrete floor, but six meters from us, he stopped midstride. Even from that distance, I saw his silvery eyes widen, and he went completely still.

The Elder disembarked from the shuttle, his three drones trailing after him like a comet's tail. The intensity of his glare should have intimidated me, but instead, it solidified my resolve. He stormed toward us. When he drew even with my friend, he staggered backward.

His voice crackled over my communication link. "What have you done?"

I raised my chin but did not answer, for I wished to tell neither the truth nor a lie.

The Elder's question seemed to loosen whatever held my friend, for James inhaled visibly and moved forward, leaving his drone behind. Once again, I stood between my first friend and the talkative Recorder, facing the man who held my future in his drone's tendrils.

"Done? Nothing," Jackson growled. "We haven't *done* anything. We told you the Recorder was still here. You didn't believe me and wasted our resources on an unscheduled trip. It shouldn't be my problem you have issues with your tech."

The Elder glowered at all of us as the crew filtered out of the shuttle, edging past Lars into the hall.

"So do we stand here looking pretty or do we get moving?" the bearded marine asked.

The Elder raised one hand, and James's abandoned drone flew back to where the Elder stood and entwined one long tendril around his arm. Behind his faceplate, the Elder's forehead wrinkled. He came no closer.

Jackson grunted and motioned for us to proceed down the hallway.

The marine watched me, his eyes asking something I did not understand, then he pivoted and left. I tapped the talkative Recorder's arm, and he turned his focus from the Elder to me and my friend.

The Recorder indicated the hall. "Shall we, then?"

Silver eyes on me, James said only, "Indeed."

With James and the talkative Recorder flanking me, I followed the bearded marine, Lars at our heels.

"Elder." Jackson's voice over the suit's tinny speaker was faint, distant. "You know what happens when a Recorder's drone gets smashed by a bug. Probably worse for someone like you. I don't really care, but unless you want to test that theory, you need to get a move on. I'll take rearguard if you don't dawdle eight meters behind."

The Elder did not answer, but the rapidity of his footfalls informed me that he complied. I did not look back.

Suddenly, the bearded marine stopped and turned around. Simultaneously, Jackson swore loudly.

"Detour," the marine explained, his eyes sweeping the corridor and ceiling. His steadiness reassured me until he added, "Bugs ahead."

James froze.

"Don't worry," Lars said. "We can handle any encroachment."

The talkative Recorder snorted.

We turned around, and Jackson, the Elder now close behind him, led us through unfamiliar passages. When we drew near enough that our devices' reach overtook the Elder, he quickened his steps and passed Jackson.

"Where do you think you're going?"

Several paces ahead, the Elder paused. His trio and James's drone linked jointed arms to form a train, the foremost wrapping its tendrils across the Elder's chest like a safety harness. He pulled the grey film of nanodevices from his dilated, hazel eyes and glared back at us.

Jackson stopped short, and Lars bumped into him.

"What—" Lars began, then whistled. "Amazing! I didn't know you could do that! Can you see like normal people now?"

The Elder ignored the questions. "I am waiting for you. If there are, indeed, insects nearby, you should not *dawdle*."

Jackson did not answer.

We had almost reached the control room when the hall lights pulsed to red and the emergency floor lights to blue.

"Pick up the pace," Jackson called over his shoulder as he broke into a run.

We, too, ran to keep up, the talkative Recorder gasping with the effort. Worry that he should reinjure his bruised ribs joined the dread that urged me forward. I took his arm, and James dodged around me to support him on the other side. I had no desire for any of us to be left in a hall where roaches had been sighted.

"Void take it," the bearded marine cursed.

"No. Timmons and Spanos have more experience. Get Morgan's team to the shuttle." Jackson's vocal cadence matched the rhythm of his pounding boots. "Engineers, yes. Don't know what they'll find."

Lars glanced at the Recorders and me. "We'll get you to safety. Don't worry."

We sped through red-lit hallways where blue baseboards glowed, but my heart's constriction was not due to exertion. Why did Nate's and Alec's experience matter?

As we approached the control room and reached the puddles of safety our devices created, the Elder's drones slowed, and he hurried through the areas where he lost connection. When our group entered the control room, the Elder halted near the double doors, where he still could communicate with his drones.

The talkative Recorder breathed heavily, and his face had a greyish tinge, so instead of asking him, I turned to the bearded marine. "What is happening?"

His jaw ticced. *"Thalassa."*

My heart stuttered. I asked, "What of *Thalassa?*"

"It's gone dark."

Images of people lanced through my mind—Edwards, Archimedes Genet, the kitchen staff, the young man from the laundry and the older one who guided him, Tia, Cam—and like a constrictor, the thoughts tightened and tightened until they blurred together into one incomprehensible ache.

With my back to the control room wall, well away from the Elder and his drones, I watched Nate, Jordan, and Alec hold a low conversation with Jackson and Zhen. James stood at my left side, still wearing a somewhat dazed expression, with the now-silent talkative Recorder next to him. A group of marines filed past on their way down the hall, and the trio in white with engineering-blue bands trailed after them.

When the engineers neared, the tiny woman touched her companions' arms, and they all stopped. The tall man, thick braids now hidden by his cap and helmet, cleared his throat, his gaze skipping between me and the Recorders.

The ginger man, whose face was now covered with thick stubble, met my eyes. "You take care, Izzy."

I nodded.

"Move," ordered a marine I did not know.

They turned to go.

I found my voice. "And you."

In unison they looked over their shoulders.

"Take care as well."

Tight smiles were their only answer.

By the time the engineers had become distant specks of blue, the talkative Recorder had caught his breath. "Izzy? A name?"

I refused to glance at the Elder. Either he heard, or he did not. "They assigned me a designation, yes."

The Recorder rested one shoulder on the wall. "An odd choice."

"As you say."

He was quiet for a few moments. "It is not the name you would have chosen?"

"It is not."

Tawny brown eyes skimmed from me to my friend. "I've chosen one."

The Elder's unveiled, hazel gaze searched the room, landing on nothing, so I turned to the talkative Recorder and attempted to raise one eyebrow.

He shrugged. "Not that it matters, not now."

"I know my name," my friend remarked quietly. "At least, in part."

"You have chosen?"

"I *know*." The words held the weight and heft of loss. "My mother told me."

Mouth open, the talkative Recorder swiveled toward James, but my friend only stared blankly across the cavernous room. I snuck another peek at the Elder, then at Nate and the others who had grouped around Zhen, near the AAVA drone. Nate's voice rose then fell, but I could not discern the words.

I left the Recorders and went to his side. The Elder scowled from his position near the door, but made no move to stop me.

"No," Jackson was insisting, "this isn't simply a malfunction in comms."

"Pirates are unlikely out here." A woman whose name I did not know indicated the display over Zhen's workstation. "We aren't near transport routes, and the nearest mining platform is a solid five or six days, at best."

Zhen scowled. "Jackson's right, though. And it can't have been lasers. Had to be an EM cannon."

"Whatever the cause," Jackson said, "they're not responding. Nothing, not even that blasted AAVA drone, is getting through. Those are all the troops I can spare, Timmons."

Nate nodded tersely. "That'll have to—"

He broke off when he saw me. Beside him, Alec's attention shifted from me to the Elder at the door, and his expression tightened.

Jackson gave an order, and the knot of people dispersed.

The gentle whir of drones sounded close behind, and I fought the urge to tell Nate once more that he was my heart. Saying so before the Elder would surely condemn him without recourse. No other words would suffice, so I remained silent. Nate's eyes sought mine. Then, he turned and left for *Thalassa* and whatever awaited him there.

All at once, it did not matter.

I could not let him go without saying something. I ran past the Elder and his drones, down the hallway after Nate, calling his name. He stopped. Three meters away, so did I.

"Nathaniel . . . Be careful. Please."

Green eyes held mine, and a smile softened his face. "We'll be back before you know it."

Then, he was gone.

I stood there, shivering in the not-cold.

"I'll look after him." Alec's voice startled me from my circling thoughts. "Eric, too."

"Thank you," I whispered.

"Don't worry. We'll all be fine." Alec put a hand on my shoulder. "Listen, have you given any thought to a name? You still need one."

Refusing to sneak another glance after Nate, I said, "I have had other things on my mind."

"Yeah." He gazed at the wall beyond me. "Arianna is a good name. It was my sister's. I don't think she'd mind if you used it. I wouldn't."

For two breaths, the honor of his offer lifted the dread compressing my heart. "Thank you. Even though"—I tempered my response—"even *if*, I do not choose it, this is one of the greatest gifts I have ever received."

In response, he held up a fist. I tapped it with my own, and he gave me a nod before following the others to the hangar and the waiting shuttle.

The empty corridor reminded me too much of *Agamemnon*'s deserted halls. The hair on my arms stood on end, and I returned to the control room.

The average trip from Pallas to *Thalassa* took ninety-three minutes, and the small green dot representing the shuttle crept slowly through Zhen's three-dimensional display. The Elder remained near the door, well clear of areas where his neural implant would not function. The Recorders stood in safety near the wall. The talkative Recorder occasionally spoke to James, who remained silent.

Thirty-seven minutes after the shuttle's departure, I pulled up a datastream next to the AAVA drone. Cyan and amber twisted together, and I began a search. The station Recorder had not been able to discover who killed Charles Tristram, but surely deep in the records—

"Moons and stars!" Zhen exclaimed. "There's someone new out there."

"What?" Jackson looked over her shoulder and uttered a vulgarity, which I hoped the Elder did not record. "That's not ours."

Jordan leaned over and slapped a panel. "Tim, get those shields up!"

"Already on it." Nate's disembodied voice pulled me from the AAVA drone as a magnet pulls iron, back to Zhen and the people now clustered behind her. "I've done this before, remember?"

Jordan glared at the display. "I'm not likely to forget it. We nearly got fried. What's your shield status?"

"On full now," Alec stated.

"Look, J, there's a rhythm to this." Nate said, and after three sharp clicks, the shuttle's background noises faded. "No need to panic. Not only do we know what we're doing, but we have a shuttle full of extremely capable marines."

The talkative Recorder moved forward, his programmed drone at his side and James two meters behind him. "What is wrong?"

Without looking away from the display, Zhen muttered, "Pirates, just like I said. If we're lucky, they've just got an EM cannon, like they used on *Thalassa*, not lasers."

Jordan, too, kept her focus on that green dot. "We don't know it's pirates."

Nate's short laugh sounded forced. "Likeliest scenario, J. There's a chance the rats might not see us if they're watching *Thalassa*. Not—"

Static took the place of his voice, and the shuttle's tiny green avatar disappeared.

I forgot to breathe.

"Tim!" Jordan's voice rose in pitch. "Alec?"

There was no response.

"Timmons." Jackson's gravelly demand was answered only by the colorless growl of static. "Spanos. Report!"

Zhen whispered Alec's name, but I could not speak, for my heart was cracking into pieces.

"We should trust that he"—the talkative Recorder corrected himself—"that they have adequately compensated for anything directed at their shuttle."

No one spoke for a fifth of a minute.

"Cut audio, DuBois, but leave the channel open." Jackson rolled his shoulders. "No need for everyone to listen to static."

Jordan closed her eyes, and her lips moved silently. Then she asked, "What's the status on the roaches?"

The woman I did not know said, "Clear. We still need to—"

All across the room, computer displays flickered, and sharp cries of protest sounded from several stations. Overhead, the lights faltered.

Someone to my left said, "You've got to be joking."

"D'you think the bugs got to the lines again?" Lars asked.

The power abruptly cut off, as if on cue, and the subdued but constant roar of circulation fans faded to silence. Emergency floor lights brightened, and the dim illumination reflected off stalactites, which seemed to bite down on us all.

Jordan's voice broke the hush enveloping us. "Elder, if you would—"

Before she finished her sentence, the Elder's drones switched on full-spectrum light, though they failed to illuminate the entire space. Even with the drones' light, however, the room seemed to contract around me. Noises blurred, and breathing became difficult.

A hand touched my shoulder. I looked up. James was at my side, the talkative Recorder behind him.

Jackson's voice coalesced into words. " . . . with Maxwell and Williams. We'll set up in the room next to Tristram's lab. Nonessential personnel will stay in secured areas."

"We must follow the Elder," James said, his silver eyes on mine, a faint divot over his nose.

Had my distress been that obvious?

The talkative Recorder's mouth quirked. "At a distance, if we want that light to work."

But James was somber as he glanced at the drones. "Yes."

The Elder said nothing as he and Jackson led the way. We marched silently through dim halls, following the drones' pools of light. Images of roaches smashing my drone, crushing Michaelson's arm, and climbing down the walls from the ceiling ricocheted through my mind. I tapped my thigh.

Nate . . .

I took refuge in prime numbers again. *Two, three, five, seven, eleven, thirteen . . .*

Though lasers no longer barricaded the hall with the infirmary, I still felt safer when marines ushered us into the room with cots. Someone had set lanterns on the tables, and the pallid light gave everything a sickly hue. Lars, who remained by the door, patted my back as I passed him, though more gently than he had before.

I settled at the farthest table, across the room from two marines who were affixing thick metal bars over the silent air vent. I clasped my hands on my lap, and James sat next to me. The talkative Recorder fidgeted on my other side. There was nothing to do, save wait, and although Recorders were trained to do so, I loathed it. In my mind, Nate's voice disappeared over and over again, and the faces of my friends from *Thalassa* repeated like recordings in VVR.

"What do we do now?" An unfamiliar marine's girlish voice halted the images, but not my distress. "With *Thalassa* gone, we're trapped down here with those spacing bugs. The shuttle can't carry us all to the nearest platform, and Krios is too far to call for help, even if we had power."

The talkative Recorder leaned past me and, when James looked at him, said quietly, "Watch over her. I have work to do."

My first friend gave an infinitesimal nod, and the Recorder pushed himself from the table.

"Michaelson could've gotten us out," declared the tallest man. "But without juice, that tank he's in is going to fail."

Lars grunted from the doorway. "Nah. We'll fry a few more bugs and get the power back on."

"We've only got enough food for a ten-day or so." The woman's voice shook slightly.

"Maybe we could roast some roaches," Lars said.

The marines were not the only ones to cringe; my stomach lurched, and James flinched.

The talkative Recorder clapped hands on the shoulders of the woman and the tall man. They startled.

"Barring his suggestion for viable protein sources, I believe Lars may have the right of it," he stated. "In which case—and since I am of little use otherwise—I want a weapon."

The woman exclaimed, "Can you do that?"

"Am I permitted? Absolutely not. But I most certainly *can*." The Recorder laughed, then winced. "Although until my ribs heal, a small weapon might be best." He grew serious. "I choose to hope you will make it off Pallas. For me, this is a temporary assignment—very possibly my last. I didn't know your Parker well, but I would not care to disappoint her. While I realize the thread is thin, I hold to hope."

"Right!" Lars already had his hand on the door handle. "Hope's what we need. Hope and incendiary rounds!" He flung the door open and strode down the hall, calling Jackson's name.

When it opened again, however, Jordan and Zhen entered with Kyleigh and Freddie, whose skin was ashen in the pale lighting.

Jackson called from the corridor, and the talkative Recorder and marines filed out. The rest of us watched the door click shut. Zhen's eyes were puffy, but she glared around the room with her usual intensity before removing her helmet and lowering herself into the chair across from mine. Jordan crossed to a pile of packs on the back wall and pulled out hers. Setting it on the table alongside the helmets, she dug through it and removed a sheathed knife, a grey rectangular stone, and a small vial.

No one spoke as Jordan poured the viscous liquid on the stone before dragging her knife across the surface. Her lips were tight, and every few seconds her jaw clenched. Other than scraping the blade over the rectangle, she was still. The sound was oddly soothing, and the movement of the metal across the dull grey mesmerized me.

"Why would you choose a knife that requires such effort?" James asked.

"Sharpening knives is like meditation." Jordan focused on the precise angle of the blade. "I left most of mine on New Triton. I shouldn't have needed any of them."

Zhen stared at the wall. "Alec gave me a ceramic knife for my last birthday."

"Did you bring it?"

"Yes."

Jordan glanced up. "Carry it."

"Right." Zhen stood and retrieved a pack from along the wall.

I moistened my lips. "Why did you not carry them before?"

"Not protocol." Zhen dug through her pack, which did not contain her knitting. "But things change."

"Yeah," Freddie murmured. "They do."

Time trailed unmarked, but eventually, Jordan pulled a sheet of paper from her pack and tested her knife. Its smooth glide must have satisfied her, for she wiped it with a small cloth and sheathed it.

Kyleigh put her hand on Freddie's back. "You should rest."

"I suppose so."

"Keep your helmet at your cot," Zhen said.

He scooped his up, gave Kyleigh a quick hug, and headed to one of the cots, which creaked as he settled. In only three and a half minutes, long, slow breaths told us he had fallen asleep.

"He was only supposed to be here for one day. His medication is all on *Thalassa*," Kyleigh said in a hushed tone.

"He'll be all right, Kye," Zhen said, then abruptly rotated to face me. "We're a lot alike, you and me."

Her words came as a surprise. I studied her dark eyes and the wisps of blue hair that had escaped from her cap. "I do not see it."

"My Grandmère took me away from my mother and raised me. She loved me. Someone should have loved you." Zhen turned to James. "And you. Although, you were wanted, at least."

"That's certainly true," Jordan said. She bent to strap the sheath to her leg, and when she sat up again, her eyes locked on James's. "He never stopped looking, you know."

His forehead furrowed, but he remained quiet.

I did not comment. It was Max's place, not mine, to tell James who he was. I tucked my hands under my thighs and faced Zhen. "It is well with me. I was never unwanted at the Training Center. It was not until I began to interact with citizens that I noticed a discrepancy in acceptance. It was more wrong for you to be rejected as a citizen."

"That type of dross is wrong." Zhen shoved herself away from the table. "I'm glad you met James when you were kids"—my friend startled, his silver eyes darting from her to me—"but playing with some kid twice isn't the same as having a real friend."

"Three times—"

The door swung open, cutting my words short. Max and the Elder entered. All five of us sprang to our feet. Once the Elder reached the jamming device's puddle, the drones trailing him slowed. He halted, then stepped back, his breath coming quickly and misting his faceplate. He pulled the nanodevices from his eyes, which went wide as Max shut the door before the drones could glide inside. The Elder's gaze darted wildly around the room.

Ignoring the Elder's obvious distress, Zhen demanded, "Any news?"

Max's movements were slow as he unfastened his helmet and set it on a cot near the front of the room. He sank down and clasped his hands. "Nothing from the shuttle or the ship. The marine generator specialist hooked up the medtank. We can't take Michaelson out until we get his infection under control."

Michaelson was ill? What else could go wrong?

"Infection?" Kyleigh squeaked. "The virus! Is he—"

"What?" Max lifted his head. "No, not the virus. The cockroach." He managed a weak smile. "I called the cats disease-carrying pests, but they're nothing compared to these insects. *E. coli* and *streptococcus*. There was enough in its saliva to keep Michaelson in the tank for half a ten-day."

Guilt tinged pointless relief that Michaelson would not succumb to Ross's bioweapon, for death would still be death, no matter the implement.

"That's not good." Kyleigh gusted a sigh. "There isn't much we can do, then, except have faith. No matter what." She glanced at the Elder, then at Freddie's sleeping form.

There seemed to be nothing left to say. We each settled on cots, but it felt as if a black hole had formed in my chest, pulling and compressing me into something small, dense, and dark. I had not truly said goodbye to Nate. Had not told him one more time that he was my heart. That memory burned like acid. I rolled onto my side and pulled the stiff thermal blanket close to my chest.

The Elder sat on the cot closest to the door, staring at nothing. Jaw tight and hands folded on his chest, Max stared up at the ceiling, casting occasional, furtive glances at his son, who breathed evenly as he slept. Zhen had curled into a ball around her pillow, while Jordan tossed and turned, and Kyleigh held Freddie's hand across the narrow aisle.

Tears seeped down my cheeks. I closed my eyes against the pale light and whispered both Kyleigh's and the talkative Recorder's words of promise.

Hope. Faith.

A thin thread, indeed.

Time dragged past, confined as we were to that one carefully guarded hallway. I listened always for news of Nate and *Thalassa*—news that never came.

The marines had made an expedition to the hangar but could not open the doors manually. Without the use of a shuttle, we were trapped on Pallas. Although, if *Thalassa* was gone, even if the doors opened, even if it had the fuel to reach Krios, the single shuttle could not have transported all of us. Out of necessity, over half would have to be left behind.

After the failed hangar foray, the marines began a thorough—and well-armed—inspection of the power lines and found no evidence of the roaches and no apparent reason for the power outage. Fortunately, the small generators kept Michaelson's medical tank functional. They were also able to purify the air in the smaller rooms, run the computers, and keep the jamming devices charged. We hid the devices, hoping the drones would run out of power first. They did.

By the second day, however, everyone was on edge. Rumors of faint, echoing voices and out-of-sync footsteps spread in whispers. Lars seemed oblivious to the uneasy glances thrown his way after his repeated suggestion that the station was haunted. Indeed, he expressed confusion when Jackson ordered him to be quiet.

The Elder rarely moved from his cot, from which he endlessly watched people sleep.

Jackson had given the marines permission to train the talkative Recorder, whose ribs had knit well enough with the help of medical nanodevices, to handle a rifle similar to the one Eric had used on *Agamemnon*. The Elder's thinned lips displayed his disapproval of a Recorder learning to handle a weapon, but he said nothing.

James had been asked to assist with adjusting a generator, and a group of marines had gone to inspect the circulation fans and scrubbers, while the others slept or patrolled the halls.

And so, Freddie, Kyleigh, and I were alone in her small laboratory with nothing to do but wait.

I was tired of waiting.

Periodically, the distant report of a weapon firing echoed up the hall. I attempted to focus on the self-appointed task of reviewing the information the station's Recorder had stored on the green datapad, but the screech of metal on concrete brought my attention to Freddie pulling out the chair across from me.

He took his seat as Kyleigh said, "Everyone does, I think."

I put the datapad down. "I beg your pardon?"

Freddie drew on the tabletop with one long, thin finger. "Ever since I could see, I wanted to show people color and light as it really is. Since we're stuck here, I guess that'll never happen. The world— it's so much more beautiful and richer than people know." He shifted uncomfortably. "I'm no good with words."

Kyleigh took his hand in hers and gave it a squeeze. "You need to paint. If I'm remembering right, there might be paint and brushes just down the hall." She jumped up and darted to the door like a butterfly. "O'Reilly? I need to get some supplies from the closet around the corner."

"What kind of supplies?"

"Art supplies." Her voice softened. "For Freddie."

O'Reilly glanced in at the young man. "Let me check with Jackson." He closed the door, but in less than a minute, it opened again. "I'm not convinced this is a good idea, but no one's seen any bugs—"

"Or heard the ghosts lately," Lars put in from his post across the corridor.

O'Reilly rolled his eyes. "Or that. Meier is just down the hall. Go ahead."

Kyleigh returned in under five minutes with a single can of paint and a two-centimeter-wide brush. "Sorry, Freddie. I forgot yours had been moved, so the choices were black and ultraviolet." She flashed him a smile. "And since I wanted to see what you paint, you just get black."

She returned to her computers, and Freddie became absorbed

in outlining shapes on the wall. I watched him until the Recorder's green datapad and its contents summoned me. Even though I had seen them so many times that once more would be fruitless, I opened the files, hoping that this time, they would distract my mind from worry and regret.

Twenty-nine minutes later, Freddie said, "Bother. I need more."

"Already?"

"The can was almost empty."

"I should've checked it, but that's easily remedied." Kyleigh sprang to her feet and threw open the door again. "Freddie's out of paint."

"Already?" O'Reilly spoke into his communication link, then motioned with his head. "No bugs. Go ahead."

We watched Kyleigh leave, then Freddie turned to me. "I'm sorry about . . ." He sighed. "Timmons told me once that you liked my mural. The one in the hall, in ultraviolet."

A lump formed in my throat. "I did, yes. Even the border was well done, but your Pegasus and Medusa were beautiful. I assume they still are." I set the datapad aside. "Why did you paint what no one else could see?"

"You saw it, and so did the other Recorder," Freddie said. "I wanted to practice, and that wall was so boring, and . . . honestly, I needed to make something for myself. That people couldn't see. That probably doesn't make sense."

"I understand." I closed the datapad's projection. "I never felt the need to show my work to anyone."

"What?" His brows lifted. "But you're—were—a Recorder."

"I enjoy art, as I told Nate last quarter. Many of us do, including your station Recorder. Drawing is a permitted leisure activity, if the subject matter has been approved." I reached for a scrap of paper and the ink pen he had abandoned in favor of paint. For five and a half minutes, I sketched Freddie himself, then stalks of lavender, but when the desire to draw eyes with perfect brows overtook me, I set the pen down and pushed the paper away.

Freddie picked it up. "This is good."

I did not reply, only reopened the datapad's files, which seemed meaningless. I checked the time, and a prickle of uneasiness crept over me.

"Freddie?" I waited for him to look up. "Kyleigh should have returned."

He checked his wrist monitor, and his face tightened. "You're right."

I followed him to the door, where he asked the marine about Kyleigh.

"You know Tristram," O'Reilly said. "She's probably chatting." He tapped the button on his suit's throat. "Meier." He tapped the button again. "Meier?"

The lack of response propelled me past the marine. Ignoring his protests, I ran down the corridor. As I cut around the corner, I accelerated, fear lashing like whipping tendrils, and skidded to a stop next to Meier's crumpled body. My heart caught in my throat. Paint sloshed across the floor in dark, uneven puddles and thick smears.

Two sets of boot prints led into the dark, and the only sign of Kyleigh was one small glove, black paint seeping into the fingers through the open cuff.

# 45

Elliott's hands fisted around his safety harness when gravity switched back on. He slouched further into the seat while Sam and Eric unbuckled themselves and quarreled in whispers over who should help Blythe, who was struggling with the straps. While the other three kids made their way to the porthole, Elliott closed his eyes and tried to pretend everything would be all right, that Dad would arrive at any minute, say they were just going to visit Julian and that he'd paid off his debts, and the three of them could be a family again.

But after the past few quarters, he couldn't quite picture Dad anymore.

Unable to put it off any longer, Elliott joined the others at the portal for his first look at the planet that would be his new home. The awkward, angular arms of Lunar Four hid some of New Triton's scabby brown surface, but perspective made the planet smaller than he'd thought it would be. He could block the whole thing with one hand.

Blythe tugged on his jumpsuit's pantleg. "Elliott? Up."

"Leave him alone," Eric said. "You're too big for that now."

"It's all right." Elliott hefted her, and Blythe lunged at the portal, nearly knocking him off balance.

She grabbed the frame and pouted. "It's ugly."

"Yeah." Stars, but his chest hurt. It wasn't that he didn't want to live with Julian. He just didn't want to go to New Triton. What if Julian couldn't keep him after all?

"Mum said your brother's already waiting." Sam's eyes were gentle. "I bet he'll be here even before we unload the ore."

"But Elliott, I want you to stay." Blythe rested her head on his shoulder, and her orange curls tickled his chin. "You can be my extra brother."

"Don't be stupid." At first, Elliott thought Eric was speaking to him, but then Eric added, "You know he has to leave, Blythe."

"There's no reason to be rude, Eric." Sam held out her arms, but Blythe clung tighter to Elliott's neck. "El, you're all packed?"

Elliott pointed to his small locker, but then hesitated. Was it rude to point? He couldn't remember. It didn't matter back on Delta5802-1007. Did it matter here? He couldn't bring himself to ask. "Yes, your mum helped me pack everything in Dad's duffel bag. I bet Julian won't want me to wear Delta's drabs, but they're all I have—" He broke off before he said anything else that'd mark him as a miner's son.

She didn't seem to notice. "And you have the datastick? The one with all your records and pictures?"

"Course he does—he's not stupid." Eric huffed at his older sister. "Don't nag."

All the same, a split second of panic had Elliott checking his jumpsuit's chest pocket, and relief washed over him. It was still there along with the ring made of Mum's hair. Those pictures of Dad, Julian, and their mother, or of him as a baby back on Ceres never seemed real to him. He didn't remember his mother at all, and even when Dad started smiling again last year, the smile wasn't the same as in the stills when he was teaching Julian to surf or dancing with their mother. They'd matter to Julian, though. Elliott turned back to the portal and New Triton's crusty surface. His stomach twisted.

"Everything I have left is right here."

"It'll be nice to be with your brother," Sam said in that almost-grown-up voice she used when she copied her mum.

Blythe caught his cheeks in her tiny hands and stared at him with her big brown eyes. "You can stay. I heard Daddy tell Mum. Jul'yan, too."

"I know, but no." His voice came out all funny with his face squished.

Blythe giggled.

He pulled his face from between her tiny hands. "Julian fought with Child Services from all the way across the system to bring me here. And got special permission from the university president so he could keep me and his status, even without a contract. I signed the documents promising to follow rules and stuff. He even got me into a decent school. I'll go."

No way would he tell them how horrible it had been, in that disgusting dorm, after Dad died and with Julian half a system away. Or how long it had taken Julian to make the university president agree to let him stay. And he wasn't sure he even wanted to know what Julian must have had to do to get him into a decent school with such rubbish records. His scores would never have gotten him out of the mines. Everyone on New Triton was sure to think he was stupid. Even Julian.

He swallowed.

A big, fat tear slid down Blythe's round cheek, and she wiggled free. As soon as her feet hit the floor, she dashed from the room.

The three of them stood at the portal for a few minutes more.

"Don't suppose you'd want to wait in VVR instead of here?" Eric motioned to the ugly planet. "Better view than that, eh?"

"Yeah."

They crossed to the locker, where Elliott retrieved the single duffel bag and his jacket.

"If Julian—when he contacts the ship, your mum will let me know, right?"

Sam studied him, then took his duffel. "Course she will. Don't worry. It'll be fine."

The three of them headed down to VVR, Eric jogging ahead so he'd reach it first. He grinned at them over his shoulder and punched in a code. The hatch slid open to a green, leafy jungle. Elliott's favorite program. At that, the tightness in his chest loosened, although he couldn't get his words to work right and thank them.

Sam set the duffel inside the door, and Elliott tossed his jacket on top. Instead of playing, this time, they walked through the projected greenery and sat against the wall.

Eric scuffed the heel of his boot against the floor, pushing it through the creeping projection of a bug. "It's been good having another kid to play with. Wish you could stay."

At the moment, Elliott did, too, even if Julian was waiting for him. "You got Sam and Blythe."

"Sam's bossy, and Blythe is four."

"Thanks, brother," Sam snipped. "And she won't always be four, just like you won't always be eight, which is a really annoying age."

Elliott startled when a projection of a bird darted across the room. He still wasn't used to sudden flashes of bright color. "But you have each other. And your parents have a VVR, so you can go almost anywhere. We didn't have that on—" He reminded himself not to talk about what it was like back—well, it wasn't home there anymore. Eric and Sam might not mind him being a miner brat, but New Triton would be different. Normal citizens all thought miners were trogs and criminals.

"What if the university changes the rules again," he blurted, "or makes Julian give me up? What if people ask about Dad or—"

"Then you tell them to stow it," Eric stated flatly, sounding a lot like his uncle Brian.

"But nicely," Sam added. "Besides, from the sound of it, Julian moved planets to get you. He's not likely to let anyone take you away."

Eric was saying something about not actually moving planets when the hatch slid open. They scrambled to their feet.

Julian stood in the doorway, even taller than before. Elliott's throat convulsed, and before he knew he was even moving, they were both halfway through VVR's jungle. Julian dropped to his knees and caught Elliott in a crushing hug. Burying his face in his brother's broad shoulders, Elliott broke into sobs.

Gradually, he straightened and scrubbed at his face with his sleeve.

Eric had followed him partway, but Sam and their mum stood in the corridor, watching. Eric dug through his pockets and found them both tissues.

Julian offered Eric a watery smile. "Thanks. I see you came prepared. Stars, Elliott, I'm so glad to see you. Ready to go home?"

Fresh tears gathered. "Do we actually have one now?"

Julian's cheeks flushed. "Yes. I . . . I convinced the powers that be that I'm capable of taking care of you."

"You don't have to go back," Eric's mum said. When Julian didn't respond at once, she continued gently, "You can both have a place here, on *Gryphon*, if you want it. Elliott is a good kid, and we've talked to you so many times we feel like we know you, too. You're both welcome."

Elliott held his breath. If only Julian would say yes. If only they could stay on a ship that felt more like home than that ugly planet would.

"Thank you." Julian straightened. "But I have verified permission to return as sole guardian and still keep my status as a student."

Eric's mum shook her head. "Uncontracted parents and guardians aren't permitted. It's a policy violation. If you have custody, you'll have to leave."

Julian set his left hand on Elliott's shoulder. "I . . . managed to get an exemption. The president has nothing to gain by dismissing me, and she has a whole lot to lose."

Elliott glanced up at his brother, but Julian's face told him nothing.

"If you say so." Her eyes zeroed in on Julian. "But if your circumstances change, young man, if you have any difficulties, let us know. We're not in the inner planets very often, but you know how to reach us."

"I appreciate your offer, but things are under control." Julian picked up Elliott's jacket and the duffel and led him and Eric out of VVR.

Eric's mum was tiny next to Julian, but she pinned him with a glare like she was twice his size. "And are you happy with whatever arrangement you've made?"

"No, ma'am, not really," he said softly, "but I'll take care of my brother. No matter what I have to do." Julian didn't hide his sigh. He repeated, "No matter what. It's what family does."

Her shoulders softened a little. "Yes. It is."

Sam led the way to the small hangar at the back—aft?—of the ship.

Their dad and uncle were waiting with Blythe, who squirmed free of her father's grip and threw herself at Elliott, then pulled back to shove what must have been the ugliest plushie in the system at his chest.

"This is Dragon," she said. He glanced up at Julian, who had a peculiar expression on his face. Blythe sniffled and dragged her wrist across her snotty nose. "She's a good dragon, and you should take her."

"Blythe, I can't—"

"Can so!"

Their mum chuckled. "Go ahead, Elliott, dear."

"Elliott?" Eric shuffled his feet. "You'll write, yeah?"

"I will. It's nice to have a friend." But that felt inadequate, so he added, "Eh?"

A grin broke across Eric's face.

Elliott tucked the plushie under his arm just in time to hug Sam, Eric, and Blythe, all at once. Julian shook hands with the grownups, then led him to the tiny transport shuttle.

"You sure?" Julian suddenly asked. "Maybe I'm being selfish. Do you want to stay? They're good people."

"I'll miss them." Elliott set the plushie into the seat next to him and clicked the harness into place. "But you're my brother. I'll always choose you."

I sat, numb, while Freddie paced the room.

"But the paint," he protested again. "You can follow the paint."

For the third time, O'Reilly said, "Jackson and the others *did* follow it to those pairs of boots. They're still looking." Then he fell silent.

There was nothing to do but wait. Meier had sustained head trauma and was under Max's care, but when James brought us something to eat, there was still no news of Kyleigh. The smell of the packaged food turned my stomach.

Freddie picked at his meal, then suddenly stabbed his fork into the oozing mess and turned to me, his green eyes wide. "Stars! You didn't see the prints!"

"Freddie," I began as patiently as I could. His agitation would benefit no one. "I saw boot prints, as did all—"

Freddie slapped a palm onto the table. "I can't believe I'm this stupid! You saw *boot* prints!" He jumped to his feet. "You didn't see what I did! I need to go back!"

"Calm down," O'Reilly said. "There's no need—"

"You!" Freddie spun to James, grabbing the chairback to steady himself. "You're a Recorder. You'll see it! Come with me."

O'Reilly peered at him from under scraggly brows. "Look, kid. We've got increased roach activity in the corridor two sections over. It's not safe."

Freddie made a strangled noise and pulled his helmet back on. "You're looking in the wrong place. You need to follow the *ultraviolet* paint."

A glimmer of hope lit in my chest.

"You can see ultraviolet?" James asked.

Freddie nodded.

James's silver eyes regarded him steadily.

"And," I said slowly, "whoever wore those boots left ultraviolet prints behind?"

"Not the boots at all, except a few traces." Freddie's eyes gleamed. "Kyleigh left handprints on the wall. And paint dribbled on the floor."

"That changes things." O'Reilly swung open the door even while he informed Jackson.

We were halfway to the corner when James said, "I am not an Elder. Without my drone and implant, I can no longer see invisible light."

Freddie was breathing heavily, but he refused to lessen his speed. "I forgot. There's a supply closet three corridors over which might have goggles." We reached the closet, and he pointed at a smear. "There. On the wall."

He reached up to about a meter and a third from the floor and splayed his fingers over a smudge on the grey concrete. He frowned and squinted into the darkness. Of all the times I had missed invisible light, none compared to this.

"Her handprints are higher as they move further down. Someone was carrying her."

O'Reilly clapped him on the shoulder. "Good work. Let's head back."

"What? No! If we go right now—"

"I said head back." O'Reilly was firm. "You did well. But you're in no shape to go chasing after whoever took her. We'll find those goggles and track her down."

"I can't just leave her to—"

"Move. Or I carry you."

The muscle in Freddie's jaw twitched, but he walked back up to the familiar hallway. Instead of returning to the laboratory, however, he threw open the door to the sleeping area and stormed to the Elder.

"Can you see them? You have eyes like mine. Tell me you can still see them."

"Calm down," O'Reilly demanded. "We'll take care of this."

The Elder raised his stare from the floor. "Do I see whom?"

"Not who. What. Light." Freddie's voice cracked. He dropped to his knees and begged, "Please tell me you can still see ultraviolet?"

Williams woke, struggled onto one elbow, and blinked at the two of them. "What is going on?"

"Kyleigh Tristram is missing," James explained in an undertone.

Williams bolted upright. "What? When?"

Freddie held up a hand, his pale eyes focused on the Elder's. "Can you?"

Slowly, as if the admission were painful, the Elder nodded.

"Then please. They won't let me look. Please find her."

"It is not my purview."

Freddie slammed his fists on the Elder's cot, and the man flinched, his eyelid twitching. An edge I had not heard before sharpened Freddie's voice. "Purview or not, you must—"

"That's enough." O'Reilly hauled Freddie up by his arms, pulling him to the door. "Apologies, Elder."

James followed after them, eyes trained like lasers on O'Reilly's back. Williams rushed out as well, leaving me alone with the man who had let Parker die.

"Elder," I began, "although you allowed Rose—"

"Theta4492807—"

"*Rose Parker.*" My temper sparked, and I fought to control my tone. "You lied to me and watched her die, and then you condemned the other two Recorders to serve here where you *knew* the roaches could destroy their drones." A tirade would not sway him, and I was being foolish. I lowered my voice. "You stopped me from inadvertently harming Rose Parker with the glass of water. Please show a portion of that compassion to Kyleigh Tristram. She was nearly gifted."

"Yet she was not. She is a citizen and not my responsibility."

"Do you not see? Only one choice makes us different. We are all human. Truly, we are one people. It is our choice to serve that . . ." I wrestled my voice under control. "Help her. If you can, please help save her."

His rate of respiration increased, and his gaze shifted to the opposite wall, but he did not move.

I left.

That afternoon, Freddie went to the water closet and never returned.

After several vehement exclamations, Jackson ordered a wider search. The marines, simultaneously incensed and relieved that Lars's ghosts were simply unknown humans, were determined to find the missing pair.

It seemed likely that the power outage was due to sabotage, rather than insectile destruction, raising our hopes that the damage could be repaired. Grim promises began to circulate, about finding the craft that had incapacitated *Thalassa* and the shuttle, about making the interlopers pay, about taking their ship and leaving them for "roach fodder."

I could no longer focus on the green datapad. Max came and sat across from me, watching James from the corner of his eye. Jordan and Zhen also returned. Zhen stabbed at her food and muttered imprecations, while Jordan sat next to Max in silence.

"Have the marines located the goggles?" I asked.

Jordan shook her head and shoved her food away.

Max turned, then, and rested his hand on her shoulder. "How are you holding up, Venetia?"

Dark circles smudged her eyes, and for half a second, it seemed as if she leaned into his hand. "I feel numb. Stars above, Max, I've lost my two oldest friends and my two newest ones in a single thirty-six-hour period."

A solitary tear leaked down Zhen's cheek.

Zhen DuBois did not cry. She never should. Neither of them should.

I could no longer sit and do nothing.

I would find Freddie and Kyleigh, and I would make the Elder help me. Zhen folded her arms on the table and rested her head. Max and Jordan's low conversation continued, even when an alarm sounded and the marine at the door stepped away. I slid the green and blue datapads and my communication device under Zhen's helmet. I could not risk the device chiming at an inopportune moment.

Someone should have stopped me, but no one did. Instead, I entered the sleeping area unobserved. Ten men and women slept on cots, but the Elder was awake, his face expressionless.

"I need your eyes, Elder." Before he could say no, I raised my hand. "You have already condemned me. That cannot be altered. But regardless of your opinion of me, you *will* help me find Kyleigh Tristram and Frederick Westruther."

"Why? It is not as if any of us will return. This was a hopeless assignment."

"When we find her, we find the people who stole her, and we find their ship."

He sat up slowly. "And we can escape Pallas after all." A faint frown appeared. "You have been assigned to serve in the Halls, if you do not die here. Your actions clearly demonstrate that you value personal freedom above service—"

"I do not value freedom above service. I value the freedom to *choose* to serve."

His hazel eyes widened, momentarily granting him the appearance of a boy fifteen years his junior. Unidentified emotions flitted behind his faceplate for the space of seventeen heartbeats. "And this, then, is the choice you make with your freedom?"

"If my choice saves them, yes."

"Even if it saves me?" He unfolded his legs and wobbled to his feet.

I caught his arm and released him as quickly as I could. "I do not do this for you."

His face shifted. "I know."

I took a torch from the frontmost pack, but nothing more, then checked the hall in both directions. Seeing no one, I slipped down the corridor to the corner, and the Elder followed.

When we reached the scene, his voice came, tinny through his helmet's speaker. "She was clever." He pointed at the wall, then at the dark congealing puddle on the floor. "This spill mingles black and ultraviolet, but while one can remains, the other is gone."

"Is it probable she took it?"

"A possibility." His forehead furrowed in concentration, eyes focused on the grey concrete, and he reached out to touch the same smudge Freddie had. The echoing slaps of distant weapons firing nearly hid his whisper. "I had not realized her hand is so small." He glanced back at me. "Zeta4542910-9545E, utilizing the torch could very well alert those who would stop us as well as those we hunt. Leave it off," he said. "For now."

I moved through the shadows at his side, torch ready for when the baseboards no longer glowed blue. His lashless eyes scanned the floor and walls while I watched the ceiling and the shadows, alert for signs of movement. The path twisted and turned through maze-like halls until we reached a hatch with a round wheel. My heart sank, for I knew what lay beyond it.

"The paint ends here," he observed unnecessarily and spun the wheel.

Nausea rose at both the musty, oily smell and the darkness that seemed to seep into the hall.

*Kyleigh. For Kyleigh and for Freddie.*

I would do this for them.

Motioning the Elder back, I stepped into the tunnels first, straining my eyes at the ceiling and walls. He closed the hatch behind us, and darkness swallowed us both.

# 47

I switched on the torch. The tunnel stretched ahead, and the single beam did little to alleviate the dark. The Elder knelt, and silt rose like clouds about the knees of his charcoal grey-and-black suit. He brushed the dust aside and lifted a paint can.

"Shine the light here."

I did, and he scooped up a handful of dust, rolling some between his thumb and forefinger. Lines of thought or displeasure etched his face. I could not tell what held his attention.

"What is it that you see?"

"Only a little blood mixed in the paint. We should hurry."

Blood? I bit my lip to keep from asking questions he could not answer.

The Elder pulled up some of his nanodevices to fill his corneas as he stared ahead into the dark. Behind his faceplate, grey swirled around his hazel irises, unsettling me. He stood quickly, sending dust into the air, and I coughed.

"Frederick Westruther also came this way, and these tracks should be sufficient." We had only walked ten meters when he added, "Particulates are less likely to bother you, if you stay at my side."

I glanced at his profile.

His eyes still fixed on the dust and silt, he said, "You should have had a respirator or a suit. I was wrong."

The confession startled me. In the history of the Consortium, had any Elder admitted error? Words of forgiveness rose, but so did the memory of Parker's death. I did not reply.

Always, always, I scanned the ceiling and walls, while he studied the floor, and the lack of insectile tracks provided little reassurance. After half a kilometer, he slowed and held up his hand. I stopped, the silt shushing under my feet.

"Slowly." The Elder's words were barely audible. "I hear them.

We are not far behind Frederick Westruther, but I do not recognize the others."

It was not long before muted voices wafted through the tunnel, rising in pitch, as if an altercation were underway.

"No!"

Kyleigh's anguished cry echoed on the tunnel walls. Without a thought, I started running, and after a second's hesitation, the Elder matched my pace. We passed side doors, ignoring the sound of our boots on concrete as the hall's particulate matter grew thinner, then disappeared.

The voices and sobs—were they Kyleigh's?—grew louder.

The tunnel's twisting and branching masked the distance, but we slowed simultaneously when light reflected off the walls ahead. I switched off the torch and put it back into the pocket on my thigh.

Somewhere ahead of us, a man said, "What's this?"

A sharp cry split the air. The Elder caught my arm to keep me from charging forward.

"That's hers," Freddie exclaimed. "Give it back!"

My eyes closed briefly in thankfulness. He, too, was alive.

Laughter resounded, and a tinny, thin soprano said, "A cross? Void it, Skip. We've got one of the elite here."

"Elite or not," threatened a man, "she'd better get working."

"I've told you"—Kyleigh's voice heaved—"I studied nanites, not virology."

Footsteps echoed, and something thudded to the floor.

"That's the last from the lab—" The familiar, rich baritone broke off, and my teeth clenched. "Kyleigh? Freddie!"

"You!" Kyleigh exclaimed.

Briefly touching my arm, the Elder whispered, "Do you know who speaks?"

"Julian Ross."

Even in the reflected light, I could see his face blanch, and he pointed back up the darkened tunnel. I shook my head and crept forward. After a faint protest, the Elder followed.

"Let us go, Ross," Freddie said. "At least let Kye go."

"Not," the soprano woman said, "until she figures out—"

"You kidnapped them?" Ross's voice rose in pitch. "Stars, Skip, let them go. I have it under control."

"Sure you do, if *under control* means killing North with the virus," sneered the man. "It shouldn't affect citizens. Little Tristram here studied under SahnVeer, so she's our best shot. She'll understand the delivery system you stole. Need someone competent working on a cure."

Edging sideways along the wall, I peeked around the corner and squinted into the bright light. The tunnel opened into a chamber lit by multiple lanterns. In the center, hooked to portable generators, computers sat on boxes and crates. His strong features half hidden behind a respirator, Julian Ross towered near Kyleigh and Freddie, both of whom knelt near a jumble of equipment. Neither wore suits, only crumpled shirts and pants. A deepening purple bruise spread across Kyleigh's left cheek, and blood crusted her jaw. She held Freddie's arm as he attempted to stand. A woman wearing Kyleigh's suit—I recognized the flowers Freddie had drawn on the upper arm—perched on the edge of a large crate, swinging one leg against the side.

"Not just kidnapping, Ross." Kyleigh's voice shook as tears streamed down her face. "They injected Freddie."

My hands fisted in anger.

"What?" Ross took two steps toward a wiry man with knives and pistols strapped to his legs and waist and a respiration mask hiding the lower half of his face. "I told you no citizens. That was the arrangement. And certainly not my brother's best friend!"

"He'll be fine." The man I assumed to be Skip brushed Ross's concern aside. "As long as Kyleigh here does her job. She needed a little motivation."

Ross's blue glare moved from a puffy-eyed Kyleigh to Freddie's ashen face, and then to the man. "Skip, you go too far when you endanger citizens."

"Stop being ridiculous, Ross," the woman in the stolen suit chided.

The Elder startled. He turned back to the dark tunnel, but a deep voice demanded, "Move."

The heat of anger turned to ice, and I pivoted to face a man who motioned with a knife. I dodged between the Elder and the knife-man, and we backed into the chamber.

I heard Kyleigh gasp.

"Look what I found lurking in the tunnel." The knife-man bared stained teeth at the Elder and me, then barked, "Turn around."

"Recorder?" Freddie's green eyes were wide and his face pale. "*Elder*?"

The woman pushed off the crate, her boots smacking the floor. "You're kidding—they're Consortium? Nah, she can't be, not with that hair, and"—she pointed—"he doesn't have drones."

"Is this your brother's unRecorder, Ross?" Skip jabbed his fingers in my direction.

Before I even realized he had moved, the knife-man grabbed my hair, jerking my head back. Cold metal touched my throat.

"A droneless Elder without grey eyes?" The woman crowed with laughter. "Well, Skip, you wanted a petri dish, and two just walked in."

"Whatever you are, Consortium, take off that suit," Skip commanded.

The Elder did not move.

"Isn't it your job to watch over Recorders?" the apparent leader taunted, and the knife-man yanked on my hair again. My eyes watered. Skip snarled, "Give me that suit."

The Elder's jaw ticced, but even though he had said he was done protecting me, he unfastened his helmet with apparent calm. He set his suit, piece by piece, on the concrete floor, until he stood only in a rumpled grey tunic, pants, and socks. When he inclined his head, a hint of pale hair and beard caught the light. Somehow, that pinched my heart.

"Good," Skip drawled. He tossed something to the woman, who caught it midair and advanced toward me. "Now, Kyleigh, I'm tired of your lack of cooperation."

"Don't!" Freddie shouted. Julian grabbed his arms, and he strained against the taller man's grip.

"Stop." The Elder's voice rang with authority, and for a moment, they all obeyed. "I have complied. You have my suit. Do not harm her."

Skip lunged. The Elder's eyes widened, and he barely dodged Skip's blow. Cursing loudly, the knife-man shoved me at the woman, and I fell to my knees. The Elder's hands curled to fists. Skip struck out again, but the Elder only blocked the rapid punches.

Before I could push myself up, a hiss and flush of heat bit my neck, and an empty jet injector tumbled to the floor in front of me.

For a fraction of a second the knife-man's blade flashed silver through the air, then it was lodged in the Elder's thigh. He cried out, and in that moment, Skip drove his fist straight into the Elder's face. Crimson blossomed over Consortium grey.

The leader bent and extracted the knife, wiping it off on the crumpled Elder's back, and handed it, hilt first, to the other man.

Less than five seconds—and it was over.

Sound echoed oddly in my ears, and the room swayed.

I had failed. Again.

We should have gone for help as the Elder had wished. Why had I not learned from previous experiences? Anger at myself and these other people wrapped twin tendrils around my heart, battling fear for preeminence. Only my tears won.

"Kyleigh, Kyleigh. All you had to do was listen." Skip *tsk'd* as he pulled another jet injector from his pocket, flipped it around, and emptied it into the Elder's neck. "Find that cure."

Tears streaming, Kyleigh choked, "You've killed them all for no reason. No reason at all."

"Recorder?" I did not even bother to look up at Elliott's voice. "*Freddie?* You're alive! But, what are you doing *here*?"

Julian Ross dropped his hold on Freddie, and Kyleigh rushed into Freddie's arms.

"Kye?" Something in Elliott's tone pulled my attention to where he stood, maskless, his gaze riveted on Kyleigh and Freddie. "Julian, what's going on?"

The woman snorted. "Back from your tunnels already, miner-boy? Bugs didn't get you?"

"Insects," Elliott said, eyes on Freddie.

The glare Ross shot at the woman would have made me quail, but she only laughed.

There was nothing to do but serve, so I wiped my tears with my sleeve. Clambering to my feet, I faced Skip. "You claim to want test subjects. Then let me tend the Elder. We are no good to you dead, even if our death is your ultimate goal."

The man merely glanced at me, as if my request meant nothing. "If you want. Elliott, do something useful for once, and take these three to that empty utility closet." Skip turned away but called over his shoulder, "And make the girl clean up the blood. Don't want to attract scavengers."

"Elliott, don't you touch him," Ross ordered.

The younger Ross brother's mouth grew taut. Ignoring Ross's command, he helped the Elder to his feet. "Too late. Freddie. Recorder. Follow me."

The knife-man fingered his blade. I took Freddie's arm, and we left the chamber.

Elliott handed me a medical kit and slid his back down the wall to sit beside Freddie. They watched me staunch the Elder's bleeding nose, while over the reddening cloth, his unveiled hazel eyes remained fixed on Elliott.

"Why'd you do it, El?" Freddie asked. "How could you go along with all this?"

Elliott drew my attention from the Elder's leg and nose when he banged his head on the wall behind him. "I didn't mean to." A long exhalation fluttered his short hair back. "Julian had started obsessing about stopping the Consortium—I swear to you, Freddie, that's all. Just stopping them. Not murder."

"Not just murder." Freddie wheezed slightly, but he pinned Elliott with a fierce look. "Genocide."

They fell silent as I tightened the bandage around the Elder's thigh. His skin already felt feverish. He murmured thanks, saying little else, only watching the three of us from under faint eyebrows. When I turned to face them, Elliott's gaze dropped from me to his hands, which fisted convulsively on his lap.

"I thought I knew you." Freddie sniffed and dragged a sleeve over his nose. "I thought we were friends. I—"

"We were! We *are*. I just—"

"Really?" Freddie shoved himself upright. "After all you've done?"

Elliott shot a sidelong look in my direction and flushed. "It's just,

Julian kept talking about transferring with bodily fluids, and well, saliva seemed the best."

"What?" Freddie scowled. "Stars, El! I'm not even talking about attacking the Recorder to appease your brother. Though if it comes to that and you were so determined to be your brother's pawn and contaminate her, you could have just spat in her drink."

The Elder shifted beside me and laid a gloveless hand on my forearm.

Elliott's mouth fell open. "I didn't think—"

"No, you certainly didn't." Freddie narrowed pale green eyes at his former friend. His jaw was tight. "My point is that the Elliott I *thought* I knew wouldn't join up with a bunch of murderers."

"I'm—"

"Julian's puppet, that's what you are," Freddie punctuated every syllable. "That was the stupidest thing you've ever done."

"Everyone—"

"Not this time, El. You aren't doing that this time. Not everyone. *You.* You're the one who attacked the Recorder. You're the one who's gone along with those . . ." He pointed at the door, then he clenched his fingers. "Stop hiding behind other people."

Elliott sputtered a reply.

But then, Freddie coughed, and scarlet dripped from his nose.

Several hours after Elliott left to answer Skip's summons, the woman who had stolen Kyleigh's suit shoved her into the closet with us and shut the door.

Kyleigh stood there, rubbing her upper arms. "I tried."

Freddie raised bloodshot, slightly swollen eyes and flashed the briefest of smiles. "It's all right, Kye. I know you did."

She gasped and dropped to her knees at his side. "Your eyes, Freddie!"

He scooted over to put distance between them. "Yeah."

"Are you—Does—" She gnawed on her lower lip.

"Colors are off, is all," he said. "Bit of a headache, but it isn't . . . it isn't bad."

"I only wanted to get you the paint to cheer you up." Her words seemed to trip over each other. "I didn't see them. I was talking to Meier, and then there was a flash, and he just fell. And I couldn't even call for help, because I still had my comm unit set to external, and they grabbed my arms and that . . . that woman took my helmet before I could switch it back."

Freddie shivered. "If it comes to that, I should've waited, convinced Jackson to listen, thought things through. But no."

The Elder's nose began to bleed again, further staining his reddened tunic. He grabbed a sodden, useless rag to quench the flow, and no one spoke until the blood stopped. Then, he rasped, "Neither did I think to use my suit's communication unit to request assistance."

For once, I could not fault him. "You are accustomed to utilizing your implant for such transmissions."

Kyleigh touched Freddie's forehead and flinched. "You've got a fever." Her glance flickered around the room and landed on the medkit on the floor next to me. "Do we have fever reducers in that thing?"

"There were three, but I dosed them both before Elliott left. Only one remains." I gave it to her.

"Not for me." Freddie held up a shaking hand and squinted at the man in the corner. "For him."

The Elder's eyebrowless forehead knotted, and slowly, he raised his head. Kyleigh cried out, and I caught my breath, for his hazel irises were crimson, and the color spread like a drone's tendrils over his corneas as if his capillaries were breaking, one after another.

Without a moment's hesitation, Kyleigh knelt at his side. "Hold out your arm."

The Elder hesitated, then obeyed. The injector popped. He loosed a ragged sigh, and his swollen, crimson eyes drifted shut.

Her shoulders hunched. "I don't want either of you to die."

Freddie struggled into an upright position. "If it comes to that, I don't want to, either." He gulped down air, but a wracking cough shook him. In a split second, Kyleigh left the Elder and was at Freddie's side, bracing him. Once he caught his breath, he tried to push her away, but she captured his hands and placed a kiss on his forehead.

"Don't—"

"I will if I want to," she whispered and cupped his fever-flushed cheek in her hand. She turned to me. "How are you feeling? Where Rose Parker hit you seems . . . darker. And unless I'm mistaken, where that horrible woman jabbed you with the injector looks bruised."

My hand lifted to my neck, and the skin felt tender under my fingers. I did not tell her that my body ached, not when Freddie and the Elder suffered more than I. But I did not want to lie, either. After three seconds, I finally replied, "Where Rose Parker hit me does not hurt."

"I suppose we'll all die," she said quietly. "I mean, the viral load in this closet would have to be off the charts." She lifted her head. "But maybe I'll be fine, and tomorrow . . . I can figure it out."

"I did not fall ill on *Agamemnon*. Cam, Tia, and Eric also were in close quarters with infected people. It is possible that you will not succumb."

A quiet knock stopped our conversation.

The knob turned.

Elliott peeked around the door. "Good. You're all awake." He pushed it halfway open. "Let's go."

No one moved.

"We don't have a lot of time," Elliott insisted. "I dosed dinner with some antihistamines, but Skip has a fast metabolism, and it could wear off."

Only the Elder struggled to his feet. At the sight of his ruined tunic, Elliott paled, but when his attention went to Freddie, his breath hissed between his teeth.

"I have to get you all out of here." Elliott checked the hallway. "We can talk once we're clear, but there isn't much time."

The Elder grimaced as he put weight on his injured leg. "There is not." He turned to me. "No matter what he has done, if he offers you freedom, take it. Make the best of what you are given."

Elliott helped Kyleigh raise Freddie to his feet, and he looked even thinner and more skeletal as he leaned on their shoulders. As quietly as we could, we filed out and followed Elliott through the central chamber, where he grabbed a flamethrower from the haphazard pile of equipment. I pulled the torch from my pocket. Sliding the strap over his shoulder, Elliott Ross led us into the tunnels.

After the second turning, I clicked on my torch. Dust again coated the tunnel's concrete floor, and the peculiar, musty, oily smell grew stronger. I eyed the flamethrower on Elliott's back. Oil, organic particulates, fire, and tunnels were not a reassuring combination.

"Good thing you have a torch, too, Recorder," Elliott said. "I only thought to bring one. We'll have to go around, take the longer way, since the others don't know it. You remember, though, Freddie?"

"Yeah." Freddie kept a trembling hand on the wall.

We pressed on, but after only twenty-nine minutes, the Elder was struggling. Elliott, intent on the path ahead and constantly checking the ceiling and shadows, did not notice. I took three more steps, then the Elder's suppressed groan stopped me.

He had refused to aid Hugo. Had punished me and threatened Nate. Had let Rose Parker die. Yet, he had also, however selfishly, helped me find Kyleigh. He, who had been so afraid of the virus that he wore a suit at all times, had given it up when I was threatened. And he had not struck back when Skip rained blows on him.

In truth, the Elder made no sense at all.

Even though my joints ached and my balance was unsteady, I caught up with him and put my shoulder under his arm. In the dim torchlight, I could no longer see the faint growth of hair, but his forehead drew down over ever-darkening eyes.

"It is well, Elder. You may lean on me."

He turned his face away and sighed, but his weight shifted. He was heavier than I had anticipated.

Elliott's torch lit the hall, the beam sparkling on the motes, but knowledge of the dust's composition destroyed its beauty. Silt rose in gentle clouds behind him, growing as Kyleigh and Freddie passed through it, and billowing when Freddie stumbled. He fell to his knees, and the Elder and I stopped. Kyleigh tried to lift him up, but he dropped back to the dust-covered floor.

"Elliott!" Kyleigh called.

He turned, and his eyes widened. "Freddie!"

"I can't help him by myself." A tear tracked down her cheek, leaving an ashy streak over the livid bruise.

"Sorry." Freddie's voice shook slightly. "Stupid—should be fine if I can rest."

"We don't have time." Elliott handed his torch to Kyleigh and shifted the flamethrower. "We can't stop. Which one, Freddie, over my shoulder or on my back?"

Freddie blinked blood-darkened eyes. "What?"

"I'm carrying you. Back it is, then."

Without waiting for an answer, Elliott hoisted Freddie onto his back and we set off again. My lungs burned, and my arms and joints ached, though whether it was because of the dose the woman had given me or exhaustion, I did not know. I began counting steps, but eventually, I struggled to remember what number came next.

With Freddie riding on Elliott's back, we progressed a little faster, until the Elder, too, began to wheeze. Kyleigh dropped back to the Elder's other side. She glanced at me over his stooped body, then put her arm firmly around his waist. Together, the three of us hobbled after Elliott and Freddie. I kept a constant check on the ceiling and walls. Elliott stayed several meters in front, casting long shadows ahead into the gloom.

Time and steps and dust and dark shadows were our whole universe then, and my legs burned from exertion.

"Here." Elliott set Freddie down next to a hatch. "If we go through here, we'll only be a few turns from the control room."

Freddie frowned. "Near the place we used to play ball and I broke the light fixtures and Gideon made me replace them myself?"

For a fleeting second, a smile ghosted across Elliott's face. "Yeah. You'll recognize it right away."

"I . . ." Freddie hesitated. "I might not."

Kyleigh eased away from the Elder, who made his way to the wall, leaned his cheek against the chilly concrete, and closed his eyes. She knelt before Freddie and touched his forehead, but he ducked from her fingers.

"I'll go first to look around." Elliott exhaled sharply. "If it's safe, you all follow. If it isn't—if there're bugs, I'll do what I can."

"But Elliott," Kyleigh protested, "if there's dust in the halls, using that flamethrower will be like setting off explosives."

Elliott's face seemed to grow older in the torchlight. "Like I said, I'll do what I can to hold them off. Otherwise, you'll have to go back the way we came, which will mean dealing with my brother and the others. So this has to work. I'll get you out."

"If that is the case," the Elder said quietly, "you will have redeemed yourself."

"I'll have done the right thing." The tunnel's gloom pressed down on us, and Elliott sighed. "Sounds the same, but it isn't."

Elliott spun the wheel and pushed the hatch open, then Kyleigh handed him the torch. Another quick glance down the tunnel from whence we had come, and then he stepped into the hall. I counted only eleven seconds before he stuck his head back through the open hatch. Some of the tension had left his face.

"We're good. Let's go."

Kyleigh and Elliott helped Freddie to his feet and guided him over the sill into the corridor.

I held out my hand. "Elder."

He allowed me to take his elbow and help him through the hatch into the hallway.

Elliott shrugged the flamethrower back over his shoulder. "I'm gonna clean out that tunnel once I reach the junction half a kilometer back, where the pheromone smell is high. Burning it should clear out the roaches and eggs. Don't go back that way just yet, though it might be a good trail to follow later."

"What?" Kyleigh jerked around.

"You're in the station proper," Elliott said. "You'll be fine."

"You can't leave us and go back to them!"

"Of course I can. No," he protested before she could finish sputtering. "Hear me out. I'm not just avoiding penalties for what I've done, though it probably looks that way."

"It certainly does," she snapped, hands on her hips.

Freddie coughed violently, then wiped his mouth with his sleeve. I tried not to stare at the dark stain left on his cuff. "You can't save your brother." In the torchlight, Freddie's eyes were almost a solid red, and his focus appeared to drift toward Elliott's left. "He has to make his own choices."

"I know you don't believe me, but he's not bad—"

Kyleigh said something under her breath.

"—and I have to try to stop them." Elliott pressed a datastick into my hand. "Recorder, I copied what I could. Do what you can." He bent suddenly to kiss Kyleigh's cheek, then clasped Freddie's shoulder and drew him into a hug. His hand was on the wheel to close the hatch behind him when he paused. "Get Freddie—all of you—to a doctor as soon as you can. Freddie, hold on, all right?" His gaze fell, then rose. He drew a deep breath. "And, I am sorry. On so many levels that it seems pointless to say it, even though it's true. If you—any of you—can ever forgive me, that'd be more than I deserve. But it would"—his voice shook a little—"it would be nice."

The hatch closed, and Kyleigh whispered his name.

Elliott was not there to hear it.

# 49

The Elder's teeth chattered. My torch's single beam revealed a dark blotch soaking through his bandage and pants.

Her voice thick, Kyleigh asked, "Which way do we go?"

"I'm not sure." Freddie cleared his throat, and he dashed his sleeve across his eyes. "If we came out where I think we did, the Recorder's room is to the left."

My heart faltered. "What?"

"Which would make the control room to the right."

"Can't you tell?" Kyleigh demanded.

He slumped and shook his head.

Flashes of memory temporarily blotted out the hall—*monstrosities skittering down the walls, jumping onto the pod containing the Recorder's remains, Michaelson falling, the talkative Recorder wielding the torch like a knife.*

I managed to keep my voice steady. "Is there another route?"

He shook his head. "Dead end."

Dead end, indeed, and all I had was a single torch.

Very well. I would get them to Jordan and the marines, and they would be safe from the roaches, even if we all died of the virus. I tucked the datastick into the pocket on my thigh and fastened it closed. If the data could be used to undo the damage Julian Ross and the others had done, perhaps this expenditure of life and energy would not have been wasted.

"Please stay close," I said. "If I tell you to run, do it. Do not look back. Do not ask questions."

"But—"

"No, Kyleigh. You will run. With no regard for the person next to you."

Freddie's eyebrows drew into a *V* at the vehemence of my command. "She's right, Kye."

"If the way is blocked," I continued, "barricade yourselves in a room until help arrives." Though, truthfully, I had no idea how they would summon assistance without communication links if the marines' explosion had sealed the corridor.

I skimmed the torchlight over the walls and ceiling, behind us and ahead. With each step, Freddie and the Elder slowed. I slipped my shoulder under the Elder's arm again and braced him, and together, we limped heavily along. We passed the fissure, and I tried not to allow my panic to show. He cocked his head as if listening, and I felt his breath catch in his chest.

In my exhaustion, counting my strides no longer had meaning, but in only one more turning, we would know if we could escape the corridor at all. If we could, if we reached the wider hallway leading to the control room, surely a patrolling marine would find us.

Meters later, we drew even with the burned drone tangled with charred, nearly unrecognizable carcasses. Kyleigh's soft exclamation seemed loud, indeed.

"What is it?" Freddie asked. "I . . ." He gulped down a breath. "I get the feeling I'm missing something."

"How could you miss . . ." Her wide eyes met mine, and what little color she had in the torch's light fled. "Freddie, what do you see?"

He held his breath, then coughed. After several more seconds he admitted, "Not much. Colors have been gone for a while, and everything is dim."

"Shh. Wait," the Elder said, and he screwed up his face in concentration. Then he added, "Faster."

"What is it?" I asked under my breath.

"I hear them," he said. "The devices in my eyes are failing, even as Freddie's are, but the cochlear nanodevices are still functional."

The hairs on my arms stood on end. "Are they coming?"

"I hear them scrabble deep inside the walls, though none too close."

"Kyleigh," I said, "Go."

In no time and yet forever later, the torch's beam showed the smooth grey floor disappearing under dust and gravel. The marine's explosion had not blocked the entire hall, but the pile of volcanic rock and concrete rose nearly to the ceiling, which was an uneven three meters high. There was no way to shift it aside.

"Kyleigh," I said, "you must go first so you can assist Freddie. The Elder and I shall go last."

She raised her chin. "I don't—"

"Take the torch." I pressed it into her hand. "When the roaches emerge, you and Freddie must be safe."

She hesitated, then began the climb, the torch casting unnatural shadows while she ascended. Freddie leaned against the wall, his eyes closed, his respiration uneven.

The Elder wobbled on his feet as he watched the darkness behind us, then sank down, breathing unevenly. Red-black stained the concrete floor under his leg.

"I know you created a jamming device," he said quietly, "and I believe I know why."

The words shot through me and out again, as quickly as a bolt of electricity. "I do not regret it, save for your current condition."

His laugh, shallow and short, ended in a low moan. "Do you regret that in all honesty?"

And suddenly, I knew that I did. "Yes."

Rocks and debris tumbled down.

"I'm all right," Kyleigh called. "Just slipped."

Freddie whispered a prayer under his breath.

"I suspected in the hangar, of course," the Elder rasped. "But I still do not know how you managed without a drone."

"Ah." What else was there to say?

Kyleigh reached the top. "I can see the emergency lights and no roaches. Here."

The torch rolled down the slope. She should have kept it, but I picked it up and ordered Freddie to begin his climb. He shuffled forward and struggled up the rubble, while Kyleigh called down directions and encouragement.

Freddie was halfway up when the Elder spoke again. "I am sure the marines will be able to arrest the people who have killed us. Before you, too, die of the virus, take my drone. Connect to the network using emergency access codes—"

"Elder." My attention switched from Freddie to the man on the floor. "You shall do it yourself."

A coughing spasm shook him. "No, you must do it for me. My leg does not have the necessary strength. I cannot make that climb."

That could not be true. It would not be true.

"You will. If need be, I will carry you."

He gave me the gentlest of smiles. "As I knew you would say."

At that moment, Kyleigh's voice rang out. "Freddie made it. We're going down the other side. We'll wait at the bottom."

Neither the Elder nor I moved. I hesitated only a fraction longer before kneeling and folding his hand in my own. His skin burned against mine.

Red eyes which should have been as hazel as Kyleigh's blinked. "Edwards is a good man. He serves well. I should not have added to his burden." His eyelids drooped. "I was wrong as well, to not treat Theta4492807-3571R, called Parker. She chose a good name. And as for you . . . I was afraid. I allowed my fear to control me, and I judged you unfairly. But no more."

He caught my face in gentle hands, pulled my forehead to his, and whispered the access codes. I repeated them three times before he released me.

Torchlight revealed a bluish tint around his lips that had nothing to do with nanodevices. "Have you chosen a name?"

The unexpectedness of the question startled me. "Not precisely."

"I have," he said slowly. "Many years ago. It means freedom."

And suddenly, I could not bear the additional burden of losing the Elder. Not after Parker. Not after losing Nate, Alec, and *Thalassa*—the cost was already too high.

"Help me!" I cried.

But there was no one who could.

He caught my hand, and I stilled.

"I hear them coming. You cannot climb and run fast enough to escape if you try to save me." His voice softened, and he said the one thing that would make me obey. "Take Kyleigh Tristram and Frederick

Westruther to safety. Take them home. I can slow you down and kill the four of us, or I can grant you time." He closed his eyes, hiding their crimson irises. "Help me stand."

Reluctantly, I did, and a fierce smile warmed his pallid face.

Behind me, a sharp, scrabbling sound caught my ear. I looked over my shoulder, but saw nothing save darkness.

"I'm coming!" Kyleigh called.

"No!" My protest echoed in the hall. "Take Freddie and run! Now!"

For a second, though his eyes remained closed, I saw his fear as if it were my own, and then, it melted away. And I understood. Fear and resignation did not drive him. Sacrifice only had meaning when it was made in love.

"My name is Lorik." The Elder faced down the hall as if he could see beyond the darkness that had swallowed his sight. "Have faith—" He stopped. "The world is beautiful, when you see the truth. This is the way I choose to serve, and within that choice lies my freedom. You will remember me?"

"Always."

He squared his shoulders and took an uneven step down the hall toward the moving shadows.

Abandoning Lorik, I scrambled up the pile of debris, slid down the other side, grabbed Freddie and Kyleigh by the hands, and ran.

Tears blurred my vision as we ran, but the red emergency lights drew closer.

Freddie tripped, pulling me to the floor, and I let go of Kyleigh's hand before she fell, too. The torch clattered on the concrete, and its beam made our shadows stretch like desperate fingers until they faded to nothing.

"Run," I panted. "Get help. Warn them—roaches."

Kyleigh obeyed and stumbled ahead with a dry sob. Somehow, I wrapped Freddie's arms about my neck and staggered to my feet, dragging him behind me.

Then, like hope, beams of light lanced through the darkness. Blinded, I raised a hand to block them and lost my grip on Freddie. I called out a warning of contamination, but the beautiful, welcome sight of blue-clad marines did not slow. Someone lifted Freddie, then I also, was caught up and lifted onto a hover gurney.

Boots thundered past.

Sudden weapons' fire and a bone-shaking explosion brought my head up.

"You're fine now." The bearded marine had appeared at my side. He tapped my arm. "We've got all three of you."

Three.

Only three.

I curled onto my side, and the bed glided under ductwork and fire-suppression units. Behind us, another explosion covered the rapid pop of weapons firing. The bed slowed, and Jordan's face replaced the marine's. Dimly, I heard her speak of quarantine and suits, but I did not understand. She covered me in a blanket, and when Max appeared, I knew I was safe.

Merciful sleep pulled me into uneasy rest.

Gloved fingers shook me awake.

"Freddie needs to talk to you." Williams's whisper sounded sharp over her helmet's speaker.

I shoved my aching body off the cot. When I wavered on my feet, she cupped my elbow and guided me to the corner, where Kyleigh sat on Freddie's hover gurney, her legs tucked underneath her.

"Zhen will be here with him in a few minutes," Williams said quietly.

He wetted his lips. "Thanks."

Freddie turned his bandaged face in our direction and held out his fist, and although tapping fists seemed inappropriate at the moment, I tapped it with my own. He caught my wrist in one clammy hand and turned it fingers up.

"Open it."

When I did, he dumped his earrings onto my palm.

"Freddie," I managed, "I have no use for—"

"Don't let this . . . go to waste."

How could I waste diamonds?

He seemed to understand my unasked question. "No, not them. Me . . . use me. Save James—" He coughed, and his thin shoulders shook. "If you can."

Kyleigh smoothed his short hair, then pressed something into his hand.

My fist tapped my thigh three times. "I do not know what you mean."

Shivering, Freddie fought for breath. "Take my place. Let him be me." He deposited a datastick on my palm with the earrings, then folded my fingers down. "It's a lot to ask . . . but could you try . . . for his sake? For Max?"

A lump rose in my throat.

"All my family information and med files. Take my I.D. bracelet, when it's done . . . My will is on there, too." He reached his other hand to Kyleigh, who took it in both of her own. "In case . . . you can't."

His breath caught, and he dropped my hand. A gagging cough forced him upright.

"Williams!" Kyleigh cried out, and Williams fired a jet injector into Freddie's neck. He slumped back onto his pillows.

Why was there nothing I could do? It was not right. And yet, there was this one thing. I could not help Freddie, but I could help James. I had experience, and I had Lorik's codes.

"I will."

Freddie's fevered eyes looked past me. I turned. Zhen had arrived with James, and they approached the bed, their boots loud in the quarantine room's quiet.

"Would you mind?" Freddie gasped. "You'd be . . . free. Should be able to . . . move about the system, if you're careful."

A crease appeared between James's faint brows. "Why would you do this? Is it a matter of efficiency? Efficiency should not dictate—"

"Because you're worth saving," Freddie's voice grew strong for a moment. "You all are. I've got the easy part." A ghost of a smile touched his lips, and he reached toward me. After a second, I took his hand. "She's got . . . the hard one."

"And I will find a way—" I stopped, the memory of the hot bite of the woman's jet injector fresh in my mind. My hand rose to the spreading bruise on my neck. "Unless death claims me first. And if it does, I shall give you the tools you need."

I extended my open hand, and the diamonds, clear as water, cast spots of color onto my fingers. James slowly nodded. I poured the datastick and Freddie's diamond earrings onto his gloved palm.

Freddie collapsed back, tension easing from his face. "We're good, then."

"I . . ." James closed his eyes for a fractured second and moved to kneel at Freddie's side. "I will endeavor to uphold your name with honor."

"I know. Just . . . no record . . . of this."

"No record will be necessary," I said, though my voice broke as I finished, "for you will not have died."

He shuddered again, but once that passed, his jaw relaxed, and he even smiled. "Not dying, anyway. Going home."

James caught Kyleigh's eye. "May I stay?"

She murmured an affirmative, and he moved to the foot of the bed, where he stood completely still.

"Recorder-that-isn't . . . you never told me"—Freddie struggled for a breath—"your name."

"I have not decided altogether, but if I had, telling people my name would endanger them."

His lips twitched into a faint grin. "Not going . . . to endanger me . . . now."

"I . . . I want a name that reminds me of my choices, what I must do, so that each time someone addresses me, I cannot but remember. I know what I want, but only part of it is . . ." I could not finish; my words and my choice were inadequate. "It is not a name at all. And I do not know whether or not I shall keep it."

"So tell me . . . what you have so far," he prompted.

I glanced up at Zhen, then whispered the single word in his ear. His grin bloomed into a smile.

"I like it. Hang on to that one."

Another round of coughing shook him, and I returned to my cot, holding my blanket to my chest while Kyleigh smoothed his short hair, Williams administered medication, and James stood like a guardian.

Though James, the talkative Recorder, and I were present, no one documented Freddie's service. As he had asked, there would never be a record.

Max choked out the standard words, his helmet's speaker lessening the gravity of his deep voice. Kyleigh buried her face in gloveless hands, but when the conveyor belt moved and the door closed, she turned to Zhen and sobbed onto her armored shoulder.

The ball of tears building in my chest unwound and seeped free, but I ignored the moisture on my cheeks. At least the roaches would not have Freddie as they had taken Lorik.

My friends gathered at the door near the marines and the talkative Recorder, who waited, armored and armed, to escort us back to the secured area. Max and Zhen walked on Kyleigh's left and right as they followed Jordan and Lars down the hall under red emergency lights.

The bearded marine set a gentle hand on my shoulder. "I'll be watching over you and Tristram both until we get out of here. And we will get out."

I could not find my voice to answer him, and my vision blurred again.

"You'll be fine. I'll believe that for you, even when you can't." He gave me a brief nod and followed the others down the short hall, turning left at the corner and vanishing from sight.

I stole a final glance at the closed furnace door and forced my own boots after the others. James fell into step beside me. The talkative Recorder and the marine's heavy footfalls rang out behind us.

Jackson's gravelly voice broke the silence. "Rumor had it you're usurping Westruther's identity. Guess it's so, since no one documented—"

I whirled around. "That is a lie."

"Rumors often are," the talkative Recorder said. "But in this case, you *are* saving your friend, aren't you?"

My exhalation was not truly a sigh. "There will be no record, for officially, he has not died. Recorder Gamma4524708-3801-1R did. Freddie gifted his identity, and there are multiple witnesses to his act of kindness, though speaking of it would condemn us all."

James put a gloved hand on my shoulder and stepped in front of me. "I accepted it."

"Easy now." One side of the talkative Recorder's mouth tipped up, but his eyes did not lighten. "I'm glad, then, for one of us."

"If you can swap identities"—Jackson's deep-set gaze bored into me—"what about creating a brand-new person? Can you do that? Or do you need a replacement to swap him with?"

The talkative Recorder's attention darted to the marine.

Even though my experience last quarter gave me the answer to his question, and even though I wanted to trust Jackson, I tempered my response. "I believe I could."

He set a hand on the talkative Recorder's shoulder, but his gaze remained riveted on my face. "If you can't, the swap will have to be me. A couple others, including Lars, volunteered, but they have families. I don't, so I can disappear into the belt, if I have to. Got the skills to handle that crowd. I'd be fine."

The talkative Recorder's jaw dropped, then he quickly shut it.

"Just get him out. Maybe make him a marine, and he can retire when we get out of this mess. We've pooled our resources."

"All of you?" One of James's faint, growing eyebrows quirked, which provoked incongruent and irrational jealousy.

Despite my ten-days of practice, I could still only raise both at once.

"All of us down here. Good thing we all shaved our heads. You'll fit right in." Jackson grinned at the Recorder. "If you want to."

I held up my hand. "You do not have all relevant information. Creating a completely new identity is more complex than making a swap. There are bound to be cracks, which would not bear up under close scrutiny by government entities or the Consortium." I met the talkative Recorder's eyes. "It is likely you will need to hide in the mining belt, which is not an easy life. Is this what you choose?"

Wordless, the Recorder nodded.

"Good," Jackson grunted. "Because you can't go back—"

"For the Eldest does not tolerate aberrations," James finished.

Determination burned through me. I would honor Freddie, Lorik, Parker—all those who had been lost, though I dared not allow myself to think of Nate. At the least, I would save these two. "I will. If I can have power enough for Lorik's drones—"

"Who?" Jackson asked.

"The Elder."

His expression tightened. "Drossing piece of—"

"No," I protested sharply. "Never that. He died so that Kyleigh, Freddie, and I . . . Forgive him."

Jackson's brows descended.

Turning to the Recorder, I asked, "What name do you choose?"

His throat worked, but still, he did not speak.

"If you want a good name," Jackson said, "we'd like you to consider Parker."

The Recorder puffed out a slow breath, and a smile spread across his face and warmed his eyes. "Parker is a good name. I'll take it. For the other one, I've always liked Daniel."

Jackson grinned broadly. "Sounds good."

Some of the weight on my heart lifted while we walked back toward the hall that had become the marines' operational center.

"Does this mean you can escape, as well?" James asked me.

"I do not know. Neither do I know—" I stopped. "James, Daniel. If I . . . if I succumb to the virus—"

Jackson cursed.

"Avoiding facts does not make them disappear. Kyleigh and I are both exposed." Sudden pressure in my throat threatened to choke me. "She was coughing a little this morning. But should I fall ill, I promise to give you the tools you need to free yourselves."

"You'll be fine," Jackson stated, as if saying so could make it true. "We'll find those trogs that killed Westruther, and they'll pay."

"Moreover," James added, "if there is any information here that can prevent further deaths, we shall find it as well."

For a splintered and hideous second, the memory of Butterfield's temporary morgue overlaid the red-lit hall before us, and I shuddered. If Ross and Skip's bioweapon left only a quarter of the population untouched, the toll was beyond what I could grasp. If we failed—no, there was no question. We could not.

"Spacing right," Jackson growled. "And if we have to steal their ship to get that antivirus or whatever it is to the hospitals on New Triton, we will."

Before I answered, however, the hall lights flickered on. Relief froze me in place, but the talkative Recorder—Daniel—cheered. The brightness lifted my spirits. We picked up our pace, but before we had traveled far, Jackson exclaimed, "What?"

My chest constricted.

"Do not worry." James pointed at his helmet, as if to reassure me that the suits' communication links still worked. "*Thalassa* is not gone. Their usual channels are down, but Portia Belisi has been sending a signal using an old code of short and long pulses, which we received as soon as the power resumed."

Jackson barked, "Transfer every scrap of power to the hangar and get those doors open!"

I set a hand on James's arm, but his expression lightened to a smile.

"Again, there is no need for worry," he said. "Nathaniel Timmons—"

"Nate?" *Oh, my heart.* Hope flooded me. "He is well?"

"He is," James answered. "The shuttle shall be—"

I did not hear him, for I was already running down the hall.

Jackson's cry of protest did not stop me, nor would even a roach dare to slow me down.

A half dozen marines were already racing toward the hangar, and more boots thundered behind us. Frigid air poured through the open hangar doors, but the cold did not matter. Clouds of exhaust and debris billowed away from the loveliest craft in the system. Someone shouted an order to stay back.

The hangar doors crept closed, but the shuttle's hatch opened. Marines charged out, weapons ready, and behind me, cheers erupted, loud even over the helmets' speakers. Jackson shouted a command to leave all helmets on, but the rest of his words blurred to mere sound because in the midst of their blue suits, I saw two figures in grey and black. Alec and—

*Nate.*

For half of a second, I could not move.

Green eyes met mine, and I was running again. Nate caught me, spun me around, then crushed me close.

He was alive and whole, and that was enough. At that moment, it was the world.

I could not hear his heart through his armored suit, but just then, I did not mind at all.

# ACKNOWLEDGMENTS

Stories have their own ebb and flow, a peculiar heartbeat of their own that might or might not comply with the author's demands. At least, they do for me. So I'll make a confession: I didn't mean to stop here. (Nate is not entirely pleased with me, though you might've guessed as much.) That said, I *am* excited about where she'll go next.

The Recorder wouldn't be anywhere at all without Enclave and you, the reader, and first, I want to thank *you*. Thanks for reading *Recorder* and now *Aberration*. Thanks as well to all of you who have cheered me on and encouraged me during the writing and editing process. There are too many of you to name! To you who have left reviews, requested it at libraries, or told friends, and to you who have made candles and lattes in the Recorder's honor, I am so very grateful!

Thank you to Orrie and everyone, to Megan, Laura, and Jenn—I am so blessed to call you friends!

Additional thanks to Sam for Lars's best line, and to CJ. At least Christine has good hair as requested, right? Even though she asked for a more villainous namesake, Parker is a lovely human being, and I couldn't write anything else. Mike, you sort of asked for this, but in no way would I wish that fate on one of the best branch managers out there!

Thank you to my Peaklings group for your wisdom and feedback: Jordan, Jon, Andrea, Nico, Jenifer, John (especially for inspiring Freddie's coffee paintings), and Jai and Rob, who not only open their home but also have dealt with my meltdowns. I appreciate you all!

Thank you to WS—Danielle, Daniel, Angie, Angel, Talis, Mindy, and so many more. All of you! Best group online!

Everyone should give a round of applause to the brave souls who were alpha and beta readers, who held my hand, helped me clarify, and showed me more gracious patience than I merit. There is no way I could ever say thank you enough, but we can pretend that saying so here is a start! Lauren, Daniel, Chrissy, Sophia, and Anne. A very special and sincere thanks to Patrice, again, for boldly going where no sane person would go and also for all the emojis.

My family has listened to paragraphs, given me sympathetic (or occasionally amused) pats on the shoulder, and borne with me during random crises over my imaginary friends, even bringing me tea and coffee when I was writing. Thank you. I love you.

As I have said, writing a book is no easy task, so thank you to the team at Enclave, and now to Oasis as well! Steve, Lisa, Trissina, Jamie, Sarah, Katie, and Megan, but most especially this time to Lisa, who has endured my rambling emails and pruned my verbosity to hone this into a tighter story. I literally could not have done this without you!

And as always, unending gratitude to the Author and Founder of faith and of the truest story.

# ABOUT THE AUTHOR

Cathy McCrumb graduated from Biola University with a degree in literature and a love for stories. *Recorder,* her debut science fiction novel, released in 2021 and has received enthusiastic editorial and reader reviews. She and her husband, whom she met while writing letters to soldiers, have five children and currently live within the shadow of the Rocky Mountains. While writing is one of her favorite things, she also enjoys reading, long hikes, naps, gluten-free brownies, raspberries, and crocheting while watching science fiction movies with friends and family. Visit her at www.cathymccrumb.com.

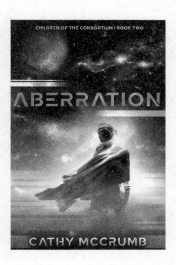